The
Daughter's
Garden

BOOKS BY KATE HEWITT

Kate Hewitt

The Daughter's Garden

bookouture

Published by Bookouture in 2022

An imprint of Storyfire Ltd.
Carmelite House
50 Victoria Embankment
London EC4Y 0DZ

www.bookouture.com

ISBN: 978-1-80314-839-7
eBook ISBN: 978-1-80314-838-0

PROLOGUE

Goswell, West Cumberland, October 1919

The rain lashes against the windows and the sky is dark with lowering clouds as she gazes out at the lawn now awash in puddles and steeped in mud. It makes her ache to remember how only a few months ago Jack was out there, toiling in the hot sun—it had been such an unusually warm summer for West Cumberland—and the lawn had been verdant, the garden so full of beauty and life. It had all looked so lovely, and her father had been so pleased.

She presses a hand to her thudding heart and turns away from the window, and the view of mud and gloom. As she walks through the house she can hear Tilly, their housemaid, humming under her breath as she moves around to stoke the fires burning in every fireplace on this grey November day. In the kitchen Mrs Stanton is starting on supper, and she can hear the busy clang of copper pots. She passes her father's study, and hears him clear his throat, and then the rustle of papers.

All is well. Or as well as it could be, in the year since Walter's death.

She walks towards the kitchen where the hall narrows. She thinks about going upstairs to change into her walking boots, but there seems little point and she does not want to have her mother call to her from the bedroom and ask her to come in and read a few verses of the Bible, a bit of poetry, something to while away the afternoon.

She won't take a coat either, or even a wrap. She stands by the kitchen door, waits until Mrs Stanton has gone into the larder and then slips like a ghost—already, she feels like a ghost, and she wonders if Walter must have felt this way, if he had *known*—into the kitchen, out the back door, into the little court-yard where the coal is kept. Through the gates and around past the old stables, along the path that leads to Bower House where Grandmama lives, on the other side of the church.

All around her the churchyard is wet and dark, the bare branches dripping with rain, heaps of soggy leaves clumped by the headstones. Jack should clear those, she thinks, before she remembers. Jack is gone.

She walks down the path and around to Grandmama's garden, the gate to the walled garden in front of her. She knows if Grandmama looked out the window of her dining room she would see her there, standing in front of the wooden door, ivy curling around its arched top. Five hundred years ago it had been the herb garden for the monks, or so her father said, before the Reformation. Now it is her garden, hers and Jack's, and it deserves her farewell.

Already she is soaked and her feet are numb. The rain is relentless, the wind from the sea cold and unforgiving. So unforgiving. Yet after a few moments she forgets the wind, the rain; she feels strangely serene and suddenly, surprisingly buoyant because she knows that there is no going back now, and that knowledge brings only relief.

She struggles with the latch to the walled garden, a few rooks wheeling and screeching above her, as if they sense her unnatural purpose. She knows that if anyone came along now they would see her soaked and shivering in the middle of a garden, wrestling with a latch. Yet even as part of her acknowledges this, another deeper part knows she will not be seen. She is becoming a ghost; she imagines if she looked down she would see her body waver, like a reflection in water. She cannot live in this world, not with the knowledge inside her, the intolerable heaviness of her own reckless cruelty.

The latch finally lifts, and she enters the garden. *Her* garden, the garden her father gave her and that Jack made. Even in the beginning of winter it is beautiful to her, the damson trees thrusting their stark branches to the sky, the borders now full of straggling weeds, although in summer they were rampant and wild, heavy with flower and fruit, which is what she had wanted. Life, pulsing, vibrant life, in all of its glory.

Now she stands in the middle of the garden and looks towards the little house, her house. Once it was warm inside enough for its fragile occupants, but now it is cold and dark and empty. There is nothing left for her here now, nothing but memories.

She leaves the walled garden and walks back through the churchyard to the vicarage, and then through the rose garden, the bushes' stark branches black with rain, and down the stone steps to the muddy acre of sheep pasture that leads to the beach road. She knows her father could see her if he just turned his head, but she feels he won't. He has most likely drawn the heavy curtains against the cold and dark.

She continues walking, the rain running down her in icy rivulets, her dress soaked completely through, and no one sees her. No one stops her.

If only it would all be this easy, she thinks. If only it was a matter of walking, one step at a time, into eternity. Walter was pushed—so suddenly, so unfairly—but she will go willingly. She will choose it. And yet she knows the entrance to eternity is not such a simple thing, although as she nears the beach she thinks perhaps it is after all. Perhaps this step is as simple as any other, if you just close your eyes.

And so she closes her eyes, and lets the rain beat over her, and everything in her demands she take that small, final step into forever.

CHAPTER 1

MARIN

It started with a door. Not just any door; a wooden door with an arched top and a rusted latch, set in the middle of a high stone wall. Marin Ellis gazed at the weathered wood in both fascination and frustration, for she'd tried the latch and rusted as it was, it wouldn't budge.

She had never been the sort to indulge in fancy. She'd long ago accepted she was practical to the point of tedium. And yet this door, and whatever lay beyond it, had, briefly at least, captured her long-dormant imagination.

"Is that the entrance to a secret garden?" Rebecca's voice carried across the icy expanse of overgrown lawn. Her boots crunched on the frost-tipped grass as she came over to join Marin, her hands thrust into the pockets of her coat. It was four o'clock on a February afternoon in a remote corner of West Cumbria, and dusk was already settling on the rolling pasture that stretched to the sea, a quarter-mile away.

"It does look like a door to a secret garden, doesn't it," Marin agreed with a little laugh. "It's probably just a door to the churchyard, or maybe to a path that leads to the beach. But in any case I can't open it."

"Let me try." Rebecca pushed at the latch for a moment, but as Marin expected it didn't move so much as a centimetre. She pressed her face against the door and peered into the crack between it and the wall. "All I see is bramble. If it leads to the churchyard, it's all grown over."

"Oh, well. It doesn't matter." Marin shivered as she turned towards the house; it looked lonely and lost in the oncoming darkness, with its blank windows and funny little turret. Or perhaps she was the one who felt lonely and lost, wondering how they'd both arrived in this place, even though she knew the answer very well.

She glanced at Rebecca, who had turned away from the door, looking as she did in these unguarded moments so young and vulnerable and impossible to reach. Marin's heart gave a little aching pulse of sympathy and grief. Rebecca had lost so much, so young... just as she once had.

"Don't be sad, Marin," Rebecca said quietly, catching her half-sister's sorrowful gaze. "This is our new start, remember."

"Yes, I remember." Smiling with effort, Marin walked back to the front door of the little house to lock up.

It had been theirs since just after Christmas, when they'd come up to the Lakes on a brief holiday. They'd been driving through the sleepy village of Goswell, on the Cumbrian coast, when Rebecca had suddenly asked her to stop the car, and surprised, she'd pulled over on the steep, narrow high street that ran through the village.

"It looks like a little castle," Rebecca had said, staring at the house that was perched on a lip of land that jutted out from the churchyard. "And it's for sale."

"It's a funny little house, isn't it," Marin had answered, nonplussed. It had long windows of stained glass and a crenellated turret on one side, a weedy bit of garden out front. From behind the house Marin could see the square Norman tower of the church.

"It's lovely," Rebecca said, a world of longing in her voice, and Marin glanced at her half-sister in wary surprise. For the last three months, since she'd become guardian of fifteen-year-old Rebecca, they'd been living in Hampshire, struggling on in survival mode, half-sisters and yet also virtual strangers, separated by twenty-two years in age and now drawn together out of necessity and grief.

Rebecca hadn't been hostile to Marin or her sudden arrival in her life, but she hadn't been overly welcoming either. How could she, when they barely knew each other? Rebecca had been born after Marin had left university and had already been estranged from their shared father for several years. She'd seen Rebecca only a handful of times since then, a few excruciating holidays and weekends where she felt like an interloper in this happy life her father had made for himself, with his new family. She had no place there.

Not until now, when all Rebecca had was her. Both her parents had been only children, their own parents dead. And so Marin had tried to keep Rebecca's life going in Hampshire: driving her to school, sorting out their father's estate, managing the housework and washing and bills. She'd thought about getting a job or going freelance, but all her energy was taken by simply dragging herself—and Rebecca—through each day.

She was, Marin knew, a sad substitute for two loving parents. She wasn't a mother. She'd only had a few semi-serious relationships in her entire adult life. To suddenly become the sole guardian of a fifteen-year-old had been shocking.

And it had, Marin acknowledged, to have been shocking for Rebecca as well; suddenly she was saddled with a thirty-seven-year old half-sister who barely knew how to fry an egg. Marin had gazed at the row of glossy cookbooks in her stepmother's gourmet kitchen in bemused incredulity, knowing she would never be able to make the kind of elegant meals Diana Ellis had no doubt regularly cooked with effortless ease. Diana had been carelessly glamorous in everything she did; she'd also only been four years older than Marin. They'd never had anything close to a relationship.

The holiday up to the Lakes had been an escape from the oppression of life in Hampshire, yet Marin had never intended to make it permanent. It had been Rebecca who had suggested it.

"We could buy it," she'd said quietly, as they sat in the car and stared at the little house, with its stained-glass windows and turret. It looked like the kind of folly you'd see in the garden of a large estate. A sign on the gate announced in grandly curling script that it was Bower House. "*You* could buy it," Rebecca amended before Marin could think to reply. "With the money from my trust."

"Buy a house in Cumbria?" she finally said, shaking her head. "Why—"

"We could start over. It's beautiful here, you said so yourself. We don't need money, not really, and if we rented out or even sold the house in Hampshire we'd be fine. You told me you could work from anywhere, if you started freelancing. Why not?"

Marin had just kept shaking her head, overwhelmed by this utterly unexpected leap in Rebecca's thinking. "The question isn't so much why not," she finally said, "as why."

"Because I'm tired of everyone looking at me funny because they know my parents died," Rebecca answered fiercely. "I'm tired of wandering around the rooms where they were and knowing they're never coming back. I'm stuck, and so are you, and I want to start over."

"Starting over won't change things," Marin told her quietly. "Your parents will still be gone." A lump rose in her throat. Her father would still be gone. And there had been so much she'd never said. "And even if you moved somewhere new, you couldn't keep their deaths secret. You wouldn't even want to, Rebecca. It would be almost like a lie, if you did."

"I know." Rebecca nibbled her lip, her face turned towards the window, and once again Marin had been struck by how young Rebecca was. How alone, except for her. In the three months since the accident Marin had never seen Rebecca cry. She'd sometimes go very quiet or sullen, but she never shed a tear.

But then neither had Marin.

"It would be different here," Rebecca said after a moment, turning back to Marin. Her jaw was set stubbornly, a flash of something like ire in her eyes. "It wouldn't be this huge shadow looming over everyone and everything, the way it is now. People wouldn't *remember* all the time."

"Maybe not, but what about your school? Your friends?"

Rebecca shrugged. "When something like this happens, you find out who your real friends are."

Marin's shoulders sagged. "Oh, Rebecca."

"There's nothing I wouldn't leave. You left your life in Boston, Marin. Why can't I do the same?"

Marin sighed again, both tempted and torn. To start over... to have something new and different to look forward to... yes, she could see the appeal, unlikely a place as this was. "This is hardly something to rush into," she said.

"Can we at least look at it? The inside?"

"I suppose..."

Rebecca had insisted on ringing the estate agent from the bed & breakfast they'd booked into that afternoon, and they'd had a viewing the next morning.

"It was built in 1905, by the vicar of the church," the agent told them as they wandered through the rooms, dust-ridden and yet with lovely proportions and elegant, tiled fireplaces. "He had it built for his mother-in-law. A sort of dower house."

"And yet it's called Bower House," Marin had observed, and the woman let out a trill of laughter.

"Yes, odd, isn't it? But in any case it was gifted to the diocese in 1929, and they let it to various tenants over the years. The garden overlooks the church—"

They hadn't spent any time in the garden, because it was drizzling an icy rain and Marin wasn't much of a gardener anyway.

"And yet completely private, of course," the woman continued. "Separated from the churchyard by a wall, so you won't have people nosing about. The vicarage was sold recently, about a year and a half ago, to an American family. Are you moving to the area?"

"Thinking about it," Rebecca answered before Marin could demur.

The kitchen, they both agreed, was the best part of the house. A large square room with sash windows that overlooked the garden, and a huge blue Rayburn that took up nearly an entire wall.

"Heats the whole house," the agent informed them cheerfully. "I know it's freezing in here at the moment, but this thing will keep everything cozy and warm when it's running."

Marin had laid one hand on top of the range, the enamel ice-cold under her hand. She had been able to imagine, quite suddenly and surprisingly, how the kitchen would look with sunlight pouring through the windows, everything cheerful and clean, a kettle whistling merrily on the range, a jar of early daffodils on the windowsill. A place of both comfort and hope, the kind she couldn't remember ever having.

Rebecca had given her a beseeching look and Marin turned to the agent. "We'll have to think about it," she said.

Over a lunch of fish and chips at the local pub, Rebecca laid out all her arguments. She was halfway through her first year of GCSEs, so the sooner they moved, the better. They could come up after February half-term; that would give them enough time to sort out the Hampshire house. She'd looked at the local secondary school online last night and it had received a very good OFSTED report.

"Rebecca, you currently attend one of the best independent schools in the country. A state school in a remote part of—"

"Don't be a snob. I can get a perfectly good education there if I apply myself, which you know I will."

Marin had just shaken her head, helpless in the face of Rebecca's determination. "I don't understand why you want this so much," she said quietly. "It's miles from anywhere, Rebecca. No shops, no museums, no distractions—"

"Maybe that's what I like about it."

"You're fifteen. Don't you want friends around and things to do? Places to go—"

"Not really." Rebecca had glanced away, her mouth turning down at the corners, her eyes shadowed. "I'm not like most fifteen-year-olds, Marin. Not anymore."

And Marin knew that all too well.

It had taken a week, but Rebecca had worn her down eventually. She'd done her own research on the village and the school, had toyed with the possibility of going freelance, setting up her own business offering website design and virtual assistant services. Nothing was keeping them in Hampshire except for Marin's reticence, her fear of taking Rebecca into something so different and unknown. Her fear, perhaps, of going there herself.

"Why don't you let the Hampshire house for a while?" Rebecca had suggested. "Then, if we decided it's an epic failure, we can go back after say, six months. We have to give it at least that long." She spoke firmly, as if she suspected Marin would sneak back as soon as she could.

And so Marin had done as Rebecca had said, and let the house out; the solicitor had approved the use of Rebecca's trust fund for the purchase of Bower House. They'd packed up their things—leaving nearly all of the furniture behind—and driven up to Goswell on a grey day in late February and now they were here, about to start their new lives.

"I can't wait till our things arrive," Rebecca said as Marin locked up the house. It was just past four o'clock and it was already dark. And freezing. Marin didn't remember it being so windy, the last time they'd been here, but now an icy wind blew off the sea, making her eyes water and sting. The windowpanes had rattled with it as they'd walked through the house. She hadn't remembered that, either. She found the rattling, along with the lack of traffic or people noise, quite unnerving.

"We don't even have many things," she told Rebecca as they headed back to the car. "We'll have to buy the basics from charity shops." They'd both agreed it was better to leave the Hampshire house furnished with all of its sleek, modern pieces, and beyond a couple of mattresses and bureaus the movers were bringing tomorrow, they hadn't anything else but their clothes and personal items.

"I can't wait," Rebecca answered cheerfully. Marin hadn't seen her so animated before, but then there had been precious little to get excited about. She wanted, for Rebecca's sake, to feel just as excited, just as optimistic, and yet as she gazed down the darkened street, the howl of the wind a lonely, mournful sound, sheep huddled miserably in the pasture by the church lane, she wondered what on earth they'd got themselves into. They weren't even in the middle of nowhere, she thought with something close to panic. They were on its *edge*.

When you were already struggling with grief, already feeling isolated and alone, was it really a good idea to move somewhere as remote as this? What if Rebecca wasn't able to make friends? What if the school was awful? What if they both hated it here, and they had no one to turn to?

They could always go back, and yet Marin acknowledged

that option wasn't all that appealing either. Life in Hampshire had become nothing more than an endurance test for both of them. She hadn't made friends there; the few neighbours who had stopped by with casseroles and sympathetic smiles had seemed cloying, unnatural. She didn't want to go back and she was afraid to go forward. Not a very good place to be.

"Tomorrow let's try to open that door in the garden," Rebecca said as Marin started the car. "I want to know what's behind it."

"Probably nothing but bramble as you said," Marin answered, and suppressed the little flicker of curiosity she still felt about that door.

"It might be something, though," Rebecca insisted. "Maybe some kind of secret garden."

"Maybe," Marin answered dubiously. She glanced back at the garden, but the door was lost in darkness.

CHAPTER 2

ELEANOR

November 1918

The telegram came on a grey day in mid-November, two days after the Armistice had been signed and everything was meant to be *over*. All morning Eleanor Sanderson had been restless, uneasy, flying from this to that, never settling to anything, as if a part of her, some deep, barely understood part, already knew what was going to happen.

"What is wrong with you today, Eleanor?" her mother asked, putting down her book of poetry as she gazed at her nineteen-year-old daughter who sat perched on a velveteen armchair in the sitting room, by the front window that overlooked the muddy sheep pasture.

"Why hasn't Father done anything with that pasture?" Eleanor asked, nodding rather truculently towards the few sheep that were huddled together under a slate-grey sky. "It's meant to be our garden, you know."

Her mother raised elegant eyebrows. "Do we need so much garden?"

The vicarage had a sizeable garden at the side of the house, with enough space for garden parties—they hadn't had any of those in a few years—and vegetables and anything else they could need. Reasonably, Eleanor knew they didn't need a muddy acre of pasture that stretched from the front of the house all the way to the beach road. Her father leased it out to a local farmer for his sheep; the dumb beasts kept lumbering up the stone steps that led from the pasture into the rose garden and nibbling on the blooms, much to Mr Lyman, the church gardener's, chagrin.

Yet as Eleanor stared out at the once grand stone steps now crumbling and covered in brambles, leading to nothing but mud and sheep, she felt an almost angry surge of feeling that things should be better than that. They should have an acre of lovely, verdant lawn on which to play croquet when the weather turned warm and Walter was home.

Walter had always liked croquet; he'd jauntily swing the mallet round by the handle while waiting for his turn and call out to Eleanor, teasing her about hitting the ball too hard.

You don't do anything by halves, Ellie. That's what I like about you.

Perhaps it was the thought that he would be home soon that was making her restless, although some had said troops wouldn't be back until near Christmas or even after. But maybe he would be able to come home sooner, since he was an officer. He'd never been much of a soldier, really; he'd studied English Literature at Oxford and had wanted, eventually, to teach.

"All you like are fusty old books," Eleanor had used to tease him, snatching whatever tome had captured his interest at that moment, and Walter would just smile and sigh.

"You should try one sometime, Ellie." She could picture the way he would lean forward and take his book back between his long, elegant fingers, perhaps ruffle her hair. "You might like it."

She'd flounce away, bored, because she'd never been much of one for books or school. "Why don't you play the piano instead," she'd plead, and eventually, as he always did with her, Walter would give in and play some ragtime before Father came in and scolded them, smiling a bit, to be a bit quieter.

When Walter was back, the house would be filled with music again. Eleanor and her sister Katherine had taken lessons, but neither of them had Walter's easy talent. Eleanor had banged out Chopin and Katherine had played every piece meticulously yet without any real enthusiasm or passion; Walter had once said, not unkindly, that Katherine approached music the way a physician approached surgery.

When Walter came back again. It felt like a prayer. When Walter came back again, the world would have righted itself. Things would go back to the way they were, the way Eleanor needed them to be. They would laugh on the lawn as they played croquet; they would have garden parties and tea dances and Walter would teach her a ragtime duet, taking over her part when her fingers fumbled with the keys, as they always did. Katherine might even come in to listen; Walter had always managed to soften her hard edges whereas Eleanor just rubbed up against them, drawing blood from them both.

The war was over; it couldn't be long now before things settled down, became just the way they were before.

"Eleanor," Anne Sanderson murmured, the word a gentle reproof, and Eleanor realised she'd got onto her knees right there on her chair, her hands balled into fists, everything in her aching for Walter to be walking up to the door right now, his officer's cap in his hand, his dark hair ruffled by the wind, that whimsical, slightly crooked smile on his face.

"I'm sorry, Mother," she said, and was about to scramble down when she saw Robbie Sykes from the telegraph office on his bicycle—he was so proud of that broken-down old thing—his cap jammed low on his head, and everything in her went terribly still.

"No..." she whispered and Anne looked up from her book again, her worn face creased into a tired smile.

"What is it now, my dear?"

Eleanor just shook her head. She felt suspended in that moment, as if by denying it she might keep them from hurtling forward into the future, when Robbie Sykes knocked on their door and handed them that telegram. When they read it. "No," she said, louder now, and Anne frowned.

"Really, my dear. You sound like a child."

And she felt like a child, a child who wanted to bang her fists and drum her heels against the floor. Who wanted to cover her ears and hide her eyes.

Robbie Sykes propped his bicycle against the side of the vicarage, his expression grim underneath his cap. He glanced up, and met Eleanor's gaze through the drawing room window before quickly looking away.

No.

She stood by the window now, her hands pressed flat against the glass, her heart beating with slow, sickly thuds. Perhaps it would stop altogether. Perhaps she'd fall down dead right here, crumpled on the Turkish carpet, just like Walter might be—

No.

She would not think like that. She couldn't, because it felt disloyal to Walter. He was alive, of course he was; the war was over and in summer she would ask Father to turn the sheep pasture into a lovely lawn for croquet. They would all play together, even Mother, if she were well enough, and Katherine would take ages to line up the ball, so Walter would do a jig to hurry her up. Eleanor would hit the ball too hard, as she always did, and Walter would pretend that he couldn't find it, that it had gone all the way into the sea, and Father would quote some obscure poet or philosopher as he stared up at the clouds, and Tilly would bring them all lemonade.

Robbie Sykes was at the door. Eleanor pressed harder against the glass, her nose nearly touching the pane, everything in her silently imploring him not to knock. Not to make them move from this last moment of sweet ignorance.

"Eleanor." Her mother rose from the chair, her pale grey day dress swishing about her ankles, and crossed to the window. "You'll smear the glass," she said, and gently removed Eleanor's hands from the windowpane. They fell limply to her side and Anne Sanderson stilled, one hand on Eleanor's shoulder, for she'd seen Robbie's bicycle.

They heard the sound of the brass door knocker, two terrible thuds.

"Shall I get that, miss?" Tilly, their downstairs maid, called in her cheerful, Cumberland brogue. Eleanor's older sister Katherine had teased Eleanor that she sounded like a local; Eleanor had been furious, even though she knew she shouldn't be. She'd been born here, after all. Katherine had been born in Wigton, which made her from Cumberland too, even if she made sure not to have a trace of accent in her clipped voice.

Anne was frozen by the window, still staring at Robbie's bicycle. It had a basket out front, Eleanor saw, and one of the leather straps had snapped so it hung crookedly.

"Yes, please, Tilly," Anne called finally, her voice a little faint, and she squeezed Eleanor's shoulder. Eleanor risked a glance towards her mother and saw her face was nearly the same colour as her dress. "Come, Eleanor," she murmured, and walked with slow, measured steps to the hall.

The door was open and a draught blew in from the porch. Robbie Sykes stood on the front step, his cap now crumpled in one hand as he offered that terrible, thin envelope with the other.

"Hello, Robbie," Anne said, stepping forward with a wan smile. "You must come inside. It's dreadful out there today."

"I won't, ma'am—" Robbie began, abjectly, and Eleanor

wondered how many telegrams he'd delivered, how many cups of tea he'd refused. There had been over thirty deaths of village boys in the last four years of fighting. Had Robbie delivered the telegrams for them all? He was the Grim Reaper, she thought with a sudden spike of bitterness and fury, dressed in a woolly jumper, flat cap, and muddy boots.

"Nonsense," Anne said kindly. "Tilly will take you to the kitchen. I believe there's some marmalade cake left over from luncheon." She smiled and with her hand trembling only slightly, held it out for the telegram.

Robbie handed it to her, hanging his head. "Sorry, ma'am," he mumbled, and with a firm hand on his shoulder, Tilly bustled him back to the kitchen.

Anne glanced over at Eleanor. "Will you read it for me please, darling?" she asked quietly.

Eleanor opened her mouth to say she wouldn't, *couldn't*, but then she saw her mother sway slightly before reaching out to steady herself on the hall table, her knuckles white as they gripped the marble edge, and wordlessly she took the telegram.

She slit the envelope and held the slip of paper in her hands without unfolding it, wanting to suspend this moment forever. Then a sudden, blazing thought occurred to her: maybe it wasn't about Walter. Perhaps it was about James, Katherine's fiancé. *Of course*, Eleanor thought in a rush of giddy, and only slightly guilty, relief. *Of course it can't be Walter.*

Walter couldn't die. Not now, not ever. He was too alive and important for that, with his crooked smile and his soft laugh and the way he'd gaze out at the distance when you were talking, but you still knew he was listening. *Really* listening, and more importantly, understanding. She thought of the way he whistled when he walked, his hands jammed in the pockets of his trousers, and how he'd ruffle her hair and slip her mint humbugs. She was his favourite; everybody knew it. Katherine said he spoiled her, but Eleanor didn't think it was true. He loved her. He couldn't be dead.

But even as these thought were tumbling wildly, desperately, through her mind, awful realisation trickled in coldly after. If it were James, the telegram wouldn't come here. It would go to his parents, in Whitehaven.

"Eleanor," Anne said, her voice sounding soft and yet somehow broken. "Please."

Eleanor opened the telegram.

"Dear Reverend and Mrs Sanderson," she began, and then her voice faltered and she felt as if she couldn't breathe.

Anne pressed a hand to her chest. "Go on."

Eleanor took a shuddering breath and continued. "It is my painful duty to inform you that a report has been received from the War Office, notifying the death of—" She broke off, not wanting to say the words, as if saying them would make them true, and Anne just nodded, her eyes closed. Eleanor forced herself to continue. "The death of Lieutenant Walter Sanderson of the Border Regiment, Second Battalion," she said, "on the Fifth of November, 1918." She lowered the telegram, unable to go on. Walter was dead. He'd been dead for *days*, killed less than a week before the war had ended. It was so unbearably unfair that Eleanor wanted to rage and rail against it, she wanted to stamp her feet and insist, like a child, that it simply *couldn't* be true.

"Finish it, darling," Anne said quietly.

"It just says a full report will be posted on receipt," Eleanor answered dully. The fury she'd been feeling left in a rush; now she felt empty inside, which was preferable, she suspected, to the grief that would surely overwhelm her, if she let it.

Anne nodded slowly. "His commanding officer will send a personal letter, I should think," she said, and took a few steps into the hall.

"I don't care about *that*—" Eleanor burst out, her voice

accusing. "How can you even think of such a thing?" Walter was *dead*. Her beloved brother with his thoughtful eyes and whimsical smile, his dark hair that stuck out every which way unless he plastered it down with pomade, was dead, never to return, never to smile at her and chuck her under the chin...

She felt the tidal wave of grief rising within her, and she whirled to glare at her mother, angry, resentful, childish words ready to spill forth about how her mother didn't even seem to *care*, but they died on her lips when she saw Anne in the hall, doubled over, one arm wrapped around her waist.

"Mother," she cried, and ran to her. Her mother sagged against her as soon as Eleanor put her arm around her; she staggered under the weight.

Tilly must have heard her cry for she came running from the kitchen, Robbie Sykes not far behind, looking alarmed and also strangely guilty, as if this really was all his fault for bringing the wretched telegram.

"It's all right, Mrs Sanderson," Tilly said quietly, and put her arm around Anne's shoulders. "All right, now." She looked at Eleanor. "Where's the Reverend?"

"Father's at the Carmichaels..." He was meeting with the grieving parents of another village boy who had died in the days before the Armistice. And only hours ago Eleanor had felt a passing flicker of sympathy for his family, no more than that. It had seemed so *unfair*, for a boy to die so close to the end. And yet the injustice of it had been trifling rather than the overwhelming devastation she felt now. She could feel the pressure of the sobs she longed to let out, a burning in her chest, and she swallowed hard.

"Miss Eleanor," Tilly said sharply. "Listen to me now. We must get your mother upstairs to bed." She glanced at Robbie, not without some sympathy. "You'd best get yourself off now, lad."

Robbie nodded, looking thoroughly miserable, and headed towards the door.

Eleanor glanced at her mother whose face was still sickly pale. Anne's health had always been fragile, although no one would guess it from the way she taught Sunday School most weeks, and had parishioners to supper and ladies to afternoon tea. She was always graciously welcoming, always putting her own needs or wants aside, even if it meant she spent a day or more in bed to recover.

Looking at her now, Eleanor wondered how long it would take to recover from this. Could you ever recover, from the death of a child? The death of a brother?

"Come on, Mother," she said, her voice trembling only a little. "We'll get you to bed, have a nice cup of tea and a hot brick for your feet."

Her mother moved woodenly, as if she were a puppet with an invisible hand pulling her strings, and jerkily at that. Her eyes were closed, her face looking so lifeless Eleanor felt a chill of foreboding. Neither of them spoke as she helped her mother up the stairs, and then down the hallway to her bedroom.

She pulled back the coverlet and helped her mother to take off her shoes; she was like a child, silent and obedient, lifting each foot in turn so Eleanor could ease the shoe off. Anne lay back on the bed, and Eleanor pulled the coverlet up to her mother's chin; her face was nearly the same colour as the pillow slip.

"Let me stoke the fire," Eleanor murmured. She took the poker and pushed at the coals rather ineffectually; Tilly usually saw to the fires. She straightened, wishing she could do something more. Wishing she knew there was something to do, to make this better.

But it would never be better; nothing could ever go back to the way it was.

Eleanor blinked, the room seeming to slide and waver

before her eyes. *Walter dead...* it was impossible, it had to be...

She could picture him the last time he'd come home for leave, in the summer. Mother had fretted a little because he'd been rather pale, seemed rather listless. And yet when they'd all sat outside when the weather had been fine, he'd agreed to a game of boules on the lawn and teased Eleanor about her hair, which she'd put up in a too-elaborate style because she'd wanted to appear grown up. She was nineteen and yet she'd had no beaux, no courtships, no mild flirtations, and even less of a prospect of any romance in the years to come with so many young men dead or wounded.

But she hardly cared about that now. She could only think of Walter, and how he couldn't be gone, and yet she knew from the horrible hollowness inside her that he was. She was afraid what might happen if she probed the emptiness inside her; it might fill up with emotions she couldn't bear to feel. And yet she knew they would come anyway, a gathering horde that would stampede over her sensibilities, make life nothing but grief.

"Thank you, Eleanor," Anne said. Her voice sounded distant and her eyes were still closed. "You must tell Grandmama, you know. And Father." She let out a tiny sigh. "And Katherine, when she returns from Carlisle."

"I can't—"

Anne opened her eyes, gave her a wan smile of sympathy. "I know it's difficult, my dear. We've spoiled you in some ways."

"*Spoiled*—" Eleanor blinked, stung. "I don't feel very spoilt now," she snapped, childish hurt easier to feel than the endless grief. "Don't make me tell everyone, Mother. It isn't fair."

Anne closed her eyes again. "Please, Eleanor. I haven't the strength. And you do. You're so young, so full of passion and fire..." Her mother's voice trailed off and in shock Eleanor wondered if she'd fainted or fallen asleep.

"Mother—"

"Please," Anne whispered, her eyes still closed, and Eleanor swallowed past the burning lump in her throat once more.

"I'll go tell Grandmama," she whispered, and turned from the room.

Downstairs Tilly and Mrs Stanton, the cook, were huddled in the kitchen, weeping. Eleanor could hear their murmured words and hushed sobs as she took her coat from the porch and stepped out into the blustery afternoon. It had been raining for days, the wind blowing it sideways, the sky dank and grey and low. Now Eleanor hunched against that unforgiving wind and walked towards the church, past the ancient, nail-studded doors, and around the corner, following the worn slates that led to Bower House.

Father had had the house built for Anne's mother just over ten years ago, after she'd been widowed. He'd come into money when his own parents had died, and he'd known Anne had wanted her mother close.

It was a funny little house, perched on a lip of property on the other side of the church, and the walled garden in the back had been said to be the herb garden for the monastery before the Reformation. Grandmama had had it dug over for potatoes and lettuces since the War started, and Tilly and Mrs Stanton had worked it with Mr Lyman, although Mr Lyman was getting too old and arthritic to manage much more than clipping hedges or offering advice.

With her heart like a stone inside her, Eleanor skirted the side of the walled garden and came out to the front of Bower House, built like a little castle, complete with a turret. Grandmama liked to call it Father's Folly; he'd named it Bower House, as a play on words of dower house.

"I always thought you had aspirations to a dukedom," Grandmama had teased once, and Father, Eleanor remembered, had swanned about for a bit, as if he were royalty. They'd always liked to tease each other, Grandmama and Father, and

Walter had often joined in; he had a flair for the dramatic, just as they did. He'd had, Eleanor corrected herself. He didn't any longer; he was gone.

Thinking about Walter was like probing a raw wound; Eleanor gasped from the sudden flash of pain. She stood immobile by her grandmother's front door, reeling from the realisation that had shocked her yet again, one hand raised to knock. She'd been about to lift the heavy brass knocker but she felt now as if she couldn't.

And in the end she didn't; Grandmama must have seen her coming and opened the door herself, her face pale, the set of her mouth resolute.

"Eleanor, my darling. Come inside before you're soaked." Elizabeth Chorley drew her granddaughter inside by the shoulders and Eleanor went as woodenly as her mother had gone to bed.

"Grandmama..." she began, and found she could not go on.

"Don't say anything, dear. Not until you're warm and dry. It's dreadful out there today. You're already soaked, and just from walking across the churchyard. I'll have some tea brought into the sitting room."

Eleanor let her grandmother lead her into the sitting room with its bow window facing the high street, now awash in mud. Mary Sutherland, Grandmama's housekeeper, bustled forward with a tea tray.

"There, now," she clucked. "Let's get something warm inside you."

Eleanor sat down and stared at Mary; she'd never given the woman much thought at all, if any, but now it occurred to her that Mary had been widowed in this awful war; her husband had died a few months ago, at Havrincourt. She had a small son too, little more than a baby; Ben, his name was. Mother had given him a silver rattle on his christening day, and Mary's sister, also widowed, watched him while she worked.

Mary pressed a cup of tea into Eleanor's hands; her fingers closed round the porcelain, registering the comforting warmth for a second before it all came rushing back.

Walter.

"Grandmama..."

"Don't say anything, not yet." Elizabeth shook her head, her lips pressed together. "Not yet," she said again, and with a jolt Eleanor understood that her grandmother already knew.

"How—" she began and Elizabeth smiled sadly and gestured to Eleanor's thin slippers.

"Why else would you come out on a day like this, with nothing more than slippers on your feet?" she asked, and when she pressed her lips together again they trembled. "I don't suppose you know the details," she said after a moment, and Eleanor shook her head.

"It was just a telegram."

Elizabeth nodded and took a scrap of lace handkerchief from inside her sleeve. She dabbed her eyes, her only concession to grief, and took a deep breath. "Your mother will take this badly," she said. "Your father will be devastated, of course. His only son..." She shook her head, took another shaky breath. "But Anne... you know she's not strong, Eleanor. Not like you."

That was the second time she'd been called strong in the space of an hour, and Eleanor wanted to fly at her grandmother, and insist that she wasn't strong at all, and she certainly couldn't be strong enough for everyone else.

Elizabeth levelled her granddaughter with a single look before she could say a single word. "You must be strong, Eleanor. For your mother's sake. Your cheerful, bright ways will do her a great deal of good. Katherine won't be able to manage, not with her own fiancé to look after."

"James isn't even back yet," Eleanor protested. "Although why he should live, and Walter die? It's his fault, you know. He insisted they join up—"

"Hush, Eleanor, you don't mean such things."

"I do," Eleanor snapped. She'd cling to anger rather than grief. "I'd rather James died than Walter! I'm not even sure Katherine loves him, anyway. They barely spoke the last time he was here on leave—"

"That is quite enough." Elizabeth's voice was like the crack of a whip. Eleanor blinked, chastised. "You are nineteen years old, Eleanor, and nearly a woman grown. You must learn to control your tongue."

Eleanor stared down at her mud-caked shoes. "It's just not fair," she muttered.

"No, but our idea of justice is not the same as God's. We want everything to go our way, and that simply isn't possible."

"Why not? If God is all powerful, He should be able to manage it."

"Oh, Eleanor." Elizabeth sank into a chair opposite her granddaughter, her face grey with fatigue and loss. "If you want to argue theology, go speak to your father. But trust that just because something bad has happened—"

"Something bad?" Eleanor cried. "The *worst*, Grandmama."

"Even the worst," Elizabeth answered steadily. "God is greater than even the worst, Eleanor."

He didn't seem very great to her at that moment, Eleanor thought, but even so she knew it was useless to argue with her grandmother, or be angry with God. It wouldn't change anything. It wouldn't bring Walter back.

"Be strong, Eleanor," Elizabeth said quietly. "For your family. For *Walter*. He'd want you to remain as bright and happy as you ever were, you know that." Her grandmother took a deep breath, gave her a shaky smile. "And when it all gets too much and you need to cry, you may come over here," she finished, and after a tiny pause, Eleanor, her throat now too tight for words, just nodded.

CHAPTER 3

MARIN

The next day dawned cold and bright, and by noon the movers had deposited all of their belongings in various rooms of the house, and Rebecca had already started opening boxes.

"We'll need a table," she said as she put dishes away in the kitchen's little larder. "And chairs. Something cozy and old-fashioned."

Marin thought of the huge glass and chrome table in the Hampshire house, and nodded. "Yes, I suppose this house really needs old pieces. But right now I need a cup of tea. If you can find the kettle somewhere in all that, I'll go down to the shops and get us some tea and milk."

"Shop, singular," Rebecca answered, grinning. "Remember what Mrs Hewitt from the B&B said? There's only one little shop in the village, and a café down by the beach."

"And a pub," Marin reminded her, smiling back. She wanted to get into the spirit of things, for Rebecca's sake. And perhaps for her own as well.

"Three pubs, actually," Rebecca answered, and then let out a cry of triumph. "Here's the kettle." She pulled the modern-looking chrome kettle out of the box, frowning as she looked at it. "Doesn't really fit, does it? We need a big brass one or something."

"That one will do for now, I should think," Marin answered, and grabbed her coat.

The village sparkled under the sunlight, and despite the cutting wind Marin's heart lifted at the sight of the sheep pasture, the tufty grass glittering with frost, and the high street that cut straight through it before meandering steeply up a hill, terraced cottages on either side.

She found the post office easily enough, a few yards up from the pub, and stepped inside, glancing around at the neat shelves of flour and biscuits and bread. A young woman behind the till nodded her hello, and Marin spent a pleasant few moments browsing her wares and thinking how weirdly and yet wonderfully different of all of this was from her life in Boston or even Hampshire, where you hardly ever saw the same person twice, and groceries were ordered online or bought from huge superstores where you were just another anonymous customer.

Not, Marin knew, that she'd bought many groceries, or ever cooked much. When living alone she'd subsisted on takeaways and toast, and that hadn't changed all that much since she'd started taking care of Rebecca. She'd managed to make a standard spaghetti bolognaise—all that had required was a jar of sauce and a pound of mince—but meals were still mostly takeaways, plain pasta, or cereal, with the occasion salad thrown in.

Rebecca hadn't minded, but as Marin thought of the cosy-looking kitchen with its tall windows and huge range, she felt a sudden urge to learn how to cook. To make nourishing meals and comforting soups for her and Rebecca. To nurse them both back to emotional wholeness and health. A silly notion, perhaps, to think food could heal, but one she still rather liked.

After she found the things she needed, she took a moment to read all the notices on the board by the door. There were the usual advertisements for housecleaning and gardening services;

a lost cat with accompanying photo; an announcement of a weekly quiz at the pub on Thursdays; and a poster for a ceilidh in the village hall that Friday.

Perhaps she and Rebecca could go to the ceilidh. She imagined kicking her heels up in a country dance, and inwardly laughed at herself. She had two left feet and would probably make a fool of herself, but she thought Rebecca might like to go. Perhaps they'd meet some people, find a way into this village and the sense of community it surely promised. Another way to heal.

Marin paid for the tea, milk and sugar at the till, exchanging a few pleasantries about the weather; the woman's Cumbrian accent seemed impenetrable at first but after a few moments Marin started to understand. She put her shopping in the little cloth bag she'd brought with her, and then headed back to Rebecca and the house.

Rebecca had finished unpacking the kitchen things and had moved onto her bedroom; she'd picked the room in front, overlooking the street, although Marin had told her the room above the kitchen was sure to be warmer.

"You have that one," Rebecca had said. "I like looking out at things."

Marin fiddled with the Rayburn for a bit, great, lumbering beast that it was. The sound of its innards flaring to life had been encouraging, and the hot plates on top had finally started to get warm. She boiled the kettle and made them mugs of tea, taking them upstairs. She stood in the doorway of Rebecca's bedroom and watched her for a moment; she was stacking her books on the floor, as they hadn't brought any bookshelves.

"We really must get out to a charity shop," she said as she handed Rebecca her tea. "Otherwise we'll be living like travellers."

"I don't mind." Rebecca blew on her tea. "But I suppose it

would be nice to have a few more things. Make the house feel cosier."

"I read some of the notices in the village shop," Marin said. "There's a ceilidh next Friday."

Rebecca wrinkled her nose. "A ceilidh?"

"A Scottish dance. Sort of like country dancing. I thought we might go, meet some people."

Rebecca, as Marin had expected her to, nodded enthusiastically. "Oh yes, that sounds brilliant."

Sipping her tea, Marin wondered how long it would take for reality to set in. For Rebecca's childish enthusiasm to wane, and for her to realise they were actually *living* here. Maybe next week, when school started back? Or would the newness of that last for a little while? Marin didn't know when it would happen, but she both feared and expected Rebecca's excitement to fizzle out, and she'd come hurtling back to earth. Back to the reality of her parents having died and her life stretching in front of her, looking utterly unlike what she'd expected it to look like just a few months ago.

"Are you going to unpack?" Rebecca asked, and Marin forced herself to push her melancholy thoughts away.

"I suppose I might as well. I didn't bring much."

"Go on, then. And when you're done we can try the door in the garden."

"You said yourself whatever's behind it is covered with bramble," Marin reminded her. "We won't find anything."

Rebecca's eyes sparkled with a mixture of defiance and determination. "I still want to open it."

Marin unpacked her things in the small bedroom over the kitchen. It didn't take long; within the space of a quarter of an hour her clothes were folded neatly in the drawers of a single bureau, the few books she owned piled on top along with her wash bag. She didn't have anything else. She surveyed her few possessions with bemusement. On one hand, it seemed quite an achievement to travel so lightly. On the other... it was, she supposed, a bit depressing. No knickknacks or mementoes. She hadn't had any in Boston, and she hadn't brought any here.

The only photograph she'd brought with her was one of her with her father, taken on a trip to the sea in Norfolk one summer. She was about fourteen in the picture, just a little younger than Rebecca, and the wind was blowing her hair into her face. She was laughing, her hands lifted to pull her hair back. It was a candid and not altogether flattering pose—her hair had gone frizzy and her nose looked too big—but the reason Marin kept the photo, had framed it, even, was because of the way her father was looking at her. He had his arm around her, just for the photo, and he was gazing down at her with a kind of affectionate amusement. She remembered when she first saw the photograph, she kept staring at her father's face, studying it, because she couldn't remember him ever looking that way at her in real life. Not, at least, since her mother had died when she'd been eight years old.

"Ready?" Rebecca appeared in the doorway, bouncing lightly on her heels.

Marin put the photo on top of the bureau. "How are we going to open that door, Rebecca? We don't have any tools."

"I thought we could try it with a kitchen knife."

"I think it's rusted too much for that."

"Let's try anyway," Rebecca answered. "And if we can't open it, we could go for a walk through the churchyard. Meet our new neighbours."

"You mean the Americans who bought the vicarage? I wonder what they think, living so close to the church."

"As close as we are."

"Yes, but we're separated by a wall, at least. The vicarage looks right out onto the church lane. I wonder if anyone knocks on the door, looking for the vicar."

Marin got her coat and wellies while Rebecca fetched a

knife and they headed out into the garden. It looked even more wild and unkempt in the bright sunlight; a horse chestnut tree was nearly choked by ivy, and the shape of the flowerbeds could barely be seen beneath the bramble and nettles.

"At least it's small," Marin said as she glanced around the square of patchy grass. "It won't be too hard to keep neat, if we hire someone to cut down the brambles, perhaps."

Rebecca wasn't listening; she was hard at work with the latch, attempting to pry it upwards with the kitchen knife. The only result of her strenuous effort was a few flakes of rust fluttering to the ground.

"I think we do need something more than a kitchen knife," Marin said. "But in any case, I'm not sure what the point is. We've enough garden to be getting on with, even if that door does lead somewhere other than the churchyard."

"Aren't you the tiniest bit interested?" Rebecca asked. She'd abandoned the knife and was peering through the space between the door and wall once more. "I really can't see anything beyond the brambles, but it *must* be a garden. A secret garden. Why would there be a door to the churchyard?"

"The house was built originally for the vicar's mother-in-law," Marin reminded her. "Maybe they put a door in the wall so they could go across more easily, rather than going all the way around the church."

"Oh, you are so boring," Rebecca said in exasperation, but she was smiling.

Marin smiled back. "Sorry, I'm afraid I always have been. Not a creative spark in my soul."

"Maybe you just haven't found it yet."

Marin laughed lightly and shook her head. "Ever the optimist, Rebecca." Although the door *had* captured her imagination, at least a little. But if it were really just brambles, she couldn't see much point in trying to open it. "Shall we have a look at the churchyard?"

They left the door and the garden and walked back to the street, following it around to the lane that led to the church, a fine Norman building with the Georgian vicarage beyond it.

They turned towards the church, walking on the well-worn path of slates past the impressive doors and around the corner to the churchyard itself; Rebecca let out a little exclamation, and pointed to a gap in the hedge where it looked as if a gate once had been. The only things left were the rusted iron posts.

"Where does that lead?" Marin asked, and Rebecca laughed.

"To our garden. We've almost walked in a complete circle."

Intrigued, Marin peered through the gap in the hedge and saw the weedy patch of grass they'd left only moments ago. "I'm all mixed up," she said with a laugh. "But how funny—it must have been put there to give quick access to Bower House from the vicarage."

Rebecca pointed to a door set in the high stone wall on the other side. "That must lead to the vicarage garden."

"We really are neighbours."

They left the remnants of the gate and turned towards the churchyard, the slate path going steeply uphill before ending at a stretch of grass dotted with mossy headstones.

It was quiet as they walked along, the only sound the rustle of the wind through the leafless trees and the chatter of a few restless rooks. Marin glanced at the headstones and realised neither she nor Rebecca had been in a churchyard since the funeral last August, when Peter and Diana had been buried in a huge cemetery overlooking a motorway. Rebecca hadn't wanted to visit their graves again; she said she didn't feel anything there.

Now Marin glanced at her half-sister in apprehension, wondering if seeing the graves would bring a fresh wave of grief, but Rebecca just looked pensive. She stopped in front of a weathered headstone and Marin joined her; the headstone was for a couple whose deaths were separated by twenty years, with the swirling inscription 'Reunited' underneath their names and dates.

"At least Mum and Dad didn't have to wait to be reunited," Rebecca said after a moment. "Really, that would be a good way to go, wouldn't it? Together?"

Marin felt her throat close as she thought of how her own parents hadn't had that. Her mother had died of cancer, just two months from diagnosis to death. Was a car accident, so sudden and brutal, better? "I suppose it spares you one kind of grief," she said after a moment, and Rebecca nodded before turning away.

Marin glanced at a few of the other headstones: one for a child, clearly beloved, who had died at only six years old, early in the last century. A little gambolling lamb had been engraved on the headstone by her name. A grandmother, 'beloved Gran', who had died only a handful of years ago.

The more recent graves were carefully tended, some with wilted posies or bouquets resting in front of them. The dearly missed grandmother's, she saw, had an ultrasound photograph in a plastic sleeve in front of it, weighted down with a rock and with a handwritten note, 'It's a boy, Gran!' attached.

Examining all these tokens of both love and grief, she felt almost as if she was spying, or at least as if she were on the outside, looking in on something she'd never had. Swallowing, Marin walked away from the flowers and photographs and glanced again at some of the older headstones, their faces faded and weeds growing round their bases.

Rebecca had already walked on, and Marin joined her, following the grassy path that ran along the edge of the church-yard, and then as they came around the corner they nearly ran smack into a man standing there with a pair of wicked looking garden shears.

"Oh!" Marin's hand flew to her chest. Rebecca smiled.

"Hello, there," she said.

"Morning." The man nodded at both of them, the tiniest of smiles quirking the corner of his mouth. He had a shock of unruly dark hair threaded with grey, and eyes just as dark and completely veiled. His face was brown and weathered, with crow's feet by his eyes and lines running from nose to mouth, but Marin guessed he was only a few years older than she was, perhaps in his early forties.

"Sorry, you startled me," she said with a self-conscious smile.

"So I did." He reached out and snipped one of the branches that twined up the wall, the simple movement managing to seem both confident and careless. He barely looked as he snipped another one, and the tips of the dead-looking branches fell to their feet.

"Do you take care of the church grounds?" Rebecca asked, and he snipped another branch.

"Aye."

Rebecca stuck out a hand. "I'm Rebecca Ellis. My sister Marin and I just moved into Bower House."

The man glanced at her hand before taking off his leather glove and shaking it. Obligingly Marin stuck her hand out too, and he shook it. His hand felt huge around hers, corded with muscle and crisscrossed with scratches despite the heavy gloves. "Joss Fowler."

"Nice to meet you," she said. There was something about Joss Fowler's contained stillness that made her feel awkward and uncertain.

"We've just been looking around the churchyard," Rebecca said. "Are you pruning the roses?" He gave one slow nod, and Rebecca continued, "Do you know the garden of Bower House? There's a door in the wall and we wondered where it led to."

"A door," the man repeated thoughtfully. He snipped another branch. "I couldn't say. Haven't been around there much, myself."

Rebecca looked rather crushingly disappointed, and Marin decided it was time to move on.

"Nice to meet you," she called, and ushered Rebecca down the path and around the corner.

"I thought he might have known something," she said with a sigh. "He sounds like he's from around here."

"That doesn't mean he knows every stick and stone," Marin answered with a smile. "And in any case, Rebecca, it's just a bunch of brambles, wherever it leads. Why are you so curious?"

"Because it's *interesting*," Rebecca answered, and for the first time she actually sounded cross. She pulled away from Marin and strode own the path, stopping in front of an old wooden five-bar gate.

Marin slowed, realisation trickling through her. Rebecca had shown her in just about every way that the garden was important to her, and Marin had kept dismissing it. If Rebecca was excited about something, then she needed to be excited too. Needed to encourage her half-sister, rather than be such a dismal voice of caution, holding her back.

She joined Rebecca at the gate and unhooked the rope from around the post, letting it swing open. "I'm sorry, Rebecca," she said stiltedly. "I don't mean to sound so negative. Let's open the door to the garden. I reckon we could do it if we found a screw-driver. Maybe there is something interesting back there, underneath all the brambles."

"Oh, what's the point," Rebecca replied wearily, and walked on.

CHAPTER 4

ELEANOR

December 1918

Katherine's fiancé James came home just before Christmas. It had been an endless, awful month, a month of dreary days that Eleanor only just managed to drag herself through. Her mother did not manage quite so much; she did not rise from her bed for a week after the telegram came. Mrs Stanton made her beef broth and toast and Tilly brought it upstairs on a tray, as if her mother was suffering from the dreaded Influenza rather than a broken heart.

They'd learned from the letter Walter's commanding officer had sent that he'd been killed in action in the taking of the Sambre-Oise canal, one of the last engagements with the Germans before the Armistice. He'd apologised for taking so long to send the telegram; things had been confused in the days before the Armistice, and many people had had the bitter experience of opening a dreaded missive after it had been signed, believing their loved ones to be safe, only to learn the terrible truth. He wrote that his death was quick, at least, and he wouldn't have suffered.

Eleanor feared that all officers assured the mothers and fathers, sisters and sweethearts, back home that there was no pain, yet she clung to that knowledge all the same because she could not bear to think of Walter suffering. For the last four years she'd had nightmares of him coming over the top and running across the muddy expanse of no man's land, felled by a single bullet or the relentless strafing of a Howitzer; he'd told her a bit about the trenches, although she'd always felt there was far more to it than he was saying, and Mother told her not to ask.

She was glad to think he hadn't lain in the mud for hours, moaning for help. She could at least save herself the torment of imagining that. And yet no matter how it had happened, he was still dead.

She asked Father, rebelliously, how he could still trust God when He'd taken Walter, and her father had looked at her very seriously and said in a quiet, broken voice,

"How can I not trust Him?"

And so Eleanor sat by her mother's bedside and urged her to take a spoonful of broth, but her mother was like a waxen effigy, pale and lifeless. She might, on occasion, manage a mouthful but more often than not Tilly collected the tray with the meal completely untouched.

Her father retreated to his study, losing himself in his books and sermons. Eleanor had had to tell him, that first day; just as with Grandmama, he'd known just by looking at her. He'd come in, hanging his hat by the door, and the smile had faded from his face as soon as he'd caught sight of her.

"Not Walter," he'd said quietly, without hope, and Eleanor had nodded. She'd wanted, in that moment, for her father to envelop her in one of his bear-like hugs, had craved that comfort more than ever. She'd felt the tears bottling in her throat and burning beneath her lids; she'd stood on her tiptoes, as if poised to hurtle herself into his arms.

But he did not embrace her. He did not even look at her. He turned away and walked slowly into his study and then with an awful, gentle finality, he had closed the door.

Katherine had been little better. She'd come home on the five o'clock train, tired from a day sorting through donated clothes for war orphans up in Carlisle. She'd been cross that morning with Eleanor for not going; Eleanor had been tired of all the busy work of volunteering that she and her mother and her sister had occupied themselves with for the last four years. Rolling bandages in the draughty village hall and knitting lumpy, misshapen socks that they packaged up with jars of sour jam because sugar had been rationed; collecting sphagnum moss and blackberries to send on trains to the Front; visiting war widows and orphans and offering what compassion they could. Mother was so gentle and loving towards every poor woman who twisted her handkerchief to shreds as she blinked back tears but Eleanor had always felt impatient, even slightly sick, as if grief were catching. She'd had enough of it all, and she'd so wanted things to be different. And now they *were* different, terribly different, and it was all much, much worse than before.

As Katherine came home Eleanor wished she'd gone with her after all. Then she wouldn't be in the terrible position of telling her, as well as everyone else, about Walter's death.

Unlike Grandmama and Father, Katherine hadn't guessed at all. She'd taken off her coat and hat, tidying her hair as she frowned at her reflection in the hall mirror, her hair, the same sandy brown as their mother's, drawn back into a plain bun that had come undone only a little.

"And why do you have such a long face, then?" she had asked over her shoulder. "You've been lounging about all day, I've no doubt, eating chocolates and reading novels."

"Eating chocolates!" Eleanor had exclaimed in indignation

before she could stop herself. "We haven't had chocolate in ages, you know that."

"Well, I don't see how you've got anything to complain about," Katherine answered tartly. "I've been on my feet all day."

"I know." Eleanor had always hated Katherine's sniping, but she couldn't feel much of anything now, except perhaps a sudden shaft of sympathy for Katherine, as well as a painful pang of envy. Her sister, for the next minute at least, was living in lovely ignorance. One last moment of innocence.

"Katherine..." she began but her sister was already heading upstairs.

"What is it?" she asked wearily, only half-turning around. "My feet are aching. I must take these shoes off. They pinch horribly."

"Katherine, it's Walter."

Katherine stilled, one hand on the bannister, her back taut and quivering. Then she turned around slowly. "No," she said, and Eleanor choked out,

"The telegram came this afternoon."

Katherine pressed one hand to the side of her head, as if she'd received a physical blow. Eleanor stood at the bottom of the stairs, her throat becoming tighter and tighter, longing for someone—even prickly Katherine—to come and comfort her. But Katherine didn't move.

"This bloody war," she said slowly, enunciating each word and shocking Eleanor, and then she turned around and walked slowly up the stairs.

In the following month it seemed that grief isolated each member of the Sanderson family, reminding Eleanor of Dante's ninth circle of hell, where those who had committed treachery were each frozen in an icy lake. And wasn't it a form of treachery, to turn away from each other when they were all hurting so much? When they all surely craved comfort?

No matter what her mother and Grandmama had said about her being strong, she did not think she possessed the fortitude to comfort others. She felt frozen herself, numb and empty, all her wild emotions and childish passions replaced by nothingness. Life went on, of course; the days blurred into one another and her mother finally rose from her bed, and concentrated on her duties, taking Sunday School classes and hosting teas, planning events to celebrate—if such a word could even be used— the Armistice.

Katherine lost herself in volunteering; she spent most of her days up in Carlisle, working with the aid society that helped orphans. Eleanor knew she should go along; her father had preached on the virtue of self-sacrifice enough for her to know she had a duty to others.

Yet she'd rather spend her days in her bedroom, rereading Walter's letters, than attempt to smile and chat as she folded winter coats or tied ribbons around donated jars of jam or lemon curd.

Although she tried to comfort herself with Walter's letters, she found them exquisitely painful to read. His humorous anecdotes, his bittersweet reminiscing, his reflections on the war, 'fighting as it seems, for a few feet of muddy ground somewhere in France'... they brought him back to her so wonderfully, and yet then she would look up, blinking, and remember all over again that he was gone, and that awful emptiness would sweep through her once more.

A month after they'd received the telegram, James Freybourn, Walter's best friend and Katherine's fiancé, came home. His parents called at the vicarage, explaining with a kind of apologetic excitement that they'd received a telegram from him; he'd arrived in Dover that morning and would be taking the train up to Goswell, to arrive after suppertime.

Eleanor had tried to compose her face into an expression of sedate interest, when in truth she'd felt a flash of rage. Why couldn't they have had a telegram like that, from Walter himself, saying he was on his way home? Why couldn't *he* be coming home, instead of jokey, arrogant James, whom Eleanor hadn't liked since he'd encouraged Walter to enlist?

His parents must have sensed something of this, for they apologised and withdrew after arranging with the family to meet the train.

"Aren't you happy?" Eleanor asked Katherine, not without malice, after they'd gone. Father had retreated to his study, and Mother up to bed.

Katherine looked away. "Of course I am," she said.

"You don't seem it."

Katherine pursed her lips, as if she'd tasted something sour. "Don't be ridiculous. It's just there is precious little to be happy about, these days."

Her mouth remained tight as she walked off with short, brisk steps. Eleanor watched her go, wondering if her sister regretted accepting James's marriage proposal back in 1914. She would never ask. Still she suspected his proposal had been a reckless act on the eve of war; Katherine and James had only been courting for a few weeks before he'd asked her to marry him, and then he'd left. Father had insisted they wait until after the war to marry, since they'd been courting such a short while. Back then everyone had thought the war would be over in a few months at most. It hadn't seemed a long time to wait.

Eleanor suspected Katherine had been surprised by James's proposal, but then he had always been a bit careless and bold; it had, after all, been his idea to join up, and so Walter, his best friend, had as well.

"You don't have to go just because James is," Eleanor had said when Walter had told her. She'd been fourteen years old and furious that he was going; she'd refused to talk to him for two whole days, until Walter had begged her to relent, since he didn't know when he'd see her again.

"I've got to do my bit," Walter had answered evenly. He looked pale yet resolute, his hair, as dark as Eleanor's, rumpled from where he'd driven his hand through it. "I don't think I'm going to much like war, though."

Eleanor had pouted. "James says it will be great fun and you'll be home by Christmas."

"Ah, James." Walter shook his head at his friend's folly and then chucked Eleanor under the chin, a gesture she jerked away from even though she'd always secretly liked it. "Let's hope he's right, eh?"

A bitter wind blew down the rail line as Eleanor, Katherine, their parents and James's all waited on the platform that evening. They were all dressed in mourning clothes, for Walter's sake, although it seemed wrong somehow, with James coming home. Eleanor's black taffeta dress's only decoration was a lace insert in the bodice; her father wore a black armband on the sleeve of his coat. A few other parents and sweethearts were waiting as well; several were also in black.

Dusk had fallen hours ago, and the night seemed endless and dark, the sheep pasture that surrounded the station stretching on into blackness. Train times had been erratic, and Eleanor thought how unnerving it was to be waiting in the dark for something but have no idea when it would actually come.

After a quarter of an hour of silence she finally heard the relentless chugging of the train as it came along the coastline from Barrow, the curl of steam from its engine white against the black sky. A wave of relieved murmurs rippled through the crowd; people shifted where they stood, dug hands in pockets to reach for handkerchiefs.

The train came slowly to a halt, the sound of its engine like a laboured breath, a last sigh. The door opened and a porter stepped out, his face set in startlingly grim lines. People shifted some more. The wind nearly blew off Eleanor's hat, and she clapped her hand to her head, hunching against the bitter onslaught.

The first soldier emerged from the train, dressed in the uniform of the Border Regiment, his kit bag slung over one shoulder. He walked with a limp. Eleanor recognised him as one of a local farmer's sons; after a moment people let out a few raggedy cheers; there was a scattered round of clapping that fell away to silence.

Then a woman stepped forward, a mother. She wore her best hat and coat put on over her housedress and apron.

"George," she said softly. The soldier's gaze moved to her, and he managed the barest of smiles.

"Hello, Mother," he said and limped towards her. The woman let out a little cry and clumsily embraced her son.

Next to her Eleanor felt Katherine tense. She could not imagine how her sister was feeling, to have her reunion with her fiancé played out on this unexpected stage. How well did Katherine know James, really? He'd escorted her to a few dances and socials, and spent several Sunday afternoons with her in the vicarage's sitting room, a cup of tea balanced on his knee as they'd made what Eleanor suspected had been no more than desultory conversation.

Since he'd joined up in September 1914 Katherine had seen him for a few hours at a time, every few months at most, when he'd come home on leave; once she'd gone to London to meet him there. Eleanor supposed Katherine loved him, although her sister was so coolly unsentimental, perhaps she'd simply accepted because James Freybourn, Cambridge-educated and soon-to-be solicitor, was a very good prospect. He was even more so now so many men had been killed or wounded in France.

Now her sister looked brittle and tense; she was clutching her handkerchief so hard she'd rent it.

Another soldier appeared from the train. "*James*," his

mother cried out, and Eleanor watched as she flung herself towards his son, and instinctively James caught her in his arms, staggering slightly. Katherine didn't move.

He looked the same, Eleanor thought in a kind of dispassionate relief. She saw no scars or missing limbs; he didn't walk with a limp. He'd been back four months ago, and he was as healthy and whole now as he'd been then. She glanced at Katherine, whose face had gone chalk-white, her eyes huge and her lips bloodless.

"Katherine," Eleanor hissed, and gave her a little push in the small of her back. Katherine stumbled forward, steadied herself, and moved towards James, a smile curving her mouth even though the knuckles of her hand clutching her handkerchief were white.

He'd been smiling slightly as he'd both greeted and comforted his mother, who had begun to weep, although the smile hadn't reached his eyes. Now Eleanor watched as for a second his face went blank when he turned to Katherine, and then his mouth curved in another smile that seemed formal, a thing of politeness rather than warmth.

"James," Katherine said. Her voice sounded faint.

James inclined his head. "Katherine," he answered, and after an endless, awkward moment, Katherine stood on her tiptoes and kissed his cheek. James went still under the brush of her lips.

They all returned to the vicarage, where Mrs Stanton had laid out a welcoming spread of food in the dining room: bread and butter, potted ham, molasses cake made with precious flour and butter. Tilly bustled around, filling teacups and offering everyone plates. Eleanor stood in the corner, watching as everyone milled around in a kind of subdued silence; joy was too hard an emotion to dredge up.

Tilly gave her a sympathetic smile along with a cup of tea.

"Drink up, Miss Eleanor," she said. "I put a whole spoonful of sugar in it, just as you like."

"Tilly, you shouldn't have. You know how little sugar there is these days."

In reply Tilly just winked, and with a rather wan answering smile Eleanor took a sip of the hot, sweet tea. Katherine and James, she noticed after a few minutes' observation, were moving around the room separately, like planets in orbit, keeping a safe distance between one another. They didn't talk or even look at each other, which caused Eleanor a ripple of exasperated unease. If they couldn't even look at each other now, how on earth were they to marry?

Yet perhaps they wouldn't marry. Was an engagement made in the shadow of war binding? James would certainly think so, Eleanor decided. He might be reckless and a bit arrogant, at least to her former, fourteen-year-old self, but he also possessed a core of honour that would forbid him from breaking any promise. It was why he, along with Walter, had joined up so early, to 'do their bit', which to Eleanor had always seemed a rather expensive sentiment to afford.

Katherine excused herself from the room and after a moment Eleanor left her tea on the sideboard and went to follow her. She found her standing by the kitchen door, one arm wrapped around her waist, her hand cupping her elbow.

"What are you doing?" Eleanor asked. "James will wonder where you are."

"You think so?" Katherine answered tonelessly, and Eleanor raised her eyebrows.

"Are you cross because he wasn't more welcoming? Because you didn't seem very pleased to see him, Katherine—"

"I'm not *cross*." Katherine answered shortly, her face averted. "What a child you are, Eleanor. You'd think I'd stormed out of the room because someone had taken my toys. We are not children in a nursery, fretting over a spoilt game. It's not about being *cross*."

Eleanor took a deep, even breath, and forced herself not to reply in the childish manner her sister no doubt expected. "Tell me what it's about, then."

She didn't think Katherine would answer; her arm was still wrapped around herself, her hand on her elbow, as if she were holding herself together. She didn't look at Eleanor. "I just don't know how to *be*," she finally said.

"I don't think any of us do," Eleanor answered. "But I can see that you wouldn't, especially. It's all so strange, the war over, nothing the way it was..." She could not quite make herself mention Walter.

"The last time he visited," Katherine said after a moment, her face still turned away from Eleanor's, "back in the summer, he seemed..." She hesitated, and Eleanor prompted gently,

"How did he seem, Katherine?"

Katherine shook her head. "Just... distant. Walter did too, don't you think? I thought it had just been the toil of war. It seemed to go on so endlessly, and no one could quite believe the end might be in sight..."

"You think it was something else?" Eleanor asked after a moment.

Katherine didn't answer, and a clatter of cups from the dining room shook her from her seeming reverie. She pressed her lips together and nodded once. "I must get back. Why don't you tell Tilly to bring in a fresh pot of tea?" She moved past Eleanor, her back straight, her chin lifted, everything about her as proud and prickly as ever.

It was that endless evening that gave Eleanor the idea of actually having a proper Christmas. Not, she knew, that Christmas could ever feel truly proper, without Walter. The last four Christmases had been subdued affairs with him at the Front; after dinner—one of the local farmers always gave Father a trussed goose—Mother would bring out Walter's letters and they'd read them aloud by the fire. Eleanor wasn't sure she could bear doing that this year.

But perhaps a few treats at Christmas would help to lift their spirits. James and his parents would be coming for Christmas dinner, and they could have roast goose with all—or most of—the trimmings, and play parlour games afterwards. For Katherine and James's sake, so they could feel just a little normal. A little more like their old selves.

And for her sake too, perhaps. For all their sakes. Because the weight of grief was so crippling, and she wanted to forget it, just for a day. She didn't think that was being disloyal to Walter; like Grandmama had said, he wouldn't want them all moping about endlessly.

The week before Christmas her mother had once more retreated to her bed, and her father to his study. Katherine spent as little time at home as possible, preferring to take the train up to Carlisle and volunteer in some freezing hall than to spend afternoons with her family—or with James. A fortnight after his arrival not much had changed, as far as Eleanor could see. James had visited Katherine at the vicarage just twice since his return; they'd sat in the parlour and spoken stiffly about meaningless things, neither of them looking at the other. Eleanor had peeked in and it had seemed awful.

If they were to have a Christmas at all, Eleanor knew it was up to her, and in fact she found it was a relief to find something to throw herself into. She spent hours poring over *Foods That Will Win The War and How To Cook Them*, to discover what celebratory things she could make with their rations. She made wartime taffy with corn syrup and vinegar; Christmas pudding with beetroot instead of dried fruit.

Mrs Stanton liked having her in the kitchen, despite Eleanor's slapdash ways with scales and spoons; by the time she was finished there was a dusting of precious flour everywhere.

"It's nice to see you smile again, Miss Eleanor," Mrs Stanton said, and carefully brushed the scattered flour into her hand, to put back in the tin.

Eleanor found a precious set of Tom Smith Christmas Crackers at Dixon's in Whitehaven, and put a good amount of care and thought into the gifts she chose for everyone. For Katherine she bought lace-edged handkerchiefs, with her soon-to-be bridal initials stitched, rather clumsily, into one corner. For Mother she'd bought a book of poems, *The Wind on the Downs* by Marian Allen. Just the first verse had brought tears to Eleanor's eyes: *I like to think of you as brown and tall/As strong and living as you used to be/In khaki tunic, Sam Brown belt and all/And standing there and laughing down at me.* For Father she'd bought a new pipe, and Grandmama would get a pair of gloves, for even after over ten years in West Cumberland, she still complained of the cold and biting wind. She bought James a set of handkerchiefs as well, and painstakingly stitched his initials in the corner. She'd never been very good at embroidery.

Christmas Day was always a busy affair in the vicarage, with it being a day of work for Father. By the time the Communion service was finished and everyone had filed out into the frosty air it was going on one o'clock, and Mrs Stanton was busy in the kitchen, preparing the Christmas dinner they would have in the early evening.

Eleanor had cajoled Mr Lyman into cutting down a small spruce from the garden and putting it in the drawing room. She'd decorated it with sweets, candles, and a few precious oranges they could eat after. She'd adorned the dining room with red and green paper chains and greenery taken from the churchyard, and she'd made a centrepiece of boughs of holly and spruce. Next to every plate she'd laid a Christmas cracker.

Grandmama gave her an approving smile as they exchanged presents in the drawing room; it took effort, but Eleanor kept up a cheerful stream of banter, flitting around the room in her best dress, one that was last year's as there was still precious little cloth for new dresses, and was now, unfortunately, a bit too tight in the bosom. Her parents, Eleanor hoped, appreciated her effort, even though they both seemed subdued. Katherine tried to contribute to the conversation, but her face was pale, lines of strain visible around her mouth. James, Eleanor thought a bit resentfully, seemed as wooden as he had since arriving home. What had happened to the jolly young man with the booming laugh and careless ways, whom Eleanor had found just a bit too loud?

He could try a bit harder, she tho"ght 's they all walked Into the dining room for dinner. He'd survived the War intact, when so many others hadn't. When Walter hadn't. He could at least be grateful for that.

She pushed such thoughts away as she showed everyone their place; she'd written out place cards in her best script, and made sure Katherine and James were seated next to each other.

"And now the crackers," she said, and Anne gave a soft laugh.

"Wherever did you get them, Eleanor?"

"Dixon's. We haven't had crackers for ages, have we, Mother?"

"I don't suppose we have."

Tentatively, with a shy smile, Katherine proffered her Christmas cracker towards James. A peace offering, Eleanor thought with both hope and triumph. A bridge. "Shall we?"

He nodded, as stiff as ever, and they both pulled. The sudden explosion of noise as the cracker came apart made James flinch, and there was an awkward moment before his father let out a forced, little laugh.

"That was jolly loud, wasn't it?"

James didn't answer, but Eleanor could see his hand tremble as he tossed the paper crown onto the table. Katherine held hers in her hand, clearly unsure whether to put it on or not.

Eleanor had wanted the mood to be celebratory, even silly, but she knew now it wouldn't be. Perhaps it was too soon for James, for everyone. Katherine dropped her crown on the table as well, and Tilly began to serve out the meal.

James's mother attempted to start a conversation, talking about a parade planned in Whitehaven to celebrate the Armistice.

"It will be good to celebrate our boys' return," she said with a smile for James, who gave a humourless laugh and answered,

"And how many of us are there, then? There's not much to celebrate, as far as I can see."

Mr Freybourn mentioned the upcoming election, to be held in just three days, and James grimaced.

"I don't trust Lloyd George's promises or any other politician's."

"Let's not talk politics," Helen Freybourn implored, her voice trembling slightly. "Not at Christmas."

"Isn't it lovely, James, that you're home for Christmas," Elizabeth tried. "I read in the papers that thousands of men haven't been demobilised yet."

James's mouth had tightened and he said nothing. Eleanor wondered if he was even glad to be home.

"I've heard there is ice skating on Bell Pond," Katherine volunteered. Her voice sounded both bright and brittle. "It's cold enough for it to freeze over, finally."

"We should all go skating," Eleanor suggested. "I haven't been in ages."

She met James's gaze and nearly flinched at how cold his eyes looked. "I don't think so," he said quietly, and then he pushed up from the table. "Pardon me, but I find I'm not very hungry," he said, and walked out of the room.

CHAPTER 5

MARIN

Even though Rebecca seemed to have lost interest in the door, Marin was now determined to open it. She suggested a trip to Whitehaven the next day, and they spent an afternoon scouring charity shops, and managed to find a few decent pieces for Bower House, including a large, square table of scarred oak, just the sort of thing the kitchen needed. Marin also stopped by a hardware shop and bought a basic set of tools, including a screwdriver. Rebecca made no comment.

Back at Bower House Rebecca retreated upstairs and Marin went to work on the door. She scraped as much rust off the latch as she could, but no matter how she tried, she couldn't make the thing move at all.

Sighing in defeat, she headed back inside. Rebecca was in her room, listening to music and scrolling on her phone. Marin hesitated in the doorway, wanting to say something, yet having no idea what—or what Rebecca needed to hear. "I tried the door," she finally ventured, and Rebecca lifted her gaze from her phone, her dark blue eyes, the same colour as her mother's, giving nothing away.

"Any luck?" she asked, and Marin shook her head.

"I'm sorry about before," she said, as awkward as ever, and Rebecca sighed.

"Forget it, Marin. It was a stupid idea, anyway." She offered her a semi-apologetic smile. "I just want to chill out, okay? It's nothing to do with you."

Marin nodded, and after another uneasy moment she retreated to her room. She hadn't had any heartfelt conversations with Rebecca in the three months since she'd taken over her care. She'd tried at first, painfully, asking her if she wanted to talk about the accident or her parents or anything, really. Rebecca hadn't, and Marin had been secretly, shamefully relieved.

But now Marin was conscious of all the things they hadn't said, all the ways they hadn't actually got to know each other. Their relationship was, in a way, as empty as this house, needing to be filled up. Made real and loving, just as this house needed to be made into a home.

Shaking her head at her own fanciful thoughts, Marin went into her bedroom.

She walked to the window, and a draught of cold air blew over her as the panes rattled in the wind. She glanced down at the garden below, the shape of the flowerbeds just barely visible underneath the tangle of bare brambles. She gazed at the door set into the wall, so blank and unyielding, and felt that tug of fascination that she'd felt earlier, that Rebecca had felt. It was just a door leading to brambles, as she'd insisted to Rebecca, and yet...

A door. A door In a wall. It was, she decided, a thing of possibility or even hope. She still wanted to open it, for her sake, perhaps, as much as Rebecca's.

She watched the wind chase dead leaves across the garden; they tangled in the long grass and swirled around the twisted trunk of a cherry tree. She hadn't noticed it before, but an old wooden swing hung from a drooping branch, and the seat creaked and swung back and forth just a little bit in the wind. Marin shivered. Everything about the garden seemed so abandoned, so lonely: the flowerbeds, the swing, the door.

As she stood there gazing down at it all she felt a sudden, powerful wave of homesickness sweep over her, although what she was missing, she couldn't even say. Certainly not anything about her life in Boston, which she'd left all too easily. She missed her father, but he'd been absent from her life for so long his death hadn't actually changed anything.

No, this sudden, sweeping homesickness was for something she'd never had, somewhere she'd never been, and for a few blinding seconds its desolation seemed to sweep right through her, leaving emptiness in its wake.

She placed one hand on the cold glass, almost as though she needed to steady herself. The rays of the afternoon sun hit the top of the garden wall, and she saw, with resounding clarity, there were actually two walls, one behind and slightly higher than the other. She leaned closer, almost hitting her nose against the windowpane. From this vantage point she could quite clearly make out that the door did in fact lead to a garden, a little walled garden. From here she could see the swathes of bramble, the bare, scraggly branches of a few trees, and not much more. The walled garden, just as she'd thought, was overgrown and forgotten.

Marin leaned forward so her nose really was pressing the glass. She thought she could see something underneath all the thorns. Something dark and mossy.

Stones, she realised after a moment. The brambles were growing over the crumbling foundations of a building set in the centre of the garden.

Excitement pulsed through her and she called over her shoulder. "Rebecca! Come here. I can see the garden from my window."

After a moment, with a laborious sigh, Rebecca came into the bedroom. "Of course you can," she said.

"I mean the walled garden." Marin pointed, and Rebecca joined her at the window, a flicker of interest lighting her eyes before winking out.

"It's just as you said. Brambles."

"No, look." Marin tapped the glass. "Underneath. Don't you see it? I think there was some kind of building back there."

Rebecca frowned and then squinted before she gave a dismissive shrug. "It was probably just a shed or a greenhouse."

Marin's excitement died down a little at that bit of prosaic practicality. "You're probably right," she said, and after a moment Rebecca turned and went back to her room.

By dinnertime Rebecca had bounced back from her little gloomy spell, which made Marin feel both relieved and a little guilty. She felt she should handle Rebecca's downturns better, but the truth was she just didn't know how. She decided to make a proper meal instead, and spent an inordinate amount of time trying to figure out how the Rayburn worked, aided by an ancient, dog-eared copy of *The Complete Book of Rayburn Cookery*, which had been left in a cupboard by the range.

The recipes In the book were woefully outdated; Marin didn't Intend to start her cooking experiment with jugged hare or whitebait in pastry. She made sausages and mash instead, which seemed easy enough although she still managed to burn the sausages, and the potatoes were a bit lumpy.

Still, Rebecca smiled when she saw the meal on the table, and despite the chilly emptiness of the house the kitchen felt cozy enough with the two of them seated there, eating the meal Marin had made. It felt like a start to their new life here, to the healing process Marin wanted them both to begin. After supper they spent a companionable hour watching TV in the sitting room; with some effort Marin had even managed to make a little coal fire in the fireplace, which provided more atmosphere than warmth. Still, it was something, that they were even both sitting in the same room of an evening. Back in Hampshire Rebecca had spent the time from supper to bed in her room.

"School starts in a couple of days," Marin announced unnecessarily when Rebecca had turned the TV off. "How do you feel about that?"

Rebecca shrugged. "Who likes school, really?"

"You must tell me if you don't like it here," Marin said. "I mean it, Rebecca. We can always go back."

Rebecca stared at her for a moment, her eyes dark. "Are you saying that for my sake," she asked, "or your own?"

And the truth was Marin didn't know.

The next morning was blustery and bright and Marin decided to go for a walk through the village. Rebecca elected to stay at home, reading, and Marin didn't push her.

"The ceilidh's tonight, remember," she said. "We'll have to dig out our dancing shoes."

Rebecca arched an eyebrow at that, but then just shrugged. Suppressing a sigh at her own ineptitude, Marin headed outside. The wind seemed to cut right through her, and made tears start in her eyes. Why hadn't she remembered this relentless wind when they'd come back in December? Or had they visited on West Cumbria's one windless day?

She dug her hands deeper into the pockets of her fleece-lined waterproof and hunched her shoulders against the wind, her head bowed so she could barely see more than the worn slates underneath her boots. She'd meant to walk up through the village and then back down along the beach, a loop Mrs Hewitt, the owner of the B&B they'd stayed at the first night, had told them about, but without even realising what she was doing, she turned into the church lane instead.

She walked past the church rather than turn towards the churchyard, coming to an uncertain stop before the vicarage. It was a lovely house, with long, sash windows and flowerpots filled with early daffodils, their yellow heads battered by the wind, on either side of the big black door. Marin hesitated, wondering just how odd it would seem if she knocked on the door and introduced herself to the American family that lived there.

Then the door opened, and a young girl, about nine or ten, stepped out, her jaw dropping rather comically in surprise as she caught sight of Marin before she offered her a wide smile.

"Hello! Are you lost? The church doors are open, if you're wanting to have a wander." The girl, Marin noticed, had a lilting accent that was part Cumbrian, part American. She'd never heard anything like it.

"Thank you, I should have a look in the church," Marin answered awkwardly. "But actually I was just coming to introduce myself..."

The girl frowned at this, cocking her head, and to Marin's relief she heard a woman's voice from inside the house.

"Merrie? Who's at the door—" A woman appeared behind Merrie; she was dark-haired and harried-looking, in her early forties, probably, just a few years older than Marin. She rested one hand on the girl's shoulder and glanced quizzically at Marin, offering an uncertain smile.

"Hello—"

"Hi, sorry to disturb you," Marin said quickly. "My sister and I have just moved into Bower House, on the other side of the church—"

"Oh." The woman's expression cleared and her smile widened. "Of course! You're our new neighbours. Why don't you come in?"

"I don't want to be a bother—"

"Nonsense." The woman stepped aside, holding out a hand. "I'm Jane. Jane Hatton. We've been here about a year and a half. What's your name?"

"Marin Ellis." She shook her hand and then Jane beckoned her inside.

"Well, come on in, Marin. Merrie, pick up the milk. I'll put the kettle on."

Merrie scampered out to pick up the two old-fashioned glass bottles of milk that had been left on the doorstep and Marin smiled, cheered by Jane's open friendliness. She followed her down the hallway, done in the same kind of patterned tile as Bower House, and around to the kitchen in the back, a room that was large and bright and friendly.

Glancing around at the huge brass kettle on the range, the children's artwork taped to the walls, the jar of daffodils on the sill by the sink, Marin was caught by a sudden, fierce tug of longing. This was what she wanted for her kitchen. Her home. Her life. She wanted the warmth and friendliness and love that exuded from Jane Hatton's cosy kitchen, with a calendar scribbled full of dates and messages, the washing hanging above the Aga on an airing rack, the warm and welcoming and full feel of it. She wanted it for her and Rebecca.

"So when did you get here?" Jane asked as she filled the kettle and plonked it on the stove. She took a packet of biscuits from the pantry—there were two, Marin saw—and slid a few onto a plate. "Sorry, I'm not really much of a baker," she said with a smiling shrug of apology towards the shop-bought biscuits.

"Neither am I. We arrived a couple of days ago, from Hampshire."

"It's very different, isn't it?" Jane said in such a tone of sympathy that Marin blinked in surprise. "It is... but you obviously like it here."

Jane let out a laugh. "Obviously? Well, that's cheering, because everyone would have said the opposite a while ago."

"Really? Why?"

Jane sat down at the scrubbed pine table and indicated for

Marin to take a chair. She propped her chin in her hand as she took a bite of her biscuit. "I didn't want to move here, to be perfectly frank. We were living in New York City, which is completely different to Goswell, as you can imagine. I loved the buzz of the city and my job..." For a moment Jane's gaze grew distant and she swallowed the last of her biscuit. "Anyway, I didn't see any reason to move, but my husband Andrew is English—he's from Keswick—and he wanted to move back here. So we did." She gave a little shrug, smiling, and the kettle started to whistle.

"But you've settled in," Marin said as Jane poured the tea. "You seem happy here."

"I am," Jane said firmly. "But it took a while. Growing pains, I suppose. Sometimes it's hard to let go of what you had. Milk?" Marin nodded and Jane bustled over to the fridge. She took out one of the glass bottles Merrie had picked up and peeled the silver foil lid off the top. "The children love it here, and I've got a job, working part-time for a children's charity. It's a little different from what I had in New York, but I've come to realise that's a good thing. We all needed a change, even if I wasn't aware of it at the time." She poured the milk in and then handed Marin her tea. "What about you? What brought you to Goswell?"

"The house, I suppose," Marin said. She was unused to talking so easily and frankly with someone, and unsure how much to say about how she and Rebecca had ended up here.

"Do you know," Jane said as she took a sip of her own tea, "I didn't even know about that house? I'd seen it, of course, but I hadn't realised it was part of the church property. The vicar built it for his mother-in-law, isn't that right? Simon told me."

"Simon?" Marin repeated and Jane explained,

"Simon Truesdell, the current vicar. Friendly man. You'll meet him soon, I'm sure."

"So this was his house, before it was sold?" Marin asked and with a laugh Jane shook her head.

"No, but I thought that exact thing when we moved here. I thought we'd turfed the poor vicar out of his home. He lives in a bungalow up on Vale Road. The diocese decided to sell this place before he came."

"It's a lovely house," Marin said. The rooms were far bigger than those of Bower House, with soaring ceilings and huge windows. It was a house made for a family, a large one, and judging from the various sounds she'd heard since coming in—someone running up and down the stairs, laughter, a shout—Jane's family filled it admirably.

Again Marin felt that sudden shaft of longing, or even of homesickness, yet for a life she'd never once known. She pushed it away, taking another sip of tea.

"I hated this house when we first arrived," Jane said. "Well, to be honest, I hated everything. The house, the isolation, the cold, the rain, the wind—"

"I have noticed the wind," Marin admitted. "The window-panes rattle with it."

"They do! It used to drive me crazy." Jane let out a little laugh and shook her head. "But you haven't told me how you ended up in Goswell. The house, you said—but aren't you from down south? What brought you all the way up to West Cumbria?"

"Well..." Marin hesitated and Jane must have noticed for she said quickly,

"Sorry, I'm being nosy, aren't I? You don't have to tell me."

"We needed a change," Jane said. "My sister, well, half-sister, especially wanted one."

"You live together?"

"Yes, I'm her guardian. She's only fifteen."

"Fifteen? That's the same age as my oldest, Natalie. Will she be starting at Copeland Academy?"

"On Monday."

"You must bring her over," Jane said. "For dinner, maybe tomorrow? It makes such a difference to have a friend before you start school."

"All right." Marin smiled with a shy awkwardness, both grateful for and surprised by this unexpected invitation. She hoped Rebecca would want to come.

"And do you know about the ceilidh tonight? That's a good way to meet some people in the village."

"Yes, I think we'll go."

"Good." Jane sat back, smiling, but then her forehead furrowed and she leaned forward and touched Marin's hand. "I know it's not easy. Even if you chose to come here, it's hard to change. To adjust. But give it time. The people here are lovely, and despite the awful weather it's really one of the most beautiful places in the world. You couldn't do better than Goswell, really, for a place to live."

"That's quite the recommendation." Smiling a bit awkwardly, Marin rose from the table. "Thanks for the tea. I ought to get back to Rebecca now. But hopefully we'll see you tonight at the ceilidh."

"Yes, definitely." Jane rose too. "And do come for supper tomorrow night, the two of you. Half past five?"

"All right, thank you." With a few more thanks and farewells, Marin moved to the front door. Merrie, the girl who had first opened the door to her, came running down the stairs, skidding to a halt in front of her.

"You will come back, won't you?" she asked and Marin smiled, touched by the girl's easy friendliness.

"Yes, tomorrow, for supper. I'll see you then."

With one last wave, Marin headed down the lane, her shoulders hunched once more against the wind.

CHAPTER 6

ELEANOR

January 1919

Christmas dinner was, Eleanor had been forced to admit, a miserable failure. There had been an awful silence after James had left the room; no one had looked at anyone else. It simply wasn't done, to leave a table like that. James had committed a terrible breech of manners, and no one knew how to respond. The war, with all of its devastation, hadn't prepared them for a moment like this. Eleanor had had a sudden, terrible urge to laugh, and then a far stronger one to weep. She put a hand over her mouth to keep herself from either reaction.

James's mother half-rose from the table, stayed by her husband's hand. "Let him be, Helen," he said quietly. "Let him be."

Finally Anne roused herself and asked her husband to serve the goose, and eventually, after a few endless, silent minutes, everyone began to chat normally, or at least with the pretence of normality. James did not return to the table.

Afterwards Eleanor felt a surge of shame for her own thoughtless folly, that she'd convinced herself a roast goose and a couple of Christmas crackers could actually cheer anyone up. The grief they all felt for the loss of Walter was too deep for that, and it seemed almost offensive that she'd thought such a paltry celebration, one of paper chains and frivolity, could make a difference.

And it wasn't, she knew, just about Walter. After the initial relief and joy that had gripped the country when the Armistice had been signed, the nation now seemed to slump back into hopelessness.

Soldiers' demobilisations had been delayed and the newspapers were full of angry or pleading letters from parents and wives and sweethearts who wanted their men back.

And the men who did come back were not the same as those who had left. They weren't the bright-eyed laughing boys who had gone off to war with a jaunty step, promising to return by Christmas back in 1914, and neither were they the smart men in khaki who talked about giving Jerry what-for. No, these men, Eleanor thought, were gaunt, hollow-eyed strangers; some of them missing limbs, others blind or scarred. And even the ones with no visible wounds at all, like James, still seemed different, somehow *less*.

In the weeks and months after Christmas James and Katherine still, at least to Eleanor, seemed strained and almost strangers to one another; Katherine had thrown herself even more into volunteering, and went up to Carlisle several times a week. James had joined his father's law practice in Whitehaven, and only came to the vicarage one evening a week, when he and Katherine would sit stiffly together on the settee with cups of tea and make awkward conversation. Once Eleanor offered to play the piano for them; Katherine had huffed impatiently but James had said, "Why not let her? I'd like to hear something lively. God knows I'd like to feel it."

This comment, made half under his breath, left a little frisson of awkwardness in its wake, and then Eleanor, rather defiantly, started playing Al Jolson's latest song from America, *Wedding Bells, Will You Ever Ring For Me?*, until Katherine stood up and nearly banged the piano lid on her fingers.

"Honestly, Eleanor, you're such a child," she snapped. "I don't even like that modern music," she added, flushing, seeming to realise she had overreacted. She went back to the settee and sat down, smoothing her skirt. Eleanor glanced at James, curious as to his reaction, but his face was blank, his gaze distant, as if he hadn't even heard the music.

It wasn't only in the vicarage that things were tense and miserable. All around the country the dreaded Influenza continued to rage, killing thousands; jobs were scarce and people were desperate. This was not, Eleanor thought, what victory was meant to look like, but then some people questioned whether the Armistice had been a victory at all.

Life in Goswell continued on, as it did everywhere. George Sanderson preached from his pulpit, and Anne went back to her Sunday School classes and visiting the poor. The winter set in, cold and icy; the puddles in the sheep pasture were frozen solid and mean little flakes of snow drifted down, not enough to cloak the world in soft whiteness, simply a reminder of how cold it was.

Still there were moments of pleasure amidst all the bleakness and sorrow. One afternoon in February Eleanor stepped past a wounded veteran selling bootlaces from a tray around his neck so she could buy a bar of chocolate—the first she'd seen in years—from the sweet shop Mrs Charters ran from the front room of her house; the window sill had become worn down from all the schoolchildren who leaned on it to look at her wares.

Eleanor held the bar of chocolate, marvelling at the sight of it, wrapped in crisp gold paper and feeling heavy in her hand. "I can't actually remember the last time I saw chocolate, Mrs Charters."

Mrs Charters nodded sagely. "It feels like the war's over properly now, doesn't it?" Her gaze slid instinctively to the man outside the shop. "That's Billy Branson," she whispered. "Lost an arm at Passchendaele. He was meant to work at the scone flour factory up the street, but he can't now, poor lad."

Eleanor nodded, her throat going tight, and on the way out she bought several pairs of bootlaces from Billy that she didn't need.

Back at the vicarage she went to the sitting room, intending to enjoy her bar of chocolate, but she found she had no appetite for it anymore. She stared out the window instead at the muted grey landscape of February: stark, leafless trees and muddy, frozen pasture. Even the sheep looked lost and forlorn, as hopeless as she felt, huddling together.

"What are you doing moping about?" Katherine asked as she came into the room with her usual brisk step; Katherine always seemed as if she were going somewhere, as if she had plenty of things to do. Eleanor roused herself guiltily; her sister always made her feel lazy.

"I was just going to eat this chocolate," she admitted. "Mrs Charters had some in today, for the first time in years."

Katherine raised her eyebrows. "And you were going to eat it all yourself, alone in here?"

Belatedly Eleanor realised how piggish that must seem. "I don't want any now," she said, and held it out to Katherine.

"Well, I don't want it," Katherine retorted, stepping back as if Eleanor were forcing her to take it. "Give it to someone who might take some pleasure in eating it—one of our returned soldiers, for example."

"I suppose I shall," Eleanor said, and placed the bar of chocolate on the table. Perhaps she should have given it to Billy Branson when she'd bought the bootlaces. Or would he have seen that as charity, and been offended? Just like Katherine had said when James had returned, she didn't know how to *be* anymore, with Billy Branson, not with anyone.

"I don't understand what's happened," she said, and Katherine glanced at her sharply.

"What on earth do you mean?"

Eleanor shook her head slowly. "The war has ended but nothing's gone back to the way it was."

"Did you suppose it would?" Katherine demanded, all impatient scorn. "Nearly a million men dead, another million wounded, and thousands now dying from the Influenza. How on earth could anything be like it was?"

"I know," Eleanor said quietly, but the truth was she hadn't known. Before Walter had died, she'd believed they could go back. She'd had to believe it, childish, naïve fancy that it had been. She'd pictured them all playing croquet on the lawn just as they had in the summer of 1914, before war had been nothing more than a passing thought, a careless whisper. Eleanor certainly hadn't paid any attention to it, and the thought that had sustained her through those long and terrible years, through the missing and wounded and killed men, from farmers' sons she'd barely known to boys in church she'd talked and teased with, had been that they could go back. They'd return to the way things were, as much as they could, at least *enough*.

But perhaps you could never go back. Perhaps there was only this endless march of time forward, and to what? She felt as if she had nothing to look forward to, nothing but more of the same, endless days marking time, doing nothing.

"When will you and James set a date for your wedding?" she asked Katherine.

Katherine stiffened, her shoulders hunching slightly before she deliberately relaxed and smoothed a hand over her immaculate hair. "Why are you asking that?"

"It would be something to look forward to, at least," Eleanor answered. "A wedding is a happy occasion."

Katherine's mouth tightened. "We haven't set a date yet."

"What are you waiting for?"

"James has only just started at the practice," Katherine said. She picked up one of the lace doilies their mother was forever embroidering and smoothed it needlessly. "And the war has only just ended. We still have butter and sugar rationed—we wouldn't even be able to make a proper cake."

A cake was hardly a reason to postpone a wedding. "Do you love him?" Eleanor asked boldly.

Katherine looked up from the doily she straightened, her eyes flashing. "Don't be ridiculous."

"Ridiculous? How is it ridiculous to ask such a question?"

"Because it implies that you think I don't," Katherine answered shortly. She tossed the doily back onto the table, where it lay, rumpled and wrinkled. She had not, Eleanor noticed, actually answered the question.

"At least you have someone to marry," she said. "I shan't find someone." Most girls her age wouldn't, Eleanor knew. There simply weren't enough men left to marry. The papers had been full of the bleak outlook for her generation.

"You might have to lower your standards a little," Katherine answered. "But you could find someone, if you were of a mind to marry."

Eleanor could not quite keep from making a face. She did not want to marry a man with a missing arm or worse. She knew that most likely made her seem snobbish and selfish and unkind, but she wanted a man who was whole in both body and soul, a man like Walter and James had been before the war, laughing as they swung their croquet mallets around by the handle, full of life and possibility and *fun*.

Katherine watched her for a moment, her face contorting in what Eleanor thought might actually be sympathy before she shrugged and straightened the doily once more. "It could be worse, you know," she said, and left the room.

February slouched into March: cold, wet months, dark and damp and joyless, at least for Eleanor. While the rest of the family went about their business, she stayed at home, rereading Walter's letters until it became too painful to do so, and then spending hours simply staring out the window at the sheep pasture which had turned into nothing but mud and puddles.

"You must get out, Eleanor," Anne chided one March morning, when Eleanor sat curled up in the window seat of her bedroom, her hair undone and an old shawl around her shoulders. She'd picked up a book of poetry but had no inclination to open it.

"Go with Katherine to Carlisle, and help with—"

"I have no desire to sort through piles of mouldy old clothing," Eleanor answered, turning her face away from her mother's.

"I don't suppose you would do it for mere pleasure's sake," Anne answered. "But think of the good of your soul."

"My soul is too weary for anything to benefit it," Eleanor replied, thinking that quite an elegant answer, but her mother would have none of it.

"Then your soul is in dire need of the medicine of good works," she replied with asperity. "You are feeling sorry for yourself, and it does no one any good, least of all yourself."

"You sound like Katherine. She berated me for buying a bar of chocolate."

"I will not deny you life's little pleasures," Anne said after a pause, "for heaven knows we all need them. But you cannot live for pleasure, Eleanor."

"I didn't even eat the chocolate," Eleanor protested. She hadn't given it to Billy Branson or anyone else, either. She'd simply left it in a drawer.

Anne gave a small sigh. "You know I am not simply talking

about chocolate." Eleanor didn't reply and she continued, "I have Mrs Belmont and her daughter Susannah coming to visit in a few minutes. You know that George Belmont has gone blind from that dreadful gas?"

Eleanor swallowed. "Yes, I knew that," she said quietly. George had been in her Sunday School class; he'd always shared his conkers with her. She had not seen him since he had returned from France a few weeks ago, one of the last to be demobbed.

Anne reached out and touched her hand. "Come down, Eleanor, for your sake as well as the Belmonts'."

"I don't think I'll be much use to the Belmonts," Eleanor said but she rose, reluctantly, and followed her mother downstairs to the drawing room.

The rain was coming down in sheets and even with the drapes drawn and a coal fire blazing in the hearth, the room felt cold. Eleanor paced restlessly while her mother went to the kitchen to make sure the tea things were ready.

"Mrs Stanton has outdone herself and made a cake," she said as she came back into the room. She was smiling, but even Eleanor could see how pale and gaunt her mother had become in the months since the war had ended. She rubbed her hands together and stretched them towards the fire.

"And Katherine said there wasn't enough flour or sugar for a wedding cake," Eleanor said thoughtlessly, and Anne's eyebrows rose.

"What's this about wedding cakes?"

Eleanor shrugged, wishing she hadn't said anything, but she felt too restless and out of sorts to stay silent, and so she continued, her voice becoming a bit strident, "Just an excuse she has concocted to delay the wedding."

"Eleanor!" Anne looked disappointed rather than shocked, which made Eleanor feel worse. "That is not a kind thing to think, much less to say."

"Well, why haven't they set a date yet?" she demanded sullenly.

"James has only been home a few months—"

"At least he came home," Eleanor returned and Anne nodded.

"That is why you are so cross, then? Because James came home and..." she faltered slightly but then continued with determined calm, "Walter did not?"

"I'm not cross," Eleanor said. She thought of how Katherine had said the same thing, back at Christmas. Her unhappiness was too soul-consuming to consider being merely cross.

"Whatever you are," Anne said quietly, "you can keep such opinions to yourself. You don't know the first thing about Katherine and James."

"What is there to know?" Eleanor asked with a flicker of curiosity, but Anne just shook her head.

From outside they heard the crunch of gravel, and Eleanor saw Mrs Belmont, dressed in a gown of green bombazine that had to be several years old, walk up to the front porch with her daughter Susannah. She grimaced as her mother went to greet them.

The next hour was, for Eleanor, interminable. Mrs Belmont made determinedly cheerful conversation about George's rehabilitation, and how he was learning new skills to cope with his blindness, "even reading, which seems quite incredible to me. But with this Braille system—all these raised dots—he could read a book one day."

Which was more, Eleanor thought, than Walter would ever do.

She didn't like the Belmonts; she'd always thought Susannah a bit of a pretender, all milky sweetness and wide, fluttering eyes. Eleanor had once seen her pull a cat's tail when she'd thought no one was looking. And Mrs Belmont was one of those women who spoke in either hushed whispers or ringing tones, with nothing in between. Her husband managed the scone flour factory, and Eleanor had always thought Mrs Belmont had pretensions to grandeur.

Now Susannah turned her milky-sweet gaze on Eleanor. "We're just so glad he's home with us," she said, tilting her head as she smiled in what looked to Eleanor like exaggerated innocence. "We've so much to be thankful for, unlike some—"

"Susannah—" Mrs Belmont hissed, and Eleanor watched with pursed lips as Susannah made a show of widening her eyes and reaching for her handkerchief.

"Oh, I'm *sorry*—" she said, but Eleanor didn't think she was. Susannah had always been jealous of her. When they'd been twelve their teacher at the girls' school they'd both attended up on the high road had complimented Eleanor on her neat handwriting, just about her only academic accomplishment, and then had held up Susannah's childish scrawl in sorry comparison. Susannah had never forgotten it.

"You needn't be sorry," Anne said quietly, and poured more tea.

Susannah's gaze slid speculatively, even spitefully to Eleanor, and without another thought Eleanor rose from her chair and walked out.

She went into the vestibule, grabbed her coat and hat and walked outside. The air was frigid and damp; the rain had thankfully stopped, but only just. She stood on the front porch for a moment, at a loss. She did not want to go into the village and see people: Billy Branson with his bootlaces or Mrs Charters with her chocolate. She did not want to make pleasantries with women whose husbands had come home, or with mothers whose sons hadn't. She was so very tired of the war, and it was *over*. It wasn't, she thought with a surge of both fury and despair, meant to be this way.

Since she couldn't face the village she went round the house into the garden instead, picking her way past puddles and churned-up mud. The garden was at its worst on this raw March day: the trees and bushes still stark and leafless, the flowerbeds bare and bedraggled.

There was nowhere to go; Bower House was dark, her grandmother out undoubtedly doing more good works, and so Eleanor simply stood there, shivering in the cold, hating the war and what it had done and equally hating herself. She could still see Susannah's smug expression as she'd left the room, glad to have made Eleanor react in such a childish fashion.

She could not go on this way. She wanted to, *needed* to change, to rise from the rut she found herself in, and yet she felt as if she didn't know how. She wasn't like Katherine, to bustle off to Carlisle and knit socks and pour tea for orphans and widows. And yet she wanted to do *something*, to offer beauty and hope where there had been none, and not just with Christmas crackers or a few boughs of holly. But what?

Eventually she heard the sound of the gate creaking open and then someone walking across the wet grass. She didn't turn around, and then her father spoke.

"You will catch cold out here, Eleanor. You must come inside."

She heard the gentle reproof in his voice and her throat clogged with tears. "I don't think Mother will want me inside, after the way I've behaved." No matter how stupid Susannah Belmont was, it didn't excuse her appalling behaviour—walking out in the middle of tea like a child having a tantrum! How could she have let Susannah Belmont get to her in such a way?

But of course it wasn't Susannah Belmont that had driven her to it; it was everything else.

"If you mean leaving the sitting room when the Belmonts were visiting," her father replied quietly, "she is more concerned than cross."

Cross. No one, it seemed, was cross. "I just couldn't bear it, Father," Eleanor whispered. Her eyes were still closed. "Any of it. Not the Belmonts, not the orphans and refugees who are so desperate, not even poor Billy Branson with his bootlaces. I can't bear any of it. I'm sorry."

"I'm afraid it's the world we live in now, my dear," her father replied, and his voice sounded tired and sad. "Like you, I wish it was not, but we cannot change what God has ordained."

"Do you really think God has ordained all the crosses in Flanders Fields?" Eleanor demanded, her voice choking. "Did He ordain Walter dying in some muddy trench, *thousands* dying—"

"Eleanor." George spoke on a sigh, sounding both weary and stern. "I cannot explain to you why this war happened. I do not know all of God's ways, and I won't pretend that I do." He was silent for a moment, and then he continued quietly, "I fear we have done a great disservice to the people of this country, preaching from our pulpits that this war was necessary or even good. Now that it is over, they are more disillusioned than ever, and worse, they feel betrayed by the people they had looked to for comfort and healing." He let out a little sigh and rested his hand on Eleanor's shoulder. "I do not want you to feel the same. I would like to see you smile again, Eleanor, in time. I know you have suffered, my dear, as we all have. But the world still has happiness in it, and more importantly, it has hope."

"I don't feel either," Eleanor answered. "But I want to. I want to do something, Father, but I don't know what." She dashed away the tears that stung her eyes with one cold hand. "What can I *do*?" she asked, her voice rising, and her father smiled sadly.

"Just being yourself brings great joy to us, Eleanor—"

"But I don't want to be myself!" she cried. "I'm dreadfully tired of myself, and my fits and failures."

"Don't be so hard on yourself, my dear," George protested. "We are all weak."

"Perhaps I need to be," Eleanor countered. Her father

would always see the best in her, and Katherine the worst. But she wanted to see clearly now, see herself and any future she could have. She gazed round the garden, muddy and dead-looking, and remembered how it had been last summer, when Walter had been home. When he'd been *alive*. The grass had been velvety and verdant, the flowerbeds bursting with blossom, with life. No one had tended to the garden since then; Mr Lyman's arthritis was too bad to do much digging and no one had seemed to care. Yet in that moment Eleanor cared; it seemed a travesty to let the garden where she'd once been happy with Walter die along with everything else.

But what use, really, was a garden?

"Come, my dear," her father implored, holding out his hand, and with a sigh of resignation Eleanor took his hand and went back inside.

CHAPTER 7

MARIN

That night Rebecca and Marin got ready for the ceilidh. The wind had started up again and rain spattered against the rattling windowpanes. Marin peered outside at the darkening gloom and wondered if it was actually worth driving the quarter-mile up the high street to the village hall.

"It's atrocious out," she called to Rebecca, who had been trying on different outfits in her bedroom. "It's almost putting me off."

"Oh, don't," Rebecca answered, flouncing into Marin's bedroom in a ruffled mini skirt and colourful tights. "It's just a bit of rain."

"More than a bit," Marin answered. She was glad Rebecca was looking forward to the ceilidh, but she didn't know how to handle her half-sister in her determinedly cheerful moods any better than in her slumps. "Are you going to dance?" she asked, and Rebecca did a little twirl.

"Of course I am, and you are too. That's why we're going, isn't it?"

"To meet people, I thought," Marin answered. She did not relish the thought of dancing; she thought it quite likely that she would make a fool of herself. But she supposed she would do it if it made Rebecca happy. Anything to distract her from her grief.

"Do you miss him?" Rebecca asked abruptly and Marin turned around, startled.

"Pardon?"

Rebecca nodded towards the photograph Marin had put on top of the bureau, of her and her father when she'd been fourteen. "Do you miss him?" she asked again and then added without waiting for Marin's reply, "Do you know, sometimes I forget he was your father too."

Marin blinked, a little stung, although she would never admit it. "Well," she answered, "I'm a lot older than you. It's an easy thing to forget."

"It's not just that," Rebecca said after a moment. "It's that you never were around much, were you."

It didn't actually sound like a question, and Marin wasn't sure if she should answer it. In any case, Rebecca answered it for herself. "I suppose you were busy with university and then jobs..."

"Yes," Marin agreed. It was easier simply to agree, and it was true, up to a point. "Yes, I was."

"But you were close?" Rebecca pressed, nodding again to the photograph. "When you were younger?"

Marin glanced at the photograph, the only time when she'd actually felt like her father cared about her, since her mother's death. Remembered that even though her mother had died, she was still alive and craved his love and attention. "We..." she trailed off helplessly. She had happy memories of her father, of her family, before her mother's death. Blurred now by time and grief, but she still held onto them. Remembered the feel of his arms around her, or tossing her in the air. But since her mother's death, there had been nothing but an awful, frozen silence she had not been able to break. An indifference that had hurt worse than any actual unkindness could have. But she didn't want to explain all of that to Rebecca, didn't want to reveal the sorrow she still felt at a loss that was decades rather than months old. "It's getting late," she said instead. "We should head over to the ceilidh."

The rain had downgraded to a steady drizzle, and after bundling up in waterproof jackets and boots they headed out into the dark night. Other people were walking along the high street towards the village hall, and despite the rain and wind, there was a convivial, expectant feeling in the air.

They ran into the Hattons coming down the vicarage lane, and Jane waved to Marin who introduced Rebecca to the family. Jane went through her own haphazard introductions; her son Ben was bouncing around and Merrie was tugging insistently on her father's sleeve. Natalie, the girl around the same age as Rebecca, gave her a guarded hello that Rebecca answered in kind, like opening moves in a game of chess. Marin hoped they would get along.

The hall was crowded with people of all ages as they entered, shedding their coats and exchanging their boots for shoes in the entry hall. Inside children raced around as the band warmed up on a makeshift stage; a bar in the corner was doing a brisk business in boxed wine and orange squash.

On the walk over, Marin had noticed, Rebecca and Natalie had begun talking about school; now Natalie led her over to the bar and they fetched glasses of squash. Marin heard Natalie say something about the biology teacher, and Rebecca laughed.

She turned away, glad for Rebecca's sake that she had a friend but feeling unsettled and a little lonely on her own. Jane and her husband Andrew had gone off to greet someone else so she stood alone. Then she saw someone standing by himself on the other side of the room, and it took her a moment to recognise who it was: Joss Fowler, the man who'd been pruning roses in the churchyard. He saw her staring and raised his glass in something of a wave; Marin smiled awkwardly back and then, having nothing else to do, she started over towards him.

"Hello," she said as she approached; she could feel an awkward, uncertain smile contorting her face and so she stopped. Joss smiled back, easy and slow.

"You all right?"

This was, Marin had learned over the last few days, Cumbrian for 'how are you?' It had disconcerted her at first, because it seemed as if people were asking because they knew she wasn't, that they could see all the uncertainty and sorrow and fear she was trying to hide. Now she was a little more prepared for it and she answered,

"Oh, yes. Yes. Fine."

"Have you sorted your door?" he asked, and after a second she realised he was talking about their garden.

"We haven't been able to open it, no. But I saw from my bedroom window that it leads to a walled garden. It looks like mostly bramble, but we're still curious."

"I could open it for you, if you wanted. Latch is rusted shut, most likely."

"Yes, it is—"

"I'm working in the churchyard tomorrow. I'll come round, if you like."

"That would be brilliant," Marin said, and this time when she smiled nothing felt awkward about it. She looked forward to telling Rebecca that they'd be able to open the door.

The band had started to play, and with a screech a microphone turned on and a man at the front began to speak.

"Welcome, everyone! Very glad you could join us at Goswell's annual ceilidh. We'll start with a basic country dance, if everyone could get into a circle..."

Marin glanced at Joss. "Are you going to..." she began and he shook his head and stepped back.

"Two left feet, I'm afraid."

She felt a strange mixture of both disappointment and relief at this admission, and was just about to confess to the same, when Rebecca hurried towards her and grabbed her hand.

"Come on, Marin. You're not getting out of this one!"

"Oh, but..." Marin began, but Rebecca was already pulling her towards the centre of the hall, where people were arranging themselves in a rather lopsided circle.

The man at the microphone guided them through the first dance, which involved walking around the circle one way, and then the other, and then going in and out. "It feels like the Hokey-Cokey," Marin whispered to Rebecca, who grinned back.

They went through several dances, each one becoming more intricate, until the band took a break and with relief Marin headed towards the bar. She hadn't minded dancing, even if she'd felt a little silly, but she'd been conscious of Joss Fowler standing behind her, watching.

Jane joined her at the bar, looking flushed and happy. "Right, that's my workout for the week!"

Marin smiled and took a glass of wine from the bar. She was terrible at making small talk, but Jane seemed determined.

"So Rebecca's looking forward to starting school next week? It's a good school, Copeland Academy. Big, but they do seem to care about the pupils. Ben was having trouble with his reading last year and they sorted him out quite quickly. Merrie, my youngest, is at the village school. It's much smaller, but a lovely place. Cosy." She let out a self-conscious laugh. "Sorry, I'm rabbiting on, aren't I?"

"It's all right," Marin assured her. "Rebecca and Natalie seem to be getting on, at any rate."

"Yes, they do." Jane glanced at the two girls, whispering together as they stood against the wall. "There's a boy, Will, who lives on the other side of the churchyard, in the old gardener's cottage. He's in the same year as Natalie and Rebecca.

They can all ride the bus together. It picks up on the Beach Road."

"Goodness, there are a lot of church buildings, aren't there?" Marin said with a smile. "It's so interesting, the history of the place."

"Oh, I think so," Jane enthused. "Do you know, when we first moved into the old vicarage, I found a shopping list? Such a small thing, and yet it fascinated me. I did a bit of research and discovered the last woman who lived in the vicarage was Alice James, back in the 1930s. She had quite an interesting life, in the end."

"Did she?" Marin thought about the walled garden, and wondered if Alice James had tended it. "What was she like?"

Jane started to tell her about Alice James, and a war evacuee called Vera, and Marin listened with interest.

"So there are church records?" she asked and Jane nodded.

"Yes, Simon's been very helpful. And there is a village historical society too—they've done a marvellous job of preserving old documents and writing up a little history of Goswell through the years."

"I'd like to read that—"

"Are you interested in Bower House?" Jane asked. "I read that the incumbent at the time sold it to the diocese in 1929. That would have been the man before David James—George Sanderson, I think his name was."

"Actually," Marin said, "I'm more interested in the garden. The walled one, between the church and Bower House."

"I didn't even realise there was a walled garden there," Jane said in surprise. "I suppose I just thought it was the church wall, separating the properties."

"You can see it from our upstairs window. There's something there, but it's all just bramble now."

"Well, you never know what you might find," Jane told her, "beneath all the bramble."

The band was starting up again, and despite Rebecca's entreaties, Marin didn't join the dancing and stood against the wall instead. Rebecca partnered with Natalie for a country reel, and as the dance started Marin wandered around the hall, looking at the old photographs of Goswell framed and hanging on the walls, each with a typed explanation underneath. The historical society was indeed alive and well.

She studied a photograph of the high street, recognising the bed and breakfast she and Rebecca had stayed in their first night, although in the picture, taken in 1909, it was a farmhouse. The house on the other side of the street, now a private dwelling, had been a poultry dealer's and greengrocer's. Fascinated by the glimpse into what Goswell would have been like all those years ago, Marin peered closer at the photograph; she could see in the background there was a sign for a tailor's and another one for a confectioner's. She wondered how many shops the village had once boasted, compared to its lone post office and few pubs now.

She moved onto the next photograph, this one of the sweep of beach, minus the café that had been built in the 1930s, and with a single, ramshackle building in the foreground that had apparently been built to house telegraph wires.

The music stopped and everyone clapped before the man with the microphone—Jane had told her his name was Derek Williams—started again with instructions. Marin moved to the next photograph.

It was of a young woman, with dark hair and striking eyes, staring straight at the camera, one hand outstretched, a butterfly having alighted onto her fingertips. She was unsmiling, with an almost wild intensity about her expression that both fascinated and unsettled Marin.

Behind the girl a young man with a shock of dark hair underneath a flat cap stood, watching her with a look of such longing on his face that Marin felt as if she'd intruded on a private moment. They were in a garden, and when she read the placard underneath the breath rushed from her lungs.

Thought to be taken in the garden of Bower House, circa 1920.

She glanced up again at the photograph, and recognised the stone walls in the background, the open door framing the picture, painted black instead of its current white. This was the walled garden. Her and Rebecca's garden.

"Marin?" Rebecca came up to her, tugging on her sleeve. "It's the last dance. You have to join in this time!"

"Rebecca, look." Marin pointed to the photograph. "It's the garden, the walled garden behind Bower House."

"Is it?" Rebecca peered at the photograph before nodding. "Wow. Cool. Now are you coming?"

Marin let herself be led towards the centre of the hall; she joined hands with Andrew Hatton and a man she didn't know on her left. As the dance started, she felt a surge of excitement at the thought of the photograph, and she reflected that now she was more interested in the garden than Rebecca was. She was looking forward even more to when Joss Fowler came and finally opened the door.

CHAPTER 8

ELEANOR

April 1919

As spring finally blossomed all over England, the mood of the country began to lift. Hope, seemingly irrepressible, was found again, albeit in small and surprising things. Anne Sanderson smiled to read in the newspaper of a new season of opera at Covent Garden; for the last four years it had been used as a furniture repository for the Ministry of Works. The nights were longer and April was one of the warmest on record, and Eleanor thought once more of the garden.

"I thought I might do a bit of work in the garden," she said one morning in early April, as they all sat down to breakfast. "It's looking so bedraggled lately."

Anne looked up with a smile. "I think that's a splendid idea."

"I don't know why we need anything particular done to the garden," Katherine said as she gave her soft-boiled egg a rather hard tap with her spoon. "It's perfectly adequate as it is. And in any case," she added, turning to Eleanor, "you've never cared a tuppence for the garden before."

Eleanor shrugged. It was true, she hadn't involved herself with any gardening work before, but she liked the idea now. She liked the idea of restoring something to the way it was before the war.

"Let Eleanor have an interest, Katherine," Anne said gently. "It will be good for her."

"She'll stop as soon as she realises it's dirty, mucky work," Katherine answered. "She's like a butterfly—she flits from one thing to another."

"Let her flit," George answered with a laugh. "It's who Eleanor is." Which didn't, she thought, sound like much of a compliment.

"Perhaps we could ask Mr Lyman for some seed catalogues," Anne suggested. "We'd need to get someone in to do the heavy digging—he's not able any longer, poor man."

Eleanor didn't much like the sound of heavy digging, and poring through seed catalogues seemed a rather dull activity, but after Katherine's criticism she knew she could hardly back out now. "It all sounds very exciting," she said brightly, and ignored the sceptical huff Katherine gave.

"If you really want a project," Katherine said to Eleanor, her gaze narrowed, "you could come up to Carlisle with me and help with the work there. Surely the poor and unfortunate are worthy of more time than a few flowers?"

"Oh, Katherine," Anne said on a sigh and Katherine jutted her chin.

"You don't disagree with me, Mother?"

"I don't disagree with the need for both things," Anne said with gentle diplomacy. "Beauty *and* service."

"I'll go with you, if you want me to so much," Eleanor said, surprising herself. She had no desire to go to Carlisle, and certainly none to spend a day in Katherine's bitter company. But she was tired of her sister's constant digs. She could prove herself charitable, she decided. For a day, at least.

Katherine looked as surprised as she felt, and then discomfited. Eleanor doubted her sister wanted to spend a day together any more than she did.

"Very well," Katherine said and rose from the table. "The train leaves in half an hour." She left the room, Eleanor noticed, without eating her breakfast. Wearily she pushed away her own plate of toast. There was no jam and she wasn't hungry anyway.

Half an hour later they were boarding the train to Carlisle, taking seats in a second class carriage. Eleanor gazed out the window at the rolling fields dotted with wildflowers, the sun shining down with benevolent promise, and wished she had not so rashly agreed to help Katherine. She did not look forward to the prospect of spending the entire day in some draughty hall, sorting through overcoats that smelled of mildew or mothballs.

"What exactly do you do to help?" she asked and Katherine looked up from her book, her expression severe and yet also strangely guarded.

"I've been volunteering with the Blinded Soldiers and Sailors' Care Committee."

Eleanor simply stared for a moment before she finally found her voice. "But... I thought you were helping with orphans. Sorting clothes and the like."

"I was," Katherine said. "But then the Care Committee started up and needed volunteers, and I think I'm more useful helping the veterans. They need to retrain to find jobs, and I help to teach them useful skills."

Eleanor was still flummoxed. "What kind of useful skills?"

"Oh, many things. Basket weaving and boot making. You'd be amazed at what they can learn. Even how to be a telephone operator or a typist."

"A typist—"

"They use special Braille typewriters."

Eleanor's mouth dropped open. "And you can help with that?"

Katherine lifted her chin. "I've learned, over the last few months. The Society is desperate for trained volunteers, so they've helped me to learn. It's quite specialist, but I've had some practice."

"Goodness," Eleanor said as she sat back against the seat. "I had no idea you were doing all that in Carlisle. I thought you were just sorting clothes."

"It's certainly more than you've been doing back at home," Katherine answered starchily, "moping about and endlessly rereading Walter's letters."

Eleanor blinked, stung. "Don't let's fight," she said in a quieter tone. "Honestly, Katherine, I'm impressed. Typing, and in Braille! I never would have thought it." Katherine just shrugged. "Does Mother know? And Father?"

She pressed her lips together and shook her head. "No. And I'd rather you didn't tell them."

"Do you think they would mind?" A few years ago, helping young men in any fashion would have been unseemly, but now? The war had changed things, but how much Eleanor didn't really know.

"I don't know, but I'd rather not find out," Katherine answered. "I like being useful, and if you saw some of these men..." She trailed off, biting her lip, and Eleanor asked,

"Does James know?"

"No," Katherine answered, looking away. "But I doubt he very much cares in any case."

Eleanor wanted to ask something more; it was rare that Katherine was so forthcoming. But something about the way her sister stared out the window, biting her lip, made her stop. Katherine looked vulnerable, even fragile, and Eleanor didn't think she would welcome any more questions, especially about James.

They didn't speak for the rest of the journey into Carlisle, and when they alighted at the station Katherine led her confidently through the throngs of people to the road outside.

Eleanor clutched her reticule, discomfited by how many people there were compared to Goswell—and how many veterans. Goswell had its fair share, of course, but here there seemed to be a man on every street corner, one with a missing limb, his trouser leg pinned neatly over the emptiness; another man with a garishly-painted tin mask covering his scarred face, looking like something out of a nightmare circus. Even the men who were whole, dressed in their Sunday best, had bitterness etched on every line of their haggard faces.

Eleanor was stunned into silence.

Katherine walked briskly across Court Square to the elegant Station Hotel; Eleanor had only been in once before, for tea with her aunt who had been visiting from Leeds.

"They're *here*—" she began in surprise and Katherine silenced her with a swift nod.

"Yes, the proprietor has given over one of the salons to the society. He's very generous." And with another nod for the bellhop who stood by the front door—the man, Eleanor saw, was missing an arm—she walked inside. Eleanor followed.

The lobby of the hotel was one of the most elegant rooms Eleanor had ever seen, with a huge chandelier and sweeping staircases leading to the floor above. Katherine walked past the few guests seated on the silk-striped divans and armchairs to a set of doors in the back; she opened them and Eleanor was greeted by an entirely different scene. The large, airy salon had been cleared of the hotel's furniture and filled with long, wooden trestle tables, each one set with half a dozen black, boxy-looking typewriters.

"But I don't know how to type," she whispered to Katherine. "And certainly not in Braillle! How can I possibly help?"

"You can watch," Katherine answered. "And if you keep at it, you can even learn, as I did. In the meantime you can distribute the tea at eleven, when they have their break." With that she hung up her coat and hat and greeted the matron who looked to be in charge; Eleanor was introduced and instructed to observe Katherine for the morning.

She did so, trying not to stare at the men who filed into the room, each with a hand on the shoulder of the man in front of him, and sat down at the benches by every table; she knew they couldn't see her but she thought they could probably feel if someone was staring. They looked, she thought, like ordinary men, neatly shaven, a bit blank-eyed, but most with ready smiles. They took off their jackets and hung them on the backs of their chairs; they chatted with one another and the matron who greeted them briskly.

Katherine, Eleanor saw in amazement, was transformed. Instead of being severe and even sullen, as she was at home, she became brisk and cheerful, moving around the room patiently showing the men how to find the keys and type out simple sentences, teasing them gently when they made a mistake, keeping them from feeling the frustration and despair that Eleanor was sure must constantly threaten. The room was soon full of the noisy sound of clacking typewriters.

Eleanor watched the men patiently learning this new skill, men who had years or even months ago been whole and healthy, able to both see and dream. Who would have ever thought they'd be reduced to this, she thought, and suddenly felt near tears.

At eleven o'clock the matron rang a bell and Eleanor went to collect the teacart. She wheeled it beside each table, pouring cups of tea from a large brown pot that was so heavy at first she struggled to lift it. The first time she simply held a cup out, and the veteran in front of her did not respond; belatedly she realised that of course he couldn't see what she was doing.

"Time for tea," she said in a weak attempt at Katherine's

cheerfulness, and with her own hands shaking she guided the cup into the man's hands.

"Thank you, Miss."

She continued down the aisle, the threat of tears still present as she continued to pour cups of tea and guide them into the waiting veterans' hands. By the time she finished serving at half past eleven she was exhausted; she sank onto the bench next to Katherine who reached over and poured them both cups, pressing one into Eleanor's hands.

"There you are," she said, and she sounded almost affectionate.

"I don't know how you do this every day," Eleanor said in a low voice. "How do you keep your heart from breaking?"

Katherine took a sip of tea and looked away. "Perhaps it's already broken," she said.

After the tea break the men exchanged typing lessons for boot making. Katherine took the opportunity to sit Eleanor down in front of one of the typewriters, and she had her first lesson.

"I don't know how you ever learned this," she exclaimed after an hour's laborious work, and Katherine laughed.

"I've been doing it for over a year."

"And you never said a word—"

She shrugged. "I don't know if Mother and Father would approve."

"Why wouldn't they?"

Another shrug and Katherine played with the keys of the typewriter. "I don't know. Perhaps I just wanted a secret. Something I could call my own."

"I think they'd be proud of you," Eleanor said. "To do so much! And James, too. If you told him—"

"Don't let's talk about all that," Katherine cut her off. She rose from her chair and smoothed her skirt. "The men are coming back in. Why don't you come and chat with them? They'll like your cheerfulness, I'm sure."

Which was as encouraging as Katherine had ever been to her. As the men came back in and sat down, Eleanor did her best to chat with a few of them.

She spoke to Harry Abrams of the Third Battalion of the Border Regiment, who had lost his sight in a gas attack when he'd been holding the village of Gheluvelt in Belgium. "But it could have been worse, Miss," he said with a crooked smile. "Forty-six of my mates and seven officers died that day."

"That's terrible," Eleanor said quietly. She had known of the war's major battles and their terrible losses, but hearing it stated so simply by this soldier made it more real, more horrible. She'd never even heard of Gheluvelt, and yet so many had died there. "And what are you hoping to do?" she asked, injecting some brightness into her voice. "Do you fancy becoming a boot maker?"

"I quite like the typing, myself," Harry admitted rather shyly. "But it takes a lot of practice."

"Doesn't it just! My sister is trying to teach me, but I feel as if I'm all thumbs. And of course I don't read Braille."

"It comes to you, eventually," Harry answered with a smile. "I'd never thought I'd get the hang of it, myself."

"You must be very clever," Eleanor said. "I was never much good at school."

"Nor was I, but needs must," he answered cheerfully, and Eleanor almost envied his optimistic determination. She could not feel it herself, and she did not have the struggles this man had.

"Have you family, nearby?" she asked, and then could have kicked herself for the man's smile faltered.

"My mother is still alive, but I don't like to worry her." He paused, and then added quietly, "And I had a fiancé. Edna." He took a creased photograph from his breast pocket and handed it to Eleanor; she glanced down at the image of a light-haired women with wide eyes and a playful, secretive smile. "She broke it off when I came back. I understood, of course. Not many women want to marry a blind man."

"More fool her," Eleanor said staunchly, and Harry's mouth lifted once more.

"It's nice of you to say, Miss. I'm glad to know that at least one pretty young lady thinks that of me."

"But you don't actually know if I'm pretty," Eleanor teased, and Harry's smile deepened, revealing a dimple in one cheek.

"Even a blind man knows when he's talking to a pretty young lady, Miss."

Eleanor laughed, even as her heart twisted. Harry's story was so heartbreakingly sad, and yet he was so cheerful. The contrariness of it made her insides ache with a strange sorrow, twined with a surprising joy.

Lunch was a vegetable stew with bread; rationing still meant meat and butter were in short supply but the food was hearty enough and the men ate it up with relish. Katherine and Eleanor ate at a separate table for the female volunteers; Eleanor simply listened as her sister chatted with several other young women who helped as she did.

By four o'clock she was utterly exhausted and yet strangely unwilling to return to Goswell and the comforting confines of the vicarage. She didn't think she would find the house or life the same again.

"Do you think you'll come again?" Katherine asked as she buttoned her coat.

"I don't know," Eleanor answered honestly. "I don't know how you stand it day after day. The hopelessness of it all."

Katherine turned to give her a sharp look. "Did it seem that hopeless to you? Those men are learning skills, Eleanor. They're finding a future. That's not hopelessness, to my thinking."

"I know that." Eleanor swallowed and thought of Harry Abrams, who had said goodbye to her as she'd gone for her coat. How he'd known she'd been near him she couldn't fathom, but he'd turned his head as she'd walked by, and lifted his hand in farewell. "They show such immense courage and resourcefulness," she said to Katherine. "But they're *blind*—"

"As are thousands of other men. At least they came back." She walked out into Court Square, and chastened, Eleanor followed.

They boarded the train in silence; the mellow, golden light of late afternoon was spreading across the countryside like syrup.

Eleanor leaned her head against the window and closed her eyes. She felt stimulated but also overwhelmed; this was why she'd stayed in her room, she knew: to hide from all the horrors of a world she no longer knew nor understood. But she wasn't a child, and she couldn't hide anymore. Katherine had seen to that, and Eleanor didn't know whether to be grateful or sorry that she had.

She felt Katherine's gloved hand on her shoulder and she closed her eyes, not wanting to cry on the train, or in front of her sister.

"It will get better," Katherine said quietly and with her eyes still shut Eleanor asked in a suffocated whisper,

"Has it got better for you?"

Katherine let out a little sigh. "A bit," she said, and squeezed Eleanor's shoulder.

As they left the train at Goswell, Eleanor thought how sleepy and peaceful the village seemed; smoke curled from a chimney towards a still-blue sky and the only sound besides the train chugging towards the sea was the gentle lowing of sheep.

Eleanor had the contradictory impulses to go back to Carlisle and stay in Goswell forever, hiding away from all the unpleasantness, all the suffering.

Katherine had started walking towards home, and impulsively Eleanor laid a hand on her arm. "Thank you for taking me," she said and Katherine just nodded.

The house was quiet as they let themselves in; Tilly bustled towards them as they took off their coats and hats in the hall.

"Your father's just gone outside," she said with an air of excitement. "It seems he might have found a gardener!"

"A gardener..." Eleanor repeated blankly. To think that morning she had been expecting to pore over seed catalogues for most of the day. Suddenly it seemed rather ridiculously trivial.

"So who has Father found?" Katherine asked. "As a matter of interest?"

"I'm not sure. I don't recognise him, at any rate. But the Begbys recommended him, it seems. He did a bit of work for them up at their farm."

Katherine nodded absently and headed upstairs. "I think I'll have a rest before dinner," she said, and then paused with one hand on the railing. "Has Mr Freybourn been to call, Tilly?"

Tilly's face fell a little although she quickly rearranged her expression into something more like a smile. "Not today, Miss Katherine, I'm afraid."

"I see," Katherine said, and continued walking upstairs.

Eleanor felt too restless to go upstairs to sit or read; her mind still seethed with all she'd seen and learned today. Impulsively she reached for her coat again.

"Miss Eleanor, you're not going out again?" Tilly exclaimed.

"Just to see Grandmother," Eleanor said. "I want to tell her about today."

Although, Eleanor reflected as she walked towards Bower House, she wasn't sure she should tell her grandmother everything she'd done today. Katherine still wanted it to be a secret, to have something for her own. Eleanor wouldn't take that away from her.

"Eleanor." Elizabeth smiled and took her hands as Eleanor came into the house. "You look tired, my dear, and a bit pale."

"I've had a long day," Eleanor admitted. "I went to Carlisle with Katherine."

Elizabeth nodded and settled herself in a chair opposite her granddaughter; in the months since Walter's death she too had become tired and pale, her face more drawn and haggard than it had been when hope had still prevailed.

"I hope it was edifying for you, at least," she said with a tired smile. "Your father has been busy, you know, with this idea of yours to liven the garden."

"Yes, Tilly said." Eleanor rose from the chair, pacing the room as she twisted her hands together. "It seems so silly now, to think about a garden, with everything the way it is."

Elizabeth raised her eyebrows. "Can we not have gardens, in this brave new world of ours?"

Eleanor smiled a bit at that. "It's just... there's so much suffering, and I can't bear to see it all, but it seems cowardly to hide behind rose bushes and seed catalogues."

I, for one, would very much like to enjoy sitting out in the garden again," Elizabeth returned. "We've had nothing but potato plants for four years, and in my old age I would like to sit on a stone bench and smell roses once more. See beauty." She stood and reached for Eleanor's hands. "Do not lose sight of the pleasure you might do others, in helping to make a garden."

"Do you really think so?"

Elizabeth squeezed her hands. "I certainly do. Your father, for one, is most enthused about the idea."

Feeling a bit better at that, Eleanor stayed for tea before she left, reluctantly, to return and dress for dinner. It was still light out as she left Bower House, the sky just starting to darken to violet as she walked through the garden towards the vicarage. She shivered in the evening chill, the garden full of lengthening shadows as she skirted around the church and then slipped through the gate that led to the vicarage's garden. She glanced round the shadowy lawn, wondering if she could rouse herself to take it in hand. She pictured a soldier like Harry Abrams out here; he wouldn't be able to see any flowers, but he could smell them, and feel the wind and sun on his face. Perhaps if she did restore the garden to its former glory, she could invite the blind veterans for an afternoon. Katherine would no doubt pour scorn on such a pointless idea, but Eleanor liked the thought of bringing beauty and pleasure, and not just usefulness, to those men's lives. They would at least be able to smell the roses, if not see them.

"Eleanor, my dear!" Her father's voice rang out through the settling twilight. "Come meet our new gardener."

Eleanor could only just make out the shape of her father coming towards her in the dusk, a man walking a step behind him.

"Father?"

"Here is our garden's salvation," George announced in a jovial tone. "He's going to dig over the flower beds and turn the lawn back into the velvet green we once loved. We shall play croquet again this June, my dear, never fear."

But not with Walter. Eleanor tried to smile; she could see the man next to her father now. He had a kind, ordinary face and a shock of dark hair underneath a flat cap. He wore a brown wool suit and a shirt with a celluloid collar, well-worn Sunday best for a working class man. He nodded a greeting.

"How do you do, Miss."

"How do you do," Eleanor answered, and George finished the introductions.

"My dear, this is our new gardener. Mr Jack Taylor."

CHAPTER 9

MARIN

Joss Fowler came to Bower House the next morning, driving up in a battered white van with 'Fowler and Son Landscaping' stencilled on the sign. Marin felt almost giddy with anticipation; she couldn't say why she wanted to open the door to the garden so much, only that she did.

"Aren't you coming out?" she asked Rebecca, who was curled up in the kitchen with a cup of hot cocoa. It was another wet, windy day; the whole world looked battered.

"Oh, I suppose, in a minute," Rebecca said. "After I get dressed."

Her sister, Marin reflected, no longer seemed to share her enthusiasm for the garden. She had not been fascinated by the photograph of the young woman with the butterfly, as Marin had; this morning she'd been tired from staying up late at the ceilidh and a little morose again, and Marin had let her be, suspecting Rebecca needed her space.

Now she stuffed her feet into wellies and reached for her waterproof jacket before heading outside. Joss had already climbed out of his van, a cap jammed low on his head.

"Quite a day for it," he remarked, and Marin nodded.

"The garden's over this way," she said, and hunching her shoulders against the wind, she led him through the bedraggled garden to the weathered wooden door.

Joss examined the rusted latch for a few seconds, and then attempted to lift it, which he couldn't. He nodded once and then took a screwdriver from his pocket and scraped at the rust. A few flakes drifted down but the door still didn't budge. Marin's heart sank a little. Would even Joss Fowler not be able to open the door?

He studied the latch again, and then to her surprise and some embarrassment, he hooked one boot under the bottom of the door and raised it up an inch. The latch lifted with a protesting screech and the door swung open.

"Now I feel a bit of a fool," she said with a little laugh. "If I'd known all I had to do was *that*—"

He shrugged. "Sometimes it's the simplest thing that works." With one work-roughened hand he pushed open the door and stood aside so she could enter the garden first.

Marin felt a lurch of anticipation even though she knew that the garden held only bramble. Still, just walking through the doorway and seeing the stone walls climbing with ivy made her heart beat a little faster. She *knew* there wasn't anything there, and yet even so the sight of a quarter-acre of untended bramble and a few twisty trees—exactly what she'd seen from her bedroom window—still managed to be disappointing. She stood there for a moment, staring at it all, unable even to enter the garden properly because of the dense thicket of thorns. She tried to think of something to say, but nothing came.

"Bit of a mess," Joss offered, and she nodded, swallowing.

"Yes—did the last resident not do anything with it?"

"No one's been in the house for ages. It used to belong to the vicarage though, if I recall aright. They used it as a garden, back in the day, I believe."

"Yes, it belonged to the old vicar's mother. I suppose it was just a vegetable garden. It's silly to be sentimental about it."

Joss raised an eyebrow. "Are you sentimental?"

"Well." Marin let out an uncertain laugh. "It just seemed... enchanting, I suppose. The door and the walls, like *The Secret Garden*. I loved that story, as a child."

"Haven't read it, myself."

"No, I don't suppose you have. It's more for girls."

"It looks like there might be something under all that," Joss said with a nod towards the thorns, and Marin felt her heartbeat quicken again.

"Do you see something?"

"It looks like the foundation of a building." He pushed some bramble away with one boot and nodded towards the ground; Marin glimpsed a few moss-covered stones.

"I saw those from my window. I thought it might have been a greenhouse or something like that."

Joss nodded. "Might have been."

"Not very interesting, then." She sighed and shook her head. "Honestly, I don't know what I was hoping for."

"Magic beans?" Joss suggested and she laughed.

"Something like that, I suppose. Or a door to Narnia."

"I've read that one."

He smiled and she smiled back, and for a second she felt... unsettled. Carefully she pushed some brambles down with her foot, the thorns snagging her jeans, and examined the mossy stones more closely. "I don't suppose I'd learn much more if I cut all the bramble down."

"You might," Joss offered. "Who knows what all is under there?"

"I suppose, but I've never actually done any gardening. I've never even had a garden before."

"Lived in flats?"

She nodded. "I was in Boston before this, in the States."

"And you came all the way to Cumbria?"

"It seemed like a good idea." She stared up at the pewter sky, rain spitting down, and let out a little laugh. "Sometimes I can't believe I'm really here."

"I know how that is," Joss said, almost under his breath, and Marin lowered her head to look at him curiously.

"Do you? Have you been doing landscaping for long?"

A shuttered look came into Joss's eyes. "About three years," he said, and he sounded strangely reluctant to impart the information. He nodded towards the garden. "So will you do anything about this, then? There are a few fruit trees amidst all that." He pointed with one soil-stained finger to some of the twisty trees whose tops she'd seen from the window. "Damson, it looks like."

"Yes..." The trees were a bit more interesting, Marin supposed, but it still all felt a bit disappointing. "I'll have to think about it. Like I said, I'm not much of a gardener."

"You could learn," Joss offered. "If you're staying."

"We're staying," Marin answered. "We bought Bower House."

"You don't sound very sure," Joss observed, and Marin looked at him in surprise.

"Don't I?" She was unsure about so many things, moving here the least of them. "Well, we are staying," she said, and she realised she sounded resigned rather than resolute. She turned back towards the door. "I should get back inside, to Rebecca. Thank you for fixing the latch—"

"It will keep sticking, on account of the rust. I can put a new one in, if you like. If you're going to be opening and closing it." The words sounded almost like a challenge, and when she glanced at Joss Marin thought she saw a glimmer of it in his eyes, golden within the grey.

Was she going to go in the garden again? Actually make something of it?

"That would be lovely," she said at last, making no promises. "Thank you."

Rebecca remained in one of her slumps for most of the day; Marin kept busy unpacking the last boxes and then tidying the kitchen and trying to learn the intricate workings of the Rayburn.

"This dial seems to control the water temperature," she said dubiously as she twirled it ineffectually. "But we still haven't had any hot water."

"Thank goodness for the electric shower," Rebecca answered and peered into the innards of the Rayburn. "Look, there's a timer." She punched a few buttons Marin had over-looked. "You have to set the heat and hot water and things—it goes on a schedule."

"So this dial is useless?" Marin surmised with a smile, but Rebecca was already drifting off. She straightened, feeling a need to be motherly or at least concerned. "How are you feeling about school starting on Monday?" Rebecca just shrugged. "The first day can sometimes be a bit difficult," she tried again and Rebecca rolled her eyes.

"Oh, Marin, don't. I'm fine, okay? And you don't need to act like my mother."

Trying not to show how hurt she was, Marin nodded. "Okay, sorry. I never was much good at small talk."

Rebecca gave her a placating, slightly patronising smile before heading upstairs and with a sigh Marin filled the kettle and plonked it on top of the Rayburn. Just over three months since she'd become Rebecca's guardian and she still had no idea how to act. How to be.

That evening the rain cleared to a flat grey sky as they headed over to the Hattons for supper. Marin had attempted to make a loaf of banana bread to bring over in a gesture of neigh-bourly goodwill, but the Rayburn seemed to cook quite unevenly and the loaf managed to be burned on the edges and raw in the middle. She took a bottle of wine instead.

"You get along with Natalie, don't you?" she asked Rebecca a little anxiously, and her sister shrugged.

"She seems nice enough."

Which was not a ringing endorsement, but Marin let it drop. She'd pestered Rebecca enough today, with her awkward, ineffectual expressions of concern.

Merrie was waiting for them as they came up the steps of the front porch; she threw the door open and greeted them with a wide smile. Marin entered the Hattons' foyer, glad to be brought into the happy chaos of a busy family. It certainly made a welcome change.

Jane ushered them into the kitchen, and Andrew fetched them both drinks. Natalie appeared in the doorway, and after a few minutes Rebecca went off with her, upstairs. Ben was playing some electronic device which Jane cheerfully rescued and told him to go stoke the fire in the dining room instead. Ben got a rather excited gleam in his eye at that, and hurried off.

"My budding pyromaniac," Jane said affectionately, and proffered a bowl of crisps. Marin took one and nibbled.

"I made the pudding," Merrie told Marin. "Chocolate mousse. Mummy only helped a little."

"I'm sure it's delicious," Marin said.

"Come sit down in the dining room where it's warm," Jane said. "Everything's already in the Aga. I don't need to do a thing."

"It smells delicious—"

"Just shepherd's pie," she said with a wave of her hand. "But it's a night for hot, simple food, I think. Come through."

Marin followed her from the cosy kitchen to a large, elegant dining room; the fire cast dancing shadows along the walls, and wooden shutters had been drawn across the windows that overlooked the garden. Despite the room's large size it was just as cosy as the kitchen, and Marin settled herself across from Jane in the windowed alcove where a sofa and a couple of chairs made a welcoming little corner. Andrew followed them in, instructing Ben to fetch more coal from the shed, and as his son sloped off he settled himself on the sofa next to Jane.

"So how are you finding it, Marin?" he asked. "Besides the dreadful weather, of course."

"I don't mind the weather that much," Marin confessed. "At least not when I'm tucked up inside with a roaring fire like this."

"We are lucky to have so many working fireplaces," Jane said. "Does Bower House have many? I've never been inside."

"We've had a fire in the sitting room," Marin answered. "I haven't checked if the other ones work. I suppose I should get a chimney sweep to come round. You must come over," she added, a bit stiltedly. "Have a cup of coffee and a look round."

"I'd love to."

"Jane's quite curious about all the buildings around here," Andrew said. "She had a grand old time researching the vicarage—"

"I've already told her about Alice," Jane said with an answering laugh. "I can't help myself."

"Did you tell her about the garden?"

Interest flared and Marin leaned forward. "The garden?"

"Andrew means the rose garden, in front of the vicarage," Jane explained. "Technically it's part of the church property. Last year we started a bit of a community project, to turn it into a memorial garden for Alice James."

"Oh?"

"She wasn't a famous person or anything like that," Jane said, "But she did make a difference, in a quiet way. I wanted people to know that, and to remember. But enough about Alice," she continued, her eyes alight. "You were telling me about your garden, last night at the ceilidh. Have you managed to open the door?"

"Yes, Joss Fowler came round this morning. It was quite simple really, he just hooked his foot under the door and lifted it a bit, and the latch came unstuck. I should have thought of it myself."

"Joss Fowler," Jane mused. "I don't think I know him."

"I've seen him round the churchyard," Andrew said. "He has a landscaping business, doesn't he?" He looked to Marin for confirmation, and she thought of the van and nodded.

"Yes, Fowler and Son Landscaping."

"So what brings you here to West Cumbria?" Andrew asked. "Jane didn't say."

"The house, I thought," Jane intervened with a questioning smile; Marin could see she looked both interested and concerned, and she knew she hadn't really explained why she and Rebecca had moved here, when she'd come round before. She was reluctant to tell the Hattons about her situation; she didn't want to invite pity, but she also knew she could hardly keep it a secret. She'd told Rebecca that would feel disloyal, even dishonest, and she knew it was true.

"My father and his second wife died three months ago," she began, and Jane and Andrew both gave the expected expressions of sympathy before she continued. "Rebecca is my half-sister, and I'm her guardian. We were rubbing along together all right back in Hampshire, I suppose, but we came up here for a holiday and Rebecca fell in love with Bower House. We decided we needed a new start."

"You've come a long way for that," Andrew said with a smile. "But I can understand why you'd feel that way. I hope you find your new start here."

"So do I," Marin answered. She tried to ignore the twinge of unease she felt at how awkward things still could be between her and Rebecca. Coming to Cumbria hadn't changed that. In some ways the isolation had made it worse.

"Are you free tomorrow?" Jane asked. "I'll introduce you to

Simon Truesdell, the vicar. Perhaps he'll be able to tell you more about your garden."

"I'd like that," Marin answered.

"Was there anything interesting, when you opened the door?"

"Just the usual brambles and weeds, and the foundations of what I suppose was a greenhouse or some kind of outbuilding. But I'm still curious about it for some reason. I know it's just a garden—"

"I know exactly how you feel," Jane said, exchanging a humorous look with her husband. "I was the same about the shopping list I found."

"I doubt I'll find anything—"

"But you might, and that's the exciting thing," Jane finished, and Marin smiled, grateful for her understanding.

"Actually, I saw a photograph of the garden in the village hall last night," she said, and haltingly explained about the girl and the gardener, although she couldn't quite articulate the unsettling intensity of the girl's gaze, the look of longing the man seemed to be giving her.

"1920..." Jane mused. "That would have been when Andrew Sanderson was the vicar. He had a family, I know, but I can't remember exactly who or what. Simon would know, though."

"Do you think it's someone from his household, in the garden?"

"Well, it stands to reason, doesn't it?" Jane answered. "Bower House would have been occupied by his mother-in-law then."

"Yes..."

"We'll ask Simon," Jane said, definitively, and rose from her seat. "I'd better get the pie out of the Aga before it's blackened. Andrew, would you call the children?"

Marin followed Jane into the kitchen, and helped bring the

dishes back into the dining room. Within a few minutes they were all seated around the large table, a loud, cheerful bunch; Rebecca, Marin noticed, seemed to be getting along with Natalie, and she was cheered by the thought.

Dinner passed in a blur of animated conversation and hearty, warming food; Marin didn't contribute much but she enjoyed the banter between Andrew and Jane, and the good-natured bickering between the children. She was feeling quite cheerful and relaxed as she and Rebecca headed back outside into the dark, still night.

"Thank goodness the wind has died down," she said as she turned the collar up on her coat. "It kept me up last night. I never knew wind could be so *noisy*." Rebecca didn't answer and Marin continued, "Jane offered to introduce me to the vicar, Simon Truesdell, tomorrow, to learn more about the garden. I thought I'd go to church in the morning, if you wanted to join me."

"Church?" Rebecca repeated, sliding her a startled glance. "Since when have you gone to church?"

"I haven't," Marin answered. "Not much, anyway. But it feels a bit rude, pestering the vicar on Sunday afternoon when you haven't been to the service on Sunday morning."

Rebecca shrugged and dug her hands deeper into the pockets of her coat. "I haven't got much time for church," she said. "Or God, for that matter."

Marin was silent, for she could understand not having time for God when your parents had been taken away from you so recklessly, so needlessly. The question of how a divine being could allow such suffering was, she supposed, as old as organised religion, and one she didn't have an answer for. But she still thought she ought to go to church tomorrow.

Back at Bower House the rooms felt cold and unwelcoming, compared to the bright bustle of the Hattons' house. Even the rumbling of the Rayburn and relative warmth of the kitchen did little to cheer Marin, and she had, she thought with a sigh, been in such a good mood when she'd left the Hattons.

Rebecca retreated upstairs without a word, and Marin put the kettle on top of the stove for a cup of tea before bed.

She drank her tea alone in the kitchen; the night was so still she could hear the ticking of the clock. Then she went upstairs to check on Rebecca, whose light was already out.

Marin retreated to her own bedroom, shivering slightly in the cold; she needed to figure out the heating a bit better. The pipes occasionally made an encouraging, clanking sound, but little heat leaked from the old radiators.

The moon had come out from behind a cloud and illuminated the tangle of garden below; Marin stood by the window and gazed at the brambles now bathed in lambent silver. She *would* clear the garden, she decided. She'd take up Joss Fowler's challenge and get rid of the brambles, find out what was underneath. Perhaps having a project would be a good thing. She could try to enlist Rebecca's help; maybe she would be more interested if Marin found out something about the garden, or even the girl with the butterfly.

Perhaps they'd clear the garden together, a joint project, a way to become closer. Cheered by these thoughts, Marin turned from the window and headed to bed.

CHAPTER 10

ELEANOR

April 1919

The next time Katherine went to Carlisle, a few days after the first visit, Eleanor decided to go with her. She half-dreaded seeing those poor men again, and hearing the relentless clacking of the typewriters, struggling to pour the tea, but she felt she needed to go, and she was looking forward to chatting to Harry Abrams and the other soldiers again.

In any case, she knew she could not hide in her bedroom any longer, pretending the world outside hadn't changed irrevocably. She thought of how disappointed Walter would be, if he knew how cowardly she'd been these last few months, and the last of her timid reluctance trickled away. Of course she would go.

Katherine looked both wary and surprised when she announced her intentions at breakfast; her mother seemed pleased but her father looked a bit concerned.

"Are you quite sure, Eleanor? I thought you were going to busy yourself with the garden."

"Perhaps she has found more important things to occupy

herself with than a garden," Katherine interjected, and Anne gave a little shake of her head.

"Do not dismiss it out of hand, Katherine," she admonished. "There are many people in this village who might derive some pleasure from our garden, should they come to visit it, and that is not even to mention how we are helping Mr Taylor, by providing him with gainful employment."

"Who is this Mr Taylor?" Katherine asked as she took a sip of tea, frowning over the rim of the cup. "Tilly said he's not from around here."

"He's from West Yorkshire," George said. "Served in the Prince of Wales's Own, Tenth Battalion." He paused, his voice turning sombre. "Seven hundred and fifty men lost on a single day at the Somme, out of a thousand. It must have been something terrible." Anne flinched a little at this and George gave her an apologetic look. "I'm sorry to mention it, my dear."

"This Mr Taylor must be a very brave man," Anne replied with a wan smile.

"But what on earth is he doing all the way over here in Cumberland?" Katherine asked. "We're a long way from West Yorkshire."

"Looking for work, same as any man," George replied. "That's something else that's changed. No one stays put anymore. They can't. Men must move around these days, looking for what jobs they can."

"There isn't much gainful employment in Goswell," Katherine pointed out. "He would have been better off to go to Carlisle, or even down to Manchester."

"He's from a farming family, and he wanted to work the land," George replied. "The Begbys had him doing all sorts up at their farm, but they don't need him now. And he's got gainful employment for the next few weeks, digging over Eleanor's garden."

"I didn't realise it was entirely hers," Katherine remarked

tartly, and Eleanor stared down at her plate. She wasn't entirely sure she wanted the garden to be hers, but both of her parents seemed pleased for her to have a project.

A few minutes later Eleanor went for her hat and coat, and she and Katherine had just stepped outside to take the train to Carlisle when she saw Mr Taylor coming up the church lane, whistling as he walked. Both women stopped short; Katherine looked at him with something like disapproval, but Eleanor smiled. It was nice to see a man looking whole and healthy and cheerful.

"Good day, ladies," he said as he approached, taking off his cap to reveal rumpled dark hair.

"Good day, Mr Taylor," Katherine answered rather sternly, and swept past. Jack Taylor looked a bit bemused, and Eleanor tried to give him a conciliatory smile as she followed Katherine.

"It looks to be a nice day for working in the garden," she offered and he nodded.

"Hot, though. But I can't complain."

"Eleanor," Katherine called, impatience edging her voice. "We'll miss the train."

"Good day," Eleanor called back to Jack, and then hurried after her sister.

Despite her initial nervousness the day spent in the salon of the Station Hotel was not nearly as bad as Eleanor had feared. Harry Abrams recognised her voice, and during his tea break he gave her some instruction on Braille. Katherine taught her a bit more typing, and later as Eleanor pushed the tea cart along, she found it much easier to chat to the soldiers, and listened as a few of them told their stories, haltingly; blinded by gas at Vimy Ridge, or being caught in a hail of shell fire somewhere in Belgium. But more than the stories of their war and wounds, they wanted to tell of the good things they remembered; of the simple pleasures of eating chocolate again, or, as one man told her with a rakish wink, "talking to a young lady with a good English accent."

Eleanor enjoyed all of their banter, their determined cheerfulness that made her own spirits lift, but by the end of the day she was as physically exhausted as she had been before, if not nearly as distraught.

"It does get better," she told Katherine as they walked back to the station. "But it can't go on forever, can it? The men will need to find jobs, and I suppose the hotel will want its salon back."

"Yes, it's likely to disband in June," Katherine answered. "At least here in Carlisle. I suppose the charity itself will go on as long as there are blinded soldiers. They have a Home near London that is their base."

"But what will you do," Eleanor asked, "in June?"

Katherine's face tightened. She did not mention a wedding. Impulsively, knowing she would lack the courage later, Eleanor asked, "Is everything... all right... between you and James?"

Katherine didn't answer for a moment; she dug in her handbag for their tickets, her face averted. "Does it seem as if it is?" she finally asked, her voice clipped, and compelled to honesty, Eleanor answered,

"No, I don't suppose it does."

"Then you have your answer," Katherine said, and marched towards their train.

Eleanor did not go to Carlisle the next day. Katherine was having tea with her future mother-in-law and so while she went into Whitehaven to visit the Freybourns, Eleanor remained at home, sitting on the settee in the dining room alcove, a pile of seed catalogues scattered around her.

She glanced at various descriptions of flowers and plants, realising she neither knew nor cared about the differences between lavender or lilac, camellia or clematis. She'd liked the *idea* of doing the garden over, creating a place of peace and beauty, but she was not, she acknowledged a bit guiltily, all that interested in helping it to come about. And yet when she thought of the blind soldiers determined to better themselves and learn something new, she knew she had to persevere. She made a few notes about different seeds to purchase, and spent a good while perusing the different kinds of roses that they might grow in Cumbria's windy climate.

Then, with a sigh, she pushed the catalogues away and stared out the window, feeling restless once more and yet for a different reason. Now her mind was full of thoughts of Carlisle, of blind soldiers and veterans who were filled with both pride and despair, of a life and a world she still didn't like but knew she had to find a way to inhabit. Despite the tension between Katherine and James, Eleanor suspected they would still marry; soon Katherine would have a full, busy life making her own household, starting her own family. But what would Eleanor do? What would her life look like?

She blinked as a figure came into view in the garden; it was Jack Taylor, a spade over one shoulder as he walked to the far flowerbed and began to dig. Eleanor watched him with unabashed curiosity for a few moments; he whistled as he worked, turning over the fresh black earth.

The day was warm, the sun bright, and after a few moments Jack Taylor removed his coat, hanging it on the back of one of the garden benches, and rolled up his shirtsleeves. He took off his cap and wiped his brow with his forearm before replacing it.

Eleanor thought he must be thirsty, toiling under the hot sun, and after a mere second's deliberation she slipped from the settee and went into the kitchen. Mrs Stanton had gone to the butcher's and Tilly was upstairs. Eleanor fetched a glass from the pantry and was about to fill it with water when she saw a pitcher of lemonade on the table, most likely prepared by Tilly for when her mother finished her rest; Anne had always liked a cool drink. Carefully Eleanor poured a glass and then headed outside.

The day was balmy, the breeze no more than a warm caress as Eleanor walked across the lawn to where Jack Taylor was still digging over a flowerbed. He turned as she approached, one hand resting on the handle of the spade before he straightened and took off his cap.

"Good afternoon, Miss."

"Good afternoon, Mr Taylor. I thought you might like a drink." She held out the glass, smiling, and after a second's pause Jack Taylor took it.

"Thank you kindly. It's hot work, this."

"I imagine it is." She glanced up at the sky, brilliant blue and cloudless. "They are saying we shall have a glorious summer."

"I hope so, Miss."

"My name is Eleanor." He simply nodded in reply, and reminded of what Katherine had said, she asked, "What is it that brought you to this far corner of Cumberland?"

"Work, Miss... Eleanor." He tacked on her name awkwardly, and took a sip of lemonade.

"You're from West Yorkshire, my father said?"

"Yes."

She paused, thinking of what else her father had said, and it felt as if a cloud had come over the sun even though the day was still bright and hot. "He said there were terrible losses, for your regiment at the Somme."

"Yes, Miss, there were."

"It must have been dreadful. Walter—my brother—was there." She felt her face contort in a way that she knew revealed too much emotion and she continued quickly, "He would never talk of it. Mother told me not to ask, and I didn't, because I didn't really want to know."

"I don't blame you, Miss. It's not something you should ever want to know."

"But you know it," she said, "don't you? And it's terrible. It seems like a burden that should be shared."

"I don't think it can be rightly shared."

"No, I suppose not. I suppose it's foolish, arrogant even, to think I could try. And I'm not sure I even wanted to try. That makes me cowardly, I suppose. Perhaps he wanted me to ask." It was a terrible thought, to consider that Walter had been suffering in silence, and she might have been able to alleviate it, if only a little.

"Women had just as hard a job of it, in their own way," Jack Taylor said after a moment. "Having to wait at home, never knowing, always afraid."

"Yes." Her voice had grown thick. "Yes, I hated the waiting. But even worse..." She stopped, not wanting to put it into words. Even worse than the waiting had been the not needing to wait.

"Everyone's lost someone, it seems," he said quietly, and she knew then that he'd been told about Walter.

"Yes," she answered after a moment, when she trusted her voice to sound steady. "Yes, I suppose everyone has, in one way or another. Even the men who come back aren't quite the same as they were, are they?"

"I don't think you could survive the war, Miss, and come back the same."

She stared at him then, his face brown from the sun, with freckles across the bridge of his nose. "Have you changed?" she asked, and Jack stilled for a moment before he gave a quick nod.

"Of course I have," he answered. "More than I wished I had." He handed her back the empty glass. "Thank you kindly for the lemonade, Miss Eleanor. I ought to get back to digging."

She knew he was right even as she was reluctant to end the conversation. She had, for some strange reason, talked more honestly with Jack Taylor than with anyone else she knew.

Perhaps that was because she didn't know him, because he wasn't quick to criticise or scorn the way Katherine was, or scold or sympathise the way her parents did. He'd just listened.

With no reason to postpone the conversation, she nodded in farewell and turned back to the house. Her heart quelled slightly at the sight of Katherine by the front porch, her eyes narrowed. Eleanor didn't know how long her sister had been standing there, but she suspected it was longer than she would have liked.

"What on earth have you been doing?" Katherine demanded as Eleanor came up the steps.

"I just brought a drink out to Mr Taylor. It's thirsty work, digging in this sun."

"Tilly could have done it."

"She was busy," Eleanor answered, and passed her as she went into the house. "I don't see why I shouldn't have done it," she added, a note of truculence coming into her voice despite her every attempt to sound measured. "You're always going on about how I should make myself useful."

"Is that what you were doing?" Katherine asked shrewdly, and then stalked past Eleanor and removed her hat, looking for a moment, so weary Eleanor almost felt sorry for her.

"How was your tea with Mrs Freybourn?" she asked after a moment.

Katherine gave a little shrug, no more than a twitching of her shoulders. "We've set a date for the wedding."

"You have?" Eleanor blinked in surprise. "Was James there, then?"

"No, his mother will tell him." Katherine patted her hair into tidiness and turned towards the stairs. "Suggest it to him, at any rate. I suppose he'll agree." She sounded so resigned that Eleanor said impulsively,

"Katherine—you don't have to marry him, if you don't want to."

Katherine stilled, one hand on the banister. "If I don't want to?" she repeated without looking at Eleanor. "Do promises not mean anything anymore?"

"I only meant—"

"Who are you to tell me what I can or cannot do?" Katherine demanded. She turned around, her face tight and pinched. "Especially when you're sneaking outside, making eyes at the gardener, for heaven's sake!"

"I wasn't making eyes," Eleanor retorted, flushing. "I was simply bringing him a drink and making a bit of conversation—"

"Hardly appropriate—"

"You're one to talk about being appropriate! You sneak off to Carlisle without telling anyone what you're up to—"

"That's different and you know it. Flirting with a gardener can't lead to anything good."

Eleanor drew herself up. "I wasn't *flirting*."

"Girls, lower your voices," Anne scolded quietly as she came down the stairs. "Your father has someone with him in his study. What do you suppose they might think, to hear you sounding like a couple of harridans in the hall?" She turned to Katherine, gentling her words with a smile. "What's this about Carlisle, my dear?"

"Nothing," Katherine said tightly. She shot Eleanor a glare that she returned with equal heat. No matter how well-intentioned she was, every exchange with Katherine seemed to end in a quarrel.

"And how was your tea with Mrs Freybourn?" Anne asked.

"They set a date for the wedding," Eleanor interjected. She knew she sounded childish but she was still fuming about Katherine's unfair comment. Making eyes, indeed. "Even though James wasn't there." A note of spite spiked her voice as she continued, "I wonder what he'll have to say about it. Do you suppose he'll be pleased?"

To her shock, Katherine let out a choked cry and hurried up

the stairs. Anne turned to gaze at Eleanor with deep disappointment clouding her eyes, and she bit her lip.

"I didn't mean to upset her."

"Didn't you?" Anne answered quietly. "I don't know why the two of you cannot get along. I suppose it is because you are so different. When Walter was here..." she faltered before continuing, "He managed to soothe the two of you, somehow. I do miss that."

Eleanor could not bear to think of Walter just then, not when she was still feeling raw from what she'd said to Jack Taylor. "What is going on between Katherine and James?" she asked as she followed her mother into the drawing room. "I don't understand it."

"And yet you keep making these little digs," Anne returned. "Eleanor, you must learn to think before you speak."

"Katherine said something unkind too," Eleanor protested and Anne turned to her, her eyebrows raised.

"And what was that?"

Eleanor didn't reply. She wasn't about to tell her mother about her conversation with Jack Taylor, or what Katherine had said about it.

"Oh, Eleanor." Anne shook her head. "Why can't you show Katherine a little compassion? Things are not, as you surely know, easy with James at the moment."

"Does Katherine not want to marry him?" Eleanor asked. It had been what she'd long suspected, judging from the way she seemed to avoid her fiancé. "Because I don't see why she should. He asked her ages ago, and the whole war has happened. Everyone has changed, not just the soldiers who came back."

"It's not like that at all," Anne returned. "But perhaps you should talk to Katherine. You could apologise, at any rate."

Eleanor did not reply. She did not want to apologise; Katherine would likely just snap at her again. And yet she knew she'd been childish, and she wanted to put such ways behind her. Helping the blind soldiers in Carlisle had made her want to grow up, if only a little, and face the world as best as she could.

"All right," she said at last, and turned from the room.

The door of Katherine's bedroom was closed and after knocking rather quietly and hearing no answer, Eleanor opened it. She would have rather just tiptoed away, but she felt spurred to action now, and determined to be different.

The room was flooded with sunlight, and she blinked for a moment in the brightness before she saw Katherine in a chair by the window, her hair undone and her face streaked with tears.

Shock left her silent for a moment as she simply stared. She'd never seen Katherine cry.

"What are you doing here?" Katherine asked irritably. She sniffed and pressed her handkerchief to her eyes. "Can't you leave me in peace?"

"I'm sorry, Katherine. I—I shouldn't have said what I did."

"It doesn't matter," Katherine answered, and turned away so her sandy hair fell against her cheek, hiding her face.

Eleanor stepped into the room, closing the door quietly behind her. "It does matter." She hesitated then asked timidly, "Is everything... is everything all right between you and James?"

Katherine let out a weary laugh that ended on a sob. "Oh, Eleanor, what do you think?" She pressed the handkerchief to her eyes once more, her shoulders shaking silently.

"Tell me what's wrong," Eleanor implored as she came towards Katherine and knelt by her side. "I'm sorry, so sorry, for what I said. But maybe I can help—"

"You can't help." Katherine dropped the handkerchief from her eyes and took a shuddering breath. "No one can. The truth is, James doesn't want to marry me anymore. I'm not sure I can even blame him."

"He... doesn't? But..."

"I love him," Katherine said simply. "I always have. I couldn't believe it when he started courting me, back in 1914. I couldn't imagine what he saw in me." She turned to Eleanor with a trembling smile. "I'm not like you, all laughter and brightness. If the war hadn't happened, Eleanor, you'd have had suitors by the dozen. Men would flock to your side, and revel in your gay ways. I've never been like that. I know I'm too serious, and even stern. I just can't seem to help it."

"And as it is, I'll be lucky to get one suitor," Eleanor answered with a small smile.

"That's all I ever wanted. One man to love me. And I wanted it to be James. He was so funny before the war, wasn't he?" Katherine leaned her head back against the chair and closed her eyes briefly. "I know he could be arrogant, a bit cocky, but he was so charming. He could always make me laugh, and that was, I'm afraid, no mean feat."

"And now?"

"You've seen him for yourself. He's serious, but it's more than that. It's as if..." Katherine bit her lip. "It's as if he isn't there, or perhaps as if he's hiding part of himself. A part I can't reach. I felt it since the summer, when he and Walter returned. They both seemed so different, then."

"A bit listless, perhaps..."

"It was more than that. It was as if neither of them wanted to meet anyone's eye. And we can't ask Walter about it, and James won't tell me."

"Perhaps in time..." Eleanor began and Katherine shook her head impatiently.

"He's been home for nearly four months and nothing has changed. He doesn't want to talk to me, much less to laugh or tease. And I'm no good for him anymore. I used to think, or at least hope, that I helped anchor him. He was so lively and full of ideas and fun... do you remember when he punted down the mud puddle in the sheep pasture? He said it was as big as a lake, and he dragged that flat-bottomed boat all the way down there! It looked ridiculous, him lounging in a white summer suit and straw hat, with the mud all around." Katherine gave a trembling smile of memory. "I convinced myself he needed someone like me, before the war. Someone to keep him steady."

"He still needs you, Katherine—"

Katherine shook her head. "Now I just bring him down even more. I'm the last thing he needs, and he knows it. He doesn't want to marry me, I can see it in his eyes. It's the only thing I *know* he feels," she said with a bitter laugh, "but he won't cry off because he's too much of a gentleman for that."

Eleanor was silent for a moment, one hand resting on Katherine's shoulder. "You could release him," she suggested, "if you think it would make you happier. And him, too."

"I should," Katherine agreed. "I know I should. I've thought about it many times, believe me. I've even thought of how I would do it. To his face, because a letter would be cowardly. And I'd want to see the relief in his eyes when I told him. I thought that would help make it more final. Amazing, really, how you can hold onto hope." She shook her head wearily, lapsing into silence.

"Well, then?" Eleanor asked gently and Katherine lifted her head to gaze at her bleakly. "The truth of it is, I don't want to release him. I still love him, you see." She drew a deep breath. "And the Freybourns don't want me to, either. They're desperate to see him settled. They think marriage will bring him out of this... this fog he seems to be in."

"Perhaps it will."

"Perhaps it would, if I were more like you. If I could cheer him up and make him laugh, tease him and pull his ears and make everything seem like such a lark. But I was never able to do that. And the truth is..." Katherine drew a quick, choked breath. "The truth is I don't want to let him go. I *can't* let him go. You could still find someone, Eleanor. You're young and pretty and lively. But I'm twenty-five and plain. No one will marry me. No one would even look at me twice. And I don't even want anyone to, except for James."

"If he loved you before the war," Eleanor insisted stubbornly, "he can love you after. He's simply got to try."

"Does love involve trying?" Katherine asked with a hollow laugh. "I didn't think it was meant to be hard."

"Perhaps not at first. But to stay with someone when life isn't what you thought, when bad or even terrible things happen... I should think that's hard."

Katherine sighed and straightened in her chair; Eleanor could tell she was withdrawing from the conversation, and most likely wishing she hadn't admitted to so much. "I don't think James would have asked me to marry him, if not for the war. It was an impulsive act of a moment, right before he and Walter went off. I don't think he meant it, but of course when I accepted he had to take it seriously. We both did." She reached up to her hair and began to shove pins back into the tangles. "Never mind," she said with a feeble attempt at briskness. "It will sort itself out."

Eleanor did not reply. She did not want to offer Katherine false hope or meaningless platitudes, and the truth was she had no idea how a marriage could sort itself out without the two parties involved at least talking.

"Do you think," she asked, "if Walter had survived, he would have been changed? Beyond what we saw, I mean. I know he seemed a bit withdrawn, a little listless, but would he... would he have been as changed as James?"

"I don't know," Katherine answered. "I think perhaps he would have been. They all had to keep themselves going during the war, didn't they? It was all so jolly in a way, getting *The Times* in the trenches and sharing out the marmalade cake we'd sent. Walter joked about your lumpy socks, didn't he?"

"He said no one would pinch them," Eleanor remembered sadly.

"But when the war ended, when there wasn't a need to keep your spirits up any longer, to stay cheerful... I think Walter might have seemed different. He was always so sensitive, wasn't he? So thoughtful." She smiled faintly, showing the creases by her eyes. "I remember when he was about fourteen he wrote an ode to the cat. 'To Smoky, As You Sleep'."

"I remember that as well," Eleanor answered with a laugh. "The poor thing died of old age. It was a bit of a joke though, that poem—"

"It was clever," Katherine agreed. "But quite heartfelt, as I remember. Some line about 'your eyes shall see no more, and there shall be peace at last.'"

"Peace from his yowling. Do you remember the racket that beast made?" She felt a burst of something in her soul, a clenching. "It's good to talk about Walter," she said. "In a way."

"Yes," Katherine agreed. "In a way. But I think the war might have affected him badly in the end, even if we never really saw it." She sighed, sitting back in her chair, her hair only half-done. "I expect the War would have changed him even more than it has changed James." She turned to Eleanor with a bleak smile. "Perhaps it's better the way things have turned out."

Eleanor drew back. "You can't mean that!"

"I don't know what I mean anymore," Katherine confessed wearily. "I want things to be different, but I don't see how they can be." She rose from her chair and reached for the wrapper laid out on the end of her bed. "I'm tired, and I have a headache. I think I'll rest before dinner."

Eleanor nodded and rose, knowing this was a dismissal. She glanced out the window at the stretch of garden still bathed in sunlight; Jack Taylor was still digging the flowerbed, the earth black and rich beneath him, the sunlight touching his bare head with gold.

CHAPTER 11

MARIN

On Sunday morning Marin headed over to the church while Rebecca remained at home, having a lie-in. A few people were walking down the lane towards the ancient building, its doors open to the weak February sunlight. Marin saw the Hattons walk over from the former vicarage, and she waved her hello.

Inside the church was dim and smelled slightly of dust; electric heaters suspended from the rafters offered a paltry warmth, and Marin decided to keep her coat on. Most of the congregation were doing the same. She accepted a hymnal and service sheet from a smiling woman and slid into a pew at the back.

The last time she'd been in a church had been her father and his wife's funeral. She still recalled the overpowering scent of the gardenias and lilies that had made up the bouquets that covered both her father and Diana's caskets. She'd had such a sense of unreality, standing at the back of the church, Rebecca pale-faced and silent by her side. Most of the people who had been coming through the doors had been strangers to both of them. Rebecca had had a scattering of friends and teachers; Marin had had no one. The rest of the mourners had been work colleagues and friends of her father and Diana; they'd smiled sadly and murmured condolences.

And then the service had started, the priest, another stranger, walking down the aisle as he spoke what Marin knew was meant to be words of comfort. *I am the Resurrection and I am the Life, says the Lord. Whoever has faith in me shall have life, even though he die. And everyone who has life, and has committed himself to me in faith, shall not die for ever.*

The words had washed over Marin without any meaning. She and Rebecca had followed the vicar down the centre aisle, conscious of everyone's circumspect stares, and then into the front pew. As the vicar had welcomed everyone to the service, his voice sombre, Rebecca had slid an ice-cold hand into Marin's. They'd held hands for most of the service; it was, in some ways, the closest Marin had ever felt to her half-sister. At the funeral, they'd both been allowed to grieve.

Now the vicar, this Simon Truesdell Jane had mentioned, came to the front of the church and offered everyone a cheerful welcome. Then the organ started and the choir began to process; Marin got to her feet as everyone began to sing a hymn she vaguely recognised from the Christmas and Easter services she'd attended over the years, but didn't know the words to. She opened her hymnal and began to sing too.

The church service was, in its own way, enjoyable; even though Marin had never been that much of a churchgoer, she found the litany of prayers and hymns to be soothing. For an hour she could simply be, without worrying about Rebecca or wondering just what she was doing in West Cumbria.

As the service ended her mind drifted back to the garden, and the vicarage's former occupants. Could the young woman in the photograph be related to the vicar named Sanderson? She thought of her intense stare, the wild rumple of her dark hair, the butterfly on her fingertips. She didn't look like a vicar's daughter, she thought even as she bemusedly recognised vicar's daughters, like any other daughters, could look however they pleased.

"There you are," someone said, and Marin blinked the world back into focus. Jane Hatton stood by her pew, a cup of tea in hand. The service had ended, and everyone was milling about in the back of the church, chatting over cups of tea and digestive biscuits. "Where's Rebecca?"

"She fancied a lie-in," Marin said and stood up. "To tell you the truth, I don't think she's very keen on church or God at the moment."

"Well, it's understandable," Jane said with a smile of sympathy. "But I want to introduce you to Simon Truesdell."

"He must be busy now—" Marin began as she eyed the man who stood by the door, wearing a suit and a clerical collar, smiling as he chatted to one of his parishioners. He looked to be in his early fifties, with curly gray hair and an open, pleasant face.

"He'll want to meet you," Jane insisted, and with seemingly little choice, Marin followed her to the door of the church. "Simon," Jane said as she took hold of Marin's arm. "I want you to meet my new neighbour, Marin—" She glanced back at Marin with a frown. "I don't actually know your last name."

"Ellis," Marin said, and held out her hand to Simon. "Marin Ellis."

"I'm pleased to meet you," Simon said and shook her hand.

"Marin's living here with her sister, Rebecca," Jane continued and Marin braced herself for the inevitable how-did-that-come-about kind of question. But Simon, perhaps sensing her reticence, simply smiled. "She's curious, like I was, about who lived in her house," Jane continued, and Marin felt compelled to correct her.

"Not in the house, actually. I know who lived there, the former vicar's mother-in-law originally, and various tenants since then. I'm more interested in the walled garden behind the house."

"Ah, yes, the old herb garden."

"Was it an herb garden?" Marin asked in interest and Simon let out a little laugh.

"Over five hundred years ago, when the church was a monastery. Since the Reformation it's surely had a different purpose."

"There's a photograph," Marin began, "in the village hall. It's of a young woman, with a butterfly resting on her fingertips. The caption says it was taken in the garden of Bower House."

"Was it?" Simon raised his eyebrows, but Marin suspected his interest was merely polite. And why should it be anything else? Why should he care about an old photograph, or an over-grown garden?

"I was thinking," Jane interjected, "that the young woman in the photo might be related to the vicar at the time—Sander-son, wasn't it?"

"I believe so. I can have a look at the register, if you like." He turned to Marin. "It seems this interest in the history of the place is catching," he teased gently. "Is Jane infecting you with her enthusiasm?" He didn't wait for an answer, which Marin couldn't have given anyway, and simply continued, "I can look up the register this afternoon. I'd be happy to stop by Bower House and drop it off."

"Oh, well, thank you," Marin answered. She was surprised by the offer, but then Goswell was a small place. She supposed it wasn't out of the ordinary for someone to offer to stop by.

After church she said goodbye to the Hattons and headed back to Bower House. The house looked forlorn and neglected, standing as it was amid the brambles and weeds. Never mind the walled garden, Marin thought; she needed to get the proper garden under control.

She let herself into the house and called for Rebecca. She came the downstairs looking sleepy, still dressed in her pyjamas.

"You're not even dressed?" Marin exclaimed with a little, uncertain laugh. "It's nearly noon."

Rebecca shrugged. "It's freezing out, and I felt like lying around."

"It is cold in here," Marin agreed. "I still don't think I've figured out the heating properly." Something else she needed to sort out, and far more urgently than any garden. She went into the kitchen and opened the door to the Rayburn's control, twiddling a few dials uselessly. "I thought I'd go into Whitehaven and get some supplies," she told Rebecca over her shoulder. "For the garden."

"What kind of supplies?" Rebecca asked. She didn't, Marin thought, sound very interested.

"Well, I'm not quite sure, to tell you the truth. Some garden tools, I suppose, to manage what's outside. I'll need something to cut down the bramble, secateurs maybe..." Although she suspected cutting down swathes of bramble with a pair of garden shears would be an incredibly time-consuming proposition. "Would you like to go with me?" she asked. "There's a home and garden store in the centre of town."

Rebecca shook her head. "No, I think I'll stay here."

Marin suppressed a sigh of disappointment. Perhaps things would be better when Rebecca started school tomorrow, or perhaps she would just notice this awkwardness less. "Is there something else you'd like to do?" she tried after a moment. "I don't have to go into town."

"Do what you like," Rebecca answered with a shrug. "I think I'll watch TV." And she disappeared into the lounge before Marin could answer.

She straightened up from where she'd been crouching by the Rayburn, glancing around the kitchen. Sunlight streamed through the window, making Marin notice the room's emptiness; besides a few dishes in the sink and the modern chrome kettle on top of the range the room looked unlived in. She thought of Jane's cosy, cluttered kitchen, and decided she'd buy a few things for the kitchen as well as the garden.

Despite her worries about Rebecca, she spent a pleasant few hours browsing through the shops in Whitehaven; she picked up an old-fashioned brass kettle and a cork board and calendar for the kitchen wall, a set of mugs and a big blue teapot. In the garden section of the store she spent an interesting half-hour browsing wares she barely knew the use for: propagators and cold frames and cloches. She felt both intrigued and intimidated, because she didn't know the first thing about any of it, and it reminded her of what a huge undertaking tackling the walled garden would be. But with Joss's and maybe Rebecca's help, perhaps they could at least clear a little bit of it.

She came away with a pair of shears, some heavy work gloves, and a paperback book called *The Amateur Gardener*. It was a start.

Back at Bower House she unpacked all her purchases as Rebecca sloped into the kitchen. Smiling, she brandished the kettle. "Look what I've got. Properly old-fashioned, this."

"I suppose it is."

"Cup of tea?" Marin asked and Rebecca just shrugged. Determinedly she washed it out and filled it, then plonked it on top of the Rayburn. "Nobody ever says no to a cup of tea, do they?"

"I guess not," Rebecca answered listlessly. She pulled out a chair and sat at the table, the sleeves of her jumper pulled down over her hands.

"Rebecca?" Marin probed gently. She knew how ineffectual her checking-in questions were, but she couldn't help herself. She didn't know what else to do. "Is everything all right?"

"It's fine," Rebecca replied automatically, and then she sighed. "I'm just... I'm just nervous about school tomorrow."

"Of course you are," Marin agreed sympathetically. "First days are always tough." Rebecca glanced up at her, her eyes dark and wide. "Did you find them tough? When you went to school?"

Briefly Marin thought of her boarding school days. "I found all of school to be tough," she said, and then wished she hadn't been quite so frank. She could hear the slightly bitter edge to her voice, that seed of resentment and hurt that still had a deep and painful root, after so many years.

"Why?" Rebecca asked. "Didn't you like school? I mean, as much as anybody likes school?"

Now Marin was the one to shrug. "Not really."

"But why?"

There wasn't, she supposed, any real reason to prevaricate. "I went to boarding school when I was eight years old," she said, her voice coming out a little more flatly than she'd meant it to. "Right after my mother died."

Rebecca's gaze widened at that. "You did? But—I didn't know that."

"There's no reason why you would," Marin answered, trying to turn her voice light, as if none of this mattered anymore. And really, it shouldn't. She was talking about something that had happened nearly thirty years ago. "It was over a decade before you were born."

"But you must have been so little," Rebecca said, "to go to boarding school. Were you homesick?"

Amazingly, Marin felt a lump rise in her throat. Yes, it had been nearly thirty years ago, and she'd done her best to make peace with her father's decisions, and yet... how quickly it could all come rushing back.

"Yes," she said, and forced herself to swallow past that awful lump. She pictured herself at eight years old, hiding in the toilets, her face tear-streaked, her heart so heavy she'd felt as if she could barely move under its crippling weight. "Yes, I was quite homesick."

"But did you come home, then?" Rebecca asked. "I mean..."

Marin shook her head. "It wasn't like that."

She turned back to her purchases, wanting, even needing to stay cheerful. "I bought a calendar for the wall. Scenes of Cumbria. They're all photos of sunny days. You'd think Cumbria was the south of France." She glanced back at Rebecca and saw that her sister was frowning as she stared at her hands, her fingers peeking out from under the frayed cuffs of her jumper.

"I didn't know that," she said slowly. "About you going to boarding school."

"Does it matter?" Marin took out the calendar and hung it on an old nail on the wall. Not quite the cosy clutter of Jane Hatton's kitchen, but it was getting there.

"I don't know," Rebecca said, looking up. Marin was startled by the bleakness in her young sister's eyes. "I don't suppose it does. But I just... I wish I'd known."

Marin couldn't think how to reply. She felt as if Rebecca had inferred something from what she'd said, something that changed things somehow, and yet she had no idea what it was. "Well, now you do," she finally said, her voice as light as she could make it, and Rebecca nodded slowly.

A knock sounded on the door, the brass lion-shaped knocker that the real estate agent had said was original to the house causing a hollow-sounding boom to echo through the house.

Rebecca raised her eyebrows. "Who do you think that is?"

"It might be the vicar," Marin answered, smiling a bit at Rebecca's double-take, and went to the door.

It was indeed Simon Truesdell, brandishing a slip of paper. "I've found the man you're looking for," he said cheerfully.

"Oh, thank you." It had started to rain, big, icy drops, and so awkwardly Marin stepped to the side, ushering Simon in. "Would you like a cup of tea? I've just put the kettle on."

"That would be lovely," Simon said, and Marin showed him to the kitchen.

Rebecca stood up as he entered, looking wary, and Simon stuck out a hand. "Simon Truesdell, resident vicar. You must be Rebecca. Jane Hatton told me about you," he explained when Rebecca looked a bit taken aback. "You're in the same year as Natalie." Rebecca nodded, and the kettle began to whistle.

Marin made the tea while Simon chatted with Rebecca; despite her guarded, monosyllabic answers, he seemed at ease, and Marin wondered in bemusement if that was a requirement for vicars. Capable in any socially awkward situation.

"So here's the man, or rather the family, you're looking for, I think," Simon said, and handed her a handwritten sheet. "I copied it out of the ledger. The church has got a list of vicars from the year dot—starting with the actual Cumbrians, back in the 800s. Urien the Unholy, or what have you."

"He doesn't sound like a very good vicar," Marin said with a smile.

"Well, I must confess I made that one up. But it does make for some interesting reading. The bloke you want is George Sanderson, vicar from 1897 to 1929."

"He was there a good long time, then," Marin said as she scanned the paper. Simon had copied the names from the ledger: *George Sanderson, Vicar. In His Household: Anne Sanderson, wife; Walter Sanderson, son; Katherine Sanderson, daughter; Eleanor Sanderson, daughter. One housemaid and a cook.*

Rebecca had roused herself to look over Marin's shoulder at the list. "One housemaid and a cook! Must be nice."

"Ah, but that was positively modest," Simon told her. "You should see the list a hundred years before then—four house-maids, a cook, a governess, a footman and a groom."

"Where on earth did they all sleep?" Marin asked. "I know the vicarage is big..."

"The top floor is the old servants' quarters. It hasn't been touched in a century or more—you can still see the bells they used to ring to call the servants. Jane showed me."

"So how much staff do you have?" Rebecca teased. Marin was glad to see her smiling and looking lively.

"Just me, myself, and I," Simon informed her cheerfully. "But fortunately I just about manage to get the job done." He nodded once more to the piece of paper Marin held. "So I hope that helps you."

"I don't know if it does or not," Marin answered. "I don't really know what I'm looking for."

"The photograph?" Simon prompted, and she nodded ruefully.

"Yes, the photograph of the young woman taken in the garden. I suppose I would like to know who she is." She almost said something about the nearly wild intensity of the girl's stare, the unsettling way she'd looked right at the camera, but then decided against it. She didn't think she could articulate, even in the privacy of her own thoughts, just what both fascinated and disturbed her about the girl.

Rebecca was peering over her shoulder once more, scanning the paper with the names. "Don't you think it's one of his daughters? Katherine or Eleanor? Look, their birthdates." She pointed to the dates Simon had scrawled under each name. "1894 for Katherine, and 1899 for Eleanor. That would have made them twenty and twenty-six in 1920, when the photo was taken."

"Circa 1920," Marin reminded her. "No one is sure when exactly it was taken. It might have been a few years before or after." She glanced back at the paper, and saw that Simon had written the dates of their deaths as well. "1918 for Walter," she said quietly. "He must have died in the war."

"Yes, I checked that," Simon told her. "His name is on the war memorial, on the bridge in the village."

Marin had passed the war memorial on her way to the post office shop, but she'd never thought to look at the names. Somehow, seeing these names written down, remembering that young woman in the photograph, it mattered more. She decided she'd look for Walter's name the next time she walked to the post office.

"Thank you for this, Simon," she said. "It is very helpful."

"So are you going to do some more digging? Find out about these people, and the house?"

"The garden," she reminded him. She liked the house with its funny little turret, but it was the garden that called to her. "Yes, I am going to do some digging. Literally. I want to clear the walled garden, and find out what's there, if anything."

"Well, do keep me informed," Simon said, and finishing his tea, he rose from his chair. Marin saw him out and returned to the kitchen to find Rebecca still looking at the list of names.

"It's strange, isn't it, seeing it written down like that," she said and Marin waited, sensing there was more. "1892 to 1918," she clarified. "He was twenty-six years old."

"So many young men lost their lives in the Great War," Marin said. She felt as if that wasn't the right thing to say, yet she couldn't discern Rebecca's mood.

"It reminds me of their gravestones," Rebecca said, and looked up from the paper. "Mum and Dad's. The dates. It's so final, isn't it? A definite ending point."

Marin nodded. They'd had the final headstones put in right before they'd come up here, and although Rebecca hadn't said anything at the time, Marin had wondered if it had hit her hard. She couldn't think of anything to say now; she could hardly refute it. Rebecca stared down at the paper again, silent, and then she suddenly looked up and said,

"Let's go out to the garden."

"You mean the walled garden—" Marin began in surprise and she nodded.

"Yes. Joss Fowler opened the door, didn't he? I haven't even seen it."

"All right," Marin said and went for her coat. It was still raining big, icy drops as they stepped outside, pulling the hoods of their coats over their heads.

Marin led the way around the back of Bower House, to the door in the wall. She hooked her boot under the bottom of the door just as Joss had, and it swung open easily, revealing the walled garden in all of its dripping, tangled glory.

They both stared at it, the endless brambles rising like a wall of thorns, the intriguing mossy stones barely visible below. Marin felt a contradictory surge of both determination and despair; what on earth was she going to do with a garden this size, even if she managed to clear away all the brambles?

"That's what happens," Rebecca said, and Marin turned to her, nonplussed. Rebecca nodded towards the garden. "It might have been beautiful once, and used and loved by that girl in the photograph, Eleanor or Katherine or whoever it was, but this is what it is now. This is what happens to everything." And with one last hard stare for the garden, she turned on her heel and walked back to the house.

CHAPTER 12

ELEANOR

April 1919

Eleanor sat curled up on a settee in the dining room alcove, which had become her favourite spot in the house. The little nook was bathed in sunshine, and best of all, it afforded her a view of the vicarage's garden.

Jack Taylor had been hard at work in the week since Eleanor had last spoken to him. He'd dug over all the flowerbeds, trimmed the shrubs and bushes, and mown the grass. The garden was like a blank canvas, waiting to be filled with colour and scent. Eleanor had spent the last few days looking at seed catalogues; she'd even sought out old Mr Lyman and asked his opinion on roses.

"Only certain varieties can thrive in Cumberland," he'd told her, "thanks to the wind and wet. Roses need a sunny, sheltered position, and good drainage."

"I can't believe any roses manage to grow here," Eleanor had answered with a laugh, and Mr Lyman had puffed out his chest.

"I managed aright, out in front of the house. Lovely roses I had there, for a time."

"Yes, I remember."

"The wind got to them out there," Mr Lyman recalled mournfully. "It's an exposed place, really, with the wind coming off the sea, but the Reverend wanted them to be seen from the church." He scratched his chin. "Roses would do better in the garden, though, sheltered by the wall. Is it roses you're thinking of then, Miss Eleanor?"

"I don't know. I'm thinking of all sorts of things, really," Eleanor answered. "The truth is, though, Mr Lyman, I never took much interest in the garden until now."

"It's good to have an interest," he remarked kindly.

"I know roses are fragrant." She thought of the blind veterans she hoped to bring one day to the garden. "I want fragrant flowers."

"Sombreuil roses have a good fragrance," he said. He pronounced it Som-brill. "You'd do well with those."

"I'll tell that to Mr Taylor."

Mr Lyman scratched his chin again. "You think that boy knows what he's about, when it comes to roses?" he asked sceptically.

"I don't know," Eleanor confessed, and laid a conciliatory hand on the old gardener's arm. "We shall rely on your expertise, Mr Lyman," she said, and was rewarded with a proud smile.

"I'll give it to you happily, Miss Eleanor. Happily."

Eleanor left feeling that another person would benefit from her project, and her heart lifted.

Now, for an afternoon, she was alone in the house save for Tilly and Mrs Stanton; Father had gone to visit a sick parishioner after lunch and Mother and Katherine had taken the train to Whitehaven to look for lace for Katherine's wedding dress.

The wedding was to be in just six weeks, on the first Saturday in June; James had agreed to the date, although Eleanor had not possessed the courage to ask Katherine if he'd seemed pleased or not. Ever since their frank conversation in Katherine's bedroom, her sister had become brittle and distant; she'd gone to Carlisle to help with the blind veterans and told Eleanor not to accompany her, as she'd just get in the way. Eleanor had felt this was a little unfair, but she decided to turn her attention to the garden.

Now Eleanor watched as Jack trundled a wheelbarrow full of manure to the flowerbed in the back of the garden; he'd taken off his coat in the hot sun and his shirtsleeves were rolled up past his forearms. Watching him, Eleanor wondered how he could seem so unchanged by the war. He didn't have the hollow-eyed look so many returned soldiers had, or the bitterness etched into his face like James. Yet Jack had seen terrible fighting. Perhaps, Eleanor mused, it was possible to suffer and come through it unscathed, or at least still whole. Perhaps Walter would have come back just as Jack seemed to have, smiling and open and easy, despite what Katherine had said.

She closed her eyes; just the thought of Walter still caused grief to rush through her. Thinking about her brother was akin to probing a sore tooth; the lightning flash of pain, though familiar, was always a surprise.

Outside a bird twittered and Eleanor opened her eyes. That rush of grief was followed by a surge of reckless defiance, and she scrambled off the settee and went for her walking boots.

A few minutes later she was in the garden, blinking in the bright sunshine as she watched Jack dig the flowerbeds over with manure.

"I've been looking through seed catalogues," she said as she walked towards him through the damp grass. "I've decided what I don't want. No camellias or gardenias or lilies. Funeral flowers, they are."

"And have you found something you do want?" Jack asked politely.

Eleanor scanned the empty flowerbeds. "Roses," she said,

"although everyone grows roses, don't they? But I want fragrant flowers. That's very important." She wondered if he would ask why but he just nodded.

"Dianthus is quite fragrant," he said. "A spicy scent, it has."

"Is it very difficult to grow here in Cumberland? With the wind and the rain, I mean. Mr Lyman, the old gardener, despairs of what has happened to his roses." She tilted her head, smiling at him; Katherine would say she was flirting but Eleanor just wanted to feel light and happy for a few moments.

"I think it would manage all right in the garden," Jack answered. "The walls provide shelter, and there should be sunlight enough along the south wall."

"What other flowers are fragrant?" Eleanor asked. "Or very fragrant, I should say. I suppose all flowers are fragrant." She let out a trilling laugh that came out a little too sharp; suddenly she felt embarrassed, exposed even, and she walked a few steps away, making a show of inspecting the empty flowerbed, the bare black earth.

"Wisteria has a nice scent," Jack said. "You could grow it along the wall. It attracts bees though, and butterflies as well. Clematis too could grow along the wall." He paused, taking off his cap to rake a hand through his hair. It stood up on end, just like Walter's used to, and Eleanor's hand twitched with the sudden desire to smooth it. "Lavender is always nice," Jack continued. "Useful, too. My mother used to grow it. She made sachets, like, for her drawers." His smile was tinged with sadness, and Eleanor repeated,

"Used to?"

"She died a long time ago. Let me see now." He replaced his cap and rubbed his jaw. "Jasmine has a strong scent. And honeysuckle smells so sweet, but it attracts the bees as well, of course. I've always liked tuberose, although some say it smells too strong." He let out a little laugh.

"You do know a great deal about flowers, Mr Taylor."

"My mother liked her garden. She knew all the names of the flowers. Had a book, even, with drawings. I liked to look at the pictures." He glanced round the garden with its expanse of lawn and empty, waiting flowerbeds. "I'd like to make a nice garden for you, Miss. For the whole family."

Eleanor stared at him, strangely moved by this clearly heart-felt sentiment, and for a moment she couldn't speak. Then, impulsively, she started forward. "Jack," she said, and she saw his eyes widen at the use of his first name, "Do you play croquet?"

"I can't say I ever have, Miss," he answered after a moment. He looked wary now, the expression in his dark eyes guarded.

"It's *such* a good game," Eleanor told him brightly. "I used to play with my brother Walter. We all played out here—" she gestured to the lawn with one arm flung wide. "But Walter and I loved it best. He could knock my ball twenty yards away, but he never did because he knew it made me cross." Suddenly her brightness went out as if it had been snuffed like a candle; she sniffed and swallowed and looked away.

"I'm very sorry for your loss, Miss Eleanor," Jack said quietly.

"So am I. But I don't want to be sorry now," she said fiercely as she turned back to him. "I'm so tired of being sorry and sad. I want to enjoy this beautiful day, the sunshine, the *promise* of it. Today's a hopeful day, don't you think?"

Jack turned his face to the sun, and for a moment he looked as if he were struggling with some powerful emotion, regret or grief. "I'd like to think so," he said after a moment.

"Did you lose anyone in the war, Jack?" Eleanor asked.

"My two brothers."

Two brothers. And she'd only lost one. "I'm sorry—"

"And my father as well." For a moment she saw the grief on his face, the sudden torment in his eyes. Then his face cleared and he gave her the easy smile she'd assumed meant he'd come through the war untouched, unscathed. Now she knew that wasn't true. "But never mind that now. You wanted to play croquet. I could set it up for you, if you like. The grass has just been cut, so it should be good playing."

"Would you?" Eleanor felt a thrill of pleasure, unexpected and sweet on the heels of her restless unhappiness. "That would be so very kind."

"Just tell me where the things are."

She pointed him towards the little shed in the back of the garden that held the croquet set and sunshades, retired for ten months of the year. She sat on a garden bench while he brought them out, and watched as he began to set up the wickets around the garden.

"No, they don't go there," she told him with a laugh, and ran to move the wicket he'd just stuck into the grass. "There's a course, you know. You can't just put them any old way."

Jack straightened, giving her a rueful smile. "Like I said, I've never played before. I've seen it done, but that's all."

"Well, you shall play now," Eleanor announced grandly, and reaching for a mallet, she proffered it to him. Jack didn't take it.

"I couldn't, Miss."

"Why not?" Eleanor smiled in what she hoped was a whimsical way. She suddenly and quite desperately wanted him to play with her, but she feared if he knew how much he would most certainly refuse. "I can hardly play alone. That's no fun."

"Even so, Miss." Jack took the mallet and put it back with the others. "I've work to do, and..." He hesitated, seeming to choose his words with care. "I don't think it would be proper."

"What's improper about a game of croquet?" Eleanor returned scoffingly. "Unless you win, of course." She swung her mallet around by the handle the way Walter used to and gave Jack a teasing smile. "One game. No one's even home, you know, except for our housemaid Tilly and the cook, and they'll hardly look out here." Too late she realised she'd made it sound as if there was something improper about them playing. She took a step towards him, her heart suddenly starting to beat rather hard. "Please, Jack. For me."

For a moment he looked torn. "I know you've had a hard time of it, Miss," he began, colour flushing his cheeks a dull red. "I know how hard it is, and especially for a young lady…" He swallowed and shook his head, resolute now. "But I can't, Miss. I'm sorry."

Eleanor let out her breath in a rush, fighting a sense of bitter disappointment that logically at least, she knew was an overreaction to his refusal. "Very well," she said with a toss of her head, knowing she now sounded childish and unable to keep herself from it. She picked up one of the balls before walking to the first wicket. Jack watched her for a moment and then, seeming satisfied that she was going to play alone, he returned to his wheelbarrow and his flowerbed.

Eleanor put the ball down on the damp grass and lined up to take a swing. This was, she realised, the first time she'd played croquet without Walter; they hadn't got the set out in years. The thought filled her with a strange kind of fury, and she took a hard swing at the ball, sending it bouncing and rolling over the lawn, straight into Jack Taylor's shin.

"Ouch!" He jumped away from the ball, clutching his leg.

"Oh, I'm so sorry!" Eleanor exclaimed. And she was sorry, both for hurting him and seeming so childish and petulant. Had she not learned anything, or grown up at all, in these last few months? She rushed over to him. "Are you very hurt? You must come and sit down—" She reached for his arm and attempted to lead him to the bench, but he shook her off and stepped back.

"I'm fine, Miss. Just a bit bruised. Nothing to worry about."

"I am sorry."

He smiled then, cocking his head as he looked at her. "You don't do anything by halves, do you, Miss Eleanor?"

It was what Walter had said to her once, and Jack Taylor said it in the same, smiling way, amusement or perhaps even affection crinkling his brown eyes. Eleanor felt as if a great, yawning chasm had opened inside her. She felt as if she could tip right into it, and never climb out again. Her face crumpled, and not wanting Jack to see her cry, she whirled away and retreated to the bench in the corner of the garden, her head bent to hide her tears, her shoulders shaking with the effort of holding back the sobs she hadn't let out since Walter's death all those months ago.

"Miss Eleanor—" Jack dropped the croquet ball and hurried towards her. Under the drooping boughs of a chestnut tree, they could not be seen by anyone from the vicarage, and he cautiously touched her on the shoulder. "I'm sorry. I didn't mean to upset you."

"You didn't. That is..." Eleanor dragged a deep breath into her lungs and searched for her handkerchief; she'd forgotten it, as usual, and so she wiped her tears away with the palms of her hands. "I'm sorry. I shouldn't have... it's just..." She felt the pressure building inside of her again, that wave of emotion she'd kept back since she'd first opened the telegram back in November. *It is my painful duty to inform you...* "Walter used to say that to me," she managed to choke out. "When I was playing croquet, even. For a moment... for a moment it almost felt like... he was back."

Distantly Eleanor realised Jack's hand was still on her shoulder; he squeezed gently before removing it, and then sitting down next to her. He didn't say anything, which Eleanor was strangely glad for. She didn't want to hear a condolence or platitude; she simply wanted his presence, solid and steady, next to her.

The only sounds were their breathing and the rustle of the breeze through the leaves above; a bird twittered and then fell silent.

"I'm sorry," she said after a moment. "I must seem dreadfully selfish. You've lost so much more than I have."

"Loss is loss," Jack answered and Eleanor turned to him.

"Yes, I suppose... do you miss them very much, Jack? Your family? Were you close to your brothers?"

"Close enough," he answered. "I miss my mother, but she died when I was a lad, well before the war. And my father..." He hesitated, and Eleanor asked softly,

"When did he die?"

"1918. Right at the end."

"Like Walter, then."

"He had a stroke," Jack continued. His gaze was distant and shuttered, as if he were replaying the scene in his mind. "Collapsed behind the plough. By the time I got there, he was dead." He fell silent, and Eleanor didn't attempt to offer some paltry platitude by way of comfort. Then Jack seemed to come to, shrugging off the memory. "I beg your pardon, Miss. I shouldn't have spoken of such things."

"I'm glad you did," Eleanor answered. "It helps knowing someone else feels as I do. Yet you seem so happy," she added impulsively. "When I first saw you, I thought you seemed untouched by the war."

Jack's mouth twisted. "No one's untouched, Miss. Not one person, man or woman or child."

"Yes," she agreed slowly. "I suppose that's true. You just hide it better."

"I don't mean to hide anything," Jack answered, and he sounded almost defensive. "I just don't see the sense in looking back. It's the future I care about. I've got a life ahead of me, which is more than most blokes who went away to fight have."

Eleanor glanced at him curiously; he sounded both bitter and defensive, and she wondered at it. Perhaps Jack Taylor hid as much grief and anger and confusion as she did.

"Do you suppose," she asked, staring down at the sun-dappled lawn, "that it ever gets better?"

Jack's face cleared, although he didn't answer for a moment. She could tell he knew what she'd meant, and was considering his response. "A bit," he said at last. "But nothing goes back to the way it was."

Eleanor closed her eyes against the fierce longing she'd had for the world to do exactly that. "I know that. I've accepted that, or at least I thought I had. But then something comes up and surprises me, makes me remember..." She opened her eyes and offered what she hoped was a smile. "Do you know, I hadn't actually wept since we received the telegram? I've been afraid to, afraid that if I started I'd never stop."

""But if you don't let the tears out," Jack countered gently, "where are they going to go?"

"*Away*," she whispered, even as she felt two more tears slip down her cheeks. Then, to her shock, Jack wiped one tear away with his thumb. Eleanor's lips parted in stunned silence; he was gazing at her almost tenderly as he wiped the other tear away. Then Jack seemed to realise what he'd done, and he straightened, standing up from the bench.

"I beg your pardon—"

"Don't," she implored. She couldn't bear for him to go back to that dreaded, awful formality. "Don't," she said again, but she knew it was too late. Jack was already walking away, and she watched from the bench as he picked up his spade and began to dig again.

She stayed out on the bench for a few more minutes, fighting a new sense of loss for something she could barely articulate, something that had nothing to do with Walter. Eventually she rose from the bench, and after carefully putting all the wickets and mallets back in the shed, she went inside. Jack had not looked at her once.

CHAPTER 13

MARIN

The first day of school, Marin got up early and attempted to make a full fry-up for breakfast. She had a desire to provide Rebecca with something warm and nourishing, to be motherly in a way she had never been before.

She still hadn't quite got the hang of the Rayburn, however; the hot plates were different temperatures in different areas, and, as with the banana bread she managed to burn some bits and undercook others. At least there was toast.

Rebecca came down in her uniform, a black blazer and trousers with a red tie, all of it with that starchy, shiny, too-new look and feel. Marin smiled and poured her a cup of tea from the new blue teapot. "Everything ready?"

"What's there to get ready?" Rebecca answered as she sat down at the table. "I'm dressed, I have a school bag. That's about it."

"Right." Marin had flutters in her stomach for Rebecca's sake, or perhaps for her own. If Rebecca had a hard time at school... if there were mean girls or simply indifferent pupils who streamed past her without so much as a glance... she didn't know how Rebecca would react, with sullen silence or breezy

determination, and she had no idea how she would react to
Rebecca's reaction, either way. It was an endless loop of uncertainty and ignorance.

There wouldn't, Marin knew, be any tears. There had been
no tears for either of them since she'd got the phone call in
Boston and had flown the red-eye to London, arriving in Hampshire less than twenty-four hours after her father had died.
She'd picked Rebecca up from the friend's house where she'd
been staying, and for a moment they'd simply stared at each
other, two strangers brought together only by tragic circum-
stances. Then Marin had stepped forward and attempted a
clumsy hug that Rebecca had ducked out of before walking to
the car.

Now Marin served Rebecca the burned bacon and runny
eggs, accompanied by several slices of toast. "I've got the hang of
the toaster, at least," she joked as she pushed the butter and jam
towards her. "Sorry about the rest."

"I'm not that hungry, anyway." Rebecca did not so much as
pick up her fork, and Marin tried not to feel stung. Perhaps it
really was that unappetising.

"You should eat a good breakfast, Rebecca," she said after a
moment and her sister shook her head.

"Don't fuss, Marin, please."

"I'm not fussing," Marin answered, trying to keep her tone
mild rather than cajoling. "But it's my duty to take care of
you—"

"I don't want to be your *duty*," Rebecca snapped, and Marin
stared at her in surprise. "I didn't mean it like that," she said and
Rebecca lifted her chin.

"Are you sure about that?"

"Rebecca," Marin said, helplessly, because she had never
encountered such unmasked hostility from her before. "Of
course you're not a duty..."

"Be honest, Marin," Rebecca cut across her. "If my parents

hadn't died, you never would have even come back to England. You wouldn't even know me."

"That's true," Marin answered after a pause. The 'my parents' rung in her ears, echoed through her. He'd been her father too, but Rebecca hardly ever seemed to realise that. "But that doesn't mean I was reluctant to do it."

"You didn't want this," Rebecca retorted, a challenge in her voice, and Marin spread her hands.

"Of course I didn't. I'd much rather you were home with— with your parents, everyone safe and well. But I'm *trying*—"

And then, all at once, Rebecca deflated. "I know you are," she said and grabbed her coat. "I need to get going. I'm meeting Natalie at the end of the church lane."

Still at a loss, Marin watched her walk out of the kitchen. Rebecca hadn't even touched the breakfast she'd so painstakingly if ineptly made. At least she was meeting a friend, she told herself. That was a good thing.

The front door slammed and Marin sighed, feeling the house stretch emptily around her. She cleared the dishes from the table and then poured herself a cup of tea, wondering what she should do now. She supposed she could get her laptop out, send a few emails mentioning her new freelancing ambitions. If she were feeling truly ambitious, she'd design her own website offering her design and administrative services, or take out some adverts online. As it was, she simply sat there and sipped her tea and tried not to feel miserable and more alone than she had since she'd first taken on the job of raising Rebecca.

It was a chilly, grey day with a wind coming straight from the sea buffeting the house as if it were a ship in a storm. She could see and even feel the glass of the windows flex, the walls shudder. The kitchen was warm, the house empty; Marin was torn between feeling both cosy and lonely. With a sigh she finished her tea and then tidied all the breakfast things, scraping the eggs and bacon into the bin.

Then she bundled up in her coat and Wellington boots, a scarf wrapped around the lower half of her face, and with her pair of secateurs in hand, she headed outside.

The wind hit her straight in the face, nearly propelling her back into the house, but she adopted the now-familiar pose of hunched shoulders and lowered head and walked into it and around to the walled garden, the frost-tipped grass crunching under her boots, and opened the door. Inside the garden it was sheltered a bit from the wind; she lowered her scarf to stare at the brambles for a moment. They still looked as impenetrable as they had yesterday, and the day before that. Forget magic beans or secret gardens; the brambles reminded her of the forest of thorns that grew up around the castle in *Sleeping Beauty*. Choking and impenetrable. Endless and life-threatening.

She stared at it all for a moment more and then, taking a deep breath and pulling on the pair of heavy-duty garden gloves she'd bought, she went to work with the secateurs.

The first snip was immensely satisfying, as was the thorny branch that fell to the ground. It only took a few minutes of snipping away for Marin to realise, however, how ineffectual her little pair of secateurs really was. And yet still she snipped, cutting a tiny swath through the endless, thorny sea, determined to do something. And, she realised, to work off the unexpected anger that had surged through her when Rebecca had walked out the door. She'd been numb for so long, since her own mother's death, and then recently so focused on what Rebecca was feeling. For most of her life she felt as if she were watching everything from a distance, as if she were always a spectator standing on the sidelines. This was the first time she'd acknowledged and accepted how she felt. How angry.

Yes, taking care of Rebecca was a duty. What had she expected, that Marin wanted to abandon her life—what little she'd had, a few friends, a handful of acquaintances—and play parent to a half-sister she barely knew? But she'd done it, willingly, and that, she thought with another savage snip, should count for something. Should *mean* something, duty or not.

"Whoa."

Marin stopped, breathing hard, the secateurs still in hand as she turned to see Joss Fowler coming through the garden door.

"You've been hard at it," he remarked as he propped one shoulder against the stone wall. "With a little pair of secateurs."

Marin let out a hollow laugh, for she could certainly see now how absurd it was, to be tackling a quarter-acre of overgrown garden with a tool meant for a much smaller task. She also realised how dishevelled she must look; her hair had come half out of her ponytail, and her face was flushed from exertion. She'd cleared less than a foot of ground.

"I didn't have anything else," she said and Joss glanced round the garden.

"What you really need is a strimmer," he said. "Or even a scythe."

She pictured herself swinging a scythe through the bramble, like some kind of green-thumbed Grim Reaper, and she shook her head. "The truth is, I don't really know the first thing about what I'm doing." And she realised, after she'd said it, that she meant that in all sorts of ways.

"Well, there's not much to clearing weeds," Joss said with a little smile. "Just have at it, but preferably with a power tool that will get the job done." He nodded towards the secateurs. "Trying to clear this lot with that is like cutting grass with a pair of nail clippers."

Marin made a face. "Ouch."

"I have a strimmer you can borrow if you like."

"To tell you the truth, I'm not even sure what a strimmer is."

"A brush cutter. You could clear this whole place in a couple of hours. Of course, then there's the matter of roots. You'd need to hire a rotovator to till the ground and make it ready for planting."

Marin sagged at this, once again realising how over-whelming a job clearing the garden would be. And she wasn't even sure why she was doing it.

"I can help you," Joss said unexpectedly. "If you want."

"You're busy—" Marin began and he shrugged.

"When I have a slow period," Joss allowed. "I don't mind. It's interesting, this." He nodded towards the mossy stones beneath the bramble, and then, frowning a little, he walked towards them and crouched down.

"Do you see something?" Marin asked, excitement mounting inside her even though she had no idea what Joss could possibly see besides what was there—weeds and rocks.

He reached through the bramble and extricated something; Marin stepped closer to see.

"It's a... pipe?" she said, frowning, and Joss sat back on his heels.

"A bit of rusted piping," he confirmed. "I imagine it provided heat for the greenhouse, if that's what this was."

"What else could it be?"

"I don't know, but a heated greenhouse would have been quite an expensive endeavour. Still." He handed her the bit of piping; flakes of rust fell off in her hands. "Worthwhile, I suppose, if they grew exotic things like melons or oranges."

Marin turned the piping over in her hands; she felt a shiver of something, although she could not name the emotion. Curiosity, or perhaps something deeper.

"Your sister got off to school today?" Joss asked and Marin looked up.

"Yes... for better or worse." He raised an eyebrow at that, and she blurted, "I don't know what I'm doing with her."

"What do you mean?"

"Her parents—my father and her mother—died in a car accident four months ago. I was appointed her guardian. But I don't have the first clue about raising a teenager, or—" She stopped suddenly, for to finish that sentence, to admit how little relationship experience she had at all, felt too revealing. Too pathetic.

Joss nodded slowly. "I think raising teenagers is hard for anyone, but you've got the deck stacked against you. She'll be dealing with grief as well."

"Yes," Marin said with a nod. "And I don't know how to handle that either. Some days she's cheerful and bright, and other times she falls into these sullen silences that I don't know how to handle. And she's never cried, as far as I know. I feel like she should, somehow." Part of Marin couldn't believe she was confessing to all this, but she needed to talk to somebody, and while someone like Jane Hatton, capable, experienced, understanding, seemed like the obvious choice, Marin didn't feel like admitting all her inadequacies to someone who, at least on the surface, seemed to have it all together.

Joss gazed at her steadily with those thoughtful brown eyes and didn't judge, didn't suggest some seemingly easy solution. He just listened.

"It'll come," he said after a moment. "Four months isn't a long time to learn to grieve."

"I never thought of that," Marin said slowly. "Learning to grieve. It's not natural, is it?"

He lifted one shoulder in a shrug. "Death is both the least and most natural thing in the world."

She sensed, from the way he spoke, that he'd some experience with death and grief, but he didn't volunteer any information and she didn't know how to ask. "Thank you," she said instead, and he surprised her by answering,

"And you need to grieve as well."

Marin stared at him, felt a lump form in her throat. No one had mentioned her loss in the four months since her father and Diana had died. It had all been about Rebecca, which she understood and accepted, because Rebecca was so young and she'd lost both her parents instead of just one. It was a far greater tragedy for a fifteen-year-old girl to become an orphan than for a thirty-seven-year-old woman to lose a father she'd already been estranged from. Marin understood that, of course she did, and yet...

"I'm not sure I know how," she told Joss, her voice little more than a whisper. The lump was growing bigger in her throat, making it hard to talk. She didn't want to cry. Not here, not in front of Joss who, as kind as he was, was still a virtual stranger.

"You'll learn, same as your sister." He gave her a rueful smile. "It's not easy."

"No." She blinked quickly, swallowed past the lump. "At least I have a project," she half-joked, gesturing to the garden.

"It is that." He frowned again, nodding towards the crumbling foundation of stones. "Seems a strange place for a greenhouse."

"Does it?"

"I would have thought it would have been up there—" he nodded towards the far end of the garden "—where it would catch more sunlight."

"Perhaps it wasn't a greenhouse, after all."

He nodded towards the pipe in her hand. "With heating, though?"

"It does seem a bit strange," Marin allowed, although the truth was she didn't the first thing about where you would put a greenhouse. "I was thinking of asking someone from the village's historical society about it. Someone might know something. There's a photo of the garden in the village hall."

"Is there?"

Briefly she told him about the picture of the girl, although she couldn't articulate how it fascinated her. "People have said it's most likely one of the vicar's daughters, Katherine or

Eleanor Sanderson. I don't know which. Of course, it could be someone else entirely."

"Yes, well it's a good idea to try someone at the historical society."

"I'll let you know if I find something out." She shifted awkwardly, aware just how much she'd revealed to him. "Thanks for the use of your brush cutter or strimmer, or whatever it is."

"I'll bring it over tomorrow if you like. I don't have need of it at the moment, and the weather's meant to be dry."

Marin nodded. She knew she should really be spending the time organising her own life, setting up her freelance business, but the garden called to her more than her laptop did.

Still, after Joss had left, she went back into the house and dutifully powered up her laptop. She sat at the kitchen table with a cup of tea at her elbow and began drafting an email to all her work contacts, informing them of where she'd moved and what she was planning on doing.

Within a few minutes she became absorbed in what she was doing; she hadn't even thought about work in months, and she realised as she considered possibilities that she'd missed it. She'd missed something that she could call her own.

She made herself a sandwich around lunchtime and kept working, and it wasn't until she noticed the shadows lengthening across the floor that she realised it was nearly four o'clock, and time for Rebecca to come home.

Guiltily Marin cleared away her laptop and papers and put her dishes in the sink. She'd wanted the house to be tidy and welcoming when Rebecca came home; she'd even thought about making cookies. But everything was as Rebecca had left it; a smell of grease from the bacon frying this morning still hung in the air.

Quickly Marin put the kettle on and opened the window to let in some fresh air. She saw some daffodils in the garden, struggling through the weeds, and she went outside and picked a few, arranging them in a water glass in the centre of the table. There. The kitchen was a little more homely, a little more welcoming now.

The front door opened and then slammed shut, and Marin heard Rebecca's footsteps coming down the hall. She pinned a bright smile on her face as her sister came into the kitchen.

"How was school?" It was, Marin thought, the question of every parent upon their child's re-entry into the home, and Rebecca's answer was probably the same as every other teenager's.

"Fine." She dumped her bag of books by the table as the kettle began to shrill. Marin whisked it off the Rayburn.

"Tea?"

"No thanks."

She'd already had several cups of tea herself, and so with nothing to busy herself, she simply stood there and tried to smile. "So tell me about it. How are your teachers? Did you meet any nice kids?" She cringed at her over-bright tone, her ignorant questions.

"Teachers are teachers," Rebecca answered with a shrug. "Kids are kids."

Which told her precisely nothing. "Do you think you're going to like it there?" Marin tried again, and Rebecca just shrugged and picked at her nails. "Rebecca..." Marin began, and her sister must have heard something in her tone for she glanced up warily, waiting. "If you don't like it here, you must tell me. We don't have to stay. I don't want you to be unhappy."

Rebecca sighed. "It's not being here," she said and Marin waited for more. "I just thought it would be different, you know?" Rebecca continued after a moment. "I thought I'd be able to start over properly. But I can't."

Marin nodded her understanding. You could change houses or towns or even countries, but you couldn't change the fact that your parents were dead. That your life wasn't turning out the way you'd expected.

"That's understandable," she said. "But you know, it's only been four months since—since your parents died." She never knew what to call her father and Rebecca's mother; saying *your parents* made Marin feel removed from their deaths, as if he hadn't been her father too, just like Rebecca had said. *I forget he was your father too. I don't*, Marin thought. *I never forget.*

"I know," Rebecca said. "Sometimes I wish I could just fast forward a couple of years, when things... when things will feel differently."

And the process of grieving would be finished—except Marin didn't think it ever finished. She still missed her mother every day of her life, more than she could say. Certainly more than she'd tell Rebecca, but then Rebecca had never asked about Marin's mother. It was as if she'd never existed.

"I was in the garden this morning," she said instead. "I cleared a bit of the bramble away. And Joss found this."

"Joss?" Rebecca raised her eyebrows.

"You remember Joss Fowler, the man we met in the churchyard? He opened the garden door?"

"Of course I remember Joss. I just didn't realise he was stopping by now, helping you with the garden." Rebecca gave her a teasing smile, and Marin started to blush.

"He isn't... I mean, not like... oh, *Rebecca*." She shook her head and Rebecca laughed.

"He's handsome, isn't he? In a rugged way. And he looks about your age."

"I have no idea how old he is."

"Well, why not fancy him?"

She shook her head again. "Because I'm not a teenager, looking for someone to have a crush on."

"But you're single, aren't you? You haven't mentioned a boyfriend before."

"Of course I'm single." And had been for a very long time. Her list of boyfriends comprised only two unremarkable relationships—one during university, and one in Boston. Neither had left her with anything close to a broken heart.

"Well, then?" Rebecca raised her eyebrows again. "He must fancy you, to stop by."

"He's not a teenager either, Rebecca. He was just helping me out." And listening to her, more than anyone else had in a long time. *Why not fancy him?* To Rebecca it was simple, but for Marin it felt incredibly fraught and complex. Because she didn't really *do* relationships, didn't know how. She'd cut herself off from true intimacy ever since her mother had died, when her father had cut himself off from her. And she didn't know how to reconnect, not in a real way. A scattering of friends whose updates she sporadically checked on Facebook or who sent the occasional, cheerfully curious email didn't count. In any case, her fumbling attempts with Rebecca were hard enough.

"I barely know him," she said, her tone final, but Rebecca just smiled and leaned back in her chair, as mercurial as ever.

"Uh-huh, sure," she said.

Marin did not reply.

CHAPTER 14

ELEANOR

May 1919

The first week of May the Sandersons went to London. Anne had long been a lover of opera, and she was keen to see the new season at Covent Garden. George agreed, thinking everyone could do with an outing, and Katherine was still in search of the elusive lace for her wedding gown.

Eleanor did not think she would particularly enjoy the opera, although she'd never been to it before, but she was looking forward to being in London. She had not gone since before the war; it was six hours by train and had been even longer during the war, when troop trains took over the rails and made passenger ones endlessly delayed.

Despite her excitement at travelling to London, she was a bit reluctant to leave Goswell—and Jack Taylor. He'd barely spoken to her since that afternoon when she'd played croquet and then cried; in fact, Eleanor had the distinct impression that he was avoiding her. She'd come out several times to give him a drink of water, and he'd taken the glass with a murmured thanks before turning rather quickly away. Eleanor had not been able to think of a reason to stay and talk, although she'd wanted to.

Part of her was ashamed and embarrassed that Jack had seen her so undone, in tears, her shoulders shaking with sobs. But another part of her was fiercely glad; she'd cried, and he had comforted her. It felt, in a strange way, like the most intimate of communications, and had created more of a connection with him than she'd felt with anyone else in a long time.

And so she boarded the train to London with some reluctance, despite all the amusements the city was sure to offer.

"You've gone rather quiet, Eleanor," Anne remarked as they settled themselves in their carriage. "I hope you're not unwell."

"You do look a little pale," George added as he sat across from his wife. "Thank heaven this dreaded 'flu is coming to an end. The government says the worst is over."

"How many times have they told us that?" Katherine interjected. She turned to look out the window, her lips pursed. "I don't think anyone can ever know if the worst is over."

Eleanor didn't answer any of them. She was too busy staring out the window as the train pulled away from the platform; as it left the station she could just glimpse the bottom of the vicarage garden, past the sheep pasture. She could see the blurred spots of pink that were the first rosebuds; she could imagine Jack Taylor bending over them, his cap and coat shed, his brown hair gleaming in the sunlight...

"Eleanor?" Anne spoke more sharply this time. "My dear, you are miles away."

Eleanor turned from the window, blinking guiltily. The train was heading towards the sea, where rail line ran along the coast, all the way to Barrow. "Sorry, Mother," she murmured. "I was miles away, as you said."

"And what were you thinking about?" Anne asked, a small smile playing about her lips. Eleanor hesitated.

"The garden," she finally admitted. "I'd like to plant a bed of herbs in the lower garden. Rosemary for remembrance."

"That's a splendid idea, Eleanor," her father said with a nod of approval. "Splendid."

Eleanor smiled, still feeling guilty. She had only just thought of the idea of an herb garden, and judging from Katherine's narrowed look, her sister knew it.

A few minutes later, when her father had snapped open his newspaper and her mother had fallen into a doze, her head resting on her hand, Katherine leaned forward and hissed,

"The garden, indeed."

Eleanor lifted her chin and whispered back, "Why shouldn't I be interested in the garden? It was meant to my project, after all."

"I know just what your *project* is," Katherine answered, and turned back to the window.

London, Eleanor decided when they left the train at Euston Station, was like Carlisle, only bigger, noisier, and dirtier. People crowded the streets, and veterans with slings and bandages and the awful tin masks seemed to be on nearly every corner. But there were other people too: women in fancy frocks and hats trimmed with lace and flowers; men who accompanied them and were whole and well and smiling; children who ran ahead of their mothers in the park with hoops and balls.

There was an energy and an expectation to the place that made Eleanor feel as if she were buzzing inside. Open-mouthed she watched a gaggle of office girls leave a building near Euston Station; two of them had shingled hair, and one wore bright red lipstick. Another girl took something from the little bag swinging from one wrist, and to her shock Eleanor saw that it was a cigarette case.

"Don't stare," Anne murmured as they passed the girls. Their laughter, to Eleanor, sounded like the cawing of the rooks that circled high above the church back in Goswell. "Although,"

Anne added, dropping her voice even further, "I do think some of these city girls seem quite fast."

They stayed at The Cumberland Hotel near Marble Arch and even that experience amazed her; Eleanor could not remember the last time she'd stayed in a hotel, and George Sanderson, as a treat for his wife, had splurged on the grand hotel that boasted the first ensuite bathrooms in any of London's establishments.

She'd been allowed a new gown for the opera, a dress of ivory silk with the new drop waist that was quite the loveliest thing she had ever owned. They were going to see the Australian soprano Nellie Melba as Mimi in Puccini's *La Boheme*, which was the exact production the Royal Opera had put on before the war had started.

"It's as if they are trying to go back to the way things were," Katherine said with a wry twist of her lips. She wore a dress of pale green crepe de chine and was fastening a gold locket around her neck as she looked in the mirror; Eleanor wore an identical one, both given to the girls by George when they'd each turned eighteen. "Don't they realise you can't?"

"Perhaps you can in little ways," Eleanor offered. Outside she could see the dark swath of Hyde Park and the blaze of lights around Marble Arch; the roads were crowded with black taxi cabs, their tops seeming to shine in the light drizzle that now fell. She watched a man snap open a black silk umbrella and step into the street, his coat flapping behind him like a cape. All of it thrilled her. "Or perhaps," she continued thoughtfully, "in important ways. We can't go back to the ways things were, not exactly, but we can hope again. We can find happiness again."

"How poetical of you," Katherine returned sardonically. "Has your little flirtation with the gardener's boy made you so eloquent?"

"He's not the gardener's boy," Eleanor returned with heat.

"He's a man in his own right, and a gardener too. He knows ever so much about flowers and their scents."

Katherine turned from the mirror and folded her arms. "And that is all you have to say?"

"It's not a flirtation," Eleanor said. She thought she should have said that first, and suppressed a pang of irritation that Katherine had somehow managed to catch her out. "The truth is, we barely know each other." And yet she'd told Jack Taylor more about herself, her own sorrows and doubts, than anyone else in Goswell, ever.

"And you'd like to remedy that situation, I suppose."

"Oh, Katherine." Eleanor shook her head, torn between weariness and anger. "Why do you care?"

"I don't," Katherine snapped and snatched her wrap. "Why should I care if you shock the village and dally with a farmer's son? Come along, Mother and Father are no doubt waiting for us. We can't be late for the opera."

From the moment she sat down in the grand theatre with its seats of plush red velvet, Eleanor was entranced. When the orchestra started, her heart seemed to stop and then suddenly leap. And when Nellie Melba began to sing in her lilting soprano that held so much power and emotion, she was completely caught.

She could not understand the Italian, of course, but she was still able to follow the general storyline of love found and lost and found again, and it spoke to her heart and the secret dreams she'd nurtured, and fed them. When bohemian Rodolfo and poor seamstress Mimi bumped in the dark, their hands fumbling over a single candle, Eleanor's heart swelled. And when the consumptive and desolate Mimi died at the end, with her lover Rodolfo weeping over her still form, she could not keep tears from slipping silently down her cheeks. It was so beautiful and powerful and sad, so overwhelming, and it captured so many of the feelings and desires she'd nurtured without daring to name them.

She sat for a moment in her seat, her handkerchief pressed to her lips, not wanting to leave the magic of the theatre and break the spell the opera had cast over her.

Anne leaned over and patted her hand. "It touches me like that too, my dear," she said. Eleanor could only sniff and nod in reply.

Afterwards they walked through the shadowy arches of Covent Garden Market to look for a cab, and Eleanor still felt as if she were brimming with emotion; she could not keep it from spilling over. She saw a veteran begging at the corner of the market, a crutch under one arm and a tin mug in his hand.

"Spare a coin, Miss?" he asked with a tired smile, and when Eleanor looked in the mug, she saw there were only a few ha'pennies rattling around in the bottom. He coughed, covering his mouth with his hand. "Begging your pardon, miss."

"Oh..." Eleanor gazed at him, her eyes filling with tears at the wretched sight.

"Eleanor," Katherine began, a bit sharply, for she more than anyone else seemed to sense when Eleanor was on the verge of being swept away by emotion.

"Here," Eleanor said, and with one swift tug she took the locket from around her neck and dropped it into the mug. The man's eyes widened.

"I couldn't, Miss—"

"You must," Eleanor insisted and turned away before he could give it back to her.

Her parents had walked ahead to a cab that waited on the corner, and as Eleanor made to join them Katherine stayed her with one hard hand on her arm.

"Tell me you didn't just give your locket—the locket Father gave you for your birthday—to a beggar on a street corner."

"A veteran," Eleanor corrected, shrugging off Katherine's

hand. "And yes, I did. Why shouldn't I? He needs it more than I do."

Katherine shook her head in exasperation. "Why can you never be measured or sensible about anything, Eleanor? He'll be lucky if someone doesn't come along and think he's stolen it. And what will you tell Father?"

Eleanor hesitated for a moment before lifting her chin and marching towards her parents. "He'll understand," she declared, although she was not quite sure she believed it. She had a terrible feeling her father would look at her with that awful disappointment in his eyes, and she would have hurt him, and for what purpose? A man on a street corner she'd never see again. "I don't care," she tossed back to Katherine as their father beckoned them towards the open door of the cab. "I don't *care!*"

She didn't speak to anyone for the entire cab ride back to the hotel; her mother and father were still discussing the opera, but for Eleanor it had all fallen flat. She feared Katherine was right, and that she shouldn't have given away her locket; she'd been impulsive and reckless once again and yet she wasn't sure if she knew how to be anything else. She thought of how Katherine had paced by the kitchen, one arm wrapped around her waist, when James had first come home. *I don't know how to be*, she'd said.

Eleanor felt the same now. *I don't know how to be in this new world of veterans and hopelessness and confusion. I don't know how to help, how to act, what to do, what to feel.* She thought of Jack Taylor back in Goswell, tending the garden, touching her shoulder. *I don't know how to be with him.* But she thought she knew what she wanted.

They left London the next morning; Katherine had given Eleanor a pointed look, knowing she had not told their father about the locket, and Eleanor ignored her. Her father hadn't noticed, and she wasn't going to tell him until he did.

Back in Goswell the sun shone on a sparkling sea; the warm

weather had not broken and Eleanor was eager to get out in the garden.

"I had an idea for an herb garden," she told Jack the next morning. She'd been sitting in the dining room alcove since breakfast, waiting for his arrival; as soon as he'd come through the gate, a spade over his shoulder, she'd hurried out. Now he stood before her, his hands clasped in front of him, his head slightly bowed, almost as if she were giving him a scolding. He wore his flat cap low on his head and his brown wool coat, buttoned now despite the warmth of the morning.

"Very good, Miss," he said and Eleanor suppressed a flicker of irritation at his almost subservient tone.

"Jack..." she began and then gave him a playful smile. "I may call you Jack, mayn't I?" A small yet telling hesitation.

"As you wish, Miss."

"Then I shall call you Jack. And you shall call me Eleanor." She felt reckless again, just as she did with the poor veteran and his tin mug, but this time it was a delicious, heady feeling. She felt as if she could fly, as if it would only take a little leap to send her soaring over the garden. "I do wish it. We're friends, aren't we, Jack?" she continued, the words seeming to spill from her lips. "You were so kind to me, the other day, when I was sad about Walter. You seemed to understand, and I know you've seen such tragedy, more than I have."

Jack's expression was still guarded underneath his cap but Eleanor thought she saw a certain softening in his brown eyes. "I understand about grief, Miss," he finally said.

"I know you do." She took a step closer to him, not quite bold enough to touch his arm as she wished to. "You lost all your family, didn't you? Have you any relatives left?"

"An aunt," he said after a moment. "But she's elderly and she never much cared for my father. But some have had it much worse," he added, his voice gruff; he lowered his head so his face was hidden by his cap.

"Yes," Eleanor agreed after a moment, "but that doesn't make it any easier, really, does it? In some ways it just makes it harder to bear."

He lifted his head then, and Eleanor saw some spark in his gaze, perhaps of interest. "How so, Miss?"

"You're meant to call me Eleanor," she reminded him. When he didn't reply, she continued, "It makes it worse because everyone just expects you to get on with things. Everyone's grieving, so why should anyone spare a moment for you? You're no different." She hesitated, and then said awkwardly, "I must sound very selfish. Talking like that."

"No, Mi—"

"Eleanor."

"It isn't," he told her, sounding as if he wished he didn't have to say it, "proper for me to call you by your Christian name."

"Why not?" Eleanor demanded. "Haven't things changed, since the war? My sister is engaged to be married but spends most of her days with veterans, teaching them how to type."

Jack looked surprised by this, and Eleanor spared a moment's regret for divulging her sister's secret so readily. "Why shouldn't I call you by your Christian name, and you call me by mine? We're working on the garden together, aren't we?"

"Yes," he said, a bit reluctantly, but Eleanor saw a small smile tug the corner of his mouth upwards. She knew she was being shamelessly forward and while part of her cringed to think what anyone would say if they could hear her—Katherine or Mother or Grandmama—another, greater part of her thrilled to speak so honestly, so boldly.

"And we are friends," she restated firmly. "So, then. Let's have no more arguments."

"Very well." But he still didn't call her Eleanor.

"And as for my herb garden..."

"Yes," Jack said with something like relief. "Where would you like it?"

Eleanor cast her gaze around the garden, with its flowerbeds of rich, black earth. Some had started to be filled; Jack had started the wisteria to climbing up the wall, its shoots still tender, fragile and young. The beds Jack had dug over were surely not big enough for a whole herb garden, Eleanor decided. She glanced at the slope that led to the churchyard and the gate to Bower House, and a sudden smile lit her face.

"I know the perfect place," she said, and started towards the gate. After a second's pause Jack followed. They walked down the path to Bower House, skirting the vicarage and the church, until they came to the gate that led to the back of the house's garden, with the walled garden in front of them. Eleanor struggled to lift the latch; it had rusted shut over the winter.

"Here." Jack stepped forward, his shoulder brushing her arm as he tried to lift the latch. "Rusted shut," he murmured, and then hooked a boot underneath the door and lifted it; the latch sprung free and the door swung open. "Does this belong to the vicarage, then?" he asked.

The garden was covered in bramble; Grandmama and Mr Lyman had not been inside since they'd harvested the potatoes last August.

"Yes, they say it used to be an herb garden, back when the church was a monastery." Eleanor stepped into the garden and tried to pull her skirt away from a thorny bramble; the delicate material snagged and she bit her lip, knowing her mother would not be pleased to see a dress rent.

"Let me," Jack said, and stooped to free her dress. Eleanor felt as if her heart were suspended in her chest as she watched his fingers gently unhook the dress from the thorn; his fingernails were rimed with dirt, as any gardener's would be, but his fingers were long and slender, like Walter's, a pianist's fingers.

"Do you play the piano?" she asked, and Jack looked up, surprised.

"The piano? No. I've got a tin ear, or so my mum used to tell me. She was one for music, though." He straightened, her dress now freed. "There."

"Thank you." She smiled at him, and Jack glanced round the garden.

"I don't know about this, Miss. It's not part of the vicarage garden proper, is it? Your father never mentioned it to me."

"But it used to be an herb garden," Eleanor returned. "And the flowerbeds in the vicarage's garden aren't big enough for what I want. A garden of remembrance," she explained, the idea growing within her as she spoke. "A quiet place of beauty where you can come to remember—or forget, as you please. And herbs are fragrant, aren't they? Like lavender, as you said." She took another step into the garden, heedless of the brambles now. "A place apart, a place where you can just *be*, however you need to." She whirled around to face him, her arms flung out, her dress snagging on a dozen different brambles.

Jack was smiling at her, a smile of amused affection and kindly exasperation that made Eleanor grin back. "Don't you see?" she demanded breathlessly. "Don't you see how we could all use a place like that?"

"I think you could use a place like that," Jack answered quietly, and he took a step towards her. The breath froze in Eleanor's lungs as she waited, although for what she could not say. But all Jack did was free her dress once more, bending down so she could see the back of his head, the dark, ruffled hair and the sun-reddened nape of his neck.

He glanced up at her, and Eleanor knew she'd been caught staring. "Your dress is quite torn. I'm sorry. You shouldn't come back here until I've cleared the brambles, if your father wishes it, that is."

"He will," Eleanor said with confidence. She stretched a

hand out to Jack to help him up, and he took it unthinkingly; his hand was warm and dry, the palms callused and rough. He straightened, withdrawing his hand quite quickly.

"Miss—"

"Eleanor."

He sighed and rubbed the back of his neck with one hand. "Eleanor," he said, and it sounded like a surrender.

Triumphant, Eleanor picked up her skirts and practically ran from the walled garden. "I'll talk to my father right now," she called back to him, and left him there amidst the brambles.

CHAPTER 15

MARIN

The week after Rebecca started school Marin worked on starting her freelance IT business every morning, and in the garden every afternoon. She liked feeling productive, both on her laptop and with a pair of secateurs in her hand. Although after that first day, she didn't use them very much; the next afternoon Joss had appeared on her doorstep with a brush cutter over one shoulder.

Marin eyed it askance. "That looks dangerous."

"Easy as pie," he assured her. "You want me to show you how to use it?"

She hesitated for a second; in Boston and in Hampshire, for her whole life really, she'd been so cautious. So careful. Yet now she felt an almost reckless sense of defiance, although what she was defying she didn't even know. Her own self, perhaps. Her own quiet, practical nature. "Yes, please," she told Joss, and grabbed her coat, shoving her feet into her already well-used Wellington boots.

Outside the sun was shining in a tentative way; the sky was a fragile blue, as if any moment it could give way to grey cloud and rain, but for the moment at least it was bright if not warm.

Marin wrapped her scarf more tightly around her neck as they headed for the walled garden.

This morning as she opened the door she felt her spirits lift instead of plummet as they had before at the sight of the overgrown tangle. Now she saw her little cleared patch of ground and smiled.

Joss fired up the brush cutter, the sound cutting across the stillness of a frosty morning. Marin watched as he sliced straight through the thorns, the branches falling to the ground, leaving nothing more than a few inches of stubble.

"Once you cut it all down," he explained after he'd cut the motor of the cutter, "you can till the ground up. And then you can plant."

"It does sound like a big project," Marin said. "And I don't even know what I'd plant." She glanced through the open door to the mess of Bower House's small back garden. "And I really should be concentrating on all of that out there."

Joss arched an eyebrow. "Are you giving me all the excuses why you shouldn't be doing this?"

"Reasons," she told him but she was smiling. She held out her hands. "All right, let me see that thing."

"Just don't take an arm off," he warned her, smiling back as he handed her the brush cutter.

It was surprisingly light and when Marin turned it on the whole thing vibrated, making her hands buzz and tickle. She took a deep breath and angled the thing towards the thorns. Even though she'd just seen Joss do it, she still let out a little laugh of delight and surprise when she was able to cut neatly through them.

"It really does work," she exclaimed, and he grinned at her, the creases deepening around his eyes.

"Do you find that so hard to believe?"

"I know I shouldn't," she answered. "I've just never done anything like this before."

"Have a go at it this morning, then," Joss said. "I'll just be in the churchyard, finishing the roses." And with a smiling salute he left her.

Marin thought she'd mind being on her own but the brush cutter was all the company she needed; she didn't think she'd ever grow tired of the way it cut so easily through the brambles. She thought she could clear the area around the greenhouse's foundations by lunchtime.

After a few hours she'd cleared most of it; she was tired and sweaty and her hands and arms ached from holding the brush cutter aloft for so long, and she had blisters on her palms. It was a light enough tool, but she wasn't used to that kind of sustained, physical activity.

The sky had started to cloud over when she cut the motor and rested it against one of the sandstone blocks that made up the greenhouse's foundation. Now that she'd cleared most of it she could see more of the bits of piping that Joss had found, old and rusting. She picked up a piece of pipe, felt the heaviness of it in her hand. It was both hard and easy to imagine the garden as it must have once been, busy and productive, with its neat beds of flowers and vegetables, the trees bearing fruit, the greenhouse full of lettuces and cucumbers and melons. Imagining it made Marin feel both hopeful and melancholy at the same time.

"You've managed quite a bit there," Joss said and she looked up to see him standing in the doorway.

"I think I'll regret it tomorrow," she said. "I haven't had that much exercise in a long time."

He held a flask aloft. "Fancy a cup of tea? It's not much, I know, and you've got your kitchen right there—"

"I'd love it," Marin said firmly, and Joss poured some of the tea into a tin mug and handed it to her before pouring some for himself into the lid of the flask.

They sat perched on the mossy stones of the foundation,

mugs cradled in their hands. The air was turning damp, a mist rolling off the sea, the fragile blue of the sky now swamped by grey. Even so Marin felt nothing but content as she sat there on the freezing stones, her hands warmed by the tea, the garden stretching all around her in a sea of bramble—but a sea that could be cleared.

"There's quite a lot of piping," she told Joss, who studied the rusting bits of metal thoughtfully.

"Yes, more than I would have expected. They must have wanted to keep this place very warm."

"Warmer than a regular greenhouse?" she asked, a hint of eagerness in her voice, and Joss gazed at her, amused.

"What would you rather it was, than a greenhouse?"

"I don't know," she admitted with a laugh. "I don't know what it could be. But something more interesting."

"You should ask the historical society about it, like you said."

"Yes." She took a sip of tea, enjoying sitting there despite the damp chill in the air and the mist from the sea that was snaking its way through the brambles, cloaking the garden in fog and turning it ghostly.

They'd lapsed into silence, and Marin found her gaze resting on Joss's hands, his long, browned fingers curled around his mug. He had nice hands, she thought, roughened and covered in scratches yet seeming capable and strong. Joss caught her staring and he lifted one hand wryly.

"Hazard of the job, I'm afraid," he said, and she realised he was referring to his dirt-encrusted fingernails.

She held up her own hand. Even with the garden gloves, her fingernails were ringed with black. "At least it's a clean kind of dirt."

Joss laughed. He had a deep laugh, Marin thought, the kind of laugh that was genuine if rare. "How can dirt be clean?"

"Country dirt. And no sheep poo back here." She'd walked

the footpath towards the beach enough already to know you had to look where you were going.

Joss nodded. "True enough."

"So you're from Goswell, aren't you?" Marin asked after another moment of companionable silence. She nodded in the direction of the church lane where his van was parked. "Fowler and Son."

"Yes, I grew up here."

"Have you lived anywhere else?"

He studied his mug of tea, his expression turning veiled, even guarded. "For a little while."

Marin nodded; he was clearly not forthcoming with details of his life, and she understood all too well the value of privacy.

"What about you?" he asked. "How long were you in Boston?"

"Four years."

"Must have been hard to leave."

"Not really." She let out a rather abrupt laugh. "I'm afraid I didn't put too many roots down there, or anywhere, actually." She hesitated, wanting to explain herself, but not quite sure how. It wasn't something she was used to doing. "I'm not good at that sort of thing," she said after a moment. Joss arched an eyebrow.

"Putting down roots, you mean?" Marin nodded and he smiled, cocking his head towards the expanse of garden. "Good thing you've got enough to be going on with, then."

She laughed at that, with a feeling of relief; revealing personal details were as hard for her as they were, it seemed, for Joss.

"I should go," Joss said, standing up from the stone he'd been sitting on. "I'm due up the village at the Hennessys' place by three."

Marin drained her tea and handed him the empty mug. "Thank you," she said, "for the tea and the brush cutter and well, everything." She smiled awkwardly, a blush touching her cheeks. For some reason her subconscious had chosen now to remind her of Rebecca's words yesterday afternoon. *Why not fancy him?* At that moment, with Joss smiling at her, it seemed as simple a thing as Rebecca had made it.

"Not a problem," Joss answered. He screwed the lid back on the flask. "Let me know when you're thinking of going to the historical society meeting. I've never been before, but I might try it out."

Marin's heart lifted rather ridiculously at that, and she nodded. "Of course, that would be great. I'll let you know."

And with a nod back Joss took his flask and his brush cutter and left the garden.

Later that afternoon Rebecca came back with Natalie; they slouched into the kitchen and raided the fridge and pantry for soda and crisps. It heartened Marin to see them together, to know Rebecca was making friends. She hadn't had a single friend over in the three months they'd been in Hampshire. Most of her friends had kept their distance; it was easier, Marin had suspected, for them to stay away than confront Rebecca's loss and grief. Maybe her half-sister had been right, and they had needed a fresh start, even somewhere as far away as this wet and windy corner of Cumbria.

"There's a swish party on Friday," Rebecca informed Marin when she and Natalie had finished their crisps and soda. "Can I go?"

"A what party?" Marin asked. She was seated at the kitchen table, thumbing through the well-worn copy of *The Complete Book of Rayburn Cookery*. She wanted to make something warm and comforting, some kind of stew perhaps, but the cookbook's offerings of rabbit cassoulet or braised venison shanks did not appeal.

"A swish party," Natalie explained. "There's one twice a year, in the village hall. You bring five pounds and five pieces of clothing, and you leave with five different pieces of clothing. Everyone swaps. It's a lot of fun. My mum went last time. I got a brilliant new top from River Island."

Marin smiled to hear how British the girl sounded, despite her American roots. Natalie had clearly adapted to life in Goswell, eighteen months on. It gave her hope for Rebecca—and for herself.

"Why don't we both go?" Rebecca suggested. "It could be fun."

"I suppose," Marin agreed. And then, thinking of her new yet unspoken resolution to defy her own sense of cautious isolation, she added, "Why not?"

That Friday saw them heading down to the village hall, just as they'd done for the ceilidh, although this time Marin had a carrier bag of clothes with her. She'd picked out five things she didn't wear very often, most of them business clothes from her Boston days. She certainly had no need of them in Goswell.

Jane and Natalie met them at the bottom of the church lane, and Jane regaled them with the story of the first swish party she'd gone to, when she'd brought her designer clothes from New York. "I felt a complete prat," she admitted, and Marin wondered if her sensible business suits were not what was needed or wanted at a swish party. A little of her hard-won optimism flagged, and Jane must have seen something of that in her face, because she continued, smiling,

"But actually people loved the clothes. It was just me who felt out of place, and honestly, that was my own fault. I didn't want to try."

Marin could not imagine Jane not trying. She seemed so energetic, so purposeful. So unlike how she felt, most of the time, drifting around, battling her own uncertainty about everything.

"Well, we'll see what they think of my clothes," she said. "They're quite boring, really. Just business suits."

"I'm sure someone will snap them up."

The village hall was set up much as it had been before, with a bar in the corner, but instead of a band on the makeshift stage there were racks of clothes. After handing over their five pounds each, Marin, Jane, Natalie, and Rebecca were ushered towards the racks and told to hang up their clothes.

As soon as Marin had finished she went to look at the photograph again. It had been over a week since she'd seen it, and she wanted to find out if it still held the same tug of fascination for her, or if that had just been the matter of a moment.

She stood in front of the photograph, and felt that same unsettling surge of emotion as she gazed at the young woman with her intense stare into the camera lens, the butterfly brushing her fingertips. The man behind her, with his look of longing or even love, made Marin feel even more disconcerted. His expression was, in its own way, just as intense as the girl's, if a bit more veiled.

Jane came to stand next to her, and gazed at the photograph for a few seconds before saying, "is that the photo taken in your walled garden?" She peered at the write-up underneath. "I can see why you're so taken with it."

"Can you?" Marin asked. She felt oddly possessive of the photograph, as if the girl and the gardener somehow belonged to her.

"She's quite beautiful, but sort of... odd," Jane said thoughtfully.

"She's not odd," Marin replied automatically. "She's lovely." She liked the girl's dark eyes and wild tangle of hair, her pale face and the wide, curving bow of her mouth. Yes, her features were perhaps a little too large for conventional beauty, and the intensity of her stare was a bit unnerving. But Marin still thought she was utterly captivating.

Jane let out a little laugh. "You remind me of myself, about

Alice James," she said. "Sounding almost possessive of someone who's been dead for fifty years or more."

"You don't know if she's dead," Marin replied, even though she knew she was being ridiculous. Of course the girl was dead. If she really was one of the Sanderson daughters, she'd been born in the 1890s. If she were alive, she'd have to be about a hundred and twenty years old. Impossible. "Anyway," she continued hurriedly, "it doesn't matter."

"Maybe it does," Jane countered, and then they were prevented from saying anything more by the organiser of the party clapping her hands and telling everyone they had five more minutes to look at the clothes before they started divvying them up.

Marin had already had a glance through the racks, and hadn't seen much of anything she really needed. She spent most days in jeans and fleeces, for both comfort and warmth. Her current lifestyle did not require any formal or business wear, and she glanced at a few sparkly tops and flouncy skirts in bemusement, knowing she'd never wear them.

"What about this?" Rebecca suggested, holding out a black knee-length cocktail dress with several tiered rows fringed with black jet.

"Where would you wear that?" she asked and Rebecca laughed and shook her head.

"Not for me, for you. I think it would really suit you."

"Me..." Marin exclaimed, shaking her head. The dress was far fancier and more frivolous and *fun* than anything she'd ever worn. "I don't need a cocktail dress, Rebecca."

"Who knows, maybe you'll have someplace to wear it," Rebecca answered mischievously. "A fancy dinner, perhaps."

Marin knew she was thinking of Joss and she shook her head again. "I don't think so."

"Why not?" Jane asked as she joined them. "It's practically

free and who knows, you might get a chance to wear it. I agree with Rebecca, it really suits you."

"How?" Marin asked in exasperation. "I've never worn anything like that in my life."

"Exactly," Rebecca answered at once, and Marin gazed at her for a moment, at all three of them, conspiring to get her a dress she knew she'd never wear.

Unless...

She banished the thought of some nebulous dinner date before it had fully formed in her mind. Best not to think of that. But why shouldn't she get the dress? Like Jane had said, it would cost practically nothing. There was no risk. No financial risk, anyway. Tentatively Marin fingered the cloth, touched one of the jet beads. The style of the dress reminded her of something a Flapper might wear, something in fact the girl in the photograph might wear, although her dress in the picture was far more conservative, a white day dress that ended just above her ankles. Still, Marin could see her in something like this.

"We'll see if anyone else wants it," she finally said, and took a step back from the dress.

A few minutes later they all took their seats as the informal auction began. The organiser Louise held up each garment of clothing and anyone who had a mind to it held up her hand; if there was more than one person interested Louise drew a name from a bowl.

"Simple system," Jane remarked to Marin, "but it works."

Marin sat back and watched as the women around her good-naturedly bid and bickered for various items. Jane had introduced her to a few of the women, mums from the school run mostly, and with a fifteen-year-old girl in her care Marin supposed she should feel some solidarity with them, but she only felt like an impostor. She wasn't a mother. She didn't have a husband. Her life, even with Rebecca in it, was so far from the cheerful chaos that these women's lives seemed to comprise. As friendly as they were, she couldn't quite feel a part of things.

Marin was jostled out of her thoughts with a sudden elbow to the ribs. "Here's yours," Jane whispered.

"It's not mine," Marin protested as Louise held up the black Flapper-style cocktail dress.

"Anyone fancy this?" Louise asked. "It's good for a night out, or even a fancy dress party. Roaring Twenties!"

Marin held back, waiting for someone else to offer for the dress. It was good quality, and she expected someone would want it, but no one seemed to. She was just about to raise her hand when a woman in the back stuck her hand up in a semi-resigned way.

"I'll take it, then," she said, "although I'm not sure it's my size."

"*Marin!*" Rebecca hissed. "You can't let her have it."

"It's not up to me—" Marin whispered back, and Rebecca rolled her eyes.

"Put your hand up," she insisted, and after a second's pause Marin did.

"There's two of you now," Louise said, looking animated; Jane had already told Marin that Louise liked a little bit of tussling over the clothes. "Makes it more interesting, apparently," she'd said. Now Louise smiled and nodded decisively. "We'll have to draw names."

She wrote their names on slips of paper and put them in the proffered bowl; Marin shifted in her seat, a bit embarrassed to suddenly be the centre of attention; so far there had been very few occasions where more than one person had wanted an item of clothing.

Louise shuffled the two bits of paper for effect and then called out in ringing tones, "Marin Ellis."

Jane, Rebecca, and Natalie all clapped as if she'd done something impressive. Blushing all the more, Marin stood up and accepted the dress. The woman from the back row gave a conciliatory wave, and Marin smiled apologetically back.

She returned to the seat, clutching the dress to her, and Jane gave her another poke in the ribs. "You'll have to wear it now, won't you?" she said. Marin did not reply.

The swish party continued, and by the end of the evening Jane had a pretty silk scarf and a pair of high-heeled boots; Natalie had some sparkly tops and Rebecca had come away with a pink cardigan. Marin had her dress.

They walked back towards the church, its squat tower looming darker against a dark sky, the moon hidden behind some fast-moving clouds. Marin breathed in the cold, still air and felt something unfurl inside of her: a seed of happiness, planted in this unexpected garden.

"That was really fun," she told Rebecca after they'd said goodbye to Natalie and Jane and were walking back to Bower House. "I'm glad I went."

"Me too," Rebecca said, and impulsively linked arms with her. Marin nearly stumbled in her shock; Rebecca had never voluntarily touched her since the funeral. And in all that time she had never touched Rebecca either.

Now she felt affection, gratitude, and bemusement all war within her, because while she was glad Rebecca had shown her some affection, she had no idea if her half-sister would, in the next few minutes, yank her arm away and stalk up the lane or keep walking like this, arm in arm. Rebecca's moods were still mercurial and impossible to predict.

But she would, Marin decided, take this moment for what it was: a moment. A moment that watered that little seed of happiness, and allowed it to begin to bloom.

CHAPTER 16

ELEANOR

May 1919

As soon as Eleanor had left Jack in the garden, she'd gone in search of her father to seek his permission for Jack to work in the walled garden. She was still seized by the reckless, restless energy that had taken hold of her while in the garden with Jack.

And so she strode through the house, threw open the door to her father's study, and hurried inside, breathless and flushed.

George looked up from his sermon notes, alarmed. His study had always been considered a private sanctum, and he was not to be disturbed except in the direst of emergencies. Tilly had been known to leave his dinner on a covered plate by the door rather than interrupt his theological musings.

"Eleanor!" He half-rose from his chair, his expression caught between alarm and anger. "What is the meaning of this?"

Too late Eleanor realised what she had done. She was still gasping for breath, and her hair had come half undone.

"Your dress is torn," George continued, his voice rising in anxiety. "What has happened?"

"Nothing, Father," Eleanor said quickly. Her dress was badly torn from the thorns, and muddy as well. She brushed at it ineffectually. "Nothing like that," she said quickly, and her father's eyebrows rose towards his hairline.

"Like *that*? And what do you imagine I was thinking of?" His voice had taken on the stentorian quality it possessed when he was in the pulpit.

"Nothing," Eleanor said, even more quickly, for she knew she was just getting herself into more and more trouble. At this rate, her father would not countenance her going in the garden ever again.

"Then what is the meaning of your bursting into my study in this hoydenish manner?" George demanded. Her father did not often lose his temper, but when he did it was a fearsome sight. Eleanor fought the urge to stammer an apology and back out of his study.

"I'm sorry, Father, but I'd just had an idea about the garden and I wanted to ask you—"

"The garden?" he interjected. He sat back down with a sigh, his temper, for the moment, curbed. "And it couldn't wait?"

"I suppose it could have," Eleanor allowed, "but it was about the herb garden. You know, the one I want to make in Walter's memory."

"Yes." George's face was solemn, all traces of his irritation gone as Eleanor knew they would be when she invoked Walter's name. And if she felt a flicker of guilt for using her brother's death to her own ends, she banished it at once. The garden *would* be for Walter's memory, after all. "What about it?" George asked and Eleanor took a deep breath.

"I want to use the walled garden by Grandmama's house. It used to be an herb garden for the monastery, and it's perfect. And the flowerbeds in the vicarage garden are too small."

George frowned. "Eleanor, my dear, that is quite a large

undertaking. And Mr Taylor has not even finished with the vicarage garden. I don't think he should take on something else, as well."

"Oh, but..." Eleanor could not think of an adequate reason to use the walled garden; the flowerbeds might be small, but they were also currently empty. It bordered on absurd to have Jack turn his hand to another garden entirely.

And yet... it was what she wanted. She could picture the walled garden full of herbs and flowers and perhaps even vegetables and fruit. Burgeoning with life and beauty, and she would help him with it all.

"Please, Father," she said, taking a step closer to him, her fingers pleated together in front of her. "The walled garden isn't used for anything anymore. It's just a big empty space, and think how beautiful it could be!" George still looked unconvinced and Eleanor thought of what she'd said to Jack. "I want it to be a place of peace and beauty, a place where anyone can go and sit and be quiet and *remember*." Her voice choked a little as she finished, "I think we all need that, don't you?"

"Oh, Eleanor..." George looked torn, and Eleanor waited, sensing her advantage now was in silence. After a few seconds he relented with a sigh as he sat back in his chair. "Very well. I shall tell Taylor that he may work on the walled garden. But I do hope you realise what you're asking him to take on—"

"I do, Father, and I'll help him. I want to get involved in the garden, I truly do." She gave him a beatific smile before turning from the room. "I'll go tell him now."

And leaving her father to ponder that, she practically flew from the room. Jack had returned to the vicarage garden when Eleanor came out; he paused when he saw her hurrying towards him, and Eleanor could not read the expression on his face.

She stopped short, uncertainty replacing the reckless excitement that had propelled her to run from garden to house and back again. She was, she knew, being incredibly forward; what had thrilled her moments ago now brought her the first stirrings of unease and even shame.

Then Jack smiled and raised his eyebrows, spade in hand. "You've already spoken to your father, haven't you?"

Eleanor laughed breathlessly. "How did you know?"

"You don't do anything by halves," Jack reminded her, still smiling, and the shame and unease melted away.

"He said yes. He thinks it's a grand idea." This, Eleanor knew, was not exactly what her father thought, but she felt reckless again, heady with the euphoria of having succeeded. "We should start right away!"

Jack shook his head. "It will take me ages to clear that garden," he said with a nod towards the walls. "It's almost as big as the entire vicarage garden, and it took me a week to do this." He nodded towards the flower beds.

"Oh." Eleanor's euphoria flagged slightly. "Yes, of course." She realised how foolish she'd been, plunging into this plan without thinking it through at all. "I didn't mean to create extra work for you..."

"I'm glad for it," Jack told her frankly. "Keeps me busy longer, maybe even through the summer."

"And then?" Eleanor pressed her hands against her heart. "Will you leave Goswell then?"

Jack shrugged. "If there's no work to be had, I suppose I'll have to."

"What brought you here in the first place? Katherine said it was an awful long way for a West Yorkshire man to go, just to find work."

Jack's expression didn't change, but Eleanor sensed a wariness in him, a certain stillness. "Did she?" he said, his voice carefully bland. "I suppose she's right."

"Was there nothing to be had, where you're from? Where are you from?" she asked, the questions tripping from her tongue. "I don't know West Yorkshire, but..." She trailed off hopefully, waiting for him to answer. She wanted to know more about Jack Taylor, even if it was just where he came from.

"Just a small village, near Halifax," he said and turned away. "I should get to these flower beds," he said over his shoulder, his gaze not quite meeting hers. "I ought to finish the job your father hired me for before I do anything with that walled garden."

Which meant an even longer wait, Eleanor realised. "I'll help you," she offered, but Jack shook his head.

"I don't think that would be a good idea," he said, his tone so final Eleanor felt she could not insist, not again. With a nod, a lump forming in her throat, she turned back to the house.

It was another week before Jack finished planting the flowerbeds, filling them with flowers and seedlings that Eleanor had picked out from the catalogue. Eleanor watched from the window as he trundled the wheelbarrow along, planting one tender shoot after another, carefully raking the dirt back over the seeds he planted.

"Have you lost interest in your garden, then?" Katherine asked one morning as she prepared to leave for Carlisle. Although she'd been busy with wedding preparations, she was volunteering again, at least until the care society stopped. "Or is it Mr Taylor you've lost interest in?" she added, a note of spite entering her voice, and Eleanor threw down the book she hadn't been able to read.

"I haven't lost interest in anything," she replied. "I'm planning an herb garden, a memorial for Walter."

"An herb garden? Where on earth are you going to put that?"

"In the old walled garden where Grandmama used to plant potatoes. Jack just has to clear it first."

"Jack, is it?" Katherine noted shrewdly and Eleanor fought a blush.

"We're friends, which I think is perfectly proper," she said with as much dignity as she could muster. "He lost everyone in the war, Katherine—both brothers and his father, and his mother before."

"So you've been having quite a few conversations, have you?"

"Oh, don't," Eleanor returned crossly. She glanced up at Katherine, her eyes narrowed. "I think you're just jealous."

"Jealous!" Katherine let out a bark of disbelieving laughter. "Of what?"

"Of the fact that I'm actually friends with a man. With someone who listens to what I say and who... who cares for me, even if just a little." A very little, perhaps, but despite Jack's reticence Eleanor felt he had cared, when he'd comforted her. He understood her as no one else had been able to.

Katherine's mouth tightened. "Eleanor, if that's true, your *friendship* with Jack Taylor is far from proper."

"It's more than you have with James," Eleanor fired back. "You barely talk to each other!"

Katherine's face closed up like the snapping shut of a fan, everything turning pinched. "I won't dignify that with a reply," she answered and Eleanor bit her lip as she remembered in a guilty rush everything Katherine had told her about her and James.

"I'm sorry. I didn't mean it—"

Katherine turned away, busying herself with fixing her hat. "You most certainly did." She let out a tired sigh. "I don't begrudge you a little happiness, Eleanor. Jack Taylor is a handsome man and he seems to have escaped the war without any scars, physical or emotional, no matter how many people he's lost." She turned back to her sister with a direct look. "But you do realise it can't go anywhere. You can't have a flirtation or even a friendship with a gardener, not even in this modern world, and kind as he may be, he might lead you quite merrily down a garden path, no pun intended." She frowned. "And too many steps down that path could keep you from making a proper alliance."

"I don't want an alliance," Eleanor protested. "Marriage never meant that to me."

"A proper marriage, then, with someone of your own class and breeding."

"You sound like such a *snob*—"

"I sound practical," Katherine corrected. "Which I must be, even if you never are." She glanced out the window where Jack was trundling a wheelbarrow towards the walled garden; Eleanor had curled back up in the dining room alcove with her book. "Why don't you come into Carlisle with me today?" Katherine asked, her voice gentling with a sudden sympathy. "The society will be running its courses for veterans for only a few more weeks. I'm sure some of the men would be happy to hear your voice. You could say goodbye to the ones you'd befriended."

Eleanor glanced out at the garden; Jack had disappeared around the corner. "All right," she said after a moment. "I'd like that."

It was strange to be back at the Station Hotel with the seated rows of blind veterans, strange but also surprisingly comfortable. Eleanor found she settled in far more quickly than before, chatting with the soldiers and pouring cups of tea. Harry Abrams had gone already; another veteran informed her he'd taken a post as a typist in Wigton, and Eleanor was glad he'd been able to find a job in the field he'd enjoyed.

She remembered how moved by pity she'd been before, thinking these poor men had nothing to look forward to but a life of darkness and drudgery; now she saw hope, just as Katherine had said. Amidst all the wreckage of the war, all the loss and pain and despair, there was, amazingly, a way forward. She felt as if she too were emerging from a cocoon of tragedy, blinking in the sunlight, stretching her still-damp wings.

"I feel different now," she told Katherine as they boarded the train back to Goswell.

"Do you?" Katherine's face was pale with strain and weariness; her wedding was less than two weeks away.

"I feel as if there can be a future for all of us, even if it doesn't look like we thought or wanted it to." She swallowed past a lump that had risen in her throat; Walter had no future. But he would have a garden, Eleanor promised herself. A place to remember him by, and she'd bring the veterans there, the ones who were still around, at least. She'd started the garden on a lark but now she felt a burning need to see it finished, to finish it with Jack.

"I trust," Katherine said acerbically, breaking into her thoughts, "that this discovered hope of yours isn't founded on the gardener."

"No," Eleanor told her firmly. "On the garden."

A week later Tilly told Eleanor that Jack Taylor had knocked on the kitchen door and asked her to come out to the garden; moments later, Eleanor flew out the front door and hurried across the lawn.

"You have something to show me?" she asked, her eyes alight, her cheeks flushed. She felt as if she could dance across the grass on her tiptoes.

"I've cleared the walled garden," he said, "and I thought you'd like to see it."

"Oh yes!" Eleanor clasped her hands together as she followed Jack around the house and church to the garden door. It opened with a creak and Eleanor stepped inside, gazing around at the quarter-acre of freshly tilled, rich, black earth. "It looks bigger somehow, now that it's all cleared of bramble," she told Jack and he nodded. "Plenty big enough, and look here." He nodded towards the small stone building in the centre of the garden. "I didn't even know that was there, until I cleared all the bramble away."

"Oh yes, it's a funny little shed, isn't it? Mr Lyman used to store some of his tools there but I don't know what it used to be for. It doesn't look old enough to be part of the monastery, does it?"

"No, I wouldn't say so."

Eleanor took a step towards the little stone building; the tiles were falling from the roof, and it had two windows, now free of glass, by a weathered wooden door. "It looks like a little shepherd's hut," she said with a laugh. "I wonder what it was for, before Mr Lyman took it over."

"I couldn't say," Jack answered, and Eleanor lifted the latch of the door and stepped inside. It was dark and musty inside, the ground no more than packed earth. She blinked in the gloom; Jack had stepped into the doorway, blocking the light.

"Careful, Miss. There might be broken glass. A storm blew those windows in, I think."

As if on cue Eleanor stepped on a shard, the glass crunching underneath her feet. "Oh—"

Jack reached for her arm to steady her, his fingers gripping the fragile bones of her wrist. "Are you all right?" he asked, his voice rough with anxiety. "It didn't go through your shoe?"

"It might have done," Eleanor admitted and quickly Jack led her out of the shed and to a pile of tumbled sandstone blocks by the wall, leftover from the days of the monastery, no doubt. He sat her down, crouching by her feet; Eleanor watched, bemused, the pain in her foot increasing. She could see now the shard of glass had pierced the sole of her shoe, and blood had welled up, staining it red. She swallowed hard and looked away.

Carefully Jack undid the buckle of her shoe and slipped it off; he glanced up at her with dark eyes, a faint flushing staining his cheeks. "You should remove your stocking, Miss," he said.

"Eleanor," she whispered back, and Jack's eyes seemed to go darker still.

"Eleanor," he agreed quietly, and Eleanor felt something

pulse between them, almost electric; her foot was throbbing, but her heart was as well. Her fingers trembled as she rolled down her stocking and exposed her bare ankle and foot. If anyone could see them, if Grandmama came out to the garden...

Suddenly she remembered Katherine's warning. *He might lead you quite merrily down the garden path.*

But she did not know who might be leading whom as Jack carefully, even tenderly, took her foot in his hands. It was strange to feel his fingers on the arch of her foot, the small bones of her ankle. His thumb pressed into her instep as he examined the wound.

"It's not too deep, thankfully," he said, his head lowered. She could not see his face. "But you ought to have it seen to properly and bandaged up."

"I will," Eleanor promised. He looked up then, meeting her gaze, her foot still in his hands. Again she felt that leaping pulse, and she did not know if it was excitement or fear. Both, she suspected; she did not move, and neither did Jack. She could still feel his thumb pressing into her instep, his fingers curved around her heel.

She felt Jack's fingers tighten briefly on her foot and she leaned forward just a little, her lips parting, everything in her straining and waiting although she did not know what for. She could not name it.

Then her gaze, so intent on Jack's face, caught sight of the flutter of wings just above his head, beyond her reach, and he let go of her ankle as she started in surprise.

"Oh look, Jack—a butterfly!" Eleanor struggled to stand, one hand outstretched to the delicate creature with its pale blue wings. "Isn't it lovely? You see butterflies so rarely here. It's usually too cold."

"It is lovely," Jack agreed. He straightened slowly, running his fingers through his hair before he settled his cap firmly back on his head. "It must be because of the warm weather. I've heard it said this is the hottest summer in twenty years."

"It's lovely," Eleanor breathed, and as lightly as the brush of a butterfly's wing, Jack touched her shoulder.

"Let me help you into the house, miss," he said. "Tilly can take care of that foot for you."

Nodding, Eleanor turned back to Jack; she felt all jumbled up inside, as if she'd had the wind knocked out of her, or missed the last step on the stair. She did not know what might have happened, or even what she had wanted to happen. She felt as if she'd come very close to the edge of a precipice, but she had not looked down, and she did not know if she was disappointed or relieved.

She tried to hobble towards the garden door but she couldn't manage it; her foot really was aching now. Coming quickly beside her, Jack put one hand around her waist and another around her shoulders as he helped her from the garden. She could breathe in the scent of him, soap and earth and a little sweat, and she felt dizzy. Their hips jostled one another as they moved.

Tilly came to the door as they approached. "What on earth has happened," she exclaimed and Jack helped Eleanor into the house and Tilly's waiting arms before replying.

"She stepped on a piece of glass in the garden. It went through her shoe into her foot." He handed Tilly the shoe, stained red with blood, and the maid exclaimed again in distress.

"Miss Eleanor, let's get you to the kitchen and wash it off," she said. She turned back to give Jack a rather appraising look; he suffered it in silence, head bowed. "Thank you for bringing her back, Mr Taylor. I'm sure there's more work in the garden for you to do."

Nodding, he stepped back, and she closed the door with a firm click.

CHAPTER 17

MARIN

One Wednesday evening in late March Marin, Rebecca, and Joss all headed to the monthly meeting of Goswell's Historical Society. Rebecca and Marin had been in Goswell for nearly a month, and Marin thought, or at least hoped, that things had settled down into a routine.

Rebecca seemed to be enjoying school, although she didn't speak much about it, and she'd made firm friends with Natalie. She hadn't had too many—or any, really—heart-to-hearts with Marin, but then Marin knew she hadn't really encouraged them. She'd focused on the practical, which was what she always did. She bought another cookbook, this one more contemporary and basic than the dog-eared *Complete Book of Rayburn Cookery*, and she mastered several easy recipes for beef stew and chicken and ham pie, potato and leek soup and sausage and bean casserole. She even learned how to bake a basic chocolate cake which met with Rebecca's approval.

She'd never had the urge to cook before; her solitary, city existence had meant she could quite happily subsist on take-aways and pots of noodles, supplemented by cereal and toast.

Often, with her work schedule, she'd eaten her meals standing at the sink.

Now, however, she was keen and even eager to make their funny little house a home; perhaps not with the bustle and noise of the Hattons' place, with children coming and going, people clattering up and down the stairs, but somewhere that was at least both warm and welcoming. She hoped Rebecca was beginning to appreciate her efforts; she ate the meals Marin made, at any rate, and she smiled when Marin joked how she hoped she was improving.

Yet even though their kitchen had become a cheerful place with the big brass kettle and the mismatched colourful mugs, the smells of something fairly delicious simmering on the stove, and a jar of daffodils on the sill by the sink, it had not bridged the chasm of silence that so often stretched between Marin and her half-sister.

Marin did not know what would achieve that. Time, perhaps, like the grief counsellors had advised, but she feared that time would simply cement them in their positions, frozen in isolated silence like Dante's ninth circle of hell.

"I don't know what teenager doesn't give her parent the silent treatment," Jane told her when she'd invited Marin over for coffee one afternoon in mid-March. "I know you're not her mother, but you are her authority figure, and it's par for the course as far as I'm concerned to have no idea whatsoever about what is going on in a teenager's head."

Marin smiled, knowing Jane meant to encourage her, and perhaps she could be encouraged that she was doing neither better nor worse than the average parent of a teen.

And yet she longed to know what Rebecca was thinking and feeling. How she was coming to terms with the grief Marin could barely acknowledge herself. What she thought of this strange little life they'd made for themselves in Goswell. What she saw their future looking like as they soldiered on here, a funny little family that had come together not by choice.

The trouble was, Marin had no idea how to get Rebecca to tell her any of that, how to ask.

The garden, at least, provided a respite from the trials of daily life, an escape from the constant unacknowledged companion of grief. With the use of Joss's brush cutter Marin had cleared a good half of it by the middle of March. As she'd worked she'd seen how things were starting to grow back; the thorny brambles had new green shoots and one morning when she came into the garden, her boots squelching in the soft mud, she saw the bright, tiny heads of crocuses peeping out from the stubbly roots.

She'd completely uncovered the foundations of the little greenhouse or shed or whatever it had been, and she could see where there had been a door. Joss had shown her where the pipes had probably been laid. She'd paced out the building and seen that it wasn't very big, perhaps half the size of her bedroom.

"A bit small for a greenhouse," Joss told her one afternoon when he'd come by to check on her progress. "Maybe it was just a shed."

"With heating?" Marin challenged, eyebrows raised, and he smiled and shook his head. "It's a mystery. Someone will know, I reckon."

Which was why they were now going to the historical society's meeting, in the hope that someone might know or at least might know how to find out about the use of the building in Bower House's walled garden.

"It would be really boring if it turned out to be something stupid," Rebecca said as they walked up the high street to where the historical society met, in the old Scout hut by the school.

"Something stupid?" Joss repeated. "What would that be?"

Rebecca shrugged. "I don't know. Just, like, a shed."

"We've already determined it can't be a shed," Marin said firmly. "But maybe someone lived there."

"In a building the size of a broom cupboard?" Rebecca exclaimed. "In the middle of a garden? Now that would be stupid."

"It's not as unlikely as all that," Joss answered mildly. "The cottage in the corner of the churchyard used to be where the church gardener lived. The diocese sold it a while back and someone's done it up into a proper house. But at one point it wouldn't have been too much bigger than our mystery shed."

Marin liked the way he carelessly used the word *our*; it implied a sense of belonging she hadn't experienced in years, if ever, or at least not since her mother had died.

"Well, hopefully we'll find out soon enough," she said, catching Joss's eye. He smiled at her over Rebecca's head.

It was still light out despite it being nearly seven o'clock; as they headed up the high street Marin could see the sheep pasture stretching to the sea, which was no more than a twinkle under the setting sun on the horizon. The sky was a pale blue streaked with long white clouds and the air felt, if not precisely warm, than at least not freezing.

"Spring's coming," Marin said, and Rebecca let out a laugh.

"It comes every year."

"It still feels like a miracle. I saw crocuses in the garden, and there are daffodils by the chestnut tree in the garden."

"The bulbs will come up year after year," Joss told her. "Even if no one tends them."

Marin liked the idea, that a flower could grow and bloom even under the most indifferent care. Bower House's proper garden was still a tangle of weeds, although Marin had managed at least to mow the lawn. She'd been spending all her time clearing the walled garden.

They finally arrived at the Scout hut, a temporary building from the 1950s that had, with the help of some minor improvements, morphed into a permanent structure. The inside smelled of sweaty socks and stale boy, and about a dozen people were seated in a circle on folding chairs. A man who looked to be about sixty rose from his chair as they came in.

"Newcomers, how delightful," he said. "I'm Allan Mayhew, Chairman of the society."

Marin introduced herself and Rebecca, and Joss gave a quick nod. Allan's gaze, Marin saw, had narrowed slightly as he caught sight of Joss.

"Joss Fowler," he said, and she had the sense he was recalling Joss's history as he said his name. "Good to see you again."

Again? Marin slid Joss a curious look; he was staring straight ahead, his expression bland. She shouldn't be surprised, she supposed; Joss had told her he'd grown up here. Yet in the month since she'd known him she'd never seen him except on his own. Even at the ceilidh he hadn't really talked to anyone but her.

"Come sit down, sit down," Allan beckoned, and someone got out a few more folding chairs. They all sat down, and after introductions the meeting began; they were talking about doing a First World War centenary display in the church.

Marin listened with interest about memorabilia and presentations and a possible lecture series on *Goswell Through The World Wars*.

Someone passed around a medal won by their grandfather in the First World War; another person had a newspaper clipping from 1915. Marin studied the tiny type, marvelling at the articles that spoke of a forgotten world: a call to collect sphagnum moss, to send to field hospitals for use as medical dressings; an advertisement for Dainty Dinah toffee to send to soldiers that, according to the ad, 'helps him to forget what he has been through—the great trials and sufferings he has undergone.' Sold, Marin saw, at all fine confectioners.

Another article outlined the house-to-house collection that had gone on in Goswell to supply funds to purchase huts for the women munitions workers.

"It's a different world, isn't it," Marin murmured to Joss as she handed him the newspaper clipping. "A different era."

"The era of the girl in the photograph," he reminded her. "And maybe our mystery shed."

After the meeting broke up Marin approached Allan Mayhew, self-conscious yet determined to see if she could find out anything more. She explained about the photograph and the garden, and Allan listened, his head cocked to one side, his bushy white eyebrows raised.

"I don't know that much about Bower House, to be honest. Just the basics, about the diocese selling it in 1929, when the incumbent at that time retired." He tapped a finger against his lips, frowning in thought. "I know the photograph you mean, though—I'm just trying to remember who it belonged to."

"I never even thought of that," Marin admitted. "Whoever had it might know more about the garden—"

"Perhaps," Allan allowed. "Although many of those photos were here in the hut, in our archives. They'd belonged to the historical society for donkey's years. But I could do a bit of digging, if you like, and ask around. Someone might remember where it came from."

"Thank you, that would be so helpful. And as for the building in the garden..."

Allan shook his head. "That I couldn't tell you about. I didn't even know it was back there. But like I said, someone might know. I'll keep my ear to the ground."

Although they hadn't found out anything about either the garden or the girl, Marin felt cheerful as they left the Scout hut and headed back down the high street towards Bower House. She'd done something, and who knew what Allan Mayhew might unearth.

As they approached the church lane where Joss had parked his van, Rebecca turned to him suddenly.

"Would you like to come in for a drink? Marin makes a mean cup of tea."

"Does she?" Joss sounded bemused, and Marin inwardly cringed at her sister's blatant attempt to push her and Joss together. Did teenagers never realise how obvious they were?

"You're welcome to, of course," she said after a too-long pause, and in the moonlight she thought she saw Joss smile.

"I'd like a cup of tea, thanks," he said, and they walked in silence towards Bower House.

Once inside Rebecca scampered upstairs with mutterings of homework, and Marin cringed again. Rebecca, she thought, couldn't be more obvious if she tried.

Joss followed her into the kitchen, and Marin felt thick-fingered and clumsy as she filled the kettle and heaved it onto the Rayburn, and then went in search of mugs and milk.

"You look well settled here," Joss said as he braced a hip against the oak table.

"Trying," Marin told him. "It's a lovely little house, the kind of place that could be a proper home, I think."

"It is, that." He arched an eyebrow. "Better than a flat in a city?"

"Yes, definitely." She put the milk on the table and closed the fridge.

"But you must miss city life a bit," Joss said. "The convenience."

"Not really," Marin answered, then amended that to, "not yet. What about you? Have you had a hankering to live in the Big Smoke?"

He laughed, the sound seeming both rich and rusty. "No, I like Goswell well enough."

"But you lived somewhere else for a bit, didn't you?" Marin's back was to Joss as she asked the question, but she felt his hesitation and she turned to see the smile wiped from his face; he looked wary and guarded now.

"Yes, for a bit."

"But you decided to come back to Goswell?" Wherever he'd lived, it clearly was out of bounds for conversation. Marin wondered if he'd been married; was there a divorce lurking in his background? Had he moved to be with his wife, and moved back again when his marriage had broken down? She knew she was being both fanciful and nosy, but she couldn't help it. She was curious about Joss Fowler, more curious than perhaps he wanted her to be.

"Yes, it seemed the right thing to do." His tone was final, but his choice of words intrigued her. The kettle whistled then, forestalling any more questions, not that Marin thought she could ask any without Joss becoming more tight-lipped.

As she poured the tea, he changed the conversation anyway. "So I think you said you do something in IT. Can you do that from here?"

"I'm trying to set up my own business," Marin answered. "Designing and maintaining websites, offering IT services, that kind of thing. Just about everyone has a website these days—"

"I don't."

"No Fowler and Son dot com?" she teased in a parody of shock, and Joss's mouth quirked upwards in a tiny smile. "Well, I could see if the domain was available, if you wanted to set one up."

He hesitated, drumming his fingers on the table, and then gave a nod. "Go on, then."

"All right, I'll just get my laptop." She hurried to fetch it, and then set it up on the kitchen table while Joss poured their tea, adding two sugars to his, which Marin teasingly raised an eyebrow at. He grinned back.

Soon they were both seated at the table with the laptop in front of them, mugs of tea by their elbows.

"So, let's see," Marin began as she logged in and pulled up a browser window. "What domain name would you like? Fowler and Son?"

"Seems best to keep it straightforward."

She typed FowlerandSon.co.uk into the browser window, and a notice popped up that the domain name was for sale. "Perfect, that means you can buy it."

"From whom?"

"A company that buys up a bunch of domain names and then sells them off."

"That's a nice little sideline."

She laughed and clicked through to get to the company's homepage. "Isn't it just." She nodded towards the screen. "There. For sixty pounds a year it's yours."

"Sixty quid? And that's just the name?"

"I think you'll find," Marin said, self-consciously adopting a businesslike tone, "that a website drives more business to you—"

Joss held up a hand. "I don't need the sales pitch. I suppose I can fork out sixty quid for a site. And whatever your going rate is for designing the website."

"Oh." Marin felt her cheeks heat. "I didn't mean you had to use me, that is, my services, for your website. I wasn't trying to drum up some business."

"Why wouldn't I have you do it? I'd rather it was someone I knew and trusted than a stranger."

"I know, but..." Marin nibbled her lip. "I just don't want you to think..."

"Don't worry about what I think," Joss cut across her. "Trust me, it's nothing bad."

And for some reason that innocuous statement made a shiver of wary pleasure go through her. "All right, then. Let's register the domain name, at least." Joss watched while she started the process, and when it came to his personal details he took over and typed them in. Joss Fowler, 2 Seaview Lane, Goswell, Cumbria.

"Where's Seaview Lane?" she asked, realising she was being nosy but still wanting to know.

"Down by the beach. I have a bungalow right by the sea."

"You must get a lot of wind."

"On a stormy day the garden, such as it is, floods. But it's worth it." He reached for the mouse to click to the next entry box, and put his hand over Marin's, which was still resting on top of the mouse. For a second his hand completely covered hers, and Marin could feel its dry warmth and solid strength before she pulled her hand away.

"Sorry," she muttered, and felt her blush return. She was thirty-seven years old and she was blushing because a man had accidentally touched her hand. Good grief.

"There we are." Joss nodded at the screen. "So Fowlerand-Son.co.uk is mine?"

"Looks like it." She smiled, conscious that she was still blushing, her hand still tingling. She felt ridiculous and yet also happy, happier than she'd been in a long while. "We can set up a time for a design consultation, and you can let me know what you want from the website—"

"I don't think I'd really have the first clue."

"Well, contact details of course, and an online form to submit requests?" He nodded and she continued, "And examples of your work, photos of gardens and landscaping."

"Sounds good."

"And if you wanted to get really high tech," she added, "you could write a blog about interesting garden projects you've done." Joss's eyebrows rose at this and Marin thought he was going to refuse, but then he said,

"What about a blog about the walled garden, and what we find? Someone might stumble across it and know something."

"What if we don't find anything?" Marin countered.

"You don't really believe that, do you?" Joss asked seriously and Marin knew she didn't. She'd had a feeling about that garden from the moment she'd seen the door. But could you really trust a feeling?

She hesitated, her hand on the mouse, and then she thought about how coming here had started to change her, how she was trying, in hesitant little steps, to come out of the shell she'd constructed and kept around herself for so long. "Why not?" she finally said. "I could set it up and link it to your site."

"Perfect. Do you have a camera?" She shook her head and he said, "I'll bring mine. We can take some photos of the garden. Too bad we didn't take an initial one when it was all bramble—"

"I think there's enough bramble left for people to get the idea."

"Good."

They stared at each other, the moment spinning out until it seemed to be turning into something else. "Thank you," Marin said at last, her tone both abrupt and awkward.

Joss raised his eyebrows. "For what?"

"For—for being a friend. I haven't actually had that many." Which suddenly felt like a far too intimate admission to make, but she couldn't take it back.

"And why's that?" Joss asked quietly.

Marin swallowed. "I've moved around because of my job," she hedged. "And I've worked long hours." Which were not the real reasons and she sensed that Joss knew it. "My mother died when I was eight," she blurted. "And my father just... shut down. You think grief brings people together but sometimes it pulls them apart."

"Yes," Joss agreed, "it does." And she had a feeling he knew what she was talking about.

"That's what happened to my father and me," she continued. It felt both good and strange to tell him more, to explain. "He completely withdrew and ended up sending me to boarding school just a few months after my mother died. I was so angry and hurt at the time, but too young to know how to confront him on it. And eventually I just started doing the same thing. Shutting people out."

"To keep yourself from getting hurt."

She swallowed hard. "Yes."

"And as an adult?" he asked after a moment. "Are you still shutting people out, Marin?"

She thought of her two failed romantic relationships, her handful of friends in Boston, and her sometimes-strained relationship with Rebecca. "I'm trying not to. Now. Here."

"I think you're succeeding," he answered. He lifted his hand and Marin held her breath as he gently tucked a tendril of hair behind her ear. It was barely the whisper of a touch, and yet it made everything in her ache and yearn; she felt as if she were stirring to life, just as the garden was, the brambles inside her finally being cleared away.

And then it was over, almost as if it had never happened, and he was standing up and taking their mugs to the sink. "I'll bring the camera tomorrow afternoon," he told her. "If you're free?"

"Yes," Marin said. She stood up too, the chair scraping across the tiled floor with a screech. "I'm free."

"Good." Another brief look passed between them that left Marin feeling strangely expectant, but also unsure. What had just happened? How much had changed between them?

And then Joss lifted a hand in farewell and started for the front door. Marin followed him, and she stood in the doorway as the cold night air swept over her and she watched Joss walk down the weedy little path and all the way to the church lane, until he was swallowed up by the darkness.

CHAPTER 18

ELEANOR

June 1919

Katherine and James's wedding day dawned bright and fair; at that point, the good weather had held for so long that everyone seemed to expect it to be fine. Anne had arranged for the wedding breakfast to take place outside, with tables and chairs set up under awnings. Jack had outdone himself with the garden; the once-empty flowerbeds were now bursting with blooms, and the warm air was fragrant with the scent of roses and dianthus, honeysuckle and wisteria.

That morning after getting dressed herself Eleanor went to help with Katherine's preparations. As bridesmaid she wore a drop-waist gown of pale pink silk with white lace underneath; it was quite the nicest thing she'd ever worn, besides the dress to the opera. Katherine's gown was even lovelier, with a high collar of white lace—they'd found it in London, after all, made by Belgian refugees during the war—and lace on the cuffs and cinched-in waist as well.

As Eleanor came into Katherine's bedroom, full of high spirits, she saw her sister's face was pale with strain.

"Oh do cheer up," she cried. "You're so pale you'll look like a ghost in the photographs." Their father had, in a moment of largesse, hired a professional photographer to take pictures of all the wedding party.

"I feel like a ghost," Katherine told her. She pressed her hands to her pale cheeks. "I feel as if I'm disappearing."

"Well, I assure you you're not. All you need is a bit of colour." Adopting the kind of briskness Katherine usually had, Eleanor pinched her sister's cheeks. "It's a shame Mother won't let you wear a bit of rouge."

"Don't be coarse," Katherine said automatically, and then a tear slipped down her cheek. Eleanor drew back.

"Oh, Katherine," she said, and patted her sister's shoulder. It was a testament to Katherine's mood that she suffered that small show of affection. "Surely it's not as bad as all that," she protested gently. "He's marrying you, after all."

Katherine wiped the tear away with trembling fingers. "Yes," she said, and took a deep breath. "There is that."

"Don't you think, in time, you may be happy?"

"I hope so. I pray so." Katherine took a deep breath. "That's what Mrs Freybourn keeps telling me. 'Just give it time, Katherine dear. He'll come round. The war was hard on him, on everyone.'" She shook her head and pressed her fingers to her eyes to prevent any more wayward tears from escaping. "Is time all one needs, do you think, Eleanor? It feels lazy to me, to just wait, but I don't know what else to do."

"Have you tried speaking with him?" Eleanor asked cautiously. "I mean, properly. Telling him..."

"Telling him what? I don't know what to say. He does all the right things. He's the perfect gentleman, respectful and solicitous and so bloody cold." She dropped her hands from her face and turned to look out the window. "I shall freeze to death," she said, her voice distant and lifeless. "Slowly."

"Please don't say that." It sounded awful to Eleanor, and yet she remembered those first few months after Walter had died, how everyone had been frozen in separate worlds of grief. She felt as if she had finally begun to break free; Jack, dear, wonderful Jack, had helped her by letting her cry, and giving her the garden. But who had helped Katherine, or James for that matter?

"I shan't say it again," Katherine told her as she turned back to face Eleanor, her expression resolute now. "I shan't say any of this again. When the vows are spoken, the thing is done. There's no point..." She trailed off, biting her lips.

"You don't have to marry him," Eleanor burst out. "If you don't think he'll make you happy—"

"Oh, Eleanor, are you still such a child?" Katherine sighed wearily and reached for her locket which she fastened around her neck, the gold heart nestling in the hollow of her throat. Eleanor still hadn't told her father she'd lost hers. "Of course I have to marry him. If I cried off on my wedding day I'd be completely ruined. No one would have me, ever, with such scandal attached to me."

"Wouldn't it be better to be alone than with someone and unhappy?"

"I don't know," Katherine answered with bleak honesty. "The trouble is, I've known happiness with James, before the war. It's the most treacherous, tempting thing. I knew it, ever so briefly, and I long for it again. Sometimes I can almost convince myself I'll find it with him now, or at least soon."

"Then speak to him—"

"It's not that simple!" Katherine's voice rose and she closed her eyes briefly, drew in a steadying breath. "If a single conversation could cure what ails us," she asked, "don't you think we would have had it already?"

"What do you think ails you? Ails him?" Eleanor asked. "He's not... shell-shocked, is he?" She'd read about the unfortunate soldiers who suffered from neurasthenia; she knew there were asylums to help the worst cases, but also that their condition was looked down on by some who condemned them as cowards. Most men simply struggled on, trying to appear normal. But James did not exhibit the usual symptoms, the 'thousand yard stare' of dazed vacancy; the lolling tongue or the jerky movements that had been dubbed 'the hysterical gait'.

"No," Katherine said after a moment. "I don't think it's that, thank heaven." She hesitated and then said, "It's almost as if something happened to him. I don't just mean the war or a battle or just the awfulness of life in the trenches. Something in particular."

"You mean because of how he was this summer. With Walter."

Katherine nodded. "I get the sense that he's hiding something from me, something he's ashamed of, almost. But perhaps I am merely being fanciful. It doesn't matter, in the end. He won't talk to me of it."

"Perhaps in time..."

"Ah, yes. Time." Katherine's mouth twisted. "That great healer." She turned to look out the window again; the sun was shining, gilding the garden in light. Eleanor could see Jack moving around, setting up chairs and tables. He was dressed in his best suit, his usually untidy hair smoothed back with pomade, and she wondered what he would think of her in her bridesmaid's dress, with a new hat besides. In the two weeks since he'd brought her into the house with her cut foot, he'd hardly spoken to her except about garden matters, and then only when she'd insisted, when she'd come out to find him and ask him about this seed or that plant, all of it no more than a pretext to talk to him again.

But he wouldn't talk, not properly, and Eleanor told herself she didn't mind because she just *knew* the thrilling truth: Jack cared for her. He had to; in that moment in the garden she'd almost thought he'd been going to kiss her.

"But if you do love him," Eleanor persisted, needing to say it, to believe it, "it will turn out all right in the end."

"Sometimes I wonder if I know what love is. Is it just that fluttering feeling you get in your middle, when you see someone?" Eleanor blushed and thought of Jack. "Or is it something rather more?" Katherine reached out and braced one hand against the windowsill, almost as if she needed help to stay standing. "If I truly love James," she continued slowly, "then I'll stand by him in this—whatever this is. Whatever he's suffering. And however cold he seems."

"And it will get better," Eleanor said bracingly. "It has to."

"Have the last four years taught you nothing?" Katherine asked with a hollow laugh. "There's no 'has to' anymore, Eleanor. There's no guarantee of a happy ending for anyone, ever."

"Don't talk like that," Eleanor begged. "Not on your wedding day, Katherine. This is a beginning, not an end. You love James, and he loves you, even if he doesn't always show it."

Katherine smiled and touched her cheek. "You're such an innocent," she said, and somehow it didn't sound like a compliment to Eleanor. "Four years of war, your brother dead, and you've seen those poor blinded soldiers. You've seen Billy Branson selling bootlaces on the street, and yet you still cling to your silly, foolish hope."

"Is hope foolish?" Eleanor replied with as much dignity as she could muster. "I don't think so."

"Then perhaps I'll take a page from your copybook," Katherine said wearily. "And be as foolish as you are."

An hour later she was married, the air inside the dark, vaulted church cold despite the warmth of the day outside. The vows were spoken, Katherine's voice ringing clear while James's tone was both flat and firm. Everyone emerged from the church into the courtyard, the ancient stones warm beneath their feet as they blinked in the bright sunlight.

Eleanor pressed one hand to her head; the cold of the church and the sudden sunshine had conspired to give her a headache.

"Are you all right, Miss Eleanor?" Jack asked, suddenly coming to stand next to her.

Eleanor gave him a distracted smile. "Yes, just a headache. And the scent of all the lovely flowers is giving me a tickle in my throat. They are as fragrant as you promised, Jack. I'll be fine." She gazed at Katherine and James, walking arm in arm towards the vicarage; they both looked stiff, like puppets or performers in a play. "Do you think they'll be happy?" she asked quietly.

Jack shifted where he stood. "It's not my place to say," he answered.

"Oh, Jack." She turned to him, all the words and thoughts she'd piled up in her head over the last few weeks spilling out in frustration. "No one is here but me," she said, for the others had gone ahead. "And I know you better than that, surely? Can't you speak honestly with me?"

He gazed at her for a moment, and she saw a struggle in his eyes. She caught her breath and held it, waiting for his answer.

"I suppose they could be happy, if they work hard at it," he finally said. "It's not an easy thing to find these days, happiness."

He sounded so weary that she frowned, catching his sleeve. "But you're happy, aren't you? Here, with..." She stopped, swallowed. "Here, I mean."

He gazed down at her hand, her white glove seeming almost silvery against his brown suit jacket. "I'm thankful to be alive," he said quietly, "even if I don't deserve to be."

Her fingers clenched on his sleeve. "Why wouldn't you deserve to be?"

He hesitated, and Eleanor had the sense that he'd said more

than he might have wished. Carefully, gently, he pulled his arm away from her hand. "It just makes you wonder sometimes. How the bloke next to you can be blown to pieces in an instant and you're still whole and well, though you're no better or cleverer than that poor sod was." He blinked as if coming to, and turned to her. "Begging your pardon, Miss. I shouldn't have said such things to you."

"I'm glad you told me," she said and dared to lay her hand on his arm once more. "I want to know such things. I've always wanted to know, because the not knowing was so terrible. I look back and I wish I could have talked more to Walter about how he felt. What he endured." She blinked rapidly as words thickened in his throat. "Do you know, the last time he came home, I made a fuss about how boring he was being? Because he wasn't as jolly as he usually was. It... *annoyed* me, which seems so petty and childish now, especially since..." She thought of James, and whatever he was hiding, and shook her head. "I was such a child, then. I'm ashamed of myself now."

For one brief moment Jack covered her hand on his arm with his own. "We were all children once, Miss," he said quietly. "The war has made men and women of us, for better or worse." He nodded towards the vicarage, where guests were milling around the garden, a small sea of bright hats and parasols mixed with the dark coats and toppers of the men. "We should go," he said. "They'll all be waiting."

The sun shone down on the wedding party as they made their way to the garden; Jack disappeared as Eleanor approached the gate, heading around the back, and she found herself near James, and moved forward to congratulate him.

"Welcome to the family, James," she said, and stood on her tiptoes to kiss his cheek. His skin was cold under her lips and when she eased back she was startled to see what looked almost like anguish in his pale blue eyes.

Before Eleanor could even fathom it his expression became

quickly veiled and his lips curved in what she supposed was a smile. "And I shall be honoured to call you sister."

It was a lovely sentiment and the right thing to say, but his voice had been toneless. Eleanor studied him for a moment, wondering just what thoughts and feelings hid behind that carefully bland expression. What hurts and scars.

"James—" she began, impulsively, and Katherine, who had been standing near him, turned suddenly and laid a hand upon his arm.

"We should go sit down," she said, her tone light and yet also implacable. "Father wants to start the toasts."

James nodded tersely and they moved off. Eleanor didn't know what she had been going to say to him just then, but Katherine had obviously not wanted her to say it.

George called for everyone's attention, and as all the guests turned to him, their coupes of champagne held aloft, he toasted Katherine. Eleanor barely heard the words; she was watching James, noticing the lines of tension that bracketed his mouth, how the expression in his eyes was veiled. Then she heard a scattering of 'hear, hear' and realised her father's toast had ended, and James stood up.

Eleanor held her breath as she watched him, saw the faint smile on his face even as his expression remained distant. She glanced at Katherine, who was smiling, but even from several feet away Eleanor could see how tightly her sister clutched her coupe of champagne.

She only half-listened as James stiffly thanked his in-laws for their generosity; her gaze had wandered to Jack, who was standing in the shadows by the walled garden, out of the way of the guests. He was there simply to shift tables and make sure nothing went amiss, but she was still glad to see him. Watching him from afar she could dwell for a moment on his features, note the contained way he held himself, see his mouth twist downwards in sorrowful sympathy as he listened to James.

How could one man go through the war, Eleanor wondered, and come out as stiff and remote as James, and another man, like Jack, seem so unscathed? Yet perhaps Jack simply hid his hurts better.

"And of course I must toast my bride." James's voice rang out a bit louder and Eleanor turned to look back at him. He lifted his glass, his gaze straying briefly to Katherine, and the faintest smile touched his lips. "To Katherine."

"To Katherine," everyone repeated dutifully, and Eleanor drank from her own coupe, the bubbles fizzing and popping on her tongue. It had not, she acknowledged, been the most romantic and loving of toasts, but at least James had got the job done.

She watched him and Katherine for another moment; they were like two stiff mannequins sitting next to each other, all tense faces and jerky movements. Despite all her determined cheer with Katherine this morning, looking at them now she had her doubts as to whether either of them would be able to find happiness with the other. And what of the anguish she'd seen in James's eyes when she'd wished him well? Had it been real or imagined?

As guests began to mingle and talk Eleanor moved off. Her headache of this morning threatened to turn into a megrim and she wanted to be alone. No one paid any attention to her as she walked away from the wedding guests and sought the sanctuary of solitude in the walled garden.

In the two weeks since she'd last been in the walled garden, Jack had made great progress. He'd used the old sandstone blocks piled in the corner, taken from the monastery long ago, to make borders for the flowerbeds, and had begun to fill them with cuttings of herbs. Eleanor recognised spiky rosemary and could smell the sharp tang of mint and the dusty scent of lavender. With the damson trees and red currant bushes that had been left from another age now in blossom, Eleanor could almost imagine how the garden would look when it was finished, full of life and beauty just as she'd wanted.

Carefully she lifted her skirt and moved through the garden. She had not walked the full length of the place since she'd been there and now she studied the old slate path that had been buried under the soil and which Jack had scraped clean. He'd shown her a few days ago, seeming intrigued by the worn slates, and Eleanor had studied them scrupulously, simply to have a moment alone with Jack.

Now she saw the path led to the funny little shed in the middle of the garden; she didn't go inside this time, although Jack had swept away all the broken glass.

Her gaze was caught by an old headstone leaning against the building; Eleanor could barely make out the faded inscription of a woman who had died in 1762. *Here Lies Isabel, Always Remembered.* The rest was lost. She shivered, wondering if the unfortunate Isabel's bones lay beneath the rich black earth.

"Eleanor."

She turned to see Jack standing in the doorway of the garden, looking serious, and her fingers clenched on the folds of her dress as anticipation leapt inside her, a wild, uncontained thing. She had, she realised in that moment, been waiting for him to come and find her.

"Is someone buried in the garden, Jack?" She pointed to the headstone. "It's rather ghastly to think of, although I know we're surrounded by graves." If she stood on her tiptoes, she could see the cemetery that stretched out on three sides, the velvety green lawn dotted with headstones.

"I asked your father about that," Jack answered as he came into the garden. "He said no one would be buried here, because it's not consecrated ground. But the old headstone would have been removed from the churchyard, to make room for new ones."

"But that's awful." She hadn't spent much time considering the fact that she lived in the middle of a cemetery, but now she suddenly had a terrible image of all the bodies beneath the soil, all the people forgotten because too much time had passed, and the headstones that had marked their place had become faded and then had been taken away. "Is there no one left to remember those people?" she asked and Jack smiled a little.

"Over a hundred years later? Probably not."

Eleanor shivered; her head was starting to ache abominably and even though it didn't make sense the thought of Isabel, with that inscription promising she would always be remembered when she'd been so clearly forgotten, and her headstone propped against a building like any old slab... it seemed quite terrible.

"Eleanor," Jack said quietly. "Your family is looking for you. Miss Katherine and Master James are leaving shortly, for their honeymoon." Katherine and James were, Eleanor knew, spending the night in Carlisle before taking a short trip to Edinburgh. Then Katherine would live in Whitehaven with James and his parents, until they were able to find a house of their own.

Eleanor didn't think she'd actually miss her sister precisely, but neither did she like the thought of her leaving.

"How did you know I'd be in the garden?" she asked.

He smiled faintly. "I just knew."

"I knew you would." Eleanor smiled back, despite the continued ache in her head. She really wasn't feeling all that well, and Jack must have sensed that for he frowned and started towards her.

"Eleanor..."

She moved towards the door, or tried to, but it seemed to swim up towards her, which she thought rather strange. Her slipper caught in the muddy earth and the whole world started to tilt and slide as she reached out with her arms, blundering now as though she were blind, just like one of those poor veterans might have done. She began to pitch forward before Jack caught her up in his arms.

"I... I don't feel very well," Eleanor mumbled, and then she closed her eyes, letting herself sink into Jack's embrace.

CHAPTER 19

MARIN

The next morning Marin spent several hours working on a possible website design for Fowler and Son; when Rebecca had asked her what she was doing at breakfast, and she'd told her, her sister's eyebrows had risen and she'd given a smirking kind of smile. Marin had rolled her eyes.

"Don't start, Rebecca. It was bad enough that you disappeared last night after inviting Joss in for a drink—it looked rather obvious, you know."

"All the better," Rebecca replied blithely. "Both of you need a good push for anything to happen."

"Maybe I don't want a good push."

"You don't want to be alone forever, do you?"

Marin frowned. "I've been alone for most of my life. It's not that bad." She'd found a small happiness in managing for herself, and surely being alone was better than being with someone and being unhappy, being hurt. Having someone you love cut you out of his life, just as her father had.

"Maybe I don't want you to be alone," Rebecca said and Marin looked up from her laptop.

"What do you mean?"

Rebecca shrugged, her gaze sliding away from Marin's. "I feel guilty for taking you away from everything," she said after a moment. "Your whole life. If you were with someone..."

Marin closed her laptop. "Rebecca," she said, "I told you before, I chose this. You. And the truth is, you didn't take me away from very much."

"Didn't you like your life in Boston?"

"It was all right." Marin rose from the table and dumped their cereal bowls in the sink. "My job was being outsourced eventually and I'd only made a few friends. I worked long hours." She was giving Rebecca the excuse she'd given Joss last night, but she didn't feel like clarifying it the way she had with Joss. She didn't want Rebecca's pity.

"Even so, it was your life," Rebecca persisted, "and it's not anymore."

"True. But I don't mind that. I'm happy here." As she said the words she knew she meant them. "You don't need to feel guilty, Rebecca."

"Maybe I can't help it," Rebecca said quietly, and Marin had the unsettling sense that her sister was talking about something else entirely.

"What do you..." she began, but Rebecca cut her off.

"I'd better get going. I don't want to miss the bus."

Marin nodded, her unfinished question sinking into the silence, and she didn't say anything else as Rebecca reached for her bag and coat and then walked out of the room; a few seconds later she heard the front door slam.

She finished doing the breakfast dishes, her mind skirting around what Rebecca had said and more importantly, what she'd meant. What did she feel guilty about? If not Marin having to give up her life, then something else, something with her parents? There was still so much they hadn't talked about, and even though Marin was trying to take steps towards bridging that chasm of silence, it was hard. Maybe she needed to take a flying leap instead, but how? It was utterly unlike her to do so.

She spent the rest of the morning working on Joss's website, glad for the distraction from her own circling thoughts. After a quick lunch of soup and a sandwich she headed outside; the sky was a fragile blue and the wind was kicking up, but she'd got used to it now, and with her scarf wrapped around her neck and her hat pulled down over her ears she felt well-equipped for the relentless Cumbrian wind.

She spent an hour clearing more of the garden; Joss had left his brush cutter with her for a few days and she still thrilled to the easy way it cut through the brambles. Another couple of hours, she reckoned, and the entire garden would be clear, albeit covered in a few inches of stubbly roots.

She was just slicing through a particularly thick branch when the brush cutter made an alarming, high-pitched noise and Marin quickly cut the motor. Pushing past the bramble, she saw that she'd started cutting into something significantly harder than a thorny branch: a slab of sandstone.

She cleared away the cut brambles and brushed off the dirt from the slab; with a shivery ripple of shock she realised it was an old headstone. But surely someone wasn't buried here? Instinctively she looked down at her feet, almost as if she expected to see a skeletal hand poking through the dirt. She really was becoming fanciful.

"What have you found?"

She turned to see Joss coming through the garden door, a camera slung round his neck. Marin nodded to the headstone.

"A grave," she said. "I think."

He came to stand next to her and then crouched down to examine the headstone. "I can't read the name," he said, "but the date looks like 17-something."

"Do you think someone is actually buried here?"

He shook his head. "Doubt it. The church has permission to

move old headstones after a certain number of years, in order to make way for new ones."

"So you mean people are buried on top of people?"

He nodded towards the headstone. "Two hundred years on and there's not going to be much left."

"Of course." But it still gave her an unsettling feeling to think about it.

Joss straightened and brushed the dirt from the knees of his jeans. "So, how about we take some photos?"

"All right."

"You've done a good job," he continued, "clearing this lot."

"It feels rather therapeutic, actually, to cut through it all." She nodded towards the growing pile of brush she'd stacked haphazardly in the far corner of the garden. "I'm not sure what to do with that, though. If it were November, we could have a roaring bonfire for Guy Fawkes."

"You could still burn it. The earth is damp enough it won't spread." He took the camera from around his neck and starting snapping photos. "How are you coming on the website?"

"Good. I'll show you what I've worked up, after you take the photos, if you like."

"All right."

Marin watched as Joss took photos of every part of the garden: the sweep of cleared earth, the dilapidated shed, the headstone, the pile of sandstone blocks, the damson trees and the red currant bushes.

Marin followed him around, seeing the garden not just as a testament to a forgotten history, but as a blank canvas. How on earth was she going to fill the space? Now that it was mostly clear, she was realising just how big it was, probably at least a quarter-acre. And she wasn't even a gardener.

"You could grow vegetables," Joss said, and Marin turned to him, startled.

"How did you know what I was thinking?"

"Your eyes went wide and you were looking around the garden with something like panic." He smiled, his eyes creasing, before he held the camera up to his face. "Smile."

"What? No!" Marin threw her hands up, pushing back her wind-blown hair and shaking her head even as he snapped the photo. "That's going to be a dreadful picture."

Joss glanced at the camera's screen, a faint smile on his lips. "Come see."

Marin joined him, and peered at the digital image. In the picture he'd taken she was squinting and only just starting to smile, her hands holding her hair back. Looking at it, she had a strange, tumbling sense of deja-vu; she was in almost the exact same pose as the picture that had been taken when she was fourteen, with her father. Just as disconcerting was the realisation that she was also in the same position as the girl in the photograph in the village hall, with the garden door framing the photograph. There was no gardener in the photo, of course, leaning on his spade, but Marin realised she could see Joss's shadow behind her, the camera raised to his face. Suddenly she shivered.

"Cold?" he asked and she shook her head.

"No... it just reminds me of the photo in the village hall."

"Of course." He glanced at the image again, nodding. "But no butterfly."

"Right. A bit too cold this time of year for those." She shivered again, this time from the cutting wind. "Shall we go inside? I could use a cup of tea and I'll show you the website design I was working on."

A few minutes later they were comfortably installed in the kitchen with cups of tea as Marin showed Joss what she'd done with his website.

"I like it," he said. "It's basic but it gets the job done."

"If you want bells and whistles, I'm happy to oblige."

"No thanks. I'm not a bells-and-whistles sort of man." He

nodded towards his camera, which he'd left on the table. "What about the photos I just took?"

"We can upload them to the blog page. I linked it to your website but also gave it its own domain—thelostgarden.com." He raised his eyebrows at this and she continued, "lostgarden.-co.uk is a walled garden up in Scotland. Penicuik, it's called."

"I don't think I've heard of it."

"I had a look at the website last night. It was a massive estate with an equally massive garden. Glasshouses for every kind of fruit—plum, cherry, apricot."

"And what happened to make it lost?" Joss asked with a little smile.

"Time and money. It was ruinously expensive to maintain, and it became overgrown sometime in the last fifty years. Even by the time of our garden it was struggling."

"Which makes you wonder how our garden really fared back then."

"I was thinking about that. The vicar, this George Sanderson, must have had some private income. He built Bower House, after all."

"That's true."

"I suppose he could have spared the money for a garden and gardener."

"The man in the photograph."

"Don't you think?"

"Yes, I do." He fell silent as did Marin; she wondered if he, like her, was thinking about the expression on the man's face. Marin wondered if he'd been in love with the Sanderson daughter, if that's who the girl in the photograph really was. Or was she being fanciful again, wanting there to be more of a story, even a romance, where there was none?

She placed her hands on the keyboard, splaying her fingers out as she formulated her thoughts. "Do you think," she asked slowly, "that there really is a story behind this all? I mean..." She glanced down at her hands. "Perhaps it's just an old garden they used for vegetables. Maybe when the Sandersons left and Bower House was let the tenants didn't need so much garden, and so it became overgrown." She glanced up at him. "Maybe that's all there is to it."

"Maybe," he agreed. "There might not be a story to the garden, but there's one to that photograph." He held her gaze for a moment and Marin felt her heart give a strange little thump.

"You mean... the girl and the gardener."

"Don't you think?" he answered, parroting her question back to her.

"Do you think..." She swallowed, wondering why this suddenly felt so personal. "Do you think he was in love with her?"

"He certainly looked like that in the photograph."

"But she doesn't even seem aware of him, only of the camera."

"And the butterfly."

"So do you think she loved him? Do you think she even knew how he felt?"

"I don't know. But maybe we can find out."

She let out a disbelieving laugh. "How could we possibly find that out, Joss?"

"The Historical Society, remember? They might be able to trace the photograph. Or we could go into Whitehaven. The library has archives on local history. There might be something there."

"It would be like searching for a needle in a haystack."

"Probably. But perhaps we'll find something in the garden."

"Buried treasure?"

"Of a sort."

She let out another laugh and shook her head. "You know, I

never used to be fanciful. I've always been tediously practical and unimaginative."

"Says who?"

"Says me. I studied business in university and have worked in IT."

"That doesn't mean you're not imaginative."

"I don't know." She lapsed into silence, sorting through the memories and thoughts that were all tangled up in her mind. "My father was the creative one in the family," she said at last, and Joss waited for her to say something more. "He was a university lecturer in art history," she finally said. "And he played the piano. My mother was an artist, a potter."

"So you must have inherited some of those artistic genes."

"You'd think so, but..." She trailed off. "I don't know. I never felt as if I did. But maybe..." She hesitated, and Joss raised an eyebrow in silent prompting. "Maybe that part of me closed off when my mother died. Maybe that's when I became... the way I am." And she knew she wasn't just talking about being creative or imaginative. She'd become closed off emotionally. Numb inside. And it was coming to Goswell, and working in the garden, that was bringing her back to life.

"Grief changes you," Joss said after a moment. "No doubt about that."

"Have you lost someone?" Marin asked. She'd sensed it before, when he'd spoken to her about grief. He'd spoken with the understanding of someone who had lived it, felt it.

Now he hesitated, and she saw a conflict in his eyes, and something else. Something darker. "My father," he finally said, and she had the feeling that he'd been going to say something else, but had changed his mind. "He died six years ago."

"I'm sorry." She thought of Fowler and Son on the van. She should have asked before, should have realised his father was gone. "I'm sorry," she said again, and then asked, "Were you very close?"

"Not as close as we should have been. He wanted me to join him in the family business, but I didn't want to."

"But you have joined—"

"After he died. I only started it up again three years ago, but people have been good about putting business my way."

"What did you do before then?"

He hesitated, and again she had the sense that he was going to say something, something important, but then he simply shrugged and said, "This and that. I tried university and ended up dropping out. I did shift work at a factory and then some construction for a while. I never seemed to find something I could stick to." He gave her a small smile, even though she still saw a bleakness in his eyes. "I was a bit of a yob, to tell you the truth. Messing about and not getting serious about anything."

"And your father's death changed that?"

Another hesitation. "Yes. I decided I wanted to keep on with the business, that it would be wrong to let it just go. So that's what I did."

"And do you like it?" Marin asked. "Are you... are you happy?"

"As happy as I can be."

And what on earth did that mean? She wasn't able to ask, however, for he leapt into the moment's silence with a question of his own.

"Are you happy, Marin? Here?"

"Yes, I am," she said after a moment. "I know things aren't perfect with Rebecca, but I'm hoping in time they might become better, at least. And I like having a house I can think of as a home instead of a soulless flat. I'm even learning to cook."

"And to garden."

She laughed and nodded. "Yes." She glanced at the clock above the Rayburn, reluctant to end their conversation but knowing Rebecca would be home any minute and Joss would have to get onto his next job. "I should start tea. Rebecca's always starving when she comes home."

"Tea, is it? You really are becoming northern."

"I suppose I am." She hesitated, then blurted, "You could stay, if you like. For tea." She held her breath, waiting for Joss's response. She'd meant to make it a casual, offhand invitation, but she'd heard both the eagerness and uncertainty in her voice, and she had a feeling Joss had heard it as well.

"That's very kind," he said as he stood up. "But I should really get on. I have a few things to get on with before dark."

"Of course." Marin smiled stiffly, the rejection of her invitation stinging far more than it should. "Thanks for all of your help."

He nodded towards her open laptop. "And thanks for your help. I like the website."

"If you email me the specifics of the content you want on it, I'll set it up."

"Great."

They both stood there, stiff and smiling, until with a nod of farewell Joss left. Marin let out the breath she hadn't realised she was still holding.

She really shouldn't feel so let down. She'd invited him to a kitchen supper with her and Rebecca, not on some romantic date. She hadn't meant it to be a date or even sound like one, and yet...

She still felt stung.

Sighing, impatient with herself, she reached for her waterproof jacket and stuffed her feet back into her Wellingtons. Forget dinner; she could clear a bit more brush before Rebecca came home.

She was hard at it twenty minutes later when Rebecca found her in the garden. "Hey," she called over the sound of the brush cutter, and Marin cut its motor.

"Hey." She swiped a few strands of her hair from her eyes. "How was school?"

"Fine." Rebecca stepped into the garden. "You've done a lot since I've last been in here." Marin hefted the brush cutter. "This thing works wonders."

"What's that?" Rebecca asked and nodded towards the headstone that was leaning against a broken bit of wall.

"It's an old headstone," Marin said. "But don't worry, no one's buried here."

"A headstone," Rebecca repeated, and a strange look came over her face, as if a shadow had passed over it. She crossed the garden to stand in front of the headstone and stared down at the faded inscription. "But it belongs to someone," she said. "Why has it been moved?"

Marin explained what Joss had told her; as she spoke Rebecca frowned, shaking her head as if to deny the truth of it.

"So headstones can just be... *moved*? After a certain amount of time?"

"If the churchyard is crowded, I suppose. But not until a long time afterwards."

"But that's still awful," Rebecca protested, and Marin could see that this wasn't just about an old headstone. "Her descendants, whoever they are, can't find her grave. Can't mourn her."

"But the headstones aren't removed for a long time, Rebecca," Marin said, trying to keep her voice gentle. "A hundred years at least, I should think. People might want to visit the grave of an ancestor, but they wouldn't necessarily mourn her."

"Still, I think it's terrible. How can people just be forgotten?"

"I'm sure there are church records to say who was buried where and when. No one's truly forgotten."

"Aren't they?" Rebecca asked, and she sounded so bleak and despairing that Marin couldn't think what to say. In any case, she wasn't given the chance because Rebecca turned and walked out of the garden. With a sigh Marin followed her. She needed to get the tea on, just as she'd told Joss.

Rebecca was quiet during dinner, a chicken and mushroom pie that Marin was quite proud of, and she retreated to her bedroom afterwards with a mumbling about homework. Marin spent the evening in the sitting room on her laptop, working on Joss's website as well as her own, advertising IT services. She'd already had a request for a quote to design a website for an interior designer in her inbox, and she made some preliminary notes on that before finally closing her laptop and heading to bed.

She paused by Rebecca's door on the way to her bedroom; the light was off even though it wasn't quite ten o'clock and she couldn't hear a sound, so she moved past to her own room.

The wind started again in the middle of the night; Marin woke up around two o'clock in the morning, startled into wakefulness first by the howling of the wind, and then the distant sound of a door banging. She reached for her dressing gown and slippers and crept through the house looking for the culprit; after some investigation she realised it was the garden door. She'd forgotten to shut it yesterday afternoon. It was dreadful out, with slanting rain and howling wind, but Marin knew she wouldn't be able to sleep for the banging. She grabbed her coat and a torch and headed outside, ducking her head against the rain as the torch's beam cut a thin swathe of light through the relentless blackness.

The wind whipped her hood back and sent her hair flying around her face before, within moments, it was plastered to her head by the rain. Even through the sound of the wind she could hear the mournful bleating of sheep in the pasture by the vicarage, and she pitied the poor animals stuck out in such a gale.

She made her way through the darkness and fastened the garden door; the latch moved easily now since she'd oiled it. She glanced at the garden and saw how eerie it looked in the darkness. By the light of her torch she could just make out the boxy shape of the little building in the centre. It looked even more desolate and forgotten in the dark.

When she came into the kitchen Rebecca was standing there, shivering in the cold despite the rolling warmth of the Rayburn.

"I couldn't sleep," she said, hugging her arms around herself. "Where were you?"

"The door in the garden was banging. I shut it." Marin shed her wet coat and reached for the kettle. "Cup of tea?" she asked and Rebecca nodded, her teeth chattering.

Marin reached for the fleece she'd draped over the back of her chair after dinner and tossed it to Rebecca. "Here. It's freezing out. The wind cuts right through the house, I think."

Rebecca poked her arms through the fleece, clutching it around her. "Are you okay?" Marin asked quietly and she jerked in response, her expression wary.

"Why wouldn't I be?"

Marin considered her response carefully, wanting so much to handle this right but afraid she simply didn't possess the emotional resources or wisdom. "Because," she finally said as she put several teabags into the pot, "You seemed upset earlier about the headstones. And we haven't really talked about things, not properly. I know what it's like to lose your mum, Rebecca. It's like... like losing your arm, or your right hand. Someone so incredibly important to you, you don't feel quite whole anymore. So if you wanted to talk about it... well, I'm here."

Rebecca didn't answer for a long moment, and Marin braced herself for one of her sullen silences. "Well..." Rebecca began, and drew a shuddering breath. Marin turned to look at her, and to her shock she watched Rebecca's face crumple and then she burst into tears.

CHAPTER 20

ELEANOR

June 1919

Eleanor blinked in the bright sunlight. She felt groggy, everything around her muted, as if she were swimming up through the water towards the light shimmering on the surface above. Finally the world came into focus, and she saw she was in her bedroom, the drapes drawn back to let in the light of a summer's afternoon. Katherine was sitting in the chair by her bed, a book forgotten in her lap as she propped her head with her hand and dozed.

Eleanor opened her mouth to speak, and nothing but a croak came out. Katherine startled to wakefulness, leaning forward to inspect Eleanor.

"Thank heaven, you're awake."

Eleanor licked her dry lips and Katherine quickly poured her a glass of water from the pitcher on the bedside table. Eleanor could see several paper twists and brown glass bottles of medicine, and she wondered just how ill she'd been.

Katherine held the glass to her lips and she managed several sips before falling back against the pillows, her eyes closed.

"You've been abed for nearly a week," Katherine told her. "With the Influenza. Mother's been half out of her mind with worry."

"I'm sorry," Eleanor whispered and Katherine brushed her words aside the way you would a fly.

"There's no need to be sorry. It wasn't your fault."

Memories filtered through Eleanor's mind, shadowy shapes that slowly gained clarity. "Your wedding..." she said, and Katherine pressed her lips together and said nothing. Eleanor turned her head; it seemed to take an awful lot of effort. Her head felt terribly heavy and it seemed as if her body was being pressed into the bed. She could not imagine walking or running or so much as moving a finger ever again.

"What happened?" she finally asked.

"I don't rightly know. Right in the middle of our wedding breakfast Jack Taylor came bolting out of the walled garden, holding you in his arms. He said you'd collapsed, and Father took you into the house. You've been in bed since, out of your mind with fever. The doctor said if it didn't break soon there was no hope, and Father went to the church and kept vigil all night long."

"Poor Father," Eleanor whispered. She lay there for a moment, trying to summon the strength to speak again. Finally she asked, "And you... and James? Did you go to Edinburgh?"

"How could we?" Katherine asked without rancour. "With you at death's door?"

"I'm sorry..."

"Stop saying that. It's not your fault. We can go to Edinburgh another time."

Eleanor turned to look at Katherine. She was bustling about her bedside table, clearing away the discarded paper twists of medicine. "And how is married life?" she asked with what she hoped was a smile. Her face felt funny too, the muscles tight and stiff.

"I wouldn't know," Katherine answered briskly. She moved Eleanor's glass and the pitcher of water, rearranging them needlessly. "I've been here since you became ill. It seemed right. You were that close to death, Eleanor."

"Did James mind?"

"Why should he?" Katherine returned, and Eleanor wasn't sure if she meant because he'd understand, or that he simply didn't care. She chose not to ask for clarification.

"Jack Taylor's come to the door every day to ask after you," Katherine said after a moment. "The kitchen door, mind. He asked Tilly who told him you were very ill and sent him away with a flea in his ear."

"She shouldn't have—"

"Even Tilly can see he's too familiar with you," Katherine cut across her. "You should have seen the look on everyone's faces when he came from the garden with you in his arms! I thought Grandmama would faint."

"Grandmama never faints," Eleanor answered. She'd closed her eyes again; she was so very tired, and Katherine's admonitions were only making her feel even wearier.

"Even so. It was shocking, Eleanor." Her sister's tone was serious rather than accusatory, which made Eleanor feel worse. "I wasn't the only one who thought so."

"I'd collapsed," Eleanor reminded her. "Was he meant to leave me lying in the dirt?" She drew a shuddering breath; speaking so much had taken a huge amount of effort and everything in her ached.

"Do you even remember what happened?" The dubious note in Katherine's voice made Eleanor open her eyes.

"You're not..." She drew another laborious breath. "You're not accusing Jack of lying, are you?"

"It's not lying I'm accusing him of, but improper feelings towards you."

"We're friends, Katherine, that's all."

"You know Father wouldn't countenance anything else for a moment," Katherine warned her. "He wasn't best pleased to see Taylor carrying you."

"I thought he would be grateful Jack came to my rescue."

"He was, but there was something familiar about the way he held you. Something... tender."

Once Eleanor would have thrilled to hear such words. Now she felt only weary. She turned her face away; she could feel sleep coming for her, the edges of her mind starting to fog.

"That's what shocked people, I suppose," Katherine continued. "If he's developed an affection for you, Father will send him away. It would be better for Taylor if you didn't encourage it."

Eleanor swallowed; her throat felt sore and swollen. "Go away, Katherine," she mumbled.

Katherine sighed. "Perhaps I shouldn't be telling you all this now," she said as she rose from the chair. "But someone has to."

Thankfully Eleanor was already drifting back to sleep.

It was another week before Eleanor felt well enough to get out of bed, seven summer days where she watched the bright green leaves of the chestnut trees dance in the breeze and wished she possessed the strength or even the desire to go outside and see the garden.

She'd felt listless and flat since waking up that afternoon with Katherine by her bedside; even the thought of seeing Jack again failed to rouse her. Their friendship, she knew, would die on the vine even as the garden he'd created blossomed and grew. Katherine had said nothing more about it, but she hadn't needed to. In the long, lonely hours of her recovery Eleanor came to the conclusion that everyone else had surely already drawn: a friendship, much less a romance, with Jack Taylor was inappropriate and impossible. She'd known that, of course, but she'd chosen to ignore the truth that was staring her in the face.

She'd enjoyed her friendship with Jack, such as it was; she *liked* him, liked the way he listened, how he understood.

But reality, she knew, was not a life or even a friendship with the gardener, and the last thing she wanted was her recklessness to cause trouble for Jack.

Her own future would most likely be a marriage to whatever half-decent man she could find. It would be like Katherine's marriage to James, an alliance that would no doubt be uninspired. Gazing out at the green leaves by her bedroom window, she wondered if she loved Jack, or even if she could love him, in time; perhaps, like Katherine, she didn't know what love was.

Finally, in the middle of June, Eleanor was well enough to go downstairs; she sat in the sitting room rather than her usual alcove in the dining room, and looked out at the lane that led to the church. Her father had been busy discussing a war memorial to be constructed by the church and listening to him talk about all the boys who had lost their lives brought Walter's death back to her afresh. It was all she could do to sit in the armchair by the window with a rug over her knees and gaze out at nothing.

"This isn't like you, Eleanor," Anne said one afternoon a fortnight after she'd woken up from her fever. "You're usually so full of joy and gaiety." Her mother came to sit down next to her, smiling although her forehead was furrowed in a frown. "I think we've come to depend on your good spirits to bolster our own."

Eleanor turned to gaze out the window. It was another brilliant day, balmy and blue-skied.

Everyone was remarking how no one had seen such a summer in Cumberland like this before, but the news hardly stirred Eleanor now. "I'm too tired to bolster anything," she said after a moment. "Nothing seems to matter anymore."

"Oh, my dear." Anne touched her arm lightly. "The world

will continue to turn, and us with it. If you rouse yourself a little, perhaps you will find something to interest you again."

"I doubt it, Mother," Eleanor replied. What was there to interest her? Days spent visiting the poor and unfortunate, or volunteering in church or with the newly formed Women's Institute? Evenings at insipid parties or dances to look for a suitable husband she didn't think she could find in herself to love? And if she didn't find a husband, which was quite likely considering the dearth of men, she would wait out her days in this vicarage, steeped in loneliness, the Sanderson spinster. When her father retired, perhaps they would all crowd into the Bower House, and she would help to care for her parents as they aged. Perhaps she would help care for Katherine's children when they came. Without the solace of her own household and children, she would have precious little to look forward to.

If she'd been more academic, Eleanor supposed she could have tried for a job, teaching in a girls' school, perhaps. Her father was old-fashioned enough not to encourage such possibilities, and even though the world was changing—Eleanor remembered the women in London with their shorter dresses and shingled hair, their swinging arms and sense of purpose, their cigarettes, even—she was not sure she possessed the strength or desire to emulate them.

A week later her father had his turn at rousing her from her glum mood. "Come out into the garden, Eleanor, and see what Taylor has done."

"I couldn't manage it, Father," Eleanor replied. She did not want to see Jack, not after Katherine's dire warning.

"But you must. He's worked ever so hard at your walled garden."

She shook her head and closed her eyes. "Even so."

"Then let me carry you out, in a chair," George insisted, and ignoring her protests, he arranged for Eleanor to be brought out in an old bath chair he'd found in the cellar.

Eleanor felt rather ridiculous, being carried out on a chair like an Indian raj in his palanquin. Her father took one side and Raymond Carr, who had just delivered the day's ice, took the other. Jack, Eleanor couldn't help but notice, had not been asked to help.

He stood to the side of the door as she was wheeled into the walled garden, and then hefted aloft when the wheels caught in the grass. Eleanor forced herself not to look at him. And in truth the garden claimed all of her attention, for Jack had truly wrought wonders with it. The ground was now laid with grass, and the borders were bursting with herbs and flowers; from Jack's tutelage she recognised the tight pink buds of thyme in flower, and the spiky clumps of anise hyssop with their purplish-blue flowers thrusting up towards the sky. And rosemary, of course, spiky and spicy-scented, for remembrance.

"Isn't it lovely," George said with satisfaction, almost as if it were his doing rather than Jack's. "But that's not even the best bit." He nodded towards the little building in the centre of the garden as he and Raymond Carr set down her chair.

Eleanor could see that the building's windows had been fitted with new glass, and they sparkled in the sunshine. The door had been fixed too, and painted; the whole building looked new again.

"Why has he repaired it?" Eleanor asked. "Is there something inside?"

"Indeed there is," her father answered. "Many things inside, as it happens. It was quite an endeavour, mind you, but I'd been planning it for some time, with Jack's help."

Eleanor turned to him. "This was your idea?"

"Well..." Her father had the grace to look a little abashed. "It was Taylor's idea, to be sure, but I gave the go-ahead. He came to me with the suggestion weeks ago, after I'd given you permission to get started in here."

Eleanor's malaise fell away as her curiosity became well and truly roused. "What on earth is it?" she asked.

"Can you walk that far?" her father asked. "Or shall I carry you inside?"

"I can walk," Eleanor said, and unsteadily she rose from her chair. It was only a matter of a dozen steps to the door of the building, but they still made her feel dizzy. Her father held her elbow, and Raymond Carr hovered on her other side. Eleanor wished Jack were there; he'd remained by the door to the garden, his hands clasped in front of him, his head slightly bowed, the very picture of subservience.

She reached the door and lifted the latch; it creaked open and she stepped inside the little room, noticing first how warm and humid it was, and then registering a strange sound, something between a hum and a flutter.

It took her a moment to adjust to the dimness of the room, although the windows let in a fair amount of light. Then with a sharply indrawn breath she saw what the building contained.

"*Butterflies...*"

Dozens of butterflies fluttered in the little room, contained behind netting so as not to escape. There were flowers, too, to provide the nectar they fed on; Jack had planted them in tubs: purple phlox and orange and red gaillardia, the tall purple spiky flowers known as blazing star.

"I had the gas man come to fix the heating," her father told her proudly. "It will be warm in here right through winter, to keep them alive."

"Oh, but that's a terrible expense," Eleanor cried.

"It's worth it to me, my dear, if it makes you happy."

"It does." Eleanor gazed in rapture at the butterflies chasing each other in their cozy quarters; she could see the bright blue wings of the same kind of butterfly she'd seen on the day she'd been here with Jack, and had thought he might kiss her.

She wanted to see Jack now, and share this with him; almost

roughly she pushed past her father and Mr Carr and went back out into the garden, the sunshine so bright she nearly reeled back. She must have staggered a little, for instinctively Mr Carr caught her arm, murmuring an apology, but Eleanor didn't listen, didn't care.

She was gazing at Jack, who had lifted his head and was staring back at her, his eyes seeming to her to blaze as brightly as the sun. Neither of them spoke, but Eleanor didn't think they needed to. The look in his eyes told her everything.

"Shall we take you back into the house?" George asked, and Eleanor shook her head.

"Oh no, please, Father. I want to stay out here and enjoy the sunshine and the butterflies." She touched his sleeve as she smiled up at him. "You've made me very happy. Thank you."

"All right, then. But tell Taylor to call me when you want to be brought inside."

Within moments her father and Mr Carr had left, and Eleanor was alone with Jack. She sat back down in the chair, for she was in fact feeling rather weak, and Jack started for the door of the walled garden.

"Don't go," Eleanor called softly, and he stopped before half-turning towards her.

"I think it's best if I get on with my work..."

"When did you think of the butterflies?" Eleanor asked. "Was it the day I cut my foot?"

He took his cap off, twisting it in his hands. "Yes."

"I thought you might kiss me then," Eleanor said, half-amazed that she was being so brazen and yet the words had come unbidden, from a deep part of her. She could not have stopped them if she'd tried.

Jack shook his head. "This isn't... it isn't proper, Eleanor."

"Don't you think the idea of what is proper is changing?" Eleanor protested. "The war has changed so much." She thought of the women in London, of Katherine teaching veterans to type. Even in Goswell surely things could change, if only a little. "If one good thing could come from so much devastation and grief," she said, "then let it be that. Let it be that two people who care for one another can do so without a regard for outdated propriety."

"That's a nice wish and no more."

"But you do care for me?" Eleanor pressed, reckless now, and determined. "Don't you?"

She could see the conflict and even the torment on his face; by pressing the point she was making him unhappy, but she would not stop. "Because I care for you," she stated defiantly, and he shook his head again.

"You don't know me."

"I do," she protested. "I know how kind and gentle and understanding you are."

He closed his eyes briefly. "No."

"Yes—"

"Oh, Eleanor." He opened his eyes then, and now he simply looked bleak. "You see the world in such a simple way, as if caring for someone is all that matters."

"Isn't it?" she demanded, stung. "It could be, at least."

"But you really don't know me," Jack said quietly. "You've only spent a handful of hours with me. You don't know who I am, what I'm capable of—"

"I know you're capable of great kindness," Eleanor returned staunchly. "You showed me great kindness, Jack, when you spoke with me about Walter. Why are you arguing with me about how I feel?"

"Because nothing can happen between us," Jack answered. "Ever."

Eleanor blinked, chastened by his final tone. Struggling a bit, she rose from her chair. "Please don't say that."

"I must."

"*Jack*—" Her voice broke on his name as she stretched one

hand out to him, all her resolutions about keeping her distance vanishing in the light of the truth she now knew. He cared for her. She would prove it to him. She took a step towards him, her knees buckling beneath her as she came over faint. With a little cry she sank back onto her chair, and Jack hurried to her.

"Are you all right? Your father will have my head if something happens to you out here." But the concern she saw on his face was not for his head, but hers. She held her arms out to him, and after a second's pause, when the entire world seemed suspended, he came to her, kneeling at her feet, his head pressed into her lap.

"Oh, Jack," Eleanor said softly. "Dear, dear Jack." She threaded her fingers through his hair; it felt soft and springy and seemed entirely natural for her to touch him in this way.

Jack lifted his head to stare at her. "I have nothing to offer you, Eleanor. Nothing."

"I don't want anything but you." It *was* simple, she thought with a fierce triumph. Of course it was, no matter what Jack had said.

"You say that now, when you have everything at your fingertips. A life with me..." He shook his head. "Your family might disown you. And I'd have nothing for you but the meanest cottage. You'd look twice your age in a matter of years, worn out from all the scrubbing..."

Eleanor laughed. "Do you really think I care about that?"

"You would."

"No." She spoke firmly, with utter certainty. Jack sat back on his heels.

"And there's something else. Something I haven't told you."

"Then tell me now."

"I... I can't."

She frowned, and Jack looked away. "Why can't you?"

"It doesn't matter. I meant what I said. I've compromised

you enough already." He stood up and she gaped at him, shocked that even now he could think of leaving her.

"So you're to decide for me?" she demanded. "About my own life? I think I know what I'm capable of, Jack. I'm stronger than you seem to think. I can manage a little housework."

"A little?" He raised his eyebrows, his mouth twisting in a funny sort of smile. "It would be more than a little, Eleanor. You'd be a—a drudge! The commonest char. And what work do you do now? A bit of embroidery? Some darning, perhaps?"

There was no scorn in his voice, only sadness, but Eleanor still felt stung. "I can learn."

"You would come to hate me, and I couldn't bear that."

"I wouldn't!" Anger surged through her and she nearly stamped her foot in rage. With effort she forced the fury back, and kept her voice calm, "That's not fair, Jack."

"You'd lose that vital, vibrant part of yourself that I love. And it would be my fault."

"But if you love me..." she whispered, still unable to believe it could end like this, before it had even begun.

"It's better this way," he answered, and Eleanor knew there would be no changing his mind, at least not now. "I'll go tell your father you want to come inside," he said, and turned to go.

CHAPTER 21

MARIN

"Rebecca..."

Helplessly Marin stared at her sister as she continued to cry the kind of noisy sobs she'd never heard from her before, jagged sounds reminding her of broken glass.

Rebecca wrapped her arms tightly around herself, her shoulders hunched so her hair fell forward and covered her face. Marin could see how they shook, and her heart ached for her sister and the grief she'd hidden for so long.

"Sweetheart," she murmured and clumsily she put her arms around Rebecca and pulled her towards her. They hadn't actually hugged since that first day in Hampshire, when Marin had come from Boston and greeted this near-stranger, both of them shocked both by grief and the knowledge that their lives were now forever entwined.

Rebecca remained stiffly in her arms for a moment before she finally, thankfully yielded, her body softening as she pressed her hot face, damp with tears, into Marin's shoulder.

Marin felt a sudden swell of emotion and affection, something almost maternal that took hold of her and brought tears to her own eyes. She blinked them back as she rubbed Rebecca's back, murmuring soothing nonsense until her sobs had subsided to snuffles.

"I'm sorry," Rebecca finally said, her voice muffled against Marin's shoulder.

"Don't be. I think you've probably needed a good cry."

"You don't even know what I'm crying about."

"I think I can guess."

"Can you?" Abruptly Rebecca pushed away from Marin, scrubbing her face with her fists like a little child.

"Why don't you tell me, then," Marin said quietly. Rebecca just stared at her, her lower lip jutted out, and then the kettle started to shrill. Sighing, Marin moved it off the hotplate. She was afraid Rebecca was already retreating, no doubt regretting her moment's outburst.

Rebecca gave a big sniff and sank onto one of the kitchen chairs while Marin busied herself with pouring their tea. "I don't know if I can," she said and Marin didn't answer, hoping that more words would come. "It's just..." Rebecca let out a shuddering breath. "It's so strange," she finally burst out.

"Joss said something similar," Marin told her as she handed her a cup of tea before sitting opposite. "He said grief was both natural and unnatural. It's a part of life, of everyone's life sooner or later, and yet it still never feels right."

Rebecca stared at her miserably, her mug of tea cradled in her hands. "You don't get it," she said and blew on her tea. "I'm not..." She lowered her gaze to her mug and again Marin waited. "I'm not grieving," she finally said. "Not really."

And what, Marin wondered, was she meant to make of that? She took a sip of tea to stall for time, but apparently that was the wrong thing to do because Rebecca gazed at her miserably, her lower lip trembling now as well as still jutting out. "You're shocked, aren't you? You think I'm awful."

"No, Rebecca, I most certainly don't. But maybe you need to help me understand what you mean."

"How else can I say it? I'm not grieving. I don't miss them!" Her voice rang out and then in seeming direct contradiction to what she'd just said, she began to cry again. She controlled herself quickly, though, sniffing hard before taking a slurpy sip of tea. "There. Now you know."

"Why don't you miss them?" Marin asked. She spoke calmly even though inside she was reeling. This was an admission she'd never expected Rebecca to make.

"I don't know. I do miss them a bit, of course I do. More than a bit. A lot. I'm not saying *that*." She looked up, clearly anxious to get this point across, and Marin nodded.

"I understand."

"But Mum and Dad... they were so wrapped up in themselves. Not in a bad way. But they had such a... I don't know, a grand passion, I suppose. I mean, Dad left his job for Mum. But of course you know that."

"Yes," Marin said after a moment. Having Rebecca say it all again was making her realise how raw she still felt about her father's second marriage. Diana had been one of his students at the university where he'd lectured, just twenty years old, and they'd both been swept up in the grand passion Rebecca had described. And this after so many years of her father virtually ignoring her, claiming he'd never forget her mother... the bitterness she'd felt still possessed a sharp bite.

Within months of meeting Diana, Richard Ellis had accepted early retirement. He'd married her and they'd gone to live in Hampshire; Rebecca had been born five years later. Marin still remembering receiving the email that she'd been born. She hadn't even known Diana was pregnant, that was how estranged they'd become. And watching her father embrace his new family from afar had only made Marin retreat all the more—away from her father, into herself.

But she couldn't do that anymore. She didn't even want to.

"I do understand what you're saying," she said to Rebecca. "But they loved you, you know. I'm quite sure of it."

"I know. I never questioned that, not really. And I loved them."

And yet Marin had questioned her father's love for her endlessly. How could he love her and send her off to boarding school the way he had? She'd begged him not to make her go, had clung to him and he'd simply set her away from him, as if she were a puppy jumping up and muddying his trousers. As she'd grown older she'd tried to both understand and justify his behaviour; she'd told herself that he was too stricken by grief to act as a proper father. Yet that small bit of comfort had been taken from her when he'd married Diana, had had Rebecca— and still hadn't reached out to her.

Now she felt all those old, unresolved feelings and memories rise up within her in a tangle of emotion; her throat had thickened and she didn't think she could speak to Rebecca, if she even knew what to say, which she didn't.

"It's just..." Rebecca said, "I don't feel the way I think should feel."

"There's no right or wrong about how you feel in this situation," Marin said after a moment, but as soon as the words were out of her mouth she realised what a meaningless platitude they were. "How do you think you should feel?" she asked.

"I don't know," Rebecca answered with a shrug. "Grief-stricken, I suppose."

Grief-stricken. To be stricken down by grief. It made Marin think of a bolt of lightning, or a smiting by an almighty hand. Rebecca didn't feel that, and neither did she. The sadness she felt was at something she'd never had, not something she'd had and lost. She just hadn't ever expected Rebecca to feel the same.

She had assumed, based on her outsider's view, that Rebecca was the adored and coddled only child of doting parents, the very centre of their world. Because her father had chosen Diana, had chosen Rebecca in a way he'd never chosen her. She'd never resented Rebecca; how could you resent a child? And yet she'd resented how her father's choices had, since she'd been eight years old, made her feel unwanted, unloved.

"What," Marin asked Rebecca, "do you think grief-stricken feels like?"

"Oh, enough with the questions," Rebecca suddenly snapped. "You're not my therapist." Stung, Marin didn't answer for a moment. Rebecca sighed impatiently. "Sorry," she said, and Marin couldn't tell if she meant it.

"I'm sorry," she said. "I don't know the right thing to say here, Rebecca." She hesitated, and then decided honesty, uncomfortable as it often could be, was needed. "I'm remarkably inept at these kinds of conversations, I'm afraid."

"Isn't everybody?" Rebecca shot back and Marin suppressed a sigh.

"Maybe. I wouldn't know, because I don't have enough experience."

Just as quickly Rebecca's mood changed again, and her face crumpled. "I'm sorry. I didn't mean to snap."

"You're entitled to snap a little," Marin said, and yet again she felt as if she'd offered a platitude, and the wrong one at that, when Rebecca shook her head, her eyes filling with tears.

"But that's the thing, Marin. I'm not."

"Why do you say that?"

"Because they were my *parents*, and sometimes I'm not sure I even miss them. When you came to stay, I didn't even feel as if anything had changed all that much. They were so wrapped up with each other, busy with their own lives... sometimes I felt like they forgot I was even there." She sighed and shook her head. "I know I sound spoiled."

"You don't."

"I wanted to move because I was tired of everyone feeling

sorry for me when I knew I didn't deserve it. They all thought that I'd had this great tragedy, and all I've ever really felt is… numb."

"I know what you mean," Marin said and Rebecca looked at her keenly.

"Do you? Because he was your father too, and yet you never seem to talk about him. He never talked about you."

Marin blinked back the hurt those words caused. "No," she said, taking a sip of tea. "He wouldn't."

"What happened? Why weren't you close?"

"When my mother died, my father withdrew from me. From life, really. He buried himself in his work." She hesitated, memories of being eight years old, confused and hurt and alone, sliding through her. Standing at her father's study door and wondering if she dared knock. And when she did knock, and she knew he was inside, there was no answer.

"Sometimes," she continued slowly, "I wonder if I've made those years before she died a bit rosier than they were. I have fond memories of my mum, but I don't have too many of him. I don't know if I've blanked them out or not." She gave a little shrug. "Memory is a tricky thing."

"But that photo of you in your bedroom. You both look happy then." Rebecca made a face. "When I saw it, I felt jealous of you, you know. Dad never looked at me that way. Sometimes I feel like they resented me, for taking them away from each other."

"Jealous?" Marin let out a short laugh. "Trust me, you've had nothing to be jealous about."

"But that photograph… you can tell he loved you, Marin."

"But it's just a photograph," Marin returned. "I didn't feel like he loved me the whole time I was growing up. So what's real—the photograph or the feeling?"

"I don't know."

They lapsed into silence and Marin thought suddenly of

the other photograph, of the girl and her gardener. She'd built so many emotions into that single image, and now she wondered if she'd made it all up, because she simply wanted them to be true. She wanted a love story; she longed for someone's happy ending.

Suddenly her entire mission with the garden seemed pointless and worse, pathetic. She was pouring so much emotional energy into discovering something that she wasn't even sure existed.

"We should go to bed," she said finally as she took both of their mugs to the sink. "You have school tomorrow, after all."

"All right." Rebecca rose from her chair. "Thank you," she said stiltedly. "I'm sorry I've been so... I don't know. Difficult."

"You haven't been, honestly, Rebecca. I just wish I was better equipped to be a support to you."

"You are a support. You moved up here even when it seemed like a really stupid thing to do."

"I'm glad we moved."

"Are you?" Rebecca looked pleased by this. "I am, too. Mostly."

"Mostly?"

"I don't like the rain," Rebecca said ruefully. "But everything else is pretty good."

Laughing a little at this, Marin switched off the kitchen light and then they both headed upstairs.

She made sure Rebecca was settled back into her bed before going to her own, yet sleep eluded her. It was nearly five in the morning before she finally gave up on trying and switched her light on. The world was still pitched in darkness and she huddled under the covers, conscious of the pre-dawn, creeping cold of the house.

Her gaze fell on the photograph of her and her father and she reached for it, studying the picture once again.

There she was, fourteen years old and a bit awkward-looking, her limbs a little long and gangly, her nose a bit too big on her face. She was laughing, and she could see the space between her front teeth that braces the next year had corrected. Her hair was blowing in the wind as she held it back, and Marin could see freckles on her nose, brought out by the sun.

Almost reluctantly she flicked her gaze towards her father. She could see the bald spot on top of his head, burnt red by the sun, and his nose was the same shape as hers; she'd never realised that before. He had placed one hand on her back, not quite a hug, but she still saw something protective and tender in the gesture. And the look in his eyes... the small curving of his lips... He looked proud and affectionate, and yet now she wondered if that expression was real. Could you trust a look? Could she take comfort from it, believing that her father had loved her as best as he could, just as, perhaps, he'd loved Rebecca? An imperfect man, a man who had not been able to balance the passions in his life, but still. A man capable of loving his children.

Grey light was filtering through the curtains when Marin finally put the photograph back on the shelf. She settled back down under the covers, and eventually she slept.

CHAPTER 22

ELEANOR

July 1919

She was going to organise a fete. The idea came to her one sunny morning as she gazed out at the garden, and thought of all the work Jack had put into it, and all the joy to be had.

And they needed joy, desperately. A week after Eleanor had risen from her bed, Katherine had moved to Whitehaven to live with James and his parents. They hoped to secure a house for themselves before too long, but it was strange not seeing her sister, not having her walk up the stairs with her brisk, light step, or frown at her across the dinner table or scold her for using too much hot water in the bath. Eleanor had not thought she would miss such irritations, and yet she found she did.

Her parents missed Katherine too. Eleanor could see it in her mother's pale, drawn face, and the way her father closeted himself in his study. Even Tilly seemed a bit disheartened, and Mrs Stanton had made Katherine's favourite cake for tea, a currant loaf, before realising she was not there to eat it.

Eleanor suspected that none of them would miss Katherine quite so much if they'd all believed her to be happy. But in the three visits she'd made since joining the Freybourns, she hadn't seemed happy at all. She'd seem brittle and edgy, her smile too bright, her hands clenching too hard on her handbag.

"What do you do all day?" Eleanor asked, not meaning it unkindly, but she did wonder how Katherine occupied herself. She was living in her mother-in-law's house, and so could not order things to her own satisfaction, and she no longer went up to Carlisle.

"Oh I lead quite the life of leisure," she'd replied with a laugh that sounded harsh rather than amused. "I read books. I tidy my room—James and I have our bedroom, of course, and then the Freybourns have allowed us another room to use as a sort of private sitting room upstairs. It's really very kind of them."

Eleanor had the most appalling image of Katherine and James sitting in their little bedroom-turned-sitting room, perched stiffly on the Freybourns' castoff settees, enduring entire evenings of silence. Was that what marriage was? She'd rather be a spinster, and yet she knew things wouldn't be like that with her and Jack.

But there was no use thinking about Jack, because he had avoided her completely since that day in the walled garden, when he'd put his head in her lap and she'd touched his hair... if she only had that moment of joy to remember, Eleanor supposed it might be enough. Almost.

But of course it wasn't really enough, not for Eleanor or anyone, and so she was determined to chivvy everyone into happiness with a garden fete. If she couldn't be happy, perhaps at least Katherine and James could, for an afternoon. She remembered how they'd been at the fete they'd had before the war; Katherine had been behind a stall, selling jam, but James had drawn her out to play the ring toss. Katherine had got it in on the first try and James had whooped and laughed. Eleanor remembered the sight of her sister looking both proud and abashed, and James being his old, exuberant self, and thought perhaps they could capture just a little bit of that again. She no longer naively believed you could go back, but surely you could at least remember.

She broached the idea at breakfast while her father was reading *The Cumberland News* and her mother a letter from a friend in Kendal. They both looked up when she spoke.

"A garden fete? We haven't had one in ages, have we, George?" Anne said. "Not since before the war."

"All the more reason to have one," Eleanor persisted. "Do you remember how they used to be, Mother—stalls in the garden, with jams and cakes and silly games? It was so much *fun*." Anne smiled indulgently at her and Eleanor continued, "I know it might sound childish and simple but I think we need a bit of fun in our lives now. Everyone is so..." She hesitated, almost afraid to put what she felt, what it seemed everyone felt, into words. "Disenchanted," she finally said.

A mood of disillusionment had crept into society in the last few months; the post-Armistice euphoria had given way first to disappointment as men were delayed in being demobilised and the soldiers who did return didn't look like the ones that had left. But as people had adjusted to that new reality, expectation had taken hold again, only to plummet as the reality stretched on and on. The front page of *The Cumberland News* was dedicated to the miners' strike; bakers were striking too, everyone demanding fairer treatment and better wages. And even people who did not work seemed to suffer from this malaise. Even the Prince of Wales had been said to feel restless, wondering what joy or adventure his life might hold.

"I think it's a grand idea," her father said with a rustle of his newspaper. "My old friend Edward Stephens and his wife are hoping to visit the weekend after next—why don't we have it then?" He turned to Eleanor. "We went to theological college together, down at Cambridge. He served in the war as a padre, all four years."

And so it was agreed.

As soon as breakfast was finished she put on her hat and walking boots and headed out to the garden. The grass was velvety-green and neatly trimmed, scattered with the fallen petals of the fading cherry blossoms.

He eyed her warily as she approached, setting down his wheelbarrow and taking off his cap. His face was completely, carefully blank.

"I've the most grand idea, Jack," Eleanor said with determined gaiety. "We're going to have a summer fete for the whole village—right here, in the garden, since you've made it look so lovely. You won't mind helping, will you, with the stalls and things?"

"Of course not."

She could not tell a thing from his tone. She searched his face for a moment, looking for some hint of the emotion he'd shown her in the walled garden, but there was nothing. "I shall have to solicit people for the raffle—and cakes, of course. There must be a cake stall. A jumble stall, too, to be sure. Everyone is in search of a bargain, these days." She let her gaze wander round the garden, imagining it lined with stalls, filled with people. "And the butterfly house will be such an attraction! We could sell tickets, couldn't we?" She turned to him with a smile. "Where did you get the butterflies, Jack? I never asked."

"I caught them," he replied. "With a net."

"It must have taken ages!" Eleanor exclaimed. "I didn't realise there were so many butterflies in all of Cumberland!"

"I sent away for some," Jack said, and settled his cap back on his head. "You can buy the chrysalides from a catalogue." He straightened, his gaze flicking away from hers. "Your father can let me know what I need to do for the fete," he said, and began trundling the barrow away while Eleanor watched.

She couldn't bear going inside just then; the day was so warm and bright and the house felt stifling in so many ways. She went to the walled garden instead, and slipped inside the butterfly house.

She'd been inside many times since her father had first shown it to her, several weeks ago. She loved the sudden flashes of beauty, and sometimes she would lift the net back and a butterfly would alight on her fingertips. Today she had a sudden, mad urge to let them all go, to see them silhouetted against the blue sky, freed from their prison.

She didn't, though, because the butterfly house had been Jack's gift to her, and she feared it was the only one he would ever give her. Instead she pressed her cheek against the cold stone and closed her eyes as her forced gaiety trickled away and tears slipped silently down her cheeks.

That afternoon Eleanor decided to take the train into Whitehaven to visit Katherine. She had been to the Freybourns' house, a Georgian townhouse overlooking the harbour, several times before when Diana had invited her and her mother, along with Katherine, for afternoon tea, but this was the first time she'd gone on her own.

She mounted the steps with some trepidation, and apologised to the maid who answered the door, flustered to have an unexpected caller and stammering that Mrs Freybourn was out.

"It's the younger Mrs Freybourn, my sister Katherine I wish to see," she said. "I should have telephoned, I suppose, but I'm still not used to them."

Her father had had a telephone installed several years ago, but Eleanor had had precious little reason to make a call.

The maid let her into the sitting room and then went upstairs to fetch Katherine. Eleanor glanced around at the house, filled with heavy Victorian pieces, every little table and dresser covered with a frilled doily or several ornaments: porcelain milkmaids and shepherdesses, and in pride of place above the mantel, a framed poem about a fallen soldier that Eleanor read silently, the last lines clutching at her heart: *Shall we, your mothers, sorrow then/As those who have no hope? Ah, no!/The Father's house is large and very safe.*

"Eleanor, what on earth are you doing here?"

Eleanor whirled away from fireplace, the lines of poetry still echoing in her head. Was Walter safe? Was he happy? She blinked rapidly and turned the corners of her mouth up in a smile as Katherine came into the room, frowning as she shut the door behind her.

"Surprise! I thought I'd visit."

"You should have telephoned. I might not have been in."

"Ah, but I thought you were living a life of leisure."

Katherine's face twisted at that and she crossed the room. "What is it you want?"

"Can't I come simply for the sake of your company?"

"I didn't think you ever enjoyed my company, or I yours, for that matter."

Eleanor recoiled at that bit of plain speaking. "That is hard, even from you, Katherine."

Katherine sank into a chair by the window, leaning her head against its back with a sigh. "I fear marriage doesn't suit me."

"Have things not improved with James?" Eleanor asked hesitantly.

"No." Katherine stared out the window. "He has nightmares," she said flatly. "Every night. He's taken to sleeping in our sitting room—but I shouldn't tell you such things. They'll put you to the blush, I'm sure."

"They won't," Eleanor insisted, but she could feel her cheeks heat all the same. It was a bit startling to hear Katherine talk of marriage and beds and sleeping. "Anyway," she said after a moment, "I came over here to ask you to help with the summer fete."

Katherine turned from the window. "What summer fete?"

"The one we're having in our garden, of course," Eleanor said with a laugh. "You must help, Katherine. You're so much more capable than I am—"

"And whose idea was this garden fete?" Katherine asked.

"Mine, of course."

"Any excuse to get into the garden, I suppose?"

Now Eleanor well and truly blushed. "It's not like that," she said stiffly. "I know... I know there can be nothing between Jack and me."

"As long as he knows it as well," Katherine answered, and then gave a long sigh. "I suppose I can help with the fete—it shall be something to do, at least."

Eleanor spent the next fortnight arranging the fete; Katherine came over to the vicarage nearly every day to help. It was encouraging to see her sister looking and acting more like herself, bossy and purposeful and just a bit irritating. Eleanor did not begrudge her anything, for she longed for Katherine to be happy, as her own happiness was surely out of reach.

The sun continued to shine as Jack helped to erect the wooden stalls that now lined the garden, and villagers brought their jars of chutney and jam to be sold. Raffle prizes piled up in the corner of the vicarage's study and Mrs Stanton saved nearly a month's worth of ration coupons to make a chocolate cake for the cake stall.

As cheered as she was by her sister's involvement, Eleanor could not keep her own spirits from sinking a little when Jack's gaze moved deliberately over her, or he carefully called her Miss Eleanor while not meeting her eyes. His stiff politeness felt like a slight, and with each bland, formal interaction she felt him moving farther and farther away from her.

Which was, Katherine reminded her more than once, as it should be, and yet Eleanor still fought against that determination, still longed for a world where propriety did not stand in the way of love.

"Your head is full of daydreams," Katherine told her bluntly when she'd caught Eleanor staring after Jack. "What do you suppose would happen? He'd marry you and you'd live in the back room of Mr Lyman's little cottage?"

Eleanor stiffened. "We'd rent a place," she said, hardly able to believe she was admitting to thinking of such things. "A cottage..."

"With what money? I imagine Jack has a few pennies in his pocket, and that is all. He's not educated, he'll never be more than a gardener's boy—"

"A gardener," Eleanor corrected fiercely. "In his own right. He designed the garden, Katherine, he thought of it all himself. He may not have the proper training or work on a grand estate, but he—"

"Even so," Katherine cut her off dismissively. "Do you want to live in some hovel and break your back scrubbing the floors?"

"Jack said much the same, and I told him I wouldn't mind—"

"What!" Katherine drew back, appalled. "He's discussed such matters with you? The impertinence! Has he... has he made some sort of offer..."

"No, no, of course not," Eleanor said quickly. She was realising far too late that she'd been terribly indiscreet. "I was the one... oh, never mind. It's all come to nothing."

"And a good thing it has," Katherine returned. "Yes, I can imagine that you were the one. You are so impulsive, Eleanor. So reckless. I wonder if you will ever learn."

"I wonder too, sometimes," Eleanor admitted, and then let out a rather shaky laugh. "But it doesn't matter, Katherine, honestly. He won't have anything to do with me now."

"He should have had nothing to do with you in the first place," Katherine answered sharply, and moved away.

The day of the fete dawned with heavy grey clouds, making Eleanor's spirits plummet. It seemed quite unfair that after months of sunshine the day for the fete would turn out so gloomy.

"Never mind," Anne told her over breakfast. "The sun might come out later, and we've had plenty of fetes where the rain has poured down! Do you remember when there was a downpour and everyone huddled under one of the stalls? Walter knocked one of the poles with his elbow and the whole thing came falling down on everyone's heads!" Anne laughed, shaking her head, and then subsided, her face now drawn in contemplative lines. "It's nice to remember," she said quietly. "Remember the good times, that is."

Eleanor nodded; for a moment she was unable to speak. Yes, it was nice to remember the good times, but it hurt too. Perhaps it would always hurt.

By ten o'clock the grey sky had thankfully lightened to pale blue, and the sun peeked out from behind the remaining shreds of cloud. People had begun to arrive, and the photographer who had taken pictures for Katherine's wedding set up his things in a corner of the garden, offering portraits for a shilling.

Eleanor had taken special care with her appearance, wearing her hair in finger waves around her ears, the rest pulled back in a knot low on the nape of her neck. It almost looked as if she'd had her hair shingled, something she knew neither of her parents would ever countenance.

Anne had allowed her a new dress of white lawn with the dropped waist that had become so fashionable. She pinned on her hat, one of soft felt rather than the huge affairs of straw and silk that were starting to go out of fashion. She looked, Eleanor decided, quite modern, but hopefully not so much as to cause her parents alarm.

Outside the air was damp and fresh, the sun just starting to dry the dew from the grass. Instinctively Eleanor looked for Jack, but she couldn't see him amidst the crowds that were starting to gather. She suspected he would do his best to keep out of her way.

She saw Katherine and James standing together, James as stiff as always, Katherine looking tenser by the second, her face pale, her lips pursed. Determinedly Eleanor walked towards them, swinging her parasol by its handle.

"Isn't this grand! We haven't had a fete here since 1914."

"Yes, I remember," Katherine answered. "Didn't you eat too many walnut whips and become sick?"

"Didn't you win the ring toss?" Eleanor countered. She would not let Katherine's sour mood spoil the day. "Perhaps you will again, if you try." She let her gaze linger on Katherine meaningfully for a moment before she turned to James. "I'm glad we've brought the tradition back," she said brightly. "Aren't you, James?"

James looked startled to be addressed; he gave a little shrug. "I suppose."

"And how are you finding married life?" Eleanor ploughed on. "Have you started looking for a house?"

"Not yet," James answered. He ignored her first question, and Katherine shot Eleanor a glowering frown, keeping her from pressing the point.

She studied James as covertly as she could; his face was so bland, his expression so blank, it seemed hard to believe he had once been jolly, fooling around with Walter. Another memory of that last fete suddenly slotted into place. "That last garden fete... you and Walter did a dance!" She thought she saw a ripple of remembrance in James's eyes but then he shook his head.

"I don't recall."

"Oh, you must. You put on women's hats and did the can-can. It was quite the laugh, even if Father pretended to disapprove. Don't you remember, Katherine?" She turned to her sister who looked torn.

"I... I'm not sure."

Eleanor felt like shaking them both. They were married; they loved each other, or had once. Why couldn't they find happiness again? Why did they have to be so infernally *stubborn*, wallowing in misery when joy was surely within their grasp if they just tried for it?

"I remember," she said firmly. "I remember it being such a jolly day even though I'd had too many sweets. Mother said it's nice to remember the good times, but I think it's important we create new memories too." She turned to smile at James. "Why don't you try the pitching game? Three throws for a penny. And if you hit the mark, you win a cake—"

James stared at her for a moment, and Eleanor thought he might relent. She thought she saw, underneath that carefully blank, oh-so-polite expression, a trace of the true James, Walter's best friend who had been filled with life and laughter.

"Very well," he said, tilting his head in acceptance, and both Katherine and Eleanor watched as he headed over to the stall. Robbie Sykes, the boy who had delivered the telegram about Walter, was manning the stall, and he gave James three cricket balls after accepting his penny.

Eleanor and Katherine both drew their breath in sharply as James threw one ball after another, as hard as he could and with deadly aim, hitting the mark three times in a row. A moment of silence ensued, stretching on until Eleanor thought it might snap.

James nodded towards Robbie, whose mouth was hanging open, and then walked quickly out of the garden.

"He didn't even take a cake," Eleanor managed after a moment and Katherine whirled on her.

"Why did you have to do that?"

"I was trying to help—"

"Help? By pushing and pushing? He doesn't want to remember the good times, Eleanor, and he certainly doesn't want to create new memories. Why can't you just leave well enough alone?" And with that Katherine walked quickly away from her.

The moment had passed and the fete continued, children running with hoops and balls; George called for children to participate in a game of The Bellman, and Mrs Hennessy, a matron of the village, went forth to judge the offerings of jam and award a first prize.

It had all fallen flat for Eleanor. She walked around, praising the produce people had brought, awarding prizes, clapping for the children, all with a bright smile pinned onto her face. Yet she felt as she had when she'd arranged the Christmas decorations and crackers for everyone back in December.

She turned and walked away from the people and the party, the noise of children's laughter fading as she headed for the only solace she could find: the walled garden. Walter's garden.

It was quiet inside the garden once she'd closed the door; the tours of the garden and butterfly house were to be later in the day. Her father had refused to sell tickets but had agreed to open the garden up to everyone in the village for the afternoon.

Now, however, the garden was empty and silent save for the rustle of the breeze through the damson trees; the plums, Eleanor saw, were small and hard, still needing to ripen.

She walked through the grass to the butterfly house, slipping inside and breathing in the warm, damp air, the almost tropical scent of the flowers. The rustle of the butterfly wings filled her ears and for a moment she could simply *be*; she didn't have to think or want or grieve.

She closed her eyes, letting everything in her absorb the moment; wanting to stay in it, never to go forward, never to go back. Then she heard the creak of the garden door and reluctantly she opened her eyes.

She thought it would be some villager hoping for a private

peek of the gardens, or perhaps her mother or father looking for her, but when she turned her head she saw it was Jack.

He stopped in the doorway, bracing one shoulder against the frame. "I came to check on things, before the garden is opened for visitors."

"I almost don't want people to see it any more," Eleanor said. "It feels like an invasion of privacy somehow." Jack didn't answer and Eleanor lifted her hand to a butterfly that was clinging by its thread-like legs to the netting. "I wonder what will happen to all these poor creatures. Even with the warmth in here, they can't live forever."

Jack didn't answer, and Eleanor turned to him with a small smile. "No one lives forever, and certainly not a butterfly. Even with this heating..." She gestured to the pipes, "They'll die."

"The butterflies will lay their eggs," he said. "On the leaves of the plants and flowers. And so there will butterflies for the house next summer, when the eggs hatch."

"Caterpillars first, then."

"Yes, it will be something to see."

She sighed, shaking her head. "I still feel sorry for them somehow. Trapped behind all this netting."

"They're safe, at least."

"Yes." She paused, her gaze still on the blue butterfly that trembled by her fingers. "What will happen to me, do you think, Jack?" she asked. He was silent for a long time but Eleanor could not think of anything else to say. She did not even know what to think.

"I only want you to be happy," he finally said in a low voice.

"Oh, I don't think I shall be happy. Content, perhaps, if I ever learn to be satisfied with what I have. But happy?" She turned to him then, too weary to feel angry or accusing anymore. "I don't think so."

"You will, Eleanor. You'll find someone... someone worthy—"

"And who will that be, do you think? Is there a man left who is whole in body and soul?"

"You think I'm whole?" he asked, his voice turning rough.

"I know you've had more than your fair share of grief, Jack," Eleanor answered. "I don't mean to suggest otherwise—"

"It's not that," he said, shaking his head. "I know I'm lucky to be alive. But I made my own luck, and I pay for it every day of my life. I've got scars, Eleanor, same as any other man who has been in France. You just don't see them."

She lowered her gaze. "Don't you know I'd take your scars, and all of you, if you'd let me?"

"You shouldn't say such things."

"I know I shouldn't. I suppose my reputation could be ruined, standing in this butterfly house alone with you. But I'll say it all the same, much difference it will make. I know you've made up your mind."

"For your sake, Eleanor—"

"If I could prove to you," she cut across him, her voice rising, "that I could manage, that I wouldn't mind, would you accept me then?"

"How could you prove such a thing?"

"I don't know." The fierce emotion that had seized hold of her for a moment subsided and she shook her head. "I don't know."

Jack laid a hand on her shoulder. "Come. Your father will wonder where you are. Where we both are, for that matter."

Eleanor didn't move and after a moment Jack left her there; she heard him walk across the grass, and then the creak of the door. Impulsively she pulled back the net; the blue butterfly clinging to it beat its wings against it and then flew free.

Eleanor let the net fall back as she watched it go; it zig-zagged through the house, bumbling around before it finally found the door and flew out into the garden.

She followed it out, watching it flutter; Jack, she saw, was standing by the garden door, but his gaze was drawn to the butterfly as it weaved its way towards him.

"I had to free it," she said, and stretched her hand out to the butterfly that seemed almost to hover in the air. "I had to let something find what happiness it could, since you won't—"

"*Eleanor*," Jack said, and she heard the anguish in his voice. Eleanor reached for the butterfly, caught between rage and despair, wanting to let the poor creature fly free and yet also longing to hold onto it.

"I've come to take snaps of the garden," Allan Dyson, the photographer, announced, and she looked up to see him standing there, smiling brightly, his Graflex 1A held out in front of him. She froze, the butterfly still hovering near her fingertips, Jack behind her. "What a picture!" he exclaimed, and held the camera up to his face. There was a snap and a pop, and then he lowered it, grinning. "Even the butterfly stayed still," he said with a laugh, but the noise had since startled it, and Eleanor saw it was now gone.

From behind her Jack made a sound and she turned, startled to see his face become leached of colour.

"Jack—" she exclaimed without a thought to how it would appear, but he didn't even seem to hear her. His gaze was on the crowd of people that were strolling towards the garden, and then he slipped through the door and walked quickly away.

CHAPTER 23

MARIN

Marin didn't expect a lightning-strike kind of change to happen after her heart-to-heart with Rebecca, which was just as well since it seemed as if nothing had changed the next morning when Rebecca came down to breakfast, pale and tired-looking and monosyllabic.

Marin had made porridge and blueberry muffins, and Rebecca picked at both before heading off to school. Marin sat at the table with her second cup of tea, wondering if she should have suggested Rebecca bunk off for the day. They could have gone to Carlisle or even Newcastle and done something fun together. But perhaps it would have been too much, seemed too forced.

She sipped her tea, her thoughts wandering aimlessly; she was tired too, having not fallen asleep until near dawn. Eventually she roused herself and cleared away the breakfast things. She was just sitting down with her laptop when the doorbell rang.

Rather to her surprise it was Joss. "Hello," she said, and stepped aside so he could enter, but he didn't.

"I can't stay long. I've got to get to grips with the churchyard now that things are growing again. But I wanted to stop by and tell you what I've learned."

"And what is that?"

Joss grinned. "Allan Mayhew traced the photograph back to its owner. James Welton, a lifelong villager. He's over eighty years old, lives in a nursing home in Whitehaven."

"And how did he come to have it?"

"Allan asked him that. He visits the nursing home to see his aunt, apparently, and stopped in to see James. Apparently his mother Flora had a few photographs from the vicarage after the Sandersons left."

Marin frowned, intrigued. "And why would that be?"

"She helped to clear out the place for the new vicar, or so James said. His mother had been close to the Sandersons, apparently, sung in the choir in the late '20s. Maybe she wanted a keepsake. In any case James remembered the one of the girl. He said he thought it was Eleanor Sanderson, and better yet, he knows what the building in the garden was."

Marin caught her breath. "He does?"

"Shall I tell you?" Joss asked with a grin and Marin laughed.

"Do you know, I almost don't want to know now? Almost as if it will spoil it, especially if it really was nothing more than an old garden shed..."

"No," Joss said. "It's far more interesting than that."

Excitement rolled through her in a gathering wave. "Go on, then. Tell me."

"A butterfly house. Just for a few years, or so he said. George Sanderson had it built for his daughter, something to cheer her up after her brother died, I think."

"A butterfly house... there was a butterfly on her fingertips in the photo! Of course." She shook her head wonderingly for a moment before turning back to James. "How does James Welton know all this?"

"It was passed down to him from his mother. She knew

quite a bit about the Sandersons, but James wasn't even born until 1929, so long after the photograph was taken."

"And the man in the photograph?"

"That I couldn't tell you, so there's still some mystery for you to solve."

"I have no idea how I'll go about it," Marin answered with a laugh. "But thank you for telling me about the house."

"You're not disappointed?"

Marin considered this for a moment. "No, I'm not. It's good to know, but it was the story I was always more interested in. About this Eleanor, and the man behind her."

"Yes, well that part we may never find out."

"I know."

They both fell silent, and Marin thought Joss would go. Then he spoke up, his gaze turning intent. "Have dinner with me? Tomorrow night?"

"Dinner..." Marin repeated, so taken aback the invitation didn't quite compute.

"Dinner, in a proper restaurant. A proper date." He swallowed. "Just to be clear."

She felt a tingling all over, as if her entire body was covered in pins and needles. "That's very clear." She swallowed too, both thrilled and unsettled by Joss's unexpected invitation. "Yes, all right. I'd like that very much."

"Good." And with a parting wave and grin he headed back down the walk.

Marin closed the door and stood there for a second, her heart beating rather hard. Joss Fowler had asked her out on a date, and she had accepted. It was a small thing for most people, but for her it felt as if she'd taken another leap forward into this life she'd been creating for herself. Coming out of her shell, learning to live. Smiling, she turned back to the kitchen.

Rebecca, of course, was thrilled when Marin told her about

the date. "Oh, you'll have to let me do your hair," she exclaimed. "And your makeup... you never wear makeup, Marin."

"I've hardly needed to," she replied. "Staying at home all day."

"And you'll wear the black dress you got at the swish party, won't you?" Rebecca continued, her hands clasped together, and Marin hesitated.

"I don't know, Rebecca. It's really rather fancy. I don't even know where Joss is taking me..."

"But it's so perfect! Especially considering it's that photo that got you together. The dress is kind of vintage, don't you think?"

"Yes, but even so..." Marin nibbled her lip. She'd bought the dress, after all, even if it had only cost five pounds. It seemed silly never to wear it. "Oh, I suppose I could," she said and Rebecca clapped her hands.

The next night Marin watched in bemusement as Rebecca assembled her arsenal of supplies in the kitchen: a straightener as well as a curling iron, plenty of hairpins and slides, and more makeup than Marin had ever owned in her entire lifetime.

"Honestly, Rebecca, I think you might be overdoing it—"

"Go put on your dress," Rebecca ordered. "While I get ready here."

Obediently Marin went upstairs and fetched the flapper-style dress from her wardrobe. She slipped it on and then looked at herself critically in the mirror; perhaps the dress really was too much. The tiers of fringed tassels glittered and winked in the light and made a little clacking sound every time she moved. She'd never worn something that left her shoulders so bare, and she shivered slightly even though the room was warm from the heat of the Rayburn below. What if Joss was dressed in jeans and a jumper? She'd both look and feel ridiculous, as if she'd made more of this date than he'd meant it to be.

But if she didn't wear it, Rebecca would be disappointed. And she'd feel a coward somehow, as if she'd stepped back from something she'd told herself she was capable of. Something she wanted.

Resolutely Marin left the dress on and headed downstairs.

Rebecca had heated up the straightener and curling iron and she guided Marin to a chair before she went to work on her hair.

"I wish I had your hair," she said as she began to style it around her ears. "It's so thick and dark."

"And so unmanageable." Rebecca had blonde, wispy hair like Diana.

"It's perfect for this style," Rebecca assured her, and Marin wondered just what style 'this' was.

It seemed an age before Rebecca had finished with her hair and makeup; finally, with a flourish, she drew back and reached for the hand mirror she'd brought down with all of the other things. "Ready to look?" she asked and Marin held her hand out for the mirror.

"Most definitely." Yet she wasn't prepared for the sight of her made-up face and styled hair when she did glimpse her reflection. Rebecca had made her eyes dark and smoky with eyeliner, giving her, Marin thought, a surprising aura of mystery. Her hair had been done, she realised, in the same style as Eleanor Sanderson in the photograph: waved over her ears and then drawn back into a low knot.

"You've tried to make me look like her," she said with a laugh, not sure if she was thrilled or horrified or both.

"I thought the dress called for it," Rebecca answered. "I think you look fab."

"Well, thank you." She cautiously touched her hair, which had been sprayed into hard-shelled conformity. She felt a bit ridiculous, but she knew she couldn't change her appearance now. Rebecca would be crushed.

Quite suddenly, Rebecca came over and threw her arms around her. "Thank you, Marin," she said, and Marin had the feeling her sister was thanking her for more than letting her style her hair and makeup. She hugged her back, savouring the moment.

"Thank you for making me look like a style icon."

Maybe this was how change happened, she reflected as Rebecca began to clean up her things. In seemingly little ways, without trumpets or fanfare. Maybe she and Rebecca would inch their way towards the kind of loving relationship Marin had felt for so long was out of her grasp. Instead of a sudden, seismic shift they would come upon it gradually, learning to like and love each other over time.

The doorbell rang, and Rebecca scurried to answer it. Marin gave her reflection one last troubled glance; it was definitely too late to change her hair or her dress, and she had a horrible vision of Joss coming into the kitchen and his jaw going slack in appalled surprise when he saw her in this over-the-top getup.

But it didn't happen that way at all. Joss came into the kitchen, dressed in a suit with an open collar; she'd never seen him in anything but jeans and jumpers and she decided he cleaned up quite nicely.

His eyes widened when he caught sight of her, but in a good way, and he smiled. "You look amazing. Eleanor would be proud."

Marin laughed and ducked her head. "It was Rebecca's idea."

"Good going, Rebecca," Joss said with a wink, and then they were heading outside with Rebecca waving them off, and Marin climbed into the passenger seat of Joss's van.

"I feel like we should be climbing into a Pullman saloon," he said, "but I'm afraid I only have my van."

"Your van will do just as well. Where are we going?"

"A restaurant in Whitehaven, on the harbourside. There's not too many options around here, I'm afraid."

They didn't speak much on the short drive to Whitehaven; the sun was just starting to set, sending long, golden rays over the rolling sheep pasture on either side of the road, but Marin could see dark violet clouds gathering on the horizon, obscuring the Isle of Man. She felt tense and expectant and definitely very nervous; despite his relaxed position, both hands loosely on the wheel, she thought Joss was nervous too.

He parked the car in a car park by the harbour and they walked to the restaurant, still hardly speaking. It was only when they were seated at a table in the back, their menus before them, that Marin blurted,

"I don't know what to say."

Joss smiled wryly. "Is this too strange? I made a hash of asking, I know. 'Just to be clear'." He shook his head disparagingly and Marin smiled back at him.

"I like clear. But I haven't... well, I haven't been on many dates recently or even ever, which is kind of a humiliating thing to admit considering my age."

"I haven't either, if it makes you feel better."

"Not even when you were young and messing around?"

"Well, I certainly didn't go to places like this." Joss looked around the restaurant at the candlelit tables; the only sound the low murmur of conversation and the tinkle of crystal and silver.

"And what about more recently?" Marin asked. "Has there... has there been anyone in your life?"

He shook his head definitively. "No."

"Why not?"

"I have a history here," he said after a moment. "And I'm afraid it's not a very good one."

"You mean messing about when you were younger," Marin stated and after a second's hesitation he nodded.

"Yes."

But just as before, she had the feeling he'd been going to say something else. Something important.

Deciding the conversation had become too intense too quickly, she moved it to other topics, asking Joss about the landscaping he'd done recently. They talked easily for a few minutes and then the waitress came to take their orders, and things started to seem normal, to feel almost easy.

After their first course had been cleared away Joss took a sip of his sparkling water—he'd offered wine to Marin but declined himself—and asked, "How are things with Rebecca?"

"They're... good. I think." She laughed a little bit and shifted in her chair, conscious of the way the beads on her dress clacked every time she moved. "We had a bit of a breakthrough the other night, and were able to speak a bit more honestly to one another."

"That's good."

"Yes... but it brought up a whole lot of things I'd rather not think about. About me." Joss just waited for her to continue and half-wishing she hadn't been quite so honest, she said awkwardly, "I always felt like my father didn't love me. The way he pushed me away after my mother died, and how he always seemed to avoid me..." She hesitated, toying with the stem of her wineglass. "But after the things Rebecca said the other night, it made me wonder if it wasn't me, so much as him. Just the way he was. And maybe he did love me, as much as he could. If that makes sense."

"Those sound like good realisations to have," Joss said and Marin sighed.

"Yes, in theory. But they make me feel sad too, like I've missed something. If I hadn't been so stubborn, holding onto my resentment over how he was with me, perhaps we could have reconciled. Maybe we could have had some kind of relationship, if I'd been willing to accept whatever he was able to give, no matter how little."

"Maybe," Joss agreed. "But you can torment yourself with what-ifs. In the end they don't change anything."

"No, and it's too late now, isn't it?" She let out an uncertain laugh. "The funny thing, or perhaps the sad thing really, is that I always meant to talk to him. To put aside our differences. But I always thought there would be time. He was only sixty-three, you know, when he died."

"How did he and his wife die?"

"A car accident. Drunk driver." Marin shook her head. "So stupid and pointless. Some young kid, about eighteen, was over the limit and driving on the wrong side of the road. They were killed instantly, and he only got three years for manslaughter."

Joss didn't say anything, and Marin wondered if she'd shared too much. He had a strange look on his face, a kind of deer-in-the-headlights look that was wiped clean away as he shook his head. "That's terrible," he said at last.

She had talked too much. She was mired in the past, when she'd been trying so hard to work towards her future. "Sorry, I'm rabbiting on. Tell me more about the landscaping project, the Hennessys—"

After a second's pause he started to do just that, explaining about the Hennessys, an old village family who had been there for centuries; their house was the big sandstone place at the top of the high street. As he went on Marin made the effort to listen attentively, or at least to appear as if she were listening attentively, but inside her spirits were sinking down, down, down. She could tell that something had shifted between her and Joss, and not in a good way.

Things now felt stilted and awkward; their hands brushed when they both reached for their glasses and Joss jerked back as if he'd been burned. When it came time to order dessert, Joss said he didn't want any and Marin could tell he was dying to get away. They both declined coffee and Joss quickly paid the bill before ushering her outside the restaurant. Standing on the pavement, the water of Whitehaven's harbour glinting under the moonlight, Marin wondered how it had all gone so wrong, so quickly.

CHAPTER 24

ELEANOR

July 1919

Eleanor didn't see Jack for the rest of the fete. She wandered around, chatting to people, smiling and laughing and playing the part, but that's all it was. A part. She felt as if she'd flown away with the butterfly, was hovering somewhere above the garden, looking down on everyone and marvelling at these people who moved about the grass in their Sunday best, holding teacups aloft and giving tinkling laughs as if it all *mattered*.

She'd ask Jack what he thought would happen to her and he hadn't answered, hadn't been able to answer. And she knew the answer anyway. It would all go on: Katherine and James's stilted marriage, her own endless days of embroidery and finger sandwiches; her father preaching from the pulpit and her mother teaching the Sunday School. The workers would continue with their strikes and discontent, the veterans would stumble down the street with their organ grinders and trays of matches and bootlaces. Nothing she did, whether it was a Christmas cracker or a locket or a garden fete, would ever make any difference to anything. And the only difference she had wanted to make, she knew, was to Jack.

By four o'clock people began to trickle away, taking their cakes and jams and raffle prizes; by five o'clock everyone was gone and the garden was littered with bits of paper and straw, as if a circus had set up among the roses.

Tilly had come out to clean up, but Eleanor didn't see Jack. Was he avoiding her to the point of shirking his duty? She helped Tilly clear the lawn of all the detritus, and brought trays of cups with their dregs of now-cold tea inside the house. She'd just finished with the cups when she heard raised voices coming from the sitting room. It was her father and his visitor, the chaplain friend, Edward Stephens.

"I must say it's very peculiar," George said. "But I do think you've got the wrong end of the stick, dear chap."

"I'd like to say the same, but I'm quite sure," Stephens replied firmly. "I never forget a face."

Eleanor stilled with one hand on the banister, wondering what on earth they were talking about.

"This is all so unpleasant," Anne interjected quietly. "If we just went and fetched him, surely it would all be resolved in an instant?"

"He'll deny it, of course," Stephens said and Eleanor felt a frisson of fear slide down her spine. Who were they talking about?

"He seems a decent sort to me," George said. He sounded aggrieved. "I really can't believe it."

"Let's just call him," Anne implored. "He must be out in the garden, mustn't he? Cleaning up the chairs and things?"

"Go ahead," Stephens said. "I'd like to see what he has to say for himself."

Unable to keep herself from it, Eleanor threw open the door and strode into the room. Everyone turned to stare at her; she realised she must look a sight, her chest heaving, her hair coming undone from its pins. "What are you saying about Jack?" she asked, striving to keep her voice calm, but her agitation must have been obvious for her father's eyebrows rose nearly to his hairline.

"You forget yourself, Eleanor," he said in a tone she had not heard since she'd been a child with torn stockings and muddy knees.

"I'm sorry, Father," she forced herself to say. "But I must know—"

"I do not see how this concerns you at all," her father retorted frostily. He did not like, Eleanor knew, being embarrassed in front of his friends. Quickly she turned towards Reverend Stephens and his wife, both of them sitting upright in the velveteen armchairs on either side of the fireplace, both of them caught between embarrassment and condemnation.

"How do you do," she said, bobbing an awkward curtsey. "I'm sorry to have come in like this, but I overheard you speaking about our gardener, Mr Taylor, and I wondered what was going on."

Reverend Stephens simply pressed his lips together, and her father explained tersely, "Reverend Stephens says he recognises Jack Taylor from his regiment."

"The Prince's Own—"

"No," her father cut across her. "The Second Northumbrian Division. And he believes Taylor isn't who he says he is. He's John Bradford, from Alnwick."

"What!" Eleanor nearly laughed at this; it was simply too unbelievable, too outrageous. "Well, surely it's a nonsense." She turned to smile with what she hoped passed as sympathy at Reverend Stephens. "I imagine it's quite easy to confuse a face, especially among the enlisted men. There were so many..."

"I assure you, I am not confusing a face," Stephens told her shortly. "I remember Bradford well, because I prayed with him when his father died, right before he was granted leave for the funeral."

Eleanor swallowed dryly. She knew he must be wrong, but Edward Stephens sounded very certain. "And what happened then?"

"Until today I believed the convoy that was taking Bradford to Le Havre, with several other soldiers, was hit by a shell and exploded. Everyone on it died." He nodded towards the open door, and presumably, Jack, wherever he was. "Now I know something else must have happened."

"But perhaps he just looks like this Bradford," Eleanor insisted. "That must be it."

"Let us resolve this unpleasantness quickly," Anne said. She looked pale and tired. "Send for Taylor, George, please."

"Very well."

"I'll go—" Eleanor offered, and her father gave her a quelling look.

"I'll go," he said, brooking no argument, and Eleanor nodded.

George left the room and everyone waited in a tense and unhappy silence. Outside the sun poured over the rolling lawns like liquid gold, but the air in the sitting room, with the windows closed all day, felt musty and cold. Even on the hottest summer day, the vicarage was cool inside.

Eleanor could hear Tilly bustling about in the hall; she'd come in from the garden and was now laying the table for dinner. If she strained her ears she could hear the clank of copper pots from the kitchen. With two overnight guests in the house Mrs Stanton would be outdoing herself for the evening meal. James and Katherine were staying as well, although Eleanor hadn't seen them. She could hardly worry about them now, though; she was too concerned for Jack.

Jack, dear Jack. Of course he wasn't this John Bradford from

Alnwick. Why, the idea was ludicrous, absurd! To think Jack had lied to them all for months now...

And yet suddenly, unwillingly, memories crept coldly into Eleanor's mind, whispered treacherously in her ear. *There's something I haven't told you. You don't know me, not really. You don't know what I'm capable of...*

But not this, surely! Not this grievous deception. He couldn't have meant something like that. The sound of the front door opening and closing had everyone straightening in their seats, gazes darting around the room. Then her father came into the sitting room.

"I couldn't find him," he said heavily. "He's not in the garden, or in the cottage he shares with our old gardener, Mr Lyman."

"I think that speaks for itself, then," Stephens said. He sounded sad rather than satisfied, but it didn't make Eleanor dislike him any less. "He's probably run off, because he saw me. I thought he had, when I was coming towards that walled garden. A queer look came over his face and he walked off rather quickly. It took me a moment to make sense of it, put a name to a face, but he knew. I'm sure of it."

Eleanor had seen that look, as well. Jack had gone so pale, and left without a word. But she still couldn't believe he'd lied the way he had. She wouldn't.

"He must be somewhere, Father," she said, trying to sound reasonable. "He wouldn't just run off like that. Perhaps he's seeing to the tables and chairs—"

"We'll know soon enough if he has gone," George said, and his tone was final, dismissive. "Let us not bother about it until we can be sure, either way." He gave Eleanor a meaningful nod. "Perhaps, my dear, you should ready yourself for dinner."

Knowing she was dismissed, Eleanor left the sitting room. But she couldn't go upstairs and put on a fancy frock, not if her life depended on it. She had to find Jack.

Heedless of her parents and their guests in the sitting room and Tilly bustling about, Eleanor turned towards the front door. As quietly as she could she opened and slipped outside. The air was starting to grow chill as she made her way around to the garden. Jack wasn't there, just as her father had said. The only remnants from the fete now were a few scraps of ribbon dancing on the breeze; they must have come loose from the jam jars they'd been tied around.

The walled garden was empty too, as was the butterfly house; with growing frustration Eleanor closed the door, wondering if she dared go to Mr Lyman's cottage in the churchyard.

"Eleanor, what are you doing out and about? I thought you would be getting ready for dinner." Her grandmother Elizabeth stood by the gate to her garden, a wrap drawn over her shoulders. In the evening light she looked older somehow, the lines of her face more deeply drawn, her hair entirely white.

"I was looking for Jack," Eleanor blurted, and her grandmother's eyebrows rose.

"Jack? Do you mean the gardener, Taylor?"

"Yes, Jack," Eleanor stated fiercely. "Father's guest says he's not who he says he is, he recognises him as some John Bradford, but it can't be true—"

"What are you raving about?" Elizabeth exclaimed. "Come inside and tell me properly."

"I can't, I must find him—"

"You will do no such thing," Elizabeth said sharply. "Have you lost all your sense? We are talking about the gardener, Eleanor—"

"I love him," Eleanor blurted. Her grandmother fell silent, her mouth hanging open before she snapped it shut. "I know you'll disapprove, but I do. We've done nothing improper, I promise you. Jack will barely speak to me now, because he doesn't want to ruin me, and he doesn't think I can manage as his wife, scrubbing and cleaning—"

"He's quite right," Elizabeth replied shortly. She still looked a bit dazed, but she'd recovered her voice and her composure. "You could not be the wife of a common day labourer, Eleanor. It is quite impossible."

"It's not—"

"I don't blame you for believing you care about him," Elizabeth continued, her voice softening. "You are young and romantic, and you have had so much sorrow in your life. Taylor is a handsome young man in his own way. Your head was bound to be turned."

"My head has not been turned!" Eleanor exclaimed. "My heart—"

"Enough." Elizabeth held up a hand to stop her, and Eleanor fell silent. "We shall have no more of this. If Taylor has gone missing, it is likely what your father's friend has said is true. He must be hiding something."

"I don't believe it," Eleanor cried. She felt seized by an emotion too strong to contain, although whether it was rage or grief or fear she didn't know. "I won't believe it," she declared, and without another word for her grandmother she turned and slipped through the gate that led to the churchyard.

Darkness was falling as she made her way through the churchyard, the headstones like silent soldiers standing to attention all around her. She'd never been to Mr Lyman's cottage, although she'd seen it from afar. It looked a mean place, no more than two small rooms, the windows' glass grimy with soot from an open fire. Her hand trembling, she knocked on the door.

She heard movement from inside, or rather, the sudden stopping of movement, and then silence, like that of a held breath, of waiting. Feeling more reckless than ever, she turned the handle and the door swung open. Jack stood in the centre of the room, a holdall in one hand, his cap jammed low on his head. His expression was wary and trapped, and when he caught sight of Eleanor he relaxed only a little, his shoulders slumping.

Eleanor took it all in: the bag, the cap, a chair that had no doubt been overturned in haste. Her heart felt as if it had had lead poured over it; suddenly it had become a heavy thing, weighing her down, an impossible anchor.

"You're going," she stated flatly, and Jack said nothing. She stared up at his face, and in the dimness of the little cottage she could not read his expression. "Tell me the truth," she demanded. "All of it."

"You've heard, then."

"Reverend Stephens was chaplain of the Second Northumbrian Division. He says you're John Bradford, from Alnwick."

For a second, no more, Eleanor caught her breath and waited, held onto hope. Then Jack gave one brief, terrible nod.

"Yes."

"Why?" she whispered. "Why did you lie to us about who you were?"

With a sigh Jack took off his cap, ran his fingers through his unruly hair. "Because I had to. Because I can't be John Bradford anymore, not since—"

"Since when? What happened, Jack? Reverend Stephens said you were in a convoy that was hit by a shell, and everyone was thought to have died—"

He nodded again. "Yes, I'd been given leave to attend my father's funeral. We had a smallholding outside of Alnwick. My father and my two brothers and I tended it, but they both died in Verdun, on the same day. I saw my brother William go down, and there was nothing I could do about it." His mouth tightened, his face closing up, and Eleanor almost reached a hand out to comfort him.

"When I got news my father had died the war was almost over—it was October, Eleanor, with just weeks to go. Everyone was saying it wouldn't be long. I couldn't take the madness of it anymore, the complete futility..." He dropped his head in his hands, and only then did she realise what he was saying. What Edward Stephens had been saying.

"You deserted," she stated, her voice thin and wavery. "That's what you mean, isn't it? You deserted."

He lifted his head from his hands, his gaze bleaker than she'd ever seen it. "I didn't plan on doing it. I was granted three days' leave, and so I went. When the shell hit the lorry we were on I was thrown clear. My head split like the very... it hurt," he amended quickly, "but the other two blokes were dead. I heard the whistling of another shell—that damned whistling—and I ran for it. When I looked back the whole convoy had exploded. There was nothing left."

"And so what did you do?" Eleanor asked. Her voice sounded hard. Unforgiving.

"I went," Jack said simply. "I didn't plan on it, not right away. But then I didn't report the explosion and I realised why I didn't. This felt like a chance, providential even—"

"Don't bring God into this," Eleanor snapped and Jack nodded his agreement.

"No," he said quietly. "No, I shouldn't do that."

"And then what happened?"

"I showed my papers, I got on the boat, and I went home. And I... I didn't go back."

"You deserted."

"Yes." He met her gaze unflinchingly, although she saw the regret etched into every line of his face. "Yes."

Eleanor drew a shuddering breath. "And then?"

"When I got back to Alnwick I buried my father. Then I left everyone in Alnwick, as if I were heading for the troop train. And then..."

"Then?" she prompted, without pity.

"I thought about going back, even then," he said. "I did, but

I just couldn't... not when my brothers and father had all been claimed by this bloody war in one way or another. I'd be facing weeks of pointlessness and maybe even dying and for what? For what?" His voice rose raggedly. "You can't imagine what it's like out there." Eleanor said nothing and he continued quietly, "I knew my CO most likely would have assumed I'd died in the convoy. I was gambling on them not checking that I'd got on the ship. Everything was a shambles then, in the weeks up to the Armistice. No one was checking anything, telegrams were delayed..."

"I know," Eleanor said quietly. "Walter's was delayed. We didn't receive it until after the Armistice."

For a moment Jack's face contorted with anguish. "Eleanor—"

"Tell me what happened next."

"I became Jack Taylor. I couldn't go back to the farm. People might have talked, word would have got back to my regiment. So I travelled around, looking for work, and I've been doing that ever since."

"And the farm?"

"We were tenants only. It's lost, as everything else is."

Eleanor sank into one of the rickety wooden chairs; she felt as if her legs could no longer hold her. "Was it worth it?" she asked eventually. "To have your freedom for those few weeks?"

"But I'm not free," Jack said. "I never have been. For the last eight months, ever since I got on that ship, I've wondered when I'll be found out. What will happen."

"And what will you do now?" She nodded towards the hold-all he'd dropped on the earthen floor. "You're running away, aren't you? But now they know you're alive."

"Yes. I suppose I'll keep running. I thought Goswell was safe enough, out of the way as it is. But maybe I'll never be safe."

"Safe," Eleanor repeated. She drew another breath; the

simple movement seemed to hurt. "You know my brother Walter died on November fifth, don't you? After you'd deserted. In the taking of the Sambre-Oise canal."

"Yes."

"He wasn't a soldier," she continued, needing to tell him, for him to hear. "He hated war. He was a poet and a musician, a thinker. He had a pianist's hands." Jack waited, his head lowered, accepting everything she said as what it was—a judgment against himself. "He wasn't like you, a sturdy fellow, used to the land. He wasn't—" She broke off, shuddering, and then made herself continue. "I don't think he could hardly bear to hold a gun. But he did, Jack. He did for four years, right to the end, and it killed him. While you... you ran away!" The tears came then, tumbling down her cheeks. She felt too angry, too enraged to brush them away. "How could you do it?" she demanded. "How could you run away to save your own skin, when men like my brother were dying every day?"

"I don't know," Jack said, his voice so low Eleanor had to strain to hear it. "I don't know. It was a matter of a moment, of... of instinct, I suppose. And then it was too late to change it."

"But you could have gone back and accepted your punishment—"

He looked up, blanching at this. "Eleanor, I would have been shot."

She blanched too; the idea was so grim, so impossible, and yet— "Not all the deserters were shot."

"A private who as good as faked his own death? Emotions were running high then. People wanted the war to end, and they were angry it wasn't. I would have been."

"You still should have done it," she insisted, although she didn't think she really meant it. "You should have accepted the consequences, for better or for worse. But now you'll just keep running away, won't you? Who will you be next? Because I suppose you can't be Jack Taylor anymore."

"I don't know." He looked wretched, miserable, and yet still she wanted to hurt him.

She stood up, one shaking hand holding onto the table for balance. "I hate you," she said very clearly. "I thought I loved you. I gave my heart to you, but I'm glad now you're going, John Bradford. Sneak away to some other village, some other vicarage!" Her voice broke on a trembling note, and with tears still running down her face, she turned and ran out of the cottage.

She could not bear to see anyone when she returned home and so she snuck in through the kitchen; Tilly and Mrs Stanton's mouths both dropped at the sight of her, but Eleanor just shook her head and held a finger to her lips.

"Don't," she whispered. "Please, I can't bear it. I'm going upstairs to bed. Tell Mother I've a headache." And she slipped down the hall and upstairs, locking her door before falling onto her bed and tucking her knees up to her chest.

She must have slept, because she awoke to sunlight trickling through the curtains, and the house stirring all around her. She pushed her hair out of her face and reached for the pitcher of water on her bedside table; her mouth felt terribly dry.

A knock sounded on the door and after taking a few hasty sips Eleanor rose to unlock it. It was, somewhat to her surprise, Katherine; she'd expected one of her parents.

"You look dreadful," Katherine said quietly. She came into the room, closing the door behind her.

"I feel dreadful," Eleanor said as she sank onto her bed. "And I don't care. What are you doing here, anyway? I thought you would have gone back to Whitehaven."

"We stayed the night, and it's just as well, considering the state you're in."

"Are Mother and Father terribly angry?" Eleanor asked, although she found she didn't much care.

"Worried. You've been terribly reckless, Eleanor, even for you."

"I had to know. I spoke to him, you know, at Mr Lyman's cottage. He told me everything." She plucked at a loose thread on her coverlet. "But I suppose he's gone now. He's run off to some other place—"

Katherine didn't answer, and Eleanor looked up, her gaze narrowing. "Hasn't he?" she said, and didn't know whether it was hope or fear she felt at the thought that he might have stayed.

"No, he hasn't," Katherine said quietly. She took Eleanor's hand in her own, and then she knew she felt fear, a dreadful lurch. "He's still here, Eleanor, at least in Goswell. He turned himself in to the police last night."

CHAPTER 25

MARIN

"So how was it?"

Marin came into the house from her date with Joss and managed a tight smile. He'd walked her to the door, but there had been no warmth in it, no kiss or even a handshake. He'd waved goodbye and retreated quickly to his van. Somehow, over the course of the evening, it had all gone wrong.

"Fine." Rebecca frowned, not fooled, and Marin shrugged off her coat. "Don't ask me to tell you about it now, Rebecca, please. I'm too tired."

"But something happened—"

"No, not really." She didn't know what had happened. One moment they'd been getting along, and the next Joss had been monosyllabic and wooden, retreating farther and farther inside himself. She must have said or done something that put him off, and she was too inexperienced and ignorant even to know what it was. "I'm going up to bed." Rebecca's face fell and Marin forced another smile. "Honestly, it's fine, Rebecca. We had a nice enough time. I'm just not sure we're suited. Please don't worry." Awkwardly she patted her sister's hand before retreating thankfully to the solitude of her bedroom.

She caught her reflection in the mirror by the bed and winced at the dress, the hair. She still had some of the crimson lipstick on her mouth, making it stand out almost savagely on her pale face. She wiped it off and then pulled the pins from her hair, unzipped her dress. She wanted to forget it all.

So much for trying, she thought as she slipped into her pyjamas, and then into bed. So much for taking those small, hesitant steps into the land of the living. She closed her eyes, tucked her knees up to her chest. At least before she hadn't had to deal with this uncertainty, this hurt.

The next morning she felt a bit battered, but she tried to be practical. She told herself she was overreacting, but the days passed and Joss didn't appear. Rebecca went to school, and Marin occupied herself with her growing business—she'd had three new clients—and the garden. She'd stayed out of the garden for a day or two at first, because somehow it all felt ruined now, but then she decided she was being ridiculous. The garden was hers, and she'd enjoyed restoring it. It didn't matter if she'd scared Joss away. She could still work on it.

So she hired a rotovator and spent three backbreaking days tilling up the roots; the sight of all the churned-up black earth made her heart swell with pride even as she caught herself glancing at the garden door, waiting for Joss to appear. He didn't.

She and Rebecca had a bonfire of all the brush and roots in the corner of the garden; the Hattons came over and it felt like Guy Fawkes Day in the spring, the sky still light and streaked with clouds of rising smoke.

"What are you going to do with all this garden?" Jane asked as they glanced over at the freshly-tilled, empty expanse, the bonfire casting dancing shadows across the earth.

"I don't know. I could put it all to lawn, but that seems a bit boring. And I don't think I have the resources to make a butterfly house."

"No, that does seem a bit impractical," Jane agreed with a smile. "But you could do some flowerbeds with plants that butterflies like. Attract them that way."

"Yes..." She liked the thought of butterflies in the garden again, restoring it just a little to how it once was.

It was mid-April, and the world was coming to life. The day after the bonfire Marin came in to find a clump of bluebells outside the garden door; they seemed to have appeared overnight. She transplanted them to the walled garden, nurturing the tender white bulbs, enjoying the way she was filling up the space, bit by bit.

Rebecca started to help her, shyly at first; they went to the garden centre and picked out seeds and bedding plants; Rebecca pointed out a few benches and a table she liked, and Marin bought it all. She felt reckless, defiant, even. *We can do this*, her heart seemed to be saying. *We can do this together, and we don't need you.*

But Joss wasn't around to hear.

He'd been absent for nearly two weeks when Marin decided to go to the library in Whitehaven and see if she could find anything about the man in her photograph. She'd solve that mystery on her own too, without Joss's help.

She spent several hours trawling through dusty boxes of donated letters and photographs in the library's archives; her head was starting to hurt from deciphering the crabbed hand-writing and tiny type from the clippings. A librarian took pity on her after a couple of hours and asked if she was looking for something in particular.

"You might want to try the Archive and Local Studies Centre on Scotch Street," she suggested. "They've got far more than we do—all the old parish records and census transcripts, and the newspapers as well. Most of it is on microfiche, so you won't strain your eyes."

Since she'd come this far Marin decided she might as well

keep going, and within half an hour she was ensconced in the Local Studies Centre, seated at a microfiche machine, blinking in the bright light as she scrolled through a decade's worth of newspapers. It was easy to get caught up in the articles about the war and the local efforts to help, but resolutely she scrolled past them to 1919, the time of Eleanor Sanderson and the mystery gardener. She didn't know what she expected to find; a gardener would hardly make the local paper. And yet she thought of that look of longing on his face and she kept scrolling.

When she found it, it took her a moment to realise what she was seeing: a photograph of the gardener, but this was a portrait of him in his army uniform, his hair brushed back with pomade, his face unsmiling and serious. But it was him, she was sure of it, and her gaze moved from the photograph on the front page of *The Whitehaven News*, July 26, 1919, to the blazing headline. LOCAL GARDENER ARRESTED FOR DESERTION.

Marin's hand stilled on the machine as she scanned the article; realising how important it all was, she forced herself to start back at the beginning and read more slowly. *The villagers of Goswell were shocked to discover a gardener and veteran had deceived many by pretending to be a soldier from the West Yorkshire Battalion. Going by the alias Jack Taylor, this scoundrel whose true name is John Bradford became dear to many until his nefarious deception was uncovered, and he was shown to be the worst kind of coward, a deserter from the Second Northumbrian Division...*

The language, for a newspaper article, seemed melodramatic and overblown, but she supposed that was a reflection of the times. And the reporter was clearly biased against this John Bradford, calling him a scoundrel. She wondered what other people had thought... what Eleanor Sanderson had thought.

Marin scrolled through several more months' worth of newspapers, and she found a few more articles. The initial furore had died down and she read how John Bradford had been taken to Alnwick where he would be court-martialed. The case seemed to have gripped the country, with people weighing in on both sides, some wanting leniency, others thinking he deserved the full measure of the law's punishment. She scrolled down some more, but the microfiche roll ended before she found out what had happened to John Bradford, and when the staff assistant went to check, the next batch of newspapers available on microfiche was for two years later.

"What happened to those two years of newspapers?" Marin asked, and the woman shrugged in apology.

"We preserve as much as we can, but invariably things get lost or damaged."

Frustrated and longing to know more, Marin headed outside. She felt too restless and keyed up by what she'd discovered to head straight home, and so she wandered through the centre of town for a bit before ending up at a café on Lowther Street. She ordered a latte and sat at the table in the window, watching the world go by, her mind on John Bradford—or Jack Taylor, as he'd been known in Goswell.

What kind of man had he been? Marin realised that she'd assumed from the photograph, he'd been a man of some feeling and depth. She'd given Jack Taylor a character reference based on nothing more than a long-ago look. Perhaps he really had been a scoundrel the newspaper had made him out to be. Perhaps she'd read far too much into that look of Jack's, just as she'd read too much into that look of affection on her father's face—and Joss's friendship.

It had been over two weeks since she'd seen him, although she'd glimpsed his van in the church lane. She'd got used to him coming round, helping her in the garden. There could be no doubt that he was avoiding her, that something had changed between them on that dinner date. She thought about confronting him, cornering him in the churchyard and demanding to know why he was keeping his distance, but every-thing in her cringed from doing something so obvious, so pathetic even. They'd gone on one date. It wasn't as if they'd even had a relationship. It had just felt to her as if they had, at least the beginnings of one.

She left the café and headed back to Bower House; Rebecca was already inside when she came in, dropping her keys on the kitchen table with a clatter.

"Where have you been?" she asked. She was sitting at the kitchen table, munching toast with chocolate spread and flip-ping through a teen magazine. The sight was so normal, so pleasant, that it took Marin out of her own gloomy mood for a few seconds.

"I was in town, doing some research," she said, and went to fill the kettle.

"Research? On what?"

"The photograph of the girl and the gardener. Well, the gardener mainly, since we hadn't found out who he was."

"Hadn't?" Rebecca repeated, her eyebrow rising. "And now you have?"

"Yes, but I almost wish I hadn't." Marin reached for a teabag, flinging it into a mug with a sigh. "Sometimes I think it's better not knowing."

"That doesn't sound good."

"It's not the happy ending I was hoping for," Marin agreed, and then she told Rebecca what she knew about Jack Taylor, or rather, John Bradford, and his desertion.

Rebecca listened, wide-eyed, her knees clutched to her chest. "That's terrible," she said when Marin had finished. "But we studied World War One in history—the shell shock and trenches and stuff like that. It was awful, for the soldiers. I don't blame him for deserting."

"Maybe not, but we'll never even know why he deserted, or whether he was punished."

"Would he have been executed, even after the war?"

"I don't know." Marin poured the boiling water into her mug and stirred slowly. "But that article in the newspaper was written on July 26, 1919—that must have been soon after the photograph was taken. James Welton said it was from a fete that summer."

"Maybe," Rebecca said dreamily, "he knew he was going to lose her."

And while that seemed tragically romantic to a fifteen-year-old, Marin thought it just sounded terrible. She drank her tea and threw together a casserole for dinner; she'd become quite adept at making a quick meal and popping it in the Rayburn. Rebecca had gone upstairs to do her homework, and after prowling around the kitchen for a moment Marin decided to go outside. She started for the garden as a matter of habit, but suddenly she couldn't face seeing it all, dealing with the memories that weren't even hers.

She turned instead to the gap in the hedge where a gate had once been, leading to the churchyard and the vicarage gardens. She walked through the churchyard, the air brisk, the sun still high overhead even though it was nearing seven o'clock. She could see a few people in the distance, walking dogs on the path that ran along the sheep pasture. The pasture was full of sheep and their lambs that had been born in the last few months, gambolling little creatures with fleeces like cotton wool.

Impulsively Marin left the churchyard and turned towards the beach; the wind kicked up as soon as she headed along the beach road, making her eyes stream and sting.

She hadn't actually been to the beach very often since she'd moved to Goswell; now she walked along the concrete promenade that ran the length of the beach, the waves crashing against it, the wind whipping her hair around her face.

She stood on the edge of the promenade, entranced by the sheer power of the slate-grey sea. Waves crested white before crashing down with a thunderous roar, and the spray flecked her face. It was a glorious and powerful sight, and the fearsome beauty of it as well as the ever-present wind at her back made her take a sudden step forward, until her toes were touching the edge of the concrete.

Her mind was full of jumbled thoughts of Joss, of Jack Taylor, of her father. Of the past and the future and the choices people made—the choices she'd made, in coming here, in trying to reach out. Was she really going to step back now, and retreat into her safe little shell? Her toes flexed instinctively, almost as if she were poised to jump. Then she felt a hard hand clamp down on her shoulder.

"What the hell do you think you're doing?"

She whirled around, blinking in surprise to see Joss standing there, looking furious.

"I was just standing here," she said defensively, and looking down she realised with a shock how close she was to edge. "I didn't realise..."

"I'll say you didn't realise." He gestured to her boots, which were wet with spray. "You could have fallen right in, and with the way the wind is now, you wouldn't have stood a chance."

A tremor ran through her at the thought. "I'm sorry," she said, and she didn't quite know what she was apologising for.

Joss's thunderous look softened and he muttered, "I'm sorry, too." And Marin didn't know what he was apologising for, either. He nodded towards a bungalow perched just beyond the promenade. "Do you want to come in? I think you could use a cup of tea."

"All right," Marin said, and followed him to the bungalow. It had no garden to speak of, just a strip of grass out front that would be covered in water during a fierce storm. Joss opened the door and she stepped inside. It was a small, homely, cluttered place, but the picture window overlooking the sea made up for its size. "What a view," she said. "I feel as if I'm suspended above the sea."

"You almost are," Joss answered, and went to the tiny galley kitchen in the back to put the kettle on. After a moment Marin followed him; the shock of the encounter was wearing off and she was remembering, rather painfully, how Joss had been avoiding her for the last two weeks. She thought she should mention it, ask him why, but the question stuck in her throat, the words feeling jagged and sharp.

"I'm sorry for avoiding you," Joss said abruptly, and Marin nearly sagged in relief that he'd got there first.

"Why have you been?" she asked, and that question felt easier, although she still had to brace herself for the answer.

Joss didn't say anything for a moment; his back was to her as he stared out the window to the muddy patch of grass behind the bungalow, facing the headland.

"Because I'm a coward," he finally said, "and I didn't want to have to tell you about my past, especially after what you told me."

This was so not what Marin had expected that she didn't say anything for a few seconds. Joss turned around.

"At dinner. When you mentioned how your father and his wife died." His face was both shuttered and grim, and Marin shook her head slowly.

"I don't understand."

"I know you don't. But the truth is I've kept something from you. I'm surprised no one in the village told you, actually. Every time I came to see you I was bracing myself for you to have heard. I suppose people can keep their mouths shut when they want to."

"What did you think I would have heard?"

He sighed and as the kettle whistled he switched it off and poured their tea. "I was in prison," he stated flatly. "I was released three years ago."

Marin blinked. "Prison..." she repeated slowly. "What... what for?"

His expression hardened and his gaze slid away. "For involuntary manslaughter. It was a light sentence, really, for what I did."

Manslaughter. She opened her mouth, but no words came out.

With a heavy sigh Joss continued. "I told you I never really got on with my father. He wanted me to settle down and work with him, and I wanted to... oh, I don't even know what I wanted anymore. To see the world, to have fun, to be stupid." He shook his head wearily and handed Marin her mug of tea, cradling his own in his hands. "In any case, I refused. He took on more jobs, worked harder than a man his age should have had to. And then he had a heart attack while digging up someone's flowerbed and died."

"Oh Joss, I'm so sorry."

"I blamed myself. I felt as if everyone blamed me, although I don't know if that was true or not." He lapsed into silence and Marin frowned.

"But that's not manslaughter," she said slowly.

"No." Joss gazed down into his mug. "At my father's funeral —well, at the reception afterwards—I drank too much. I wasn't over the limit, but it was close. Too close. And I drove too fast on my way home and hit an eight-year-old girl." His throat worked, his gaze turning both shuttered and bleak. "She died instantly."

Marin's mouth dropped open. "Oh, Joss..." she began, and then stopped. She did not know what to say, what she could say.

"She darted out from behind a car. Someone saw that, apparently, which is why I got a lighter sentence. It could have happened to anyone, my defense counsel said. But I'd been going too fast, there was no question about that. I killed her."

"And you served your sentence."

"Three years, out of five." He sighed. "And I came back

here because I felt like I needed to face everyone. I didn't want to run away, and I wanted to keep my father's business going. But..." He looked up at her, his gaze bleaker than ever. "But nothing changes what I did. Nothing will bring that little girl back."

"I know." She swallowed hard and continued, "I can't imagine what it's like to live with that, Joss. To deal with it."

"It's something I'll never forget. Never escape."

"And that... that's why you've avoided me?"

"I wanted to tell you, but then when you told me your father had been killed by a drunk driver..." He shrugged helplessly. "How could you ever see past what I did?"

"It's not the same—"

"Isn't it?"

"I don't know," she said after a moment, honestly. Her mind was reeling from all Joss had just told her. "I don't know anything anymore. But it doesn't seem right to punish us both for something that happened a long time ago, something you've already paid for."

"How can you see past it..."

"I've lived with a lot of hurt and anger over the way my father treated me," Marin said. "And I don't want to live that way anymore. I don't want to hide away with nothing but my own hurt to keep me company."

"Even so—"

"I'm not the one who needs to forgive you, Joss," Marin said quietly. "You need to forgive yourself. Or maybe ask the family of that little girl to forgive you. Maybe that will help everyone move on."

"I did that," Joss said after a moment. "After I got out of prison. And they were..." His voice thickened, and he swallowed. "Very gracious."

"Then perhaps you need to be gracious," she said quietly. "To yourself."

"It feels like it shouldn't be that easy."

"I didn't say it was easy."

He gave her a ghost of a smile then and suddenly, inexplicably, Marin felt near tears. "I wish you'd told me this before," she said, her voice choking. "Do you know how miserable I've been these last two weeks?"

"Oh, Marin." He pulled her into a hug, and she rested her cheek against the rough wool of his jumper and closed her eyes. "I told you I was a coward," he whispered and kissed her hair. "I'm sorry."

"So am I. For a lot of things."

They remained like that for a moment, and then Marin eased back. "I found out about our mystery gardener," she said, and Joss raised his eyebrows in expectation. "It's not a very nice story," she said. "But maybe, just maybe, they still found their happy ending somehow." Maybe happy endings could be found, even through all the grief and loss and pain.

"Tell me," Joss said, and so she did.

CHAPTER 26

ELEANOR

July 1919

It was all so terrible. Eleanor stared down at the newspaper article that called Jack a scoundrel, condemning his 'nefarious deception', and then thrust it away with a shudder. She'd never wanted this.

Yet what had she wanted, when she'd told Jack all those dreadful things? When she'd called him a coward and worse, and acted as if she hated him? She didn't hate him at all, yet she didn't know what she felt now besides an unending misery for all they'd both lost.

In the days and weeks that followed Jack's arrest her parents maintained a dignified silence on the subject. Eleanor's wayward behaviour was not discussed, and she forced herself to become more involved in the church and village, as a kind of penance for her reckless foolishness. Oh, but she'd been so very reckless. Katherine had chided her for it, everyone had, and she'd actually thought she'd grown up a bit. But she'd shown her true colours in the moment she'd shouted at Jack, and forced him away from her forever.

She took a Sunday School class, and spent hours embroidering handkerchiefs and knitting socks. She mastered the art of turning a heel, though it gave her no satisfaction. She even visited dreadful Susannah Belmont, whose barbed remarks thankfully bounced off her; she felt too numb, too dead inside to be hurt by someone's petty spite.

No amount of good works could fill up the terrible emptiness inside her, though, and even when her hands were busy with whatever task she'd set herself, her mind seethed with fear and regret. The newspapers were full of Jack's desertion, and with the country caught between hope and grief, the story of a soldier's desertion captured everyone's imagination. It seemed as if half the world wanted him either hanged or shot, and the other half was tired of all the needless death and misery and wanted to show some sort of mercy. But everyone, it seemed, agreed that he should pay somehow.

Stories were trotted out, stories of soldiers who had endured far worse losses than Jack—or rather, John—had. Soldiers who had stayed at the Front when their whole families had been felled, farms lost. It was clear that Jack was not to be excused— or pardoned.

"What do you think they will do to him?" Eleanor asked Katherine, several weeks after Jack had turned himself in and been taken back to Alnwick.

"I don't know," Katherine answered frankly. "They're saying he might be court-martialled, even though he's been demobilised, since it happened during the war."

"And if he is?" Eleanor asked through numb lips.

"He won't be executed, not now," Katherine told her with what Eleanor suspected was meant to be bracing cheer. "But he might receive a prison sentence... I don't know, Eleanor. The mood of the country is so strange these days. Up one minute and down the next."

"The courts shouldn't be dictated by mood," Eleanor

protested and Katherine nodded soberly. "I know. But the fact is, they are. And Jack might be made an example of." It was the first time, Eleanor noted, that her sister had called Jack by his Christian name.

She stopped reading the local newspapers, because she couldn't bear to see Jack vilified in such a heartless way... and yet she knew she'd done the same thing, and to his face. If only she hadn't been so reckless, so impulsive and thoughtless and *cruel*...

But it was too late. Jack was gone. And the walled garden was gone, too, left to weeds and ruin. A week after Jack had been taken back to Alnwick her father turned off the heat for the butterfly house. Eleanor knew her father felt betrayed by Jack too, and hurt. When he'd asked her about the garden, she'd simply shaken her head. She couldn't bear even to think about it anymore, which felt like another loss.

After her father turned off the heat, Eleanor went in the butterfly house herself and drew back the netting, watched with wretched despair as the butterflies bumbled their way to freedom, a thousand tiny wings silhouetted against the sky before they were gone. How long would they last? Some had been used to tropical climes. But then, how long did anything last?

She shut the door of the garden and no one went in there again; it was as if it had never been ploughed or planted. As if none of it had happened; her parents never spoke of Jack once.

Summer lurched into autumn, and the weather grew cold, the skies dark and overcast. The newspapers continued to print stories of Jack, peppered with melodramatic accounts of other soldiers who had suffered and not deserted. Eleanor didn't read any of it, but one afternoon in early October Katherine came to her and told her what she'd heard.

"He's to be court-martialled," she said, taking Eleanor's cold hand in hers. "I don't know what the sentence will be, but..." She hesitated, her eyes full of sympathy and sorrow. "It will be serious. At least we'll know what's going to happen in a few days."

Eleanor nodded; her throat had closed up too much for words. She didn't know if knowing would make her feel better or worse.

And then the verdict came, and she realised it was worse, much worse. She was up in her bedroom when Katherine came to tell her, her face so serious that Eleanor knew it was bad.

"Not..." she began, and then found she could not continue.

"No," Katherine said quickly, "not that. No one wants that anymore, I don't think. But ten years of penal servitude, Eleanor. I'm sorry. He's to be sent immediately to Reading Gaol."

Ten years. A decade of his life. And who knew what he would be like when he came out, his health broken, his name still blackened, his life in ruins? And it was all her fault.

If she hadn't challenged him, *condemned* him, he could have escaped. Left a free man, even if he'd have had to keep running.

"Thank you," she finally said. "Thank you for telling me."

She could not sleep that night. She could not set to anything the next day, to read or eat or even think. Her parents went on with their duties, and Katherine returned to Whitehaven, as if everything had returned to normal. Eleanor suspected her parents were actually relieved. The thing was done, and they could move on.

But how could she move on, knowing what she did? How could she live with herself, enduring endless, pointless days, on and on, with no respite in sight? She wrestled with the question for a week; it tormented her thoughts in every waking moment, and sleep was nearly impossible. She watched her parents moving about the vicarage as if they were actors in a play; listened to Tilly and Mrs Stanton chatting in the kitchen, as if everything was fine, as if life could just go on. And on. And on.

The answer, when it came, seemed simple, even easy. She couldn't go on like this. She didn't want to. She'd asked Jack what would happen to her, and now she knew. She would not wait to grow old, wracked by guilt and filling her days with meaningless pursuits; no, she would choose her destiny. She liked that thought, found comfort in it.

This, then, would be her last reckless act, except it didn't feel impulsive or thoughtless. It felt like the only choice left to her.

The rain was sleeting down as she walked through the house in a final, silent farewell. She could hear the rustle of papers from her father's study, the clang of copper pots from the kitchen. She stepped out onto the porch without even a wrap; her indoor slippers were soon soaked. And still she walked. First to the garden, lifting the latch that had almost rusted shut in the months since Jack had gone. It was bare and bedraggled now, the branches stark and leafless, everything left to ruin. She wondered who would open this gate one day in the future. Another girl, another gardener? Would they fill it with flowers, even butterflies? She almost smiled to think of the garden being redeemed and loved again. It would not happen in her lifetime.

She left the garden then, and slipped through the gate to the churchyard, and then down to the sheep pasture, the world growing dark around her, the rain coming down steadily, soaking her and freezing her to the bone. She felt nothing.

All the way to the beach, each step making her more sure, more purposeful. This was her choice. This was what she wanted.

She stood on the edge of the headland, the waves crashing below her, sending up their icy spray to douse her face. The ground was slippery with mud; it would be so easy to take that last little step. She might even do it by accident, slipping in the mud, windmilling to the waves below.

She should do it, she thought. Now, before her courage

failed her, before she slunk back to the vicarage ashamed and as empty as ever.

Now...

A hand suddenly clamped down on her shoulder. Her feet slid in the mud and her legs gave out from under her. For a second she was suspended, as close to falling, to death, as she'd ever been, and in that moment she knew she did not want to die. She wanted to live, not just for her own sake, but also for Jack's.

And then that hand on her shoulder was pulling her backwards, an arm wrapped around her waist, yanking her away from the edge of the cliff so they both fell with a grunt and a gasp onto the muddy headland; she at least was cushioned by the body below her.

"Are you all right?" The voice was rough with anxiety and emotion, and Eleanor turned in shock to stare at the face of James Freybourn.

"What..." For a moment she could not speak. "What are you doing here?"

"I was driving through town and I saw you," he said. He sat up, and then helped her up, draping his sodden coat around her shoulders. "You were walking to the beach in nothing but your day dress, soaked through and looking like a ghost."

But she hadn't been a ghost, after all. She'd been seen, by James of all people, and she was thankful. "I thought..." James looked away. "I thought you might be going to do yourself some harm." He spoke quietly, without censure or anger or that peculiar coldness that had become unpleasantly familiar in the last year. He spoke, Eleanor thought, almost like the old James.

James stood up, reaching a hand down to her. "Let me get you home. I have the motorcar."

"I can't go home like this. I can't face it—"

"Then I'll take you to Whitehaven. My parents are out, and only Katherine is home. She can attend to you."

Wordlessly Eleanor nodded, and they walked to James's motorcar, parked haphazardly on the edge of the beach road.

"What were you doing, out on a day like this?" Eleanor asked when she'd got into the passenger seat. She had started to shiver violently, and she wrapped her arms around herself.

"Sometimes I like to go for a drive," James said and then added, almost reluctantly, "I just need to get away."

"James..."

"I know," he said, his tone abrupt, his hands clenched on the steering wheel as he stared straight ahead. "I know what you were going to do, Eleanor, because I've nearly done it myself."

It took a moment for his words to penetrate the dazed fog of her mind. "When..."

"That last summer, '18. You know, it's easy for people to shake their fingers at Taylor, or Bradford, or whatever his name was. Easy to say he was a coward because they've got no idea what it was like. How terrible it was." He closed his eyes briefly, his pale face etched with strain. "Walter wasn't a coward. He hated the war, and it affected him badly. He'd started to have the shakes, poor man. But he wasn't afraid. Not like I was."

"Being afraid doesn't make you a coward," Eleanor said softly.

"But it did me, because I wanted to end it." He held up two fingers, barely a breath of space between them. "I came this close. *This close.* Walter found me."

"What..."

"I was going to shoot myself," he stated baldly. "After the Battle of the Lys, in Ypres. Thousands of men, *hundreds* of thousands of men died, but they called it a victory because the Jerries lost more." He shook his head slowly. "Over half my men died on that one day and I just couldn't... it was all so *pointless*, so utterly wretched. I was sending men to their deaths over and over again. They knew it as I well as I did." He let out a shuddering breath and continued. "Walter found me holding my service pistol... well, never mind. He didn't tell anyone, even though I could have been court-martialled. Disgraced, my family disgraced. He never told anyone. He just took the pistol out of my shaking hand."

Eleanor saw tears starting in his eyes, and she laid a hand on his arm. "Oh, James. Is this... is this why you and Katherine..."

"I can't bear to look at myself. How could she, if she knew?"

"You must tell her. The agony you've both gone through! If the war leaves us any legacy, it should be to snatch at happiness —and not just snatch, but fight for it. There has been too much sadness, too much grief and loss and death." She spoke fiercely, but James just kept staring straight ahead.

"Katherine loves you, you know," she said in a quieter voice. "Desperately."

"I know." James's voice was low, his head bowed. "And I couldn't bear it if she stopped."

"She won't," Eleanor protested. "She's far more constant than I ever was—" She broke off, the pain of losing Jack as fresh as ever, and James turned to place a hand on her arm.

"I'll take you back to Katherine," he said quietly. "She'll know what to do."

Eleanor gave a gulping kind of nod, and with a small, sad smile James got out to turn the crank to start the car.

CHAPTER 27

MARIN

One Year Later

The sun shone brightly down on the walled garden, the grass a velvety stretch of green thanks to Joss's ministrations. The flowerbeds burst with life, a riot of colour that Rebecca and Marin had chosen together.

The little building in the centre of the garden had been turned into a summer house, with a table and chairs; Joss had even put a skylight in the roof to let in more sunshine.

And today was a day of sunshine, of spring breezes and warmth and hope. Marin and Rebecca had invited friends over for a picnic, the Hattons and a few other families from the village and school, people they'd got to know in the year they'd been living in Goswell.

It hadn't always been easy. In fact, Marin thought, none of it had been easy. There had been uncomfortable, awkward conversations with Rebecca as they both came to terms with the grief they felt at the loss of their parents, and the sorrow for the relationships they'd never had with them. There had been more tears in the night, more sullen silences, but there had always been more steps, tiny, tottering ones, like learning how to walk, towards each other.

Marin spread a blanket out on the grass as Joss came into the garden with a picnic basket. Things hadn't been easy there, either, but they'd been good. More steps, learning to forgive, to let go, to move on. They'd been dating for a year and Jane had started asking veiled and then not-so-veiled questions about whether a proposal was in the offing. Marin didn't know, but she didn't mind, either. She could wait. She could enjoy what she had, accept what life had given her. And it was good.

She sat on the blanket as Joss started unpacking the picnic things and more people arrived, spreading their own blankets. Ben Hatton started kicking a ball around, and the other kids joined in. Marin leaned back and closed her eyes, let the sun bathe her face in warmth.

Then she felt a tap on her shoulder. "Look," Joss whispered, and she opened her eyes, blinking in the bright sunshine.

A butterfly had flown into the garden, and was resting on an open bud of honeysuckle, its pale blue wings outstretched.

"A Common Blue," Joss said. "They're usually seen on the coast."

"I knew they'd come, if we planted the right flowers," Marin said, her voice a hushed whisper. "I knew they'd come if we waited." And smiling, she reached out with one hand to touch it.

CHAPTER 28

ELEANOR

Reading, Berkshire, 1930

Eleanor stood shivering in the chill autumn air, the pavement slick beneath her boots. It had been a cold, dull November, the whole world still gripped in the awful depression that had hit almost exactly a year ago. Yet today Eleanor felt nothing but hope.

The last ten years had not been easy. With Katherine's help, she'd applied to a typing course, and been accepted. Her parents had accepted this change of plans with some chagrin, but in the autumn of 1921 they had allowed her to leave Goswell and take up a position as a typist for a solicitor, down in London. She'd found lodgings in a perfectly respectable boarding house and wrote her parents every week.

And for nine years she'd worked hard and gone once a month to visit Jack—she could only think of him as Jack—in Reading Gaol.

In the last ten years much had changed. James and Katherine had reconciled, and moved into their own house in Whitehaven. They now had three children, and Eleanor had travelled up on the train to visit them as often as she could. Her mother's health had broken down over the last decade, and two years ago her grandmother had died. Last year her father had retired, and Bower House was empty now, the vicarage about to be occupied by the new vicar, a single man named David James.

And Eleanor's life was finally about to begin. The doors across from where she waited on the street corner opened, and her heart lurched. She started forward, only to stop when she saw it was a stranger. She stepped back, her heart still beating hard. She'd been waiting a long time. She could wait a little longer.

Another ten minutes passed, and it began to rain a needling sort of drizzle. Eleanor pulled the brim of her cloche hat farther down and hunched her shoulders against the cold.

The door opened again, and here at last he was, looking older and thinner in the street clothes he hadn't worn in a decade, his coat hanging off his shoulders. He was no longer the robust young man, healthy and hale, who had given her a garden, but he was still the man she loved. He glanced around, and Eleanor started forward.

He turned, and recognition and relief softened his haggard features. He smiled and began to walk towards her.

"Jack," she said, and stepped into his arms.

A LETTER FROM KATE

Dear reader,

I want to say a huge thank you for choosing to read *The Daughter's Garden*. If you found it thought provoking and powerful, and would like to keep up to date with all my latest releases, just sign up at the following link. Your email address will never be shared and you can unsubscribe at any time.

www.bookouture.com/kate-hewitt

The Daughter's Garden was inspired by the walled garden behind the old vicarage I used to live in, in a village much like Goswell. Like Marin, I was fascinated by the history of the garden, and the foundation of a building in its centre. Sadly, I never discovered the true purpose of that building, but I greatly enjoyed making up my own story about it!

I hope you loved *The Daughter's Garden* and if you did, I would be very grateful if you could write a review. I'd love to hear what you think, and it makes such a difference helping new readers to discover one of my books for the first time.

I love hearing from my readers—you can get in touch on my Facebook page, through Twitter, Goodreads or my website.

Thanks again for reading!

Kate

KEEP IN TOUCH WITH KATE

www.kate-hewitt.com

facebook.com/KateHewittAuthor

twitter.com/author_kate

Lightning Source UK Ltd.
Milton Keynes UK
UKHW031035031122
411569UK00003B/71